Love and Loss Series, Book 1

BLACK ICE

CLAUDIA WHITSITT

BLACK ICE
Copyright © 2021 Claudia Whitsitt
Published 2021 in the United States by Twisted Vines Press

ISBN: 978-0-9963436-9-5

Cover Design by Champagne Book Design
Book Formatting by champagnebookdesign.com
Editor: Jean Jenkins

This is a work of fiction. Names, characters, places, and incidents either are the product of the author's imagination or are used fictitiously, and any resemblance to actual persons, living or dead, businesses, companies, events, or locales is entirely coincidental.

FOR JEAN JENKINS
my fairy godmother
who spent countless hours encouraging
and mentoring my work

OTHER TITLES BY
CLAUDIA WHITSITT

THE LOVE AND LOSS SERIES
BLACK ICE (BOOK 1)
LAKE FOG (BOOK 2)
LINGERING CLOUDS (BOOK 3)

MYSTERY TITLES by Claudia Whitsitt
THE WRONG GUY

THE SAMANTHA SERIES
IDENTITY ISSUES (Book 1)
INTIMACY ISSUES (Book 2)
INTERNAL ISSUES (Book 3)
INHERITED ISSUES (Book 4)

THE KIDS LIKE YOU SERIES
BETWEEN THE LINES (Book 1)
BEYOND THE LINES (Book 2)
BROKEN LINES (Book 3)
BATTLE LINES (Book 4)

Visit Claudia at: www.claudiawhitsitt.com
Facebook: Claudia Whitsitt
Author Twitter: @claudiawhitsitt
no Instagram: claudiawhitsitt

CHAPTER ONE

Brea

BREA WATSON STARED AT FORTY, HATING WHAT SHE SAW. She ached for a thirties do-over—life had passed her by. For the most part, she'd successfully suppressed her longing for that special someone. She tamped down her emotions and desires when they prickled, rationalizing that some people were placed on this earth to be cheerleaders. Today, the truth threatened to drown her, much like a fierce undertow. No matter how hard she tried, she couldn't come up for air.

She'd skipped all the Cinderella milestones—the loving marriage, the two perfect children, the old-fashioned swing set tucked into a quaint backyard next to the vegetable garden. Not because she didn't long for a family, but because she'd opted for an all-consuming career and settled for a married lover. She should have given up on silly, stupid fairy tales by now. At least that's what she told herself.

So far, the drive north from Hilton Head had been fraught with endless road construction and patches of inclement weather. The thought of turning around held tons of appeal for all kinds of reasons, but she'd promised Beth she'd come.

Brea had been groomed, or perhaps groomed herself, as her sister's caretaker. Watching over Beth was a familiar and comfortable habit, and in its own twisted way, Brea delighted in being the older, wiser sister, and loved Beth unconditionally. She and Beth had always been—and would be—besties for all time. In a fleeting bittersweet moment, Brea wondered if she'd given up too much.

Her stomach clenched the farther she drove, even though she couldn't wait to see her sister. She winced at the "Welcome to Michigan" sign, easing her foot back from the accelerator. For six months, she'd echoed a convoluted mantra. *Peter is history. More ancient with each passing day. I'm over him.*

Yet when Ann Arbor exits appeared on Highway 23 thirty minutes later, Brea's heart battered against her ribs. She'd fooled herself into believing she had shed the heartstrings that tied her to Peter. She'd been fine for six solid months—the move to South Carolina had served her well. But if her exodus had truly satisfied her need to end things with him, why did she have to fight the temptation to veer off the highway at Main Street and stop by Peter's office before he went home for the night? She fought the memory of his lips pressed to hers, the shimmer of his fingertip as it traced a path from her shoulder to her breast. Dangerous, ugly thoughts.

Recriminations rocked her with the fierceness of a sucking wind—*you slut, you senseless ass, you wuss.* Only a senseless woman would throw her life away on a married man.

Her story had become a messed up Lifetime movie. *Get a grip, Brea.*

Nausea rose in Brea's throat, threatening an unexpected stop at the next rest area. She squelched bile and skimmed her tongue over her teeth in a feeble attempt to quell the bitter taste. Thankfully, light snow had begun to fall—the dusting on the roadway both a warning and convenient excuse to halt a spiral into black space. She placed her focus back on the road.

She shook off a sudden chill and shifted to thoughts of Beth. Nothing had been the same with her sister since Brea's move. In the past months, Beth had become distant and hollow-eyed. A gray pallor dulled her alabaster skin.

From Brea's end, leaving Beth and the kids was a loss far more painful than she'd ever imagined. The void had left her numb and robotic some days. Beth now had the full-time responsibility of raising two young kids while her cardiologist husband, Jeffry Marks, whose practice had skyrocketed thanks to the clogged arteries of overly stressed executives, spent his entire life at the hospital.

But Beth's demeanor suggested far more than a lonely, harried mom. A pang struck Brea's heart. If Beth had withheld news of an incurable illness, Brea would never forgive herself for abandoning her family.

Beth couldn't be sick. Life had to be fairer than that. Brea splayed her fingers, released her hold on the steering wheel and unclenched her jaw.

Only a few hours more and she'd lay eyes on her twin. While Beth could recite a litany of excuses for her appearance and distance—"I'm distracted. I'm exhausted. There aren't enough hours in the day," her defense when they Skyped—she couldn't hide secrets when the sisters were together.

One glance into her sister's emerald eyes and she'd know. She'd be certain if her worries warranted sleepless nights, or if the weight of anxiety and guilt was playing tricks on her. Again, she forced herself to relinquish her death-grip on the wheel.

An hour past Ann Arbor, Brea pulled off the freeway, gassed the car, and cruised through a fast food restaurant for a diet cola. She dialed Beth to let her know of her expected arrival time, but the call went to voicemail. Before she merged onto the freeway, she texted Beth. *Be there by 8. Boil the water. I'll need tea.*

Brea boosted the car's temperature and punched the button for the heated seat. The northbound Interstate had been well-salted, but the road commission could do nothing about the vicious bite in the air. She switched on a podcast and lost herself in a documentary on the Innocence Project—for the life of her, she couldn't decide if the high school boy had mutilated his girlfriend or not.

Once she reached Highway 22, Brea white-knuckled the steering wheel over slick roads. The two-lane highway hugged Lake Michigan. Scenic vistas and twinkling lights against the inky sky teased a single gaze out the passenger window, but Brea didn't dare allow her eyes to drift for more than a second, especially after a blowing horn jerked her attention back to the winding road. Finally, she spotted a "Welcome to Northport, Michigan" sign, then a nail-biting ten minutes later, a familiar mailbox. Tension eased from her shoulders. The half-mile gravel drive was marked by a single reflective pole jabbed into a mountainous snow stack, the topper, a tattered neon fabric triangle that flapped in the wind like the first flag on the moon—a lone symbol of civilization amidst a vast wilderness. She negotiated a slow, calculated left turn as ice-glazed pebbles crunched beneath the tires. In a tunnel formed by rows of pines, she guided the car up the stretch of stone. Far beyond the pitch-black darkness, she caught the glint of the moon off Lake Michigan's endless ice, then spotted a solitary light glowing on the porch of her sister's cottage. Her heart swelled as the first of her birthday wishes was granted. She'd arrived safe, and right on schedule.

Odd, though, that no lights were on in the house. But once Brea's gaze found the garage, she understood. The automatic door rose, revealing Beth's SUV, high beams blazing. Beth had plans—ones that didn't include a piping cup of hot tea in front of the cozy fieldstone fireplace.

She beeped the horn and motioned to Brea before rolling down her window. "I have boots and a winter coat for you. Hop in!"

Brea shuddered at the bitter cold, but as soon as she caught sight of her sister's face, warmth flooded her. Nothing calmed her twisted life like time with her twin.

Brea hadn't been wrong though—the sallow cheeks, the manic affect, the hint of avoidance in Beth's averted gaze—they stared back at her this very minute.

"You're impossible. Let me hit the john and we'll go."

She met her sister's flat green eyes in the glow of moonlight.

Inside the house, Brea discovered further evidence of Beth's derailment. As if a cyclone had blown through, papers lay scattered on countertops; wood shavings from fireplace logs littered the floor in a trail from the deck to the hearth. Food-crusted dishes cluttered the sink. Brea had seen quite enough, and dashed back to the car.

She clambered into the front seat and gathered Beth in a lingering hug. After she inhaled Beth's scent, she backed away a smidge to push her sister's hair out of those still vacant eyes. Being with Beth always made Brea feel home again.

While calm embraced her, Brea couldn't ignore the obvious.

Beth looked wretched, but Brea offered light-hearted banter instead of concern. "Stubble's?" she asked. The sooner they settled into a booth at the local pub, the sooner she would unearth the source of Beth's angst.

Beth rattled on about burgers as she veered down the curved driveway with precision honed by years of practice. The stable SUV grabbed the road in ways Brea had merely dreamt of on her slippery journey north. With the blast of music and hum of the heater fan, Beth howled down the back roads of upper Michigan, a bandit running with a prize. When the Jeep Cherokee fishtailed to a halt directly in front of the neighborhood dive, Brea's heart settled back inside her chest.

She linked her twin's arm and they strolled into the bar, picking up, for a moment, right where they'd left off. They moved in unison, the same wiggle to their walk, the same toss of the hair, the same sea green eyes, the same half-moon smiles, the same lilt to their laughter.

Mirror sisters.

Beth searched for a corner table. "There, in the back. We need an ashtray and privacy."

"An ashtray?"

Beth leaned close and whispered. "They still let you smoke here. A perk of living in the boondocks."

A frown settled and thinned Brea's lips.

As they made their way to the rear of the bar, a male voice boomed out, "Hey, you two identical?"

"Brilliant," Beth mumbled. "Mensa members drink here." She flashed a snide smirk and raised her voice. "Seeing double, are you? Perhaps you've been over-served."

Brea led her sister away from the tattooed bar flies. "Sarcasm already? You do need a beverage and a smoke."

They sank into vinyl chairs at an out of the way, well-worn oak table. Beth fished a cigarette and lighter out of her designer bag and lit up.

"Okay, you're beyond hyped. What's up?"

Beth ignored the question as Brea waved smoke away from her face.

As if on cue, the bartender strode over to their table. "Hi, I'm Art. Get you ladies a drink?"

Smoke swirled over Beth's head like a genie loosed from a bottle. "Hi Art. You're new here, aren't you? I'm Beth, and this is my sister, Brea. I'll have a Grey Goose martini, on the rocks. Dirty. Filthy dirty."

"And you, Brea?" The recognition of their twinship etched behind his eyes, he seemed to sense Beth's edge and kept his thoughts to himself as Brea ordered a burger and brew. Back in two minutes, he delivered drinks, set them on cork coasters with the deftness of a magician, then disappeared.

Brea tasted her beer, set her glass back on the tabletop, and leaned forward, her chin cupped in her hands. "Spill."

"I'm stressed is all." Beth directed another swirl of smoke overhead. She tilted the tumbler to her lips, poured vodka down her throat, and took another deliberate drag on her cigarette. "I had to let the housekeeper go. I'm so far behind I can't stand it."

Brea cursed under her breath, irritated at her sister's evasiveness. "Let's get this straight. Thanks to technology, we see each other all the time. But I haven't locked eyes with you in six months. Not really. You insist you're fine, and you say the kids are great. But here's the thing. Far as I remember, you haven't smoked in twenty years."

Brea sipped her Stella, rocked back in her seat, rested her hands in her lap, and waited. She'd learned a long time ago her sister would tell all. But Beth liked having control, so divulging more would happen in her own good time.

While she waited for Beth to 'fess up, Brea hit her mind's replay button. When they were born in 1981 to the last two Republicans on the planet, she'd been first out of the gate. Being the oldest awarded her several privileges as far as she was concerned: the upper hand, responsibility and bragging rights over her baby sister, and the common sense inherently afforded the eldest child. While their parents dressed and treated them identically, her first-born status revealed itself in subliminal ways. Brea hovered over her baby sister like a mother hen, often standing in the background watching while Beth tested every limit. She became her guardian and protector, on the playground, in the cafeteria, at those teen gatherings in Kensington Park. Kind of a shadow, now that she replayed their youth.

She had taken the role far more seriously after their parents died in a car/train collision one week after the girls' eighteenth birthday. Beth fell apart, completely and totally to bits, and Brea played dual roles—she attended all their college courses and navigated them both through their freshman year. Then, and in the years since, Brea had firmly adopted the role of older and wiser sister, or better, pseudo mom. Right up until Brea left Beth to fend for herself. The initial results haunted Brea. Self-reproach crept up her spine.

Beth, a constant jangle of activity, wiggled two fingers at the bartender. He delivered another round. "Keep 'em coming, Art." She flashed a twenty-dollar bill at him.

A hot fire blazed in her eyes. "My darling husband is boffing another woman. Wait, I'm too kind. My testosterone-on-overdrive husband is screwing a slut. Surely, you could have guessed." She sucked another deep drag from her cigarette. "I followed him this morning. After I dropped Jack and Ella at the sitter, I stopped back by the house to pick up some papers I'd left on the kitchen counter. He pushed past me at the door, headed out for a run. Shit, in January. Five below zero. He knows I'm headed up here today to celebrate my—Sorry—" She hung her head in apology, "—our birthday. You know what I mean.

"He doesn't even wish me happy birthday. Elbows past me, and bolts out the door. I've had a feeling. Gut instinct."

Brea winced as Beth tossed down the rest of her drink.

By some supernatural fluke, another martini appeared in front of Beth as Brea's burger arrived. Beth offered Art a thumbs up. "Art the b…ART…ender." She pointed and chuckled as he stepped away.

"Go on," Brea ordered, taking a substantial bite of her sandwich.

Beth closed her eyes and tipped her head to the ceiling. "Why do bad things always happen to me?"

Brea pushed aside the plate and folded her hand over her sister's for a brief moment.

"I followed him. From a distance." Beth's eyes grew glassier with every word. "About a mile down the road, he brakes, like a deer leaped in front of him. Stops dead. At a corner. He's bouncing up and down, running in place. But there's no traffic, right? So, I pull over and spy on him like the typical scorned wife. A car snuggles right up to the curb. He hops in, and guess what? He starts a make out session with some bimbo. Right there, in broad daylight. Parked, in a car, like a hormone addled teenager."

"Are you sure? I mean, could you see from a distance?" Beth had this propensity for drama.

"I'm not blind. Or stupid. I pulled up close enough to see their heads smashed together." Beth's eyes shot flames and she flapped her arms in frustration. "Steam fogged up the windows."

Brea reached out and laid a soothing hand on her sister's arm. "There must be some kind of explanation." At least she hoped so.

"Yeah. He's having an affair." Beth's voice rose. "T.H. comes up on his texts. There's a nurse at the hospital. Tammy Hawthorne," she spat out the woman's name as if she'd swallowed venom.

Brea shushed Beth as her own heart skipped. "A reasonable explanation."

Brea inched back as expletives swirled in her head, forming

judgments and accusations she couldn't voice. She'd long had doubts about Beth's husband. After all this time, she still grit her teeth at the mention of his name. Beyond handsome and obviously intelligent, Jeffry charmed even the most resistant snakes. He said the right things, all the time. Acted as he should, all the time. The too-good-to-be-true type. Brea swore the man ate charisma for breakfast.

But at the same time, he kept his distance, his primary investment being his three favorite people—me, myself, and I. Not unusual for a doc of his stature to develop a God complex, holding life and death in his hands every day. She'd long hoped the signals she picked up from him would prove false, because she wanted things to work out for Beth. But then there were those times—the way he'd tapped her on the butt when Beth dipped out of sight, the hasty apology that trailed his wandering hand. He professed his mistake—he couldn't tell them apart. And he'd kissed her under the mistletoe two years ago, sneaking the tip of his tongue between her lips. Impossible to ignore.

"Maybe we should head back to the house," Brea suggested, her mother hen roosting. "You're sloshing a bit."

"One more." Beth signaled Art for another Grey Goose. Her purse hung off the back of her chair and she twisted her arm around to drag out her cigarettes, lit one, then set the pack on the table and stared into her drink. "You still like olives?"

"You know me. I haven't changed." Brea vacillated between disgust and compassion. *Get a grip, Beth.*

"Here." Beth fished three of them out of the bottom of her glass. "I'm full."

Brea gestured to Beth's untouched burger. "You haven't eaten anything."

"Yes, I have. Olives."

Brea popped a green oval into her mouth, hoping her nonchalance would even out her twin. "We'll figure this out."

"Yeah. Sure, Pollyanna. Easy as pie." Beth balanced her cigarette on the edge of the table and yanked off her diamond engagement ring and wedding band. They tinkled as she flipped them into the grimy ashtray. "There. Problem solved."

Brea scowled and blew out a steady puff of air. Rather than scold her sister, she snaked the bands out of the ashes, wiped them clean with her napkin, and held them out to Beth.

After downing another drink, Beth's snicker built to a full-blown laugh, a sneer riding on its heels. "Don't need those anymore," she said, waving toward the rings.

Brea fought her own nagging thoughts. All she'd ever wanted was a husband and family. If she were married and had the endearing kids Beth had, she'd use super glue to hold on. She swallowed hard. "Listen to me. You and Jeffry will figure this out."

"In divorce court." Hurt lay behind Beth's fury.

Brea gazed at her sister with sympathy. "Sweetie, don't jump to conclusions. You have two beautiful children together. Kids count for a lot."

"What good are the kids if they have to grow up in a broken family?"

"You don't mean that. Slow down, for goodness sake."

"We'll wind up in court, fighting over visitation. I'll see my kids on alternating holidays. That's how it always happens with docs and the wives they leave behind." Beth dropped her head in her hands and wavered in her chair, the alcohol assuming a firm grasp on her, body and soul.

"There are other solutions. You could try counseling."

Disgusted, Beth bit her lip. "Spoken like a true shrink. You know I hate talking to anyone about my issues. You're the one who loves figuring yourself out, not me."

Brea held her temper against Beth's caustic tone and fought to remain calm. "And you tend to be a tad pessimistic. I know the kids seem like small consolation, but if the worst were to happen and you and Jeffry did divorce, you'd still have them. That ship has sailed for me." Brea patted her sister's arm. "I'm not trying to make light of the situation, but having kids is a blessing. Try to focus on Jack and Ella."

"Me…on my own? I haven't worked since I had Ella. How on earth will I manage? I'm not the supermom type."

"Take a breath, would you? Try not to get ahead of yourself." Brea picked at the last of the French fries and broke off bits of her burger. "Put your rings back on and let's get out of here. A good night's sleep will do you good."

Beth lurched forward, threw her arms up in defeat, and almost lost her balance. "This isn't just a bad day. Don't you get it?" Her words slurred as she tipped back in her chair.

"You might be drunk."

"He's a dirt bag. Like every other man on the frigging planet. Promise me something. If anything happens to me, take care of my kids."

"You know I will."

This wasn't the first time Beth had asked and Brea knew it wouldn't be the last. She rolled her eyes. She knew her sister better than anyone. As soon as a crisis loomed, Beth worried about not being there for her kids and pictured catastrophic events when the slightest problem arose. Beth. The-sky-is-falling sister.

Brea steamed. Personally, she could put up with a lot. But when somebody hurt her sister, there would be hell to pay. She imagined herself in Beth's situation with a husband like Jeffry, armed with whetted kitchen shears, a penis and testicles in her hand, carving them off with one swift curve of the blades.

She covered her mouth to stifle a snicker.

"What's so funny?" Beth's words slurred.

"I had a private thought. I have those every now and then."

"No, you don't. Let me guess. You're castrating Jeffry, right? Already been there."

Damn Jeffry. Brea attempted to quash her loathing with a slug of beer. "Let's get some rest. Tomorrow, we're going to pretend we're Scarletts, or Scarlett and her twin Scarletta, if you require autonomy, and forget about your troubles till another day. We'll sleep 'til noon, eat handfuls of birthday cake, take a long walk on the beach, and climb over the proverbial hill. The ride down the back forty has to be smoother."

"Be right back." Beth's words came out garbled. She snatched her keys from the table and tripped over the leg of her chair as she stood.

"Where…?"

Brea eyed her sister as she stumbled to the bar and tapped the shoulder of the biker who'd teased them on their way in. "Next time you see double, call a cab, asshole. Laws are stiff for drunk drivers." Beth's heated voice shattered the friendly air. Reality hit Brea. The state of the cottage, her twin's appearance, her anger and spite. She'd come undone.

Mortified, Brea pushed her arms through the sleeves of her coat as she raced to her twin's side. "Excuse my sister. Rough day."

Brea draped Beth's coat around her shoulders and turned her toward the door. "Hand over the keys," she demanded. "You are not driving. And zip up your coat or you'll freeze."

Beth fiddled with her zipper until Brea reached over and fastened it for her, then tucked a stray lock of hair beneath her sister's wool cap. Not like this was the first time they'd been in a similar predicament.

When Beth glanced up, tears rimmed her eyes, her voice barely a whisper as she swayed toward Brea. "I'm pregnant."

Brea steadied her. "Hold on. I have to get our bags." As she spun away toward their table, Beth's words took root. "Wait. You're what?"

"Pregnant, goddamn it. Got a bun in the oven…"

"Wait right here. Don't move." Brea hurried to grab their belongings, slung the purses over her shoulder and jammed Beth's rings on her finger as she noticed her twin spill out the door. She sprinted to catch her sister before she wandered aimlessly into the street.

Brea clutched Beth's arm a moment before she stepped off the curb. "I love you," she said as she kissed her sister's cheek. *Pregnant. Drinking. Smoking.* Shit. Double shit. "We'll figure this out—" her heart sunk as she checked her watch, "—and, hey, happy birthday."

Beth smiled back weakly. "Happy Birthday. Happy Baby."

Brea eased her hammered twin inside the Jeep, then settled herself behind the wheel. She glanced over.

Beth turned away. "It's not so great. He hits me sometimes."

Brea inhaled sharply. She couldn't believe her ears. Yet…when she glanced back over at her twin, soft snores filled the space between them. Beth. Carrying a baby? An abusive husband? The Beth she knew would never tolerate being manhandled. The Beth she knew had been more than content with her two perfect kids, one boy and one girl. The perfect nuclear family. She didn't want another child. The Jeffry she knew, a self-absorbed lout, couldn't possibly hurt his pregnant wife, then screw another woman in the next breath. Or could he? Maybe Beth hadn't had the chance to tell him about the baby yet. Maybe when she said he hits, she meant he broke her heart. Maybe she'd misheard Beth. Drunks say things they don't mean. For the life of her, Brea couldn't believe she had missed Jeffry's anger issues. Yet, dark secrets festered behind closed doors. And they could be doozies. Tomorrow she'd get answers. Nothing more could be accomplished tonight.

She swerved onto the back road, almost missing her turn as rural darkness shrouded her. At the last second, she caught a dancing shadow on the right, and jammed the brakes to avoid hitting some forest creature. Only sheer luck prevented its demise. Her foot slid off the pedal and she clambered to find it again, cut the wheel too far and nearly slid off the road's shoulder. Brea gasped. *Jesus, that was close.* Her nerves were already on edge—from the long drive, to say nothing of her sister's state, to say nothing of being in the same state with Peter for the first time in half a year. *Could the rest of the night not cut her a break?*

She pulled to the side of the road and tipped her head to her chest in a futile attempt to unleash the ever-tightening knots from her neck. After a long pause, she started down the road again, slow and steady, and placed a few taps on the brakes, the SUV's response feeling foreign under her boot. She had all the time in the world to get back to Beth's place. *Better safe than dead.* She continued down the

13

track of asphalt, on the lookout for road ice or other animals on the move, squinting to tune in her night vision, a tense grip on the wheel.

In the distance, the moon danced behind puffy clouds, outlining them in silver, sending deep shadows across snow-covered fields. Memories flickered—standing up in Beth's wedding, secretly yearning for a lightning strike to keep her sister from marrying, period, much less marrying the schmoozer. She reached over and clutched her sister's hand. A vision of Beth's face came to mind, how she'd beamed through exhaustion after giving birth to Ella.

How could so much have changed in the short six months she'd been away?

She glanced over at her lightly snoring sister, cursed Jeffry and wished for an easy fix. Beth didn't deserve any of this. Plus, she already had two little kids to worry about. God, she'd like to throttle her brother-in-law. Another reason to add to her Stay Single List. *Men. The bastards.*

Beth mumbled in her sleep. "Take care of me. Take care…of the kids. Jeffry…" She drifted off again.

Brea patted her sister's wrist and glimpsed the copper curls that spilled out over her shoulders. The deep fear that lived inside Beth's soul—of losing anyone she loved, Brea had witnessed firsthand. When Mom and Dad died, she'd tapped every ounce of strength to keep Beth within arm's reach of the rails, much less on them. Another loss might mark Beth's final collapse. To say nothing of the added hormones accompanying her sister's swelling middle.

Brea's gaze returned to the road. From the crest of a hill, blinding lights barreled toward her. She slammed the brakes.

A looming semi spiraled. Spun on the ice-covered road. Sped at the SUV like a projectile.

Brea's right arm flew across to shield Beth. Her left hand braced the wheel. Horns blared. Torn metal shrieked. Blood-curdling screams pierced the night. Then, the awful crunch of weight against frozen ground.

CHAPTER TWO

Grant

THE CALL CAME OVER FROM DISPATCH AT 2:00 A.M.—AN ungodly hour even if you were accustomed to staying up all night. Northport police had reported a fatal MVA involving an Ann Arbor resident. A fax clicked and whirred through the machine, feeding Detective Grant Fulton the accident report. He recognized the name of the victim.

He scanned quickly. SUV versus semi. Minutes after midnight. Black ice. Two-lane highway. Semi lost control. Hit passenger vehicle. Two women in the Jeep and in the truck, a lone driver. One of the women, Elizabeth Marks, a resident in his jurisdiction, had been transferred to a nearby hospital in Traverse City, her condition critical. The passenger died at the scene.

The news—the names—hit him like a wrecking ball.

Normally, a uniformed officer would handle the notification, but once he knew, his heart weighted with lead, Grant couldn't fathom a stranger delivering the news. "Wanda," he said solemnly to the night dispatcher, "I'll make the call."

He would personally visit the survivor's husband and inform him of the accident, his wife's condition and location. Then, tell him about the deceased passenger, Breanne Watson, from Hilton Head, South Carolina.

The deceased. He repeated the words several times, disbelief echoing in his brain. Breanne Watson—his high school sweetheart.

He'd lost track of Brea a long time ago, but wished he hadn't. He prayed this wasn't the same girl, but his gut knew better. Brea and Beth had always been a matched set. Until now.

Focus Dammit. Do your job.

While Grant knew Dr. Jeffry Marks directly as a result of his mother's illness, the rest of Ann Arbor recognized him as a celebrity of sorts. The entire city, perhaps the entire Lower Peninsula, knew Marks' face from print ads. The University hospital had recently sponsored cardiac screenings, complete with free checkups for all local high school athletes, as a means to detect hypertrophic cardiomyopathy, a hidden killer. Dr. Marks, a leading cardiologist and thoracic surgeon, served as the program's spokesman and "heart" of the effort. His model good looks covered billboards throughout the Detroit metropolitan area. With squared off shoulders, thick ebony hair, a chiseled jaw and deep-set cobalt eyes, Jeffry Marks bore a face every regular guy in America hated. And most women loved.

Grant wound his way into prestigious Barton Hills and pulled into a circular drive. The older brick home, statuesque on its acre of land, adorned the bitter night. High pillars graced the entrance of the estate while floodlights illuminated the red brick façade. Grant hunched his shoulders against the bitter wind as he pushed the doorbell, and waited impatiently for the chimes to finish their song.

After several long moments, teeth chattering, he knocked and rang again. He listened carefully and detected movement inside. Shuffling from foot to foot, cold biting past the soles of his shoes, he shoved his hands deep inside his pockets.

The porch light flicked on. A bolt tumbled but the chain lock remained fastened. As the door opened, he noted a slender hand and the bold maize "U of M" imprint on an oversized navy blue sweatshirt. A young lady peered out at him, obviously struggling with the hour.

"Yes?"

Grant flashed his badge. "I'm Detective Grant Fulton with the Ann Arbor Police. Is Dr. Marks home?"

"Sorry. He isn't here right now. I'm the babysitter."

"Can you tell me where I might find him?"

"He's usually at the hospital."

"Thanks. I'll check there. Sorry to have awakened you."

Grant adjusted his coat collar and hustled back to his service vehicle. He headed south to the same hospital where he'd spent so many days just a few weeks before. His mother had been on the cardiac floor for a triple by-pass. He'd first met the good doctor then and observed his habits. If Marks wasn't home at this hour, Grant knew precisely where to find him.

Grant dragged himself into the hospital. He hated this place and everything it represented. He'd been here far too many times in the past couple of years. First, when he'd lost his partner Dave in a shootout and later over the long months of care his mother had required. In. Out. In. Out. It seemed like every time he turned around, she was hospitalized. The medicinal smell about knocked him flat as he stepped off the elevator. More than that, the antiseptic odor left him feeling helpless, powerless. He'd rather walk into a crime scene any day. He actually preferred the scent of decomposing bodies that reeked to high heaven to this. At least in those situations there was a problem he could untangle. He'd had no luck solving anything in this godforsaken place. He wasn't in control, but at the mercy of a system he despised.

I'm here for Brea, he told himself. At least I can do this one last thing for her.

Grant acknowledged the familiar nurse at the fourth floor station. "Seen Doc Marks around?"

"He may have left for the night. I can try to page him though."

"Thanks." Grant peeled off his heavy wool coat and draped it over his arm. "I'd appreciate that."

As she dialed, footsteps advanced behind him.

"Detective Fulton," a male voice resonated. Grant flinched reflexively as a hand slapped his shoulder. "To what do we owe this late night honor?"

"Dr. Marks." Grant arched his brows, surprised the doctor remembered him. They'd met several times, but a guy like Marks had to meet hundreds of family members. "Good to see you. Any place we can talk?"

"Sure." Jeffry Marks ambled down the bright hallway. "Let's try the lounge. This late at night, we should have the place to ourselves."

As he followed Marks down the hall, Grant remembered his first meeting with the guy. He had seemed too good to be true, but he couldn't put his finger on why. Here, at nearly 3 a.m., the doctor appeared ready to take on the day—fresh-shaven, bright-eyed, and cheerful. Grant frowned, unable to allay a nagging suspicion. From his years as a beat cop, he'd learned to heed these feelings, often garnering more from what didn't fit than from what did.

Something didn't fit with Marks.

Grant's gaze traveled from top to bottom. Marks presented a prime physical specimen, his looks photo-shoot perfect—no need for touch-ups or airbrushing—the perfect pie from Betty Crocker's oven. Marks' height matched his, 6-foot-4. His eyes, deep blue and flecked with gold, his handshake solid, his smile wide and inviting, and his affect genuine. He wore a plain gold band on his smooth, polished left hand.

Hard not to like the guy. Charm dripped off him like foam from a chilled beer mug. Not flawless, but awful damn close. The poor schmuck. Must be hard to be perfect.

Dr. Marks stopped inside the door of the stark hospital lounge and turned to face Grant. "What can I do for you?"

Grant took charge. "Let's have a seat." He gestured to the utilitarian loveseat to his left.

"Is there a problem?"

"Your wife, sir. She's been in an accident."

"Beth?" Marks' brow furrowed, but he remained composed. "Are you sure? Elizabeth Marks?"

Grant took an invisible step back. He'd witnessed reactions like this before. When he delivered tragic news, family members often repeated a loved one's name, as if to verify they spoke about the same person, the right person. He sympathized while confirming the dreadful details.

"Yes, sir," Grant continued. "I received an accident report. On 201 near Northport. Your wife's SUV collided with a semi. Unfortunately, road conditions are treacherous tonight from Traverse City north. Black ice."

Concern etched Dr. Marks' brow. "What's her condition?"

"She's been transported to Munson Medical Center in Traverse City. She's unconscious, I'm afraid. Her condition is critical."

"Shit," Dr. Marks said, his voice flat. "The kids."

Grant heard the words, but sensed a lack of emotion. Could be shock. Could be something else. Second-guessing people, a hazard of the profession, had hooked its claws in him eons ago.

"The children weren't with her, sir. I just came from your home and spoke with a young woman who identified herself as your babysitter. And, according to the call I received, there was only one passenger in the car, not a child." Grant's eyes narrowed as he observed Marks' clenched fists. Seemed odd the guy wouldn't know where his wife and kids were.

"A passenger? Who? You're sure the kids are home?" Marks fidgeted with his ring, then tipped his head side to side, as if trying to loosen a noose.

"Breanne Watson. Do you know her?"

Marks' mouth gaped for a moment, then, as if his memory had cleared, he set his shoulders back. "My wife's sister. They were meeting for the weekend at our home Up North. A birthday weekend. Guess I lost track of time." After a measured breath, he blew out a puff of air. "This is horrible. What's Brea's condition?"

"I'm sorry, sir, but she didn't survive. She was thrown from the vehicle. Dead at the scene."

"Oh God, no. Brea is her twin—her only surviving relative, her best friend. They're everything to each other." Marks' face fell. "This will kill my wife."

Grant's heart sank. Now he knew for sure—his Brea, dead. As he rose, pain stabbed his midsection. He reached inside his shirt pocket for a business card. "Is there anything I can do? Make a call? Can someone make the drive with you?"

Marks clamped his hand over his mouth and scrubbed his jaw, a blank stare fixed on his face.

"I'm sorry, sir," Grant continued. "Local authorities are waiting for me to notify you in order to determine who else needs to be advised."

"I'll handle the notifications. My wife and her sister lost their parents years ago. They have no one. Just me and the kids."

The pieces fell into place, and the grip of Grant's grief deepened. "A husband, perhaps? Was Ms. Watson married?"

"No, Brea never married. She always said the good guy got away. She's single. I mean…was single."

The deafening roar of his heartbeat stilled Grant.

"Munson Medical Center?" Marks confirmed.

Grant snapped back to the present and handed his card to the doctor. "Anything I can do, please let me know. I knew Beth and Brea in high school. I can't tell you how sorry I am."

"I should get to my wife," Marks said. With that, the doctor turned on his heel and marched down the hall. As Grant watched, his antenna recalled something else that didn't fit.

He'd seen the doctor late one night when he'd stopped by to visit his mom. Marks had leaned across a nurse's station and peered back over his shoulder like a kid up to no good. Grant may have been overly suspicious, but he knew better than to let a signal go unheeded. Moments later he had witnessed Marks and a nurse waltz down the hall together, then dart into a room. A patient's room? A supply room?

He chewed his cheek.

Grant drove back to the station, his brain on autopilot. He shivered in the gnawing deep freeze as he made his way inside. In a fog, he shuffled to his cubicle, sank into his chair, and Googled Breanne Watson's name. Plenty of hits, but none with new information about the Breanne Watson he'd known. Next, he typed in "Elizabeth Marks." Twenty-three hits came back which allowed him a glimpse into Brea's life. One, an engagement announcement from 2010.

Elizabeth Marie Watson and Dr. Jeffry David Marks are engaged. Elizabeth's sister, Breanne Watson, announced the engagement at a private dinner party held at The Earle restaurant on June 3, 2010. Elizabeth attended the University of Michigan and graduated Phi Beta Kappa, with a degree in Journalism. Dr. Marks is a cardiologist with the University of Michigan Medical Center. They will be wed in November of this year.

A photo of Beth, Brea's identical match, and Jeffry, accompanied the announcement. Beth Watson married Jeffry Marks, but Brea had never marched down the aisle. The guy she wanted had gotten away. While he hoped he'd been that guy, it sickened him to think that.

He signed out and left for home. Hopefully, Mary hadn't surprised him by spending the night at his place as she sometimes did. He needed a beer and some time with his memories.

CHAPTER THREE

Jeffry

JEFFRY STRODE DOWN THE HALLWAY TO THE NURSES' STATION. Perturbed, he caught himself scowling, then donned his usual mask, pasting an even expression on his face. He spoke to the clerk with a well-rehearsed calm. "Get me Munson Hospital ER on the line, please. Traverse City." He leaned against the counter while he waited. After a few moments, the clerk passed him the phone.

He introduced himself, then shot questions into the receiver: "How's my wife?" He rubbed his temple. "I'm a physician at the University of Michigan Medical Center. Medivac her here as soon as she's stable. Road conditions won't allow me to travel." With robotic efficiency, he recited his cell number, then handed the phone back to the clerk.

Jeffry stopped for a vending machine latte on his way out of the building. He drew in a sip, a ragged breath, and sauntered to the parking garage. The remote clicked under his thumb, and he slid into his silver Audi sedan. He turned on the radio, headed out of the parking structure, merged onto 23-North, and dialed his Bluetooth.

"Hey," he said, tossing his head back as the call connected. "Something came up. Be there in twenty minutes." He paused and listened.

"No, we're still on. Beth's been in an accident. She's in Traverse City. At Munson. They'll ship her back when she's stable. She'll keep until Monday. I'm not about to interrupt our plans." He swallowed a sip of steaming froth, fighting to ignore the vise gripping his chest. "Yeah, the roads are hazardous, too dangerous to head north now. She can be transported to the U after the weekend. Soon enough and better for everyone that way. Right now, I could use a drink and a good f…cuddle. See you in a few."

Monday morning, Jeffry smiled with satisfaction. He'd made the best decision for Beth, and for the kids. The timing of her air ambulance arrival fit smack into the middle of his morning rounds. Perfect.

Once nurses settled Beth in her ICU hospital room at the U, Jeffry's frame filled the doorway. He perused her chart. A dismal picture: broken jaw, wired shut. Concussion. Dislocated hip, broken arm. Contusions and edema. Burns from the air bags on her chin, neck and chest. Normal stuff for a cataclysmic vehicle crash. Bottom line, she was damned lucky to be alive.

He entered the room, closing the door behind him.

"Beth," he said, eyes glued to her chart. "Welcome home."

Jeffry placed the chart on the bottom of the bed, moved to his wife's side and patted her hand with the methodical rhythm he used with all patients. He eased the stethoscope into his ears and manipulated the circular orb beneath her hospital gown, onto her chest. "Good strong heartbeat," he announced.

He tapped her forearm. "Beth. Wake up."

She didn't respond. Jeffry pulled up the requisite vinyl visitor chair, an unnatural shade of turquoise, and sat. He exhaled. His head fell to his chest. No one watched him here. He could take a moment.

His body swayed, a foreign reaction for a man sure of himself every minute of every single day. He couldn't assuage the nagging thoughts. While he should be grateful the mother of his children had survived, life would have been simpler if she had died. Easier. He couldn't remember the last time he and Beth had had a real conversation, shared a loving moment, and certainly could not recall the last time they'd had sex. Six months ago, maybe. Her death would have been an easy answer. That said, nothing had ever come easy, and he'd never been particularly lucky.

He released another puff of air and attempted untwisting the tension from his neck. No dice.

Brea. Dead. He had made certain no one delivered the news to Beth. He would be the one. A bitter taste filled his mouth. Should be enough she lay mangled and broken but word of Brea's death would break Beth in other, more profound ways. Like he needed more problems with his wife.

Brea had made more white noise than anything. He hadn't been close to her, yet stood here about to tell Beth they had to bury her twin. He tried to recall what he knew about Brea. Cheerful. Helpful. The stronger of the twins, both emotionally and psychologically. His wife played the role of tender soul, and even though she sought to be the life of the party, clearly life had mistreated her every step of the way. Brea mopped up her sister's messes and everyone else's too. She specialized in child development, a psychologist who took on the hardest cases, the most wounded and traumatized kids. The autistic. The mentally ill. The abused. She'd helped Beth with their kids all the time. Probably knew them better than he did. Other than that, he didn't know much about her. She didn't make a difference in his life, other than easing his wife's anxiety over raising two little kids. For that, he was grateful.

Six months ago, after Brea moved away, Beth bitched at him more than usual. Jeffry cursed the shrink his sister-in-law had the affair with. If the jerk had married her, Brea wouldn't have left town.

Earlier, Jeffrey had instructed police to release Brea's body to Muehlig's, the funeral home at the corner of William and 4th Street. The mortuary director told Jeffry he'd prepare the body and hold Brea's remains until the family made further decisions on arrangements. Great. Bury someone he barely knew. One more thing to do because no one else could, or would. One more responsibility. *Totally twisted.*

Jeffry stood, leaned over the bed rail, and stared at Beth. He hadn't looked at her—really looked—in a very long time. He barely recognized her. Her face resembled an overripe squash, purple and grey, spongy where her cheeks should have been firm and pink, bleeding and raw where the air bags had abraded her chin. "You were in an accident. Going to be a while before you feel like your old self, but you're going to be fine."

The door to the room opened. A nurse peeked in.

"Sorry. I didn't know you were here, Doctor Marks. I'd like to check Mrs. Marks' vitals and deliver more pain meds, but I can come back later."

Jeffry urged her inside. "No, you're fine." He glanced down at his hands, noting a slight tremor in his fingers, and balled them into fists as he grappled for composure. "I'm just leaving."

CHAPTER FOUR

Peter

D R. PETER MAGNESS DROPPED HIS TALL, LEAN FRAME INTO the leather office chair and cradled his face in his hands. He took a moment to absorb the news. Brea. Dead. Times like this, he believed in fate. After he'd decided to simplify his life, Brea had meant a complication he no longer needed. And even though he hadn't seen her in six months, somehow knowing she thought about him plagued him, as if she possessed a Voodoo doll she plunged pins into with a deep and biting hatred. He felt her stabs on a daily basis. Right up until the moment he'd read the news about her death. Now, nothing.

Free from another headache, he should be ecstatic, but instead, he wanted more. To be rid of all of them.

His gaze swept across the framed diplomas on his wall, Bachelor's degree. Master's. Ph.D. The gold calligraphy and embossed seals lent credence to the framed covers of his books. Funny how he had achieved such respected success in one aspect of his life, and in another, proved to be such a colossal failure.

Cynthia made more noise than usual these days, perhaps since the time of Brea's death now that he remembered, yapping about the fact he spent too many hours away from home, when he'd actually been home more. She'd whined nonstop about her loneliness and her disconnection from the universe; she'd decided to quit taking her anti-depressants recently as well. His hands were overly full. He wished the cosmos would see fit to have lightning strike twice.

Short of wishing his wife meet a painful end, he'd be happy enough to ship her off to her sister's place out east, so he could catch his breath and decide what to do next. Somehow life had spun out of control, yet he still had a full schedule of speaking engagements, book signings, and appointments with clients whose own paltry marriage fiascos he was expected to manage. His clinical therapy method, arising out of a research study, was so successful, eighty percent of his clients who had threatened divorce on their first office visit were still together two years later, and cited Dr. Magness's techniques as the cure for their ailing marriage. He didn't dare lose clients now, but listening to them drone on and bitch about their spouses was the last thing he wanted to do. If only his avatar could handle his afternoon appointments.

The intercom light flashed before his secretary's voice sounded. "Dr. Magness? Your three o'clock has arrived. The Kerfoots are in the waiting room." Her voice grew soft. "They're already fighting."

"Be right there." Peter sighed, pulled his latest book down from the shelf, *Fix Your Marriage in Five Easy Steps*, and positioned the title on the inlaid coffee table between where he and his clients sat. He located an exercise in his workbook for them to role play. See if he could help them remember a time when they liked each other. The practice seemed worth a shot. And far easier than inventing an on-the-spot tactic.

He pulled his phone from his pocket. Still no response from Beth. Maybe she had lost track of her phone after the accident. He'd read the reports in the Ann Arbor News, but hearing an actual account from someone he knew and trusted meant more. He wondered if Brea had said anything about him before she died. The reports said she had died instantly, but maybe she'd mentioned his name, asked for him. How would Beth have reacted if Brea called out for him? She'd harbored her own feelings about his relationship with her sister.

Three soft taps on his door. Martha had this way of reminding him to stay on track with his appointments. Subtle, yet effective. Peter opened his office door and studied Jim and Ann Kerfoot. A couple in their sixties, you'd have thought they'd be happy since their children had left the nest and they had the house to themselves. But no, all they could do was finger-point and name-call. If Peter could, he'd send them back to kindergarten and teach them to play nice.

"Hello, Jim. Ann. Come in."

Jim, with a full head of white, mad-scientist hair and beady little eyes, and Ann, with her round fleshy face and lips pulled into a tight wire, were indeed, unhappy. They assumed seats next to each other on the narrow loveseat but pulled into themselves as if trying to escape the tension produced by such close proximity.

Peter assumed a seat across from them and folded his hands in his lap. "How are things since we last met? We were focusing on using "I" messages rather than starting every sentence with blaming words. Any luck?"

Jim narrowed his eyes and glared at Ann. "She still starts every sentence with 'You always,' even when I remind her what you said."

Ann shot daggers at Jim. "And he answers the same way each time. 'If you hadn't done blah, blah, blah, I wouldn't act like this.' Every word out of his mouth is a farfetched accusation."

Peter inched forward and rested his elbows on his knees. "For the next," he glanced at his Rolex, "forty-five minutes, we are going to practice "I" messages. Ann, you start. Tell Jim how you feel."

Ann twitched, but spoke just the same. "I feel furious when you rationalize your asinine behavior and claim all that you say and do is my fault. There, how's that, Doc?"

Peter disregarded her sarcasm. "Nice work, Ann. Can you share with Jim what would work better for you?"

Ann dissolved into tears. Peter slid the Kleenex box toward her and leaned back in his chair, waiting for her to compose herself. He knew from experience, either a quiet few seconds or several long minutes would be required. Jim picked at his fingernails like a nervous kid. Peter would like to say he cared, but his own crumbled marriage nagged at him like a raw heel blister. If he weren't a national best-selling author and authority on marriage, he might be able to weather a divorce. Damn Doctor Phil and his television show. Did he really need to parade his wife around like a pull toy? Blasting his whiter than bread life in everyone's face. No one's life was so perfect.

Pressure to live the ideal life proved a source of daily torment for a lot of people, especially Peter. ABC had been in touch with his agent, inquiring about his interest in appearing on Good Morning America as a featured guest for their series "Creating Lasting and Healthy Marriages" three months down the road. He couldn't turn them down, but he had to get Cynthia under control first. Her threats should have stopped after he agreed and followed through on ending things with Brea. The fact that he'd supplied his lover with the ways and means to leave town eased his own guilty conscience, but Cynthia still seethed with rage. She couldn't—or maybe wouldn't—relinquish her resentment. He'd thrown money at her, too, hoping another day at the spa, or something to add to her already overflowing wardrobe or a dozen or so pair of those spiked heels she liked so much would make her happy, but no luck. Headed toward broke, he couldn't seem to put on the brakes.

He supposed he could try an "I" message or two of his own. "I hate you" were the first words that came to mind though. "I want a divorce," the second. Maybe he'd better hold off until he could think of something nice to say.

The day Cynthia had confronted him about his affair with Brea flashed like heat lightning. She'd been waiting up for him, her hair in a tight bun like a scolding schoolmarm. Sitting in the dark of the living room and scaring the shit out of him when he arrived home still smelling of sex and Brea's perfume. His wife kept it simple to start, the words a recitation rather than an indictment. "I followed you to your lover's condo tonight. You should tell her to pull the blinds. Unless you consider it an obligation to educate the neighbors on the various positions one can use to screw his mistress."

"I never slept with that woman." Christ. He sounded like Bill Clinton. He winced in spite of himself.

"Nice try." Cynthia sat like a statue on the Queen Anne sofa, calm and poised.

Peter's chest deflated. He scrambled for a convincing story. "I stopped by Dr. Watson's to discuss a custody case that goes to court next week. Your imagination is playing tricks on you."

"Again? Seems I have an overactive mind, doesn't it? No worries, I'll continue to be your wife. How about this? Your career can't afford a divorce right now, and I can't afford for you to lose this possible deal with the network. You'll split the money with me. Right down the middle."

Peter stifled a retort. A startling chill broke over him.

Cynthia sat back and snarled. "What worries me is this. One of these women, or their spouses, will kill you someday. The thought of a lengthy estate settlement holds no appeal."

At least she'd chosen the cold as ice approach, rather than her usual screaming banshee tantrum. He silently thanked her for that.

She rose, crossed the room and placed her nose to his, nostrils flaring. "Just remember. I'm in charge now. I call the shots."

She had him by the short hairs. He couldn't afford a divorce. Still. Blackmailed by his own wife? Little did she realize, she wasn't the first.

Peter's professional demeanor kicked back in when Jim coughed. "Let's try this." He strode to his desk where he picked up two legal pads and two freshly sharpened pencils, then handed one to Ann and the other to Jim. "Write down everything you can remember about the first time you met." Ann pursed her lips and frowned. "Come on, now," Peter continued. "You love each other and we need to cut through the anger and fear. You're afraid to risk closeness again, so you continue to lash out at each other. Let's break the cycle."

Jim reached out a hand, and paused just before he touched Ann's arm. "Honey? Can we at least give this a try?"

Peter's mouth dropped open. The guy had been a self-absorbed prick during each and every visit for the past two months. Maybe he'd been making headway with this couple after all.

Ann blinked, either shocked by her husband's words, or suspicious.

Jim grinned at his wife, a dimple deepening on his right cheek. "Remember when we first bumped into each other at the Union? You wore a pink blouse, the one with the ruffles, and a tight black skirt. I couldn't tell you then, but those hips of yours caught my eye. The curve at the end of your spine. Whew. Sorry, Doc. I'm getting hot and bothered thinking about what a vision she was."

"Forty years ago, but seems like yesterday. You had tons of hair." Ann glimpsed Peter and explained. "He's always had more hair than is fair for any man to possess, and his mop grows like grass. Back then though, Jim had auburn hair. Can you imagine? My Jim with shocks of red throughout his entire mane. And his eyes reminded me of Paul Newman. He'd glance my way and I'd melt, my legs would turn to jelly. He was my first, you know."

"You have some fond memories quite close to the surface here. Tell me more about your wife, Jim."

"She laughed all the time." Jim gazed at Ann and then locked eyes with Peter. "She loved my jokes. At least I think she did."

"I did," Ann said. "You were funny."

"Where did you spend your honeymoon?"

"Niagara Falls." A smile crept across Ann's face. "We were something then, weren't we?"

Jim took his wife's hand. He cocked his head Peter's way. "We didn't spend a lot of time gazing at the falls, if you get my drift."

Peter sat back. Smug. He'd worked his magic. Again.

He could try to rescue himself. Rescue Cynthia. Admittedly, there came a time in life where you had to face the facts, although his wife, a complicated mess, with a list of diagnoses a highway long, seemed beyond repair. And his own narcissism, impossible to escape. He craved constant approval, the unceasing attention and adoration of a woman. Not Cynthia, but someone more intact and capable of real passion. Now that Brea had died and her seemingly daily punishment had ceased, he could concentrate on the one woman he desired. Sadly, she remained out of his reach. At least for the time being.

And then he remembered the damned letter he needed to deal with.

Time's running out, Doc. Heal thyself.

CHAPTER FIVE

Brea

THE SMELL OF DISINFECTANT SEEPED INTO HER NOSTRILS and stimulated her awake. She squinted as she attempted to gain her bearings. Stiff and swollen at the same time, she tried to stretch. Pain shot through her body. Every inch of her hurt—bones, muscles, a simple wave of her eyelashes—the slightest move produced searing pain. Brea Watson winced as she traced the wires clamping her jaw shut. She tried to speak, but her words slurred. She listened for a few moments to muffled voices, beeping machines, running water, and clinking metal.

She opened her eyes, moving them rather than her head, and studied her surroundings. The walls, painted a stark white, other than holding a dry erase board with two names written in marker and a flimsy magnetic strip, were bare and unfamiliar. Out the window, winter clouds hung low over city rooftops. Gloom seeped inside. She inventoried stainless steel poles and rails, gray on gray, silicone tubes and computerized monitors, and wrestled to make sense of her environs. Her arm, casted from elbow to fingertips, itched to the point of distraction. A pulley contraption of some sort hung from the ceiling above her body.

After several long moments she glued the pieces together. Hospital. Strapped to a bed. Her heart began to race, and her breathing came in quick, shallow gasps.

Then, in short flashes, the accident flickered in her memory.

She blinked as furiously as she breathed. Beth. The bar. Pitch black. Bitter night. She closed her eyes—blinding lights, smashing metal, the screech of her own screams. A void filled her with emptiness. *Beth. Beth. Beth.* Tears spilled down her cheeks until she slipped back to sleep.

Every now and then, one nurse or another ducked into her room, fiddling with a tube, adjusting a lead. When an aide checked her IV, she roused a little. They called her Beth. A common mistake. She stayed quiet, kept her eyes shut and her breath even. She only wanted to sleep, and to escape the pain.

Two days later, she awoke to voices. First, a sound she soon recognized as children's laughter. Then, soft crying and apprehension, followed by a soothing female tone. Brea lay motionless, eyes closed, and eavesdropped on her niece and nephew.

"That's not Momma." Ella sniffed. "I'm scared. I want to go home."

A gentle voice soothed. "Don't be afraid, Ella. Remember when you fell off your bike and your knee looked like raw hamburger goo?"

Infectious giggles tumbled from Ella's mouth. "Hamburger goo?"

"Yes, hamburger goo. Well, Momma's got lots of hamburger goo on her face, and all over her body. She's got buns on some of her burger, too. Some are made out of cloth, those giant bandages on her face, and some are made out of hard plaster and fiberglass. I bet if you and Jack are good, Momma might even let you knock on her cast. You can say, 'anybody home?'" The voice chuckled. "Give your Momma some quick kisses then I'll take you to the inside playground on our way home."

"I wanna go now," Ella whined.

"You made a pretty picture for Momma, remember? We want to pin your masterpiece on this board. I'll hold you up so you can give Momma a kiss."

"Momma?" a gravelly little voice called.

"Jack," the female voice directed, "stay right here, sweetie. I'll pick you up next, and you can kiss Momma, too."

"Momma," Ella's frightened voice called from a distance, "want me to kiss your booboos and make them better?"

A chair screeched over the floor's surface. Small limbs scrambled up and rocked the bed rails. Brea caught sight of Ella's strawberry curls. They softly brushed her skin as the sitter suspended her over the side of the bed for a kiss. Ella recoiled, pressing her head into the sitter's shoulder.

Ella spoke again, asking, "Momma, do you hurt?"

Brea moaned and blinked back tears. Little Ella thinks I'm Beth. They've confused us again.

Brea remembered Dana, Beth's babysitter, and turned toward her. The girl took one look at Brea's face and shuddered. She lifted the children down, one by one, and quickly dragged chairs to the foot of the bed. "Here, guys," she said. "Climb up here so you can be close to Momma, but don't climb on her. She needs air onto her boo-boos in order to get better."

As Jack toppled over the rail and onto Brea's legs, he squealed with delight. "Momma," his gruff little voice rang out. Brea stifled a wail as excruciating pain shot through her. She didn't want to scare the little guy.

Dana scooped him up again, and stood him on the bedside chair, folding his chubby hands around the top of the rail. "I hope you don't mind, Mrs. Marks," she said. "They missed you so. Jeffry, I mean, Dr. Marks, hired a full-time housekeeper, and with you expected..." she smoothed Ella's hair "...to be away for a while, everything's unfamiliar to them. I asked him if I could bring the children to see you. They know about the accident and worry about you. I'm not sure when you'll be well enough to come home. I thought seeing you with their own eyes would make things easier on them. At least I hoped so."

Brea lay motionless, paralyzed by more than just her broken body. Her head began to clear. As memories resurfaced, beating her like a battering ram, she wished they would stop. A sinking feeling claimed her chest.

"Don't try to talk," Dana said, leaning over the bed and gazing at Brea while Ella and Jack chattered and grabbed at the tubes and wires. "We won't stay long." Dana replaced the pulse oximeter Jack had freed from Brea's big toe.

In a stunning moment of lucidity, Brea focused her gaze on the fat pad covering the back of Jack's two-year-old hand. She inhaled the sweetness of baby shampoo drifting up from his strawberry-blond wisps and couldn't help but marvel at the freckles scattered across his cheeks like sprinkles on a cupcake. His green eyes sparkled. She shifted her eyes. Gazing at Ella was like peering at a young version of Beth.

Ella climbed down from the bedside chair and searched through the bag Dana had slung over her shoulder. "Where's my painting? I want to give Momma her picture."

Dana reached into the bag and slipped the creation into Ella's hand. "Here, sweetie. Show your watercolor to Momma. I'll hang it up for her afterward. That way Momma can see the beautiful colors from her pillow."

Ella pushed the chair to the side of the bed, clambered up, and leaned over the side rail. "See, Momma? There's you and me and Jack."

Brea struggled to focus on the drawing. She deciphered three stick figures. One, taller than the others, wore a triangle skirt and held the hands of the two smaller forms, a curly-headed girl, as evidenced by her geometric skirt, and the smallest, a round little boy with a misshapen orb of a body. All three faces held wide smiles with boxy Crayola-colored clothing covering their middles.

The door to the room creaked open. A tall, broad, well-toned young man entered the room in a tight t-shirt and jeans. Brea didn't recognize him.

"There you are, Derek," Dana said, turning to kiss his cheek. "Hard to find a parking place?"

"Yeah, the structure is packed." Derek caught Brea's gaze and winked.

"We're ready to go," Dana said. "Beth needs rest."

Where are you, Beth? I need you. Your kids need you.

CHAPTER SIX

Grant

GRANT WITNESSED SEVERAL DEATHS A YEAR. EACH ONE affected him. Infuriated him when an innocent victim lost their life. Pierced his heart when he had to deliver tragic news to a parent. Numbed him when death hit too close. But he'd seen enough that he learned to push past his feelings in order to do his job. Brea's death struck him differently. Even though he hadn't been at the scene, he wished he had. Being there would have made losing her more believable. Grief rooted in his gut, endlessly twisting. A week had passed, but he couldn't refocus. His thoughts remained on Brea.

If Grant hadn't volunteered to take the midnight shift for a friend with a wife due to deliver any day, he would have been home in bed when the news of Brea's death came in to dispatch. That might've been easier to take, hearing it on the news or in talk around the squad room, but who knew? A seasoned detective, he didn't believe in coincidences. Everything happened for a reason.

Brea. Dead. When the thought came, as if he'd been sucker punched, he couldn't catch his breath. He'd busied himself with odd jobs all day, trying to push away the unease and the sorrow. Never happened. Finally, he gave up, popped open a beer, settled into the overstuffed mahogany leather recliner, a gift to himself last Christmas, and kicked up his feet. Brea's death was surely a sign.

He mulled things over, tracing his lip with an index finger. On paper, Mary met all the criteria. Pretty, trim, intelligent, and good-hearted. She also had a great sense of humor. They should have been the perfect couple. From the start, they'd liked each other well enough. She represented comfort and security. But he had to face facts, she was a good friend but he didn't love her. She'd become a habit.

His choice became crystal clear. Life with Mary wasn't okay any longer, and she wasn't enough. He picked up the phone and dialed her cell. She answered.

"Hey," he said. "We need to talk."

"Why? What's wrong?"

"Everything."

"Be there in twenty minutes. I'm just leaving the gym."

Darkness settled early, one of those oyster gray midwinter afternoons, which quickly turned the world pitch black. Grant sat in the dark, frozen in some kind of trance.

Mary knocked thirty minutes later. He pushed himself up from the chair and opened the door. "Why'd you knock?"

"I'm not sure." She stood motionless. "Seemed like one of those calls."

Grant glanced at his beer. "Want something to drink?"

"No." Mary shoved her hands into her coat pockets. "Tell me what's wrong." She perched on the edge of the nearest chair.

He sat on the ottoman. "Nothing. Everything."

"What are you talking about? You don't look well. Are you sick?"

"No. But I think…" he paused, hoping some higher force would stop him, some infinite power would either drive him to say the right words or shut him up altogether. "We should stop seeing each other." He let out a weighted puff of air. "Sounds trite, I know. I don't have a great explanation. We've been together a long time, but this isn't working anymore."

"We're friends with benefits. Not much more."

Grant sat back. Her agreement surprised him.

Mary went on. "There's something missing. I go back and forth all the time. We get close, then pull apart. We've never been able to take the final step. I can't even keep more than a day's worth of clothing here and feel right. People stopped asking us a long time ago when we were getting married. Have you noticed?"

Grant's stare drifted from Mary's gentle brown eyes to his balled up fists. He turned away. A second later, he locked Mary's gaze. "This seems too simple," he said.

She clenched her jaw before she spoke. "I'm the one who keeps trying. You gave up on us a long time ago."

An audible sigh later, Grant muttered. "Unbelievable."

"That's for sure."

She rose and headed to the bedroom, resignation in her well-placed steps. She opened drawers and banged them shut. Ten minutes later, she reappeared in the living room, her possessions crammed into a small overnight bag. "You haven't been the same since the shooting. Something inside you died when you lost Dave."

"I suffered a flesh wound, for Christ's sake. Quit psychoanalyzing me."

"I'm not talking about a superficial wound." Mary paused. Grant watched her hesitate then forge ahead, resolute. "I'm talking about grief. Your partner was killed, Grant. I'm talking about an open wound. A wound of the heart."

"It was a long time ago. I've put that behind me."

"Keep telling yourself that. When anyone experiences a trauma like you did, they have mourning to do. You lost your best friend. Your partner. You act like nothing happened. Shelving feelings closes a person up. You're in denial. And I've watched you withdraw. From me. From Shaun…"

"You're trying to place blame, turn the tables."

Mary glared at him. "Stop right there. Just because you feel guilty, doesn't entitle you to lash out at me."

Grant abandoned the ottoman and faced her. "This sucks. I don't want to hurt you. You're terrific, Mary. You always have been."

Her eyes conveyed hurt and resentment, tears pooling at the edges. "Don't you dare pacify me," she ordered.

"It's not you is all I'm trying to say. It's me."

"Knowing I'm terrific makes breaking up a helluva lot easier."

She stood rigid before him. He reached out in an attempt to comfort her. "Stop," she said. "Just let me go."

"Do you want to talk?"

"Talk about what? The fact that you've been remote for over a year, although I've been patient and supportive, waiting for you to get your shit together? Talk about the time I've wasted, my biological clock ticking like a time bomb? Talk about the fact life passed me by while I waited for you to get back to normal?"

"Mary, please." He took a step toward her.

"Don't touch me."

He closed his eyes. "I never meant to hurt you." When he opened his eyes and peered into hers, they ached with sorrow. "I'm sorry. But you said you knew things weren't right between us. I thought you agreed…"

Tears spilled down her cheeks. "This has nothing to do with agreeing. I'm sad." She wiped her eyes and sniffed. "I'm sorry. I shouldn't be striking out at you. You're right. This hurts. I'm hurt."

Grant wrapped his arms around her and held on tight. "I'm sorry."

"I know. Me, too," she choked out between sobs.

He kissed the top of her head, her shiny black hair tousled and faintly laced with sweat from her recent yoga session. The air between them turned leaden. Grant sighed. What the hell had he done?

"Goddammit, Grant. I need to go," Mary said.

He released her and stepped back.

Mary paused in the open doorway, gazed back at him with tear-filled eyes and said, "Goodbye, Grant."

He stared at the closed door, losing track of time and space as he stood rooted in the single spot.

Grant tossed and turned all night, images of Brea haunting him—her easy smile, shiny copper curls, sparkling green eyes. With each breath, he smelled her honey-scented fragrance. He scrubbed his hand over his face, as if a simple swipe would wash away his memories. No such luck. They wouldn't fade. Finally, he sat up, threw his legs over the side of the bed, and sighed.

He flicked on the light and examined his bedroom. Nothing had changed, not the dark oak dresser, the oversized bed, or the shirt draped across the chair in the corner. Mary. Gone. Her leaving had been too damn easy. He pushed himself to his feet, wandered into the shower, and adjusted the water temperature. The bathroom quickly filled with steam. As he lathered his hair, he laughed—a long, ironic cackle. He'd given up the real thing for his dead high school sweetheart. *There was evidence of solid thinking.*

After he dressed, he snatched his leather coat from the chair nearest the door. On his way out, he greeted Saul Epstein, his neighbor.

"Howdy do, Detective Fulton. Off to work early today." Saul's gnarled fingers curled around his cane. His body trembled as he leaned down on the stoop to grab the morning paper.

Grant strained to hide his concern as he beat Saul to the task. He dusted snowflakes off the frigid newsprint, folded and handed the paper over.

"Good to see you, Saul. No work today, got a day off."

"Care for a cup of coffee?"

"Wish I had the time."

"I can have Elsie fix you one of those 'to go' cups she loves."

"No, thanks. Gotta run."

He slid down the ice-glazed sidewalk to his SUV, and headed north on US 23 toward the University Medical Center. The thought of heading back inside the place turned his stomach. But Beth was as close to Brea as he could get. Worth the agony. The drive took twelve minutes, barely time to melt the ice from his windshield.

Inside the hospital, he flashed his badge. "Have a patient named Beth Marks? Elizabeth, maybe." He spoke to the woman wearing a blue volunteer jacket at the information desk, then folded his badge over and replaced the case in his inside pocket.

She perused the long list of M's in front of her, then handed him a sticky rectangular label. "Just peel off the back and wear the pass on your jacket. The room number is in the upper right hand corner."

"Thanks." Grant followed instructions and headed to the elevators, all the while questioning why he'd come. He hated to admit he acted out of pure selfishness. Pure curiosity. His grief over losing Brea was his alone, not Beth's concern. Still, offering sympathy seemed right. Motivated by his own loss and some ridiculous delusion, he recognized he could reckon with or rationalize those facts later. He hesitated in the doorway of Beth's ICU room.

A nurse noticed him and said hello.

"Beth Marks' room?"

"Yes," the nurse said. "I gave her some pain meds a minute ago. She's been a bit more alert lately, but with what I've given her, she'll be pretty groggy."

"Thanks for letting me know." Grant stepped aside as the nurse left the room. He strode to the bedside and spoke softly. "Beth?"

The woman's eyes flickered, confusion momentarily filling them.

Grant registered her bewildered expression, made more difficult to read from her swollen purple flesh and mangled body. He immediately regretted the impulse that had led him here. He backed away, but she ever so slightly cocked her head at him. Imagining her trying to place him, he drew a chair to the bedside and gently took her hand.

"Sorry, I probably shouldn't have come, but I'm an old friend of your sister. Grant Fulton. You remember me. I dated Brea back in high school. You probably think I'm crazy, showing up like this… but I had to…"

Her gaze narrowed.

"I've been awake all night," he continued, "and I apologize. Just showing up like this, some guy from the past." *Get a grip, idiot. Look at her. She can't even speak.*

He peered into her eyes, hoping for a sign. A hint of recognition creased her brow.

She continued to stare at him.

"I had to see you. Don't ask me why." *I do know why. I wanted there to be a mistake. I wanted Brea to be alive.* "Since I heard about the accident, and once I realized Brea had died…" Grant rubbed his temples, struggling to push back the pain "…I needed to speak to you." He spiraled, aware of his babbling, but unable to stop. "Tell you that I loved her."

Grant slumped back in the chair and all the air whooshed out of him. There. He'd said it. He took a moment to sit and settle with his thoughts. Brea's death changed him. In an instant, he realized. Made him frantic to hurry up and live the life he wanted, not necessarily the one he had. He regretted so many things. Maybe Mary had been right. Maybe he needed to face his losses, and slam headlong into them instead of running away. He wanted the simplest of things. To love and be loved. But those he loved most were gone.

Despair and emptiness flooded him. Tears pooled in his eyes and his face flushed as he fought them back. "I still love her." He blinked and swiped at a single teardrop escaping down his cheek.

Beth studied him, her eyes spilling over with tears. He foraged the clean handkerchief from his pocket, reached out, and tenderly dabbed at her face. He sat back and reached for her hand again.

She kept her gaze locked on him, as if to reassure him that she welcomed his presence.

"I remember so much about her. Like we were together yesterday." He recalled how Brea's green eyes softened when she smiled at him, how silky-smooth her lips were when they met his, how he warmed when he touched her freckled skin, playing connect the dots. "Maybe I'm sentimental because she was my first love, but I've got to tell you, if she were alive today, I'd hunt her down and convince her to give me a second chance." He saddened at the broken possibility. "Silly, I know."

Grant rested a fist against his forehead, his gaze settling on Beth. Her breath evened out, and she appeared to be listening. The enormity of her loss, and his own, stabbed him like a sharp blade.

"I can't help but wonder…"

A flood of tears drenched Beth's cheeks, startling him.

"Oh no. I'm making things worse."

Grant sank back in his chair and rammed the toe of his shoe into the floor. Like him, Brea hadn't had a spouse or kids. They'd both missed out.

"Brea loved you more than anyone. I knew her well enough to tell you she'd want you, above all, to know she was glad you're the one who survived. You're the one with the kids, the family. She'd be happy you're still here to raise your kids."

Then he leaned forward, took the woman's hand in his again, and stroked her skin, for a moment imagining a gentle squeeze in return. He envisioned holding Brea's hand for the last time.

CHAPTER SEVEN

Brea

WHILE CHAINED TO HER CONSTANT COMPANIONS, THE blinking monitors and adhesive leads, Brea studied the clock. Two in the morning. She wrestled with time, dreams, reality, hallucinations. Grant Fulton. He had been here, in this room. No. Not possible.

Whether she'd dreamed his visit or not didn't matter. Real or imagined, thoughts of being with him made her feel more complete. Like hope lived somewhere—off beyond the horizon. She slowly inhaled, then let out a deep and deliberate breath. A clean, relaxed breath. She replayed the dream in fits and starts, listening again to Grant's tender words, the information he'd shared. He'd confirmed her greatest fear.

When her memory floated to what he'd said about Beth, she gasped, frozen with shock. Beth had died in the accident.

Beth. Dead. She wanted to have misheard him. Maybe she had. Too many drugs had caused her to hallucinate. Again.

Brea squeezed her eyes shut, her standard attempt to block the agonizing pain. She slept again, tortured by nightmares and nausea. When she awoke, the flashes of memory continued to haunt her— the explosion of breaking glass, the paralyzing flood of headlights. To move away from them, she sought clarity—a rewind of the days since she'd been in the hospital. When her nurse arrived at 7:00 a.m. with a fresh vial of medication, Brea muffled words through a wired jaw, "No…more…meds." She fixed her gaze on the vials dripping into her IV, then locked eyes with the nurse, determined not to give in.

"Oh, honey. Don't stop yet. Take them a few days longer. Your jaw will give you fits, to say nothing of the other injuries."

"Only…night," Brea grunted, tired of the mind-muddling drug fog.

The nurse rested a hand on her arm. "Are you sure?"

Brea nodded. She watched the nurse place the filled syringe on the tray table, jot some chart notes, pick up the unused medication, and turn down the lights as she left the room. Still tense with pain, Brea willed her mind and her body to relax. Calling to mind the Yoga meditation she'd once practiced, she breathed in and out, steadying her pulse, focusing on the inside of her eyelids.

As she inhaled, she smelled Grant's cologne, a mix of oak and spice, the same scent he'd worn years ago. She hadn't dreamt or imagined a thing. He had been here. He'd filled out some, but had the same strong jaw, deep dimples, and, she imagined, heart-warming grin. The thick blond hair and deep-set blue eyes that made her fall for him in the first place hadn't faded. She had loved how he towered over her, tall and strong. She'd felt secure in his shadow.

She missed those days. Wished she could find a time machine and take a quick trip back to the beach, or the championship football game. She missed Grant, but she ached for Beth.

After several minutes, she opened her eyes and attempted words. "Oh, Beth." Sobs wracked her. "Come back to me."

Determined to get some answers, she opened and closed her un-injured hand while she practiced trying to speak. "My sister. I want to see her." Her words came out like gibberish, even to her, and her throat filled with tears. With a basketball-sized face, a jaw wired shut, and a leathery tongue the size of a spatula, fluent language came up short. Twelve minutes later, she glanced up at the illuminated hands of the clock. Nothing had changed. She still couldn't talk. Too drained to move. Beth still dead. Exhausted. Raw. Muddled.

She awoke to dancing shadows as they flickered from the pulse of lights on her monitors. Once they had soothed her, a welcome sign of life. Now, they itched behind her eyes. She ached to jump out of bed, to move her body without pain. She practiced talking and flexed her muscles for five minutes longer this time before she floated into a memory, a sharp stab of guilt along with the recollection. She'd never shared the episode with Beth, or with anyone other than her own therapist almost twenty years before. She ground over the timeline in her head, and guessed fifteen years or more had passed since she stopped blaming herself. At least she'd thought she had.

Dad had found the letter Brea carelessly left atop her dresser instead of tucking the evidence back into the hiding place at the rear of her underwear drawer. He'd ambled into her room to say goodbye before he and Mom left for their twentieth anniversary weekend on the Miracle Mile in Chicago. Beth had gone to play practice. Dad, packed and ready to go, came in to kiss Brea goodbye and leave last minute instructions.

She should have been more careful. Even now the recklessness made her wince. Perpetually curious, Dad always checked out every piece of paper in the house as if it were meant for his eyes. He never missed a chance to snoop. She'd been lying on her bed, leaning on her elbows, legs kicked up behind her, with ankles threaded like a pretzel knot, pretending to read *Lady Chatterley's Lover*, trying to think how she'd confront Mom if this special weekend didn't work, didn't make her forget…whoever he was.

As usual, she ignored her dad when he strode in, a typical eighteen-year-old. Brea had stumbled across the note while in search of a postage stamp—a letter Mom had written to her lover. Brea intended to confront her mother with the note, and convince her that marriage and family mattered more than some torrid fling. And after the shock of the daunting news, she'd blocked out removing the page from her mom's desk drawer. Denial on steroids. She'd been so young. She could hardly expect to wage control over her mother's passion for another man. But she had learned that lesson the hard way, and only in hindsight.

Dad lifted the letter. "What's this?"

A moment later, his words registered. By the time Brea glanced over her shoulder, he'd put the pieces together. His outrage shot through the house like cannon fire. Her mom, startled and scrambling, had tried to calm and soothe him with a litany of lies, but he was inconsolable. She tried to shush him, and begged and pleaded in vain that they wait until later to discuss "it."

The vicious fight, the awkward goodbyes, those fiercely tense moments marked the last time Brea saw her parents alive. More nights than she cared to remember, she'd lain awake, shivering under the weight of three blankets, unable to forgive her mistake—causing her parent's death, Beth's loss, a life gone haywire—for years. The trauma led to her choice of careers, her life alone, her fear of love and commitment. Then finally the counseling had registered, at least in a logical sense; none of those consequences were her fault. If Mom hadn't left the letter lying around… Plus, Brea grew up. Funny how things changed when viewed through adult eyes. Still, the scar tissue remained. Thick as armor.

Then, again, the hairs on her arms prickled with remorse. A knot the size of a small country grew in her stomach. A mother's sin bequeathed to her daughter.

A jolt of insight assaulted her. She'd always focused on her mother's betrayal and protecting her sister from the truth. Beth had had the luxury of mourning their parents' deaths naturally, while the pain and guilt chewed at Brea for years. She questioned whether pushing the pain away had cost her more than letting it consume her in the way Beth had. Who had chosen the better route? Her heart shattered. Now she'd lost Beth, too. She'd lost everyone, and at her own hand. Gone. All of them. Wracking sobs consumed her for the first time in twenty-some years. If only she could trade places with them. Death would be a welcome gift.

Once the tears ran dry, drugs took over, and her mind and body floated in a trance-like state.

Muffled voices entered the periphery of her subconscious. She feigned sleep and listened, picking up a word here and there. Instinct spiked the hair on her neck.

"She'd be better off dead." A woman's voice. Unrecognizable.

"You shouldn't be here," Jeffry warned.

"Just imagine," the woman said. "If she'd died instead of her sister, we could get married. I could be your wife. A real wife. I could be mother to your children. We could have a family of our own. Maybe you could slip her something. Or just hold this pillow over her head. She can't fight back."

"Shhh. Unconscious doesn't mean deaf." Jeffry hissed in a whisper. "You can't be here. I'll call you later. We'll make plans then. Not now."

"Easier for her to go tonight with a clot, or maybe she drank the wrong thing. She's too drugged to catch on. And with that head injury…"

Jeffry's voice turned firm. "You're being evil," he said, then taunted, "and a wicked temptress."

Brea peeked out as the door latch clicked. She glimpsed the flash of a nurse's uniform as Jeffry led the woman into the hall.

This woman, this nurse, Jeffry's mistress no doubt, wanted Beth dead. Goosebumps rose on her flesh. How could he have even allowed her into the room and listened to her sick desires? Practically colluded with her. The coldness of the woman's words brought a shudder as Brea fought to keep her body still and free from pain. In spite of the leftover drug fog, a burst of adrenalin coursed through her.

Trapped by more than her broken body, Brea grappled to make sense of what she'd heard. She blinked and assured herself time passed as she watched the second hand travel around the clock's face. Maybe Beth had a premonition. Maybe this time she had known something. She'd made Brea promise to care for the kids.

What if this woman came back alone, without Jeffry to temper her actions? Or worse…Jeffry unleashed the monster Beth described.

No way would Brea allow Jeffry to raise those kids. They weren't just his blood, they were hers too, and all she had left. Over her dead body would she permit another woman to step into Beth's shoes. No way would she let that woman near Jack and Ella. She'd sooner die than have Jeffry's mistress take Beth's place. Sooner die than lose what remained of her family. Besides, if Brea did step back, what new wife would accept her sister's identical twin as part of the family? Brea would surely lose Jack and Ella if that were to happen.

Memories assaulted her in jagged shards, like shrapnel from an explosion. Then booming realizations, as if she'd stepped on a land mine. Brea remembered a former client who died of leukemia leaving two toddlers behind. Her husband had married his mistress less than six months later.

Brea grasped the bed rail with her left hand and tried to sit up, but she had no strength. With her dominant arm broken and casted she couldn't grip a thing. She needed to make plans, face reality, clear the cobwebs from her brain. Piercing pain halted her. If only she could somehow escape this madness, in some way fashion the reality of Jeffry's mistress and her death threats into a dreadful nightmare. Screw Jeffry and his mistress. She would not give in to the pain. She would not let anyone take Beth away from her children.

Breathe. In and out.

A moment later, the door opened. Jeffry, clad in a white coat complete with a stethoscope draped around his neck, paraded in, alone, a smile pasted on his face. "You're awake. You look different. Better. You're gonna be stuck with those wires for a month or so, depending how things heal. But there's clearness in your eyes I haven't seen for quite some time. Good progress." He set her chart down on the end of the bed and placed his hand around her wrist, taking her pulse.

Brea couldn't face him. She despised him—his phony bedside manner, his lies, his callousness toward Beth. The man had brought his mistress into this room. Talked about killing *her*. Discussed his "plans" in front of his wife. Her inner psychologist kicked in. *He's a sociopath. Certifiably crazy. A maniac.* At first glance, he hadn't looked sinister. But Beth's final words stuck with her. *He hits.* For seven years, Brea had missed the clues. She'd somewhat admired his polished charm. But…

"How long?" Brea asked. For once, the words were intelligible. Amazing what rage produced.

Jeffry arched his brows. "Oh, good, you're talking." He busied himself with her chart. "I guess wondering about time is right. You've lost track, haven't you?"

Brea offered him the slightest of nods as fury ripped at her gut.

He glanced up. "You've been back in Ann Arbor a little over a week. Almost two weeks since the collision."

She glared at him. *Who is this man?*

He busied himself as he copied numbers off monitors and re-arranged tubes. "I'm sorry, but Brea didn't make it. This was an act of God. Nothing more. Nothing less. While you may think I sound harsh, really Beth, you have to accept the facts. You'll have a tough time, I know, but you have to move on. For the kids' sake. And for Brea's, too. She wouldn't want you to mourn."

Tears pooled in Brea's eyes. This man, colder than the Canadian tundra, had been her sister's husband. Poor Beth.

He answered her unspoken horror with a matter-of-fact pat on her hand. "C'mon now. With time, the pain will ease."

Brea recoiled. This man is poison. He's talking to me like he's reporting the morning commute—yes, life is a bit of a traffic jam right now, but if you tap the brakes, slow down a tad, everything will work out just fine. Soon you'll be sailing down the road.

Wrong. All wrong. The fact that Beth was dead, which she still couldn't allow herself to believe. The fact that he'd discussed offing her with his mistress. The fact that Jeffry didn't know the difference between his wife and her twin.

Look at me, idiot. I'm Brea.

He recited in a flat monotone, "You'll be fine."

"What's wrong with you?" she mumbled in a rage.

Jeffry tilted his head, unable to decipher her words. "I don't understand."

Brea begged him to see her. Brea.

"You want to know about your injuries, don't you?" He sighed as he perused her chart. "You did quite a number on yourself. Broken jaw, a pelvic ligament tear. Those can be quite painful and lay you up for a while." He bit his lip as he flipped the pages of her chart. "And then there's an ankle fracture as well as a broken arm. Concussion. Contusions and edema. Actually, your swelling is down. Your face was quite bruised and distended when you arrived from Munson." Jeffry studied something behind her head. "Knowing how concerned you are about appearances, you'd be mortified. You've got a ways to go, but you look a bit more like yourself today." He examined her face more closely and recoiled. "Maybe not quite yet, but no worries…soon, I hope."

Chills racked her body. "I'm…Brea."

"Free? You're a bit optimistic. But I like your attitude. A hopeful patient heals the fastest."

"Jack." Brea punctuated her speech. "Ella."

"They're fine."

"Who?"

"Who's with them?" Jeffry anticipated her question, finally looking at her without flinching. "Judith's back. I know she's not your favorite, but we need the help. Oh, Julie's brought food over, too. And Dana and Derek are a huge help. They pitch in non-stop. Everyone's been great."

The names confused her, probably a result of medication fog. Judith? Julie?

"I want to see them." Brea's cheeks flushed with anger and fear. Jeffry could be filling the house with threats for all she knew. If she could see the kids…

"Don't try to talk. You'll get worked up, and I can't understand what you're saying. Don't worry about the kids. They're fine. Feed 'em. Play with 'em." He patted her foot. "They're fine."

Exasperated, Brea turned her head to the wall. With each second, the weight of her grief grew, as if she dragged an anchor. She missed her mom and dad more than she'd ever imagined possible. And Beth.

"B…" she mumbled involuntarily as a grimace contorted her face.

"Brea? I had her taken to Muehlig's. We can plan a service once you're well. I had one of the girls at work notify her office. Her bills should all be online and automatic, so no worries there. We'll deal with the details later. Right now, nothing more is important than you. Concentrate on healing, so you can get home to the children. No worries allowed. I've taken over the bills, the grocery shopping, the laundry, the cleaning." He flashed a sheepish smile. "At least I'm giving the housekeeper instructions."

Brea focused on Jeffry's teeth—the whitest, straightest teeth she had ever seen. He stroked her hand, his fingers like talons. She fought to escape, pull herself up and away from the scene. The pain of being alive gripped her like a noose. She squeezed shut her eyes for what she thought was a second. When she opened them, he was gone.

She woke to the nurse delivering pain meds. Desperation tapped her shoulder. Plant a distraction. If Jeffry or his mistress returned to kill her…she needed a warning. She gestured to the nurse to move the tray table in front of her, the water pitcher to the edge of the table and place the call button in her good hand. Narcotics flooded her bloodstream and swept her off to Neverland.

CHAPTER EIGHT

Brea

BREA SLEPT THROUGH THE AFTERNOON AND NIGHT. She woke to searing pain shooting down her legs, but was so stinking glad to wake up, she tamped the suffering. She made note of the date, written on the white board, checked the time, and called to mind the days of ESP. When she and Beth were little girls and had spent their first days apart in different kindergarten classrooms, they played a game. They each concentrated on the other so they didn't feel alone and afraid. Brea summoned Beth, or Beth beckoned Brea. With closed eyes, they sent telepathic messages. Either as a part of their twinship, their fierce imaginations, or the strength of their bond, one often felt the presence of the other.

Brea lay stone still and concentrated so hard her brain hurt. Nothing. No Beth. She heaved a deep breath, calmed herself and envisioned her sister—her slender fingers, the warmth of her touch, her impish grin. Nada.

She'd bemoaned never having fostered a relationship with Jeffry. If she'd been less superficial with him and formed a real connection—not that you could connect with Jeffry—her predicament would be so much easier to handle. She could simply explain the horrible mistake and count on him, count on everyone to act reasonably. With the unveiled threats from Jeffry's mistress to deal with though, and his reported wicked temper, she wondered if she could clear up the confusion, come clean about the mistake, so the risk of a lethal injection or a pillow over the face might be less likely. As far as she knew, Jeffry had no need to rid himself of Brea.

What a joke. If she believed in miracles, she'd believe Jeffry to be a stand-up man like Grant, trustworthy and fair. Plus, she'd promised Beth to care for the kids. This was the best way to stay close.

Grief overcame her like a rogue wave, a current of sadness pulled her under and held her hostage. She'd never reach the surface. Never breathe again.

Brea let the pain and emptiness consume her. Tears filled her throat. Jack and Ella. *I'm all they have left. They're all I have left.* Brea turned her head and gazed at the photos someone had hung on the magnetic strip on the wall. Beautiful candid photos of Jack and Ella, playing in the yard, their eyes alight with innocence and wonder. *Her kids now.*

After Beth married Jeffry, Brea had focused on guarding her relationship with her sister. When they spent time together, Brea invariably craved the good old days, and huddled close to her twin. Jeffry, an up-and-coming surgeon, had a bright future. Beth didn't expect to see him often. She had instead thrown her life into raising the kids, decorating, and fitness. Brea never minded tagging along, and the kids loved an extra mom, one for each of them.

Her mind wandered to Peter Magness and his arrival in her life. She hadn't involved herself in a serious relationship in all the years since Grant Fulton. She hadn't known enough to trust Grant, or recognize true love at the tender age of seventeen. Her college beaus had been fun, but just idle crushes. No one had swept her off her feet since high school. Correction, Peter had, but he turned out to be painfully unavailable. A mistake she'd paid for far too long. She had focused on keeping Beth's head above water after their parents died. Then, she concentrated on school, completed her doctorate, and found the job she loved. She let so many years pass, settled for a married man, all the while believing she deserved nothing more. No reason to hold onto false hope.

Peter had entered her life unexpectedly. They'd met at an early Monday morning staff meeting when he was introduced as the new consulting psychologist in the practice where she worked. When Peter stuck his head into her office a few hours later, she was startled. She hadn't expected him to be so available, so... friendly. A big deal, this man. A New York Times best-selling author, paid attention to her. Blond curly hair fell just below his shoulders. As she took in his tall, slim build and the gentle pale blue eyes, the pull of sexual tension rushed between them, as undeniable as the pull of gravity.

"As you heard, I'm new in town," he remarked. "Think you could help me find a place for lunch?"

"There are great restaurants on Main Street," she offered. "All within walking distance."

He grinned, his affable smile illuminating his face. "Show me?"

He had her, right then and there.

She shoved her feet into boots, grabbed her coat and scarf, pulled on mittens, and slung her bag over a shoulder. "Sure. Why not?"

Minutes later, he guided her through the restaurant door and pressed his hand against the small of her back. Electricity fired up her spine despite a frigid wind whipping beneath the hem of her long down coat.

Although they lingered over a lengthy lunch, her face glowed well before the first glass of Chardonnay.

She listened attentively while he described his idyllic childhood, stellar college career, thriving practice, and groundbreaking papers in the field of relationships. He had amassed some of the most authoritative studies on marriage, on how to save a failing relationship. He'd published his first book a year earlier, already a bestselling self-help hard cover. He was forty. She, thirty-two.

He won her over with his assessment of deteriorating marriages. Years easily erased the delight of falling in love. Too many couples took each other for granted. Lost track of their vows, wandered off with a lover rather than take a few minutes to repair the damage. This was a wise man. Without knowing, Peter summed up Brea's feelings about her parent's marriage. If they'd just taken the time to recall and honor the strength of their initial attraction, they would have had it made. No fights. No death.

If Peter had been around when her parents were struggling, if they'd worked with him, he might have been able to save their marriage. In that moment, Brea knew she and Peter were the same as her parents had once been. Soul mates.

Now, eight years later, irony smacked like a hand to the middle of her forehead. Peter was married. She wasn't so different from Beth. How easily they'd both been smitten by smooth-talking men. Blind. Seeing what they wanted rather than what was right in front of them. Foolish, like men. Freaking hormones ruling their lives.

Before heading back to the office, Peter had loaded all her pertinent information into his phone: email, home address, and cell numbers. The same night, when her phone rang about 7:30 p.m., she didn't recognize the number on the caller ID. Against her better judgment—she never answered calls she didn't recognize—she picked up. He was parked outside her condo. Did she like Chinese takeout?

She'd slid under his spell like sand through a sieve. Sweat-soaked in workout gear, her face flushed, she opened the door. He wore a leather jacket and a smile that deepened the dimples in his cheeks. His extended hand offered a large brown grocery bag.

"This is a welcome surprise." She took the bag and ushered him inside. "Let me take your coat."

He handed her his jacket and stepped out of his shoes. He

rubbed his bare hands together, blew on them, and kept his eyes locked on her. "I hope you don't find me presumptuous," he said.

"As a matter of fact," she answered, a touch self-conscious, "I'm starving."

She set out plates while he lifted the takeout containers from the bag and strategically placed napkins and chopsticks on the table. Right at home, as if they'd been friends forever.

"I hope you like Moo Goo Gai Pan," he said.

"Don't even know what it is." She tittered like a schoolgirl. "But I'm ravenous." *For you.*

"Incredible."

"What?"

"You. You're refreshing. I loathe women who worry about how they look, who can't do anything spur of the moment, who have to primp and plan."

For a renowned psychologist, he'd totally misdiagnosed her. She was the ultimate control freak. Obviously, he hadn't caught on yet. He'd bestowed upon her the qualities he hoped to find in a woman. She decided not to burst his bubble, settled into her chair, and devoured her meal.

"And you eat with chopsticks, too." He filled her wine glass with a delectable Chablis.

"My sister and I traveled to Japan with our father when I was in high school. Dad went on business, and as a gift for our sixteenth birthday, she and I toured with him for two weeks. We spent time in Nagoya and Tokyo, and we both became quite accomplished with chopsticks."

"Twins?" he asked.

"You're quite astute, Dr. Magness," she teased. "Yes, my sister Beth and I are identical."

"So, did you play all those twin games? Trading places, telepathic messages?"

"We sure did."

"Are you still close?"

"Absolutely. Our lives have taken different paths, she's married and getting ready to have a family." *And I'm not.* "But we're still close. We talk every day and spend time together whenever we can."

"Tell me your best twin story."

"I never share our secrets."

He reached across the table and settled his hand on hers. "I can't tell you how much I like Ann Arbor."

His touch sent waves of warmth to all the right places. *Oh, God. Trouble.* "Where are you from originally?"

"Massachusetts. But I studied at Columbia, then NYU. I lived in San Diego before college, surfing and all that. Then the East Coast. Now, here. This past year, I've been everywhere. London, Paris. Of course, I've been on the road more since the book's on the New York Times bestseller list."

Brea's only travel outside of Michigan had been her trip to Asia. Impressed by his worldliness and accomplishments, she tried to still the drumming of her heart. Maybe this time, she'd fall in love. Maybe this was destined to be more than casual companionship. Maybe she really had met her soul mate. At thirty-two, she'd begun to settle into the idea a marriage might not happen. Single life was less complicated, but deep down she still longed for the day-to-day intimacy of a loving relationship with the right man. Kids. A family. The whole shebang.

Maybe Jeffry's affair had started in the same way. Maybe he'd been lonely. She stopped, horrified she'd gone from thinking of Peter to identifying with her brother-in-law's damned affair. A psychologist should know better.

A bass voice interrupted her memories. "Has P.T. been in yet?"

Brea jerked, startled by Jeffry's unexpected appearance. She waited for him to fill in the blanks.

"Physical therapy," Jeffry said, his tone brusque. "I've instructed them to get you moving. You're healed enough. The kids miss you. We need you at home. If you're too sick, we can send you to rehab for a while. What would you prefer?"

She wanted to scream. She was Brea, not Beth. But gut instinct stopped her. When they were kids, about to get in trouble, Beth could silence her with a single glance. Brea had always been the one who believed in 'fessing up and accepting her fate, but Beth had stepped in more times than she could count, as if to say, "Pick your battles, Sis. Not this one. Not now." Somehow, this was like that. Beth held up her hand, urged her to keep quiet. ESP had worked after all. Beth was just a tad late showing up.

Brea responded with one word. "Home." The word sounded like an obscenity, her exact intention.

"If going home is your number one priority, get to work."

CHAPTER NINE

Brea

EVERYONE ALREADY THINKS I'M BETH. THERE'S GOOD REASON to let them.

The thought festered like a bedsore.

Pure madness. The meds must be to blame. Or maybe grief clouded her judgment. Perhaps she'd suffered brain damage. In spite of the fact she ached in places she never knew existed, numbness consumed her. A tiny voice cautioned her, "think about you. Think about your plans." She ignored the message. There would be plenty of time to worry about her future later. As much as she wanted to high tail it out of here, she couldn't. And she'd made a promise. She wasn't about to break her word.

Her breath fell in ragged gasps. She longed for her mom, as she hadn't in years. If only she were here to tell her what to do. Mom had never really advised her. Channeled her, sure, when she needed guidance, but more like Mom expected Brea to know what was best, to be Beth's compass. Brea stared at the photos of Jack and Ella, their sweet, innocent faces staring back at her, begging her to be their mom. Becoming their substitute mother seemed like the smallest of sacrifices, especially if leaving them to Jeffry and his snake of a mistress was the alternative. When I feel better, after the kids get older, then I can…

Once when Brea and Beth were around eight years old and had mastered riding their bicycles, they took off on a bright Sunday afternoon, racing down the street with handlebar streamers flying in the wind. Mom had said a ride around the block in the fresh air would do them good. Adventurous Beth decided they should cross the street and go further than they were allowed. Brea tried to talk her out of it, but the idea held a lot of appeal for her too. The girls walked their bikes across the street, rationalizing that they were acting safely in spite of breaking the rules. Soon caught up in pretending they were super girls with super powers, they had ridden several blocks away. Only when they decided to turn around and head home did they realize they had no idea where they were or how far they had gone. All those familiar landmarks were gone—the boulder on the corner, the apple tree in the schoolyard they climbed at recess, the lazy winding roads. A traffic light flashed at them and cars buzzed by them at a frightening speed.

Beth started to cry, even though she'd been the mastermind. Brea had parked with her kickstand and stepped over to her sister, draping a scrawny arm around her sister's shoulder. "Even if we don't get home, we still have each other."

Even if Brea couldn't go home, she'd have the kids. And they'd have each other. And her.

She pondered the reality of daily life. Could she pull it off? Her last visit to Beth's, the summer before her move, Jeffry was frequently absent. His hospital schedule made his time at home sporadic at best. She'd rarely seen him, no matter what time of day or night she stopped by. *Would people notice the differences? No, I've been in that house. I know Beth. I know what she'd do. I can be her.*

From then on, Brea pushed herself. To stand. To walk. To dress herself. To bathe.

Even James, the P.T., was astounded.

"For someone who's been lying in bed for almost three weeks, you show amazing strength. I'm impressed." The young man smiled at Brea.

Brea continued to inch forward. James held the gait belt steady around her waist, but she felt tipsy with even the slightest movement. Her balance wavered every time she picked up a foot.

"Shit," she muttered.

She clenched her teeth, pain shooting through her jaw. The sooner she went home, the better. God only knew what the kids were living with. While Brea had only briefly met Judith, she remembered Beth complaining about her being a nosy, judgmental pain in the ass, a bible-thumping radical. She closed her eyes and hoped she'd be able to schmooze the vile woman into a cooperative relationship. Brea had always prided herself on her ability to accommodate and collaborate. And in spite of her fiery independence, Brea knew she'd require help when she assumed the role of mother and wife.

Patterning movement over and over, she winced with each baby step but didn't stop until James demanded she take a break. "Again? Tomorrow?" Brea hated to finish their session.

"Every day if you want," James said. "Our goal is to get you up and keep you up."

Brea agreed. Drained but dogged, she refused to surrender to her broken body.

"Tomorrow," she repeated, more audibly.

The next two weeks dragged by. Brea forced herself to walk with a cane, focused on one thing only, getting home to the kids ASAP. With her casted arm braced in a waterproof sling, she learned to shower one-handed, adapted to dressing and feeding herself, and somewhat mastered speaking through her wires, intelligible when she spoke in an abbreviated fashion, enunciating each word. Tasks which once went unnoticed became insurmountable and exhausting.

She also woke each morning to Jeffry's slack form sleeping in the chair next to her bed. When she began to stir, he would awaken, rub his eyes, and cast a concerned expression her way.

The night before her scheduled discharge, Jeffry slowed in her doorway at dusk. Brea sat in the vinyl recliner, her chair angled toward the window where she'd watched the sunset fade below the horizon some time ago. His quick five-minute visits at the end of the day had become habit and much unlike the late night visit she'd overheard with his mistress. Even though the visits were often short, Brea read an unmistakable growing care and concern in his eyes each time he stopped by. Or did she imagine it? As she turned to glance back at him, she wondered if he was still seeing his lover, if the accident had brought him closer to home, or if his mistress' threats to kill his wife had scared him silly. Undeniably, something had shifted.

"I can come home soon," she said, articulating each word as best she could, hoping he would understand.

Jeffry stood before her, shoulder resting against the window frame.

"Good." He forced a half-smile.

Brea studied the dark circles carved beneath his eyes, the hollowed out gray space. "Tired?" she asked.

"Whipped."

"Go home. Rest."

"That's the plan," he said. "But first, I want to spend a little time with the kids. I think I'm going to kick out the nanny. Read *Wild Things* to them. Dad's gonna tuck them in tonight, not some stranger." He came to life as he spoke of the kids.

This man was becoming a source of constant confusion. Beth said he'd abused her. And one minute he'd allowed his mistress into his wife's hospital room, the next he acted like the doting husband and father. *Who was he?* A sociopath or merely a man in the midst of a midlife crisis. She hadn't witnessed him with the children in a long time and wondered how he behaved with them. Maybe he had changed over the years. Maybe since the accident.

She put herself in Beth's shoes and speculated. Beth might be surprised to see him this way. In all the years Beth had spent with Jeffry, she'd never described him as a family man. The more time

Brea spent around Jeffry, the more of a puzzle he became. "Ready for Mom?" she teased. "You'll…share them."

"I'm the rookie. You're the expert. They miss you. They'll be glad to have you back. Thrilled, actually. If Ella tells me one more time, 'that's not the way Momma does it'…" He snickered at the memory.

"Kids. Need. A. Dad," Brea said. "My. Being. Away…has been good…for…the three of you." Every cloud had a silver lining. If possible, she would line this cloud.

Jeffry ambled over to her and planted a kiss on top of her head.

"I'll…sleep…in the guest room," Brea said, trying to sound casual.

"Of course. You can't climb stairs yet."

"No."

"Let me know if there's anything else you need at home."

Brea had no idea what she needed. Every time she considered her discharge from the hospital, her stomach flipped uncontrollably. Best not to think about "home." Forge ahead instead.

"Well, then," Jeffry said. "I'll let you get some rest."

There was no denying the exhaustion etched in his gaze.

Brea braced herself and pushed up from her chair, Jeffry moving to her side to steady her and help her to the bed. She couldn't prevent herself from welcoming his touch. An eternity ago, she'd relished the comfort of human contact. Even the warmth from his hand—a stranger's hand—reassured her. She leaned into him, inhaling his aftershave. The scent smelled earthy, a mixture of citrus and oak. Rather than tilting back, she tipped her head into his shoulder and deeply inhaled the rich aroma, letting the tang soothe her. She knew better, but she'd been so alone for so long…

"Thanks." Brea eased down onto the bed and stared at him.

"Welcome." He beamed sheepishly. "I'm outta here," he added with a wave.

"See you." Brea stared after him, wondering about his awkwardness.

CHAPTER TEN

Brea

WITH EACH BREATH, BREA BECAME MORE AGITATED. Jeffry zoomed in and out of traffic in his late model Audi like a paramedic intent on delivering a critically ill patient to the hospital, rather than a husband returning his recovering wife home. While Brea was determined to block any memory of the accident, being in a car unnerved her. She white-knuckled the door handle with every shift of the gears.

"Can you…slow down?" she begged.

Her body still fragile, she bit her lip bloody. Starting a new life petrified her. She shivered in spite of the fact the heat vent blasted in her face. She longed for a recognizable sight, her belongings, and the stupid meaningless objects that centered her. Nothing she would find in her sister's house, certainly.

"Sorry." He eased the pressure on the accelerator. "I forgot."

"For…got?"

"That you hate my speeding."

She had no idea Beth had chastised Jeffry for his race-car-driving. Brea uttered a grateful moan, relieved he seemed oblivious to the differences between she and Beth, happy for now they were more alike than not. If only this blind luck would continue. She tipped her head skyward and prayed for strength, worried Ella and Jack might see through her upcoming performance. Experience had taught her kids were hard to fool.

The last of the snow mounds were melting in the golden sunshine as Jeffry took a sharp right turn into the neighborhood. Brea re-familiarized herself. A mature, high-end section of Ann Arbor, Barton Hills boasted towering oaks, splendid pines, and ivy curving with delicate strength along the rooftops. As they neared home, though, her heart rate quickened. She had been away for seven months and had no idea about the household routine. Navigating a schedule she knew nothing about would prove challenging, to say the least.

Jeffry slowed, pulled into the driveway, and waited for the garage door to lift. Then, he unexpectedly shoved the gear into park.

Her heart rate increased tenfold as a stark realization pierced her awareness. She'd now live in fear of being discovered. At every juncture. "Why are you…stopping?" Brea asked.

"Let's use the front door. I don't want you to maneuver the garage."

He hurried around to the passenger side, opened the door, and waited as she turned her body in the seat, anticipating her every need, staging the walker in front of her and offering to help, still the caring guy from the past few weeks.

They inched slowly along the winding brick path, avoiding the last few patches of ice and recent melt, finally reaching the stoop. Jeffry rang the front doorbell. An instant later, Brea heard excited voices from inside.

"Momma's home!"

"She's here!"

Brea's anxiety was replaced by joy for three solid minutes as Jeffry opened the door and the rambunctious youngsters bounded outside.

"Inside, hooligans," Jeffry ordered with a friendly tone.

Brea inched forward, tipping her head to examine the door of her new home. The door had to be twelve feet tall. Why had she never noticed this before? The bars over the arch-shaped window reminded her of a prison, one she was about to voluntarily enter for…the rest of her life. The gargoyle on the doorknocker snarled at her. Locks galore, meant to keep the bad guys out, would now trap her inside.

Now you're acting like Beth. Catastrophizing. Jeffry has been nicer lately. There are two sides to every story.

Brea stepped through the door, an anchor still weighing her down. As soon as she crossed the threshold, there'd be no turning back. The weight of the role sapped what little strength she possessed.

The house looked different. Imposing. She stood in the front hall, and took in the giant foyer with the marble floor, the rich alabaster staircase, and the winding stairs. She studied the two children springing up and down like baby kangaroos in front of her.

Realization hit her like a sledgehammer. No one would call her Brea again. The sweet sound of hearing her name, the belonging, the recognition of her individuality, how she fit in the world, none of that would ever happen again. The dizzying insight turned her legs to jelly.

"How's. My. Guys?" she asked, all the while questioning what Beth would say, wracking her brain for Beth's words. She hoped she was overthinking things, worrying too much. Her bruises and swelling had faded, but she still didn't look or sound like anyone in particular, and she felt like a nearly mute haphazard arrangement of bones.

"Momma, Momma!" Ella grabbed Brea's hand and started to tug.

Jeffry stepped in, loving but firm.

"You can't yank on Momma 'til she's all better." He scooped Ella into one arm and Jack into the other. "Into the kitchen, you two."

He marched ahead. Judith, the nanny/housekeeper, resembled an Amish woman—with long graying hair twisted into a firm bun at the nape of her neck, a full-length calico dress covering her portly figure, black utilitarian tie-up shoes molded over large feet, and a weathered face. She stood back unpleasantly as Jeffry took the helm. Clearly, she was more comfortable being in charge. No Mrs.

Doubtfire here. The poor kids. No wonder Jeffry was in a hurry to get home to them each night.

"Hello, Mrs. Marks, how are you?" Judith frowned, hands tightly folded in front of her as if Beth had invaded her space.

"Well. Glad…home." The words came slowly, but she managed, and offered a twisted smile.

"Yes. Derek, the sitter's boyfriend, arranged the guest bedroom for you. He's put clean sheets on the bed and fresh towels in the bath."

Brea straightened her shoulders. "Thank you."

"I told Dr. Marks I can stay on as long as you need me."

"Yes," Brea said, frustrated by the energy required to speak. She'd been home less than five minutes and all she wanted was a pillow and bed. As much as she wished the woman gone, she needed her.

Jeffry shifted Jack in his arms. "Go home for tonight, Judith. I'll be home the rest of the day. I want Mrs. Marks to have some time with the kids."

Brea's heart stuttered in her chest. Alone with Jeffry and the kids? The room began to spin.

"I'll say goodbye then." Judith gathered her belongings and headed to the door.

All her ideas about making nice with Judith were put on hold. "Nice…to see you." Brea could barely speak, and for more reasons than just her wired jaw. Judith knew all about Beth. Judith knew some about Brea. Having Judith around full-time posed a daily threat to being discovered. Sweat trickled down her spine. *God, help me pull this off.*

"Yes, ma'am," Judith said. "And ma'am?" She gathered her satchel and hesitated as she stepped out the back door.

Brea gazed at Judith expectantly.

"I'm sorry about your sister."

Emotion closed Brea's throat as Judith closed the door behind her. Beth. Her home. Her children. Her husband. Without warning, her legs began to give way. She wobbled and swayed, grasping the top rail of a kitchen chair for support.

"Beth? Beth?" Alarm sounded in Jeffry's voice. "Beth!"

A strong arm slid around her waist to steady her. The room went white, her ears rang and her body went slack. After a long moment, her heart rate slowed and air seeped back into her lungs.

"Better?" Jeffry asked.

Brea exhaled softly. "Yes. Thank you."

Jeffry whispered. "I've got you covered."

For a man who often seemed like an arrogant self-involved jerk, he now performed the role of savior. Not only did Brea need Judith, she needed Jeffry.

"Momma needs a nap. This was her first big outing, so I'm going to help her to bed."

As Jeffry helped her down the hall, Ella looked puzzled. "Why are you taking Momma to Auntie Brea's room instead of your bedroom?"

Brea's breath caught in her throat and she stopped moving. She rubbed her nose, her telltale nervous habit rearing its head.

"Momma can't do the stairs. Remember, her climbing bones aren't healed yet."

Brea offered him a grateful glance, and let him lead her into the bedroom. "Need help?" he said as he pulled back the covers of the bed.

"No," she said, her throat obstructed by anxiety. She backed away, her gaze hitting the floor. The thought of him helping her undress terrified her. She needed distance, permanent distance. But she needed him. "Thank you."

"Not a problem," he said as he closed the shades then pulled the door shut behind him.

Brea's head hit the pillow. This was too much. There had to be another way. She longed to turn back the clock, but how to go back and how far to go seemed an impossible task. A dull headache threatened to blossom into a full-on migraine as the impossibility of her situation took root. She closed her eyes to fight the pain. Could she leave? Could she explain the mistake? No. Trapped and unable to pace or move a single limb without pain, she lay immobile and stared at the ceiling.

She must have finally dozed off. Sunlight crept in beneath the shades and as her eyes grew accustomed to the light, she became reacquainted with the room. The creamy yellow walls, cabbage rose flowered curtains and country cottage décor, all choices she and Beth had made together, warmed her for the span of a few minutes. She'd spent many nights here. Her home away from home. Yet, she missed the security and confines of the hospital, her secluded safety net. She missed her condo. She missed the ease of movement. She missed the ease of her former life. Funny how everything looked simpler in hindsight.

Brea managed to turn on the bed lamp and noticed a school bell sitting on the nightstand. A note next to the bell read, "Ring me for first class service."

Her throat constricted. Jeffry was full of surprises. She knew better than to succumb to his charms, yet she felt desperate for a connection to the world. She told herself she was grieving, recovering from an abundance of injuries, but she had to remain smart, not fall prey to her vulnerability. Before she realized what had happened, she rang the bell. The entire family showed up at the door, the kids rushing in to climb on the bed.

Jeffry warned them off. "Careful, careful. Go easy now."

Brea extended her hand to the children, reeling them in. They could be her comfort. Her salvation.

"Momma, can I cuddle with you? Please?" Ella pleaded.

"Yes." Brea snuggled the child close while Jeffry helped Jack onto the opposite side of the bed. He planted himself on the pillow next to hers, shoving his thumb into his mouth and twirling a lock of her hair, as he'd done with Beth since he was eight months old.

"Can I bring you some tea?" Jeffry asked.

Brea blinked hard to fight off tears. Jeffry patted her hand. "Back in a jiffy."

Ella ran her finger along Brea's brow. "Momma, you look different."

Brea swallowed hard and her blood froze to ice. "Because…of my boo-boos."

Ella scrunched her face. "You look like Auntie Brea."

"Twins look…the same."

Jack unplugged his thumb from his mouth. "Momma is pretty."

Brea shifted her gaze to him. "You're cute…too."

Jeffry returned with a mug of tea and shooed the kids to the side of the bed while he propped Brea's pillows, then handed her the drink.

She sat motionless for some time, her head throbbing. Could she trust him not to spike her tea?

"I've called Dana," he said. "She offered to bring Derek with her. They're on their way."

Brea's eyes sought an explanation.

"We need help. This way, I can be with you if you need me, and we won't run out of gas managing these two rug rats. Judith will be here Monday through Friday from nine 'til five. Laundry, cooking, cleaning, helping with the kids, she does it all."

"Why her?"

"I know she's odd, and if I'd had more time, I'd have chosen differently. She's the only one available at the agency right now. We'll replace her when we can. For now, we have to settle."

Brea didn't want anyone in the house, especially Judith, as she remembered Beth's horror stories about the intrusive woman, but there was little choice.

"You seem tired," he said. "Should I take these guys out of here?"

"Not. Yet." Brea took in the scene, bizarre, but somehow reassuring.

Jeffry began to pace. "I'll put cartoons on for them. They'll be right next door in the family room. We need to talk."

The oxygen left the room.

Oblivious to her panic, Jeffry said, "C'mon guys. TV time."

They bounded off the bed.

Brea imagined how this would go. Jeffry would confront her, she'd be ousted on the front stoop, hopefully with a cell phone so she could call for a cab and find lodging for the night. Hell, she didn't even know where her purse or credit cards were. Her cell phone had disappeared too. Brea mulled over a thousand different scenarios during Jeffry's absence. One replayed in her mind above the rest. She could write Jeffry an explanatory note and leave the kids with Dana. Call a cab and catch the next flight to Hilton Head. *Chicken's way out.* But just the thought of navigating the airport, much less the entire trip, proved daunting. She could barely totter the length of the house for the moment. No way could she manage traveling alone.

When Jeffry returned, he cracked open the door and came to sit on the side of the bed, not at all ready to attack her as she had envisioned, but scratching his jaw, a sign Brea had come to interpret as nervousness or apprehension. Still, she pulled into herself.

"You…seem on edge," she said.

He rubbed his hands together and laced his fingers. "No, I'm fine."

Brea shifted on the bed, bending at the hips to ease the pain pulsing through her abdomen. Her breathing became shallow. "I…" She broke off, not knowing what to say.

"Brea," he said.

Her heart arrested. She tipped her head down, avoiding his gaze.

"We need to talk about Brea."

Brea closed her eyes and prayed Jeffry missed seeing the wave of relief wash over her. A web of knots strangled her gut. She'd never pull this off, not without having a heart attack or a grand mal seizure.

"Not yet."

"Listen, Beth. I don't want to upset you, but we need to make some decisions about a funeral. Some kind of memorial service."

Brea stared at him. Bury me. Bury Beth.

She couldn't think straight.

"Shit, I didn't mean to upset you. Can I get you something?"

"I feel…strange." She wished he knew how strange, how far outside her body she'd gone, how suspended everything had become, as if gravity had vanished, floating images of dead people, or living people who looked dead, was all she could see. Ringing filled her ears.

Jeffry studied her with a clinical look. "Your color's a little off." His fingers found the pulse point at her wrist and he paused.

She willed deep, cleansing breaths, relaxed muscles and a slower heartbeat.

The patter of little feet raced down the hallway and forced Brea to calm more. The sight of Jack's squat body, his piano straight white teeth, the dusting of freckles across his nose, his tiny feet snuggled into footie pajamas, rooted her back in reality.

"Derek put my jammies on," he said as Jeffry helped him onto the bed. He snuggled in next to Brea with a simple "Momma" and a sigh. He stuck his thumb into his mouth, reached for a lock of her hair with his free hand, and began to twirl the tresses around his stubby fingers. Tears streaked her cheeks, and she swiped at them with the back of her hand. She didn't want the kids to see her cry.

She cradled Jack close, soothing him as he soothed her.

Ella skipped over to Brea and waved a sheet of color-splattered paper in her hand.

Brea reached out to admire the gift. "For me?"

"I made one special. For you." Ella scrambled to the foot of the bed, using the frame to clamber onto the coverlet. She climbed in next to Jack.

"Pretty." Brea examined the bright, happy splashes of color, then leaned over to the nightstand and propped the artwork against the bedside lamp, each movement insufferable.

Jeffry stroked Jack's hair with tenderness, which seemed to catch him off guard. Moving in, then abruptly pulling away.

Maybe he really had loved Beth, but lost those emotions somehow. Brea had witnessed many clients and friends struggle to show affection. She knew little about Jeffry's childhood or family. Although she'd witnessed the adoration the medical community showered on him during her hospital stay, she'd never seen him show much affection for his family. She checked her thoughts. This could be an Academy Award performance.

Jeffry crossed the bedroom and paused in the open doorway, hands stuffed deep in his pockets. She peered at him, a question in her eyes.

He reentered the room and paced a path in the floor. "Will you guys be okay for a while? Dana and Derek are in the kitchen if you need anything. You can just have one of the kids run and get them, or," he gestured to the nightstand, "use the bell."

"Why?"

"I have to make a call. I'll just head out to the garage for a few minutes."

The garage? Brea searched for the clock. Eight o'clock on a frigid February night. It wasn't like they lived in a matchbox. She couldn't help but think about his mistress.

❧

The following morning Brea made her way to the kitchen with the aid of her walker. A cane didn't provide enough support for longer distances, and even though she was unable to use crutches, she was determined to be as independent as possible, in spite of her walking cast. She discovered Jeffry pulling two mugs from the shelf, his eyes brightening when she shuffled into the room.

"Hey, I know we need to make some decisions," he said, "but I might have been rushing things. I've been feeling like an insensitive ass all night."

Brea eyed him with distrust. For the life of her, she could not figure him out. Then she studied him. She read compassion on his face. She decided to play along.

He set a cup of coffee down in front of her. "Black?"

Her eyebrows shot to the ceiling and she caught herself. "Yes."

"About Brea…" he said.

"We'll decide soon," she said as she sipped the coffee in front of her.

"I've hesitated mentioning it, but..."

"What?" Brea asked, noticing the shift in Jeffry's demeanor. She watched as he paced, evidently his go-to MO before he shared uncomfortable topics. Brea struggled to assess his behavior. He seemed unsure, or embarrassed, or something.

"Did you know Brea was pregnant? Did you know she'd been drinking?"

Brea clutched her stomach. *Not Brea. Beth. With your child.* She glared at Jeffry, fury growing in her gut. "Why does this matter? Why an autopsy?" She struggled to voice the two short questions.

"Everyone's blood was tested. In a cataclysmic crash like this, it's procedure."

Brea bit back tears as a flame ignited inside her. "I...had three sips...I...drove. My...sister...dead...and...a baby? Oh...my...God. No."

"You were all taken to Munson first thing, even though Brea died at the scene. They tested the semi driver too. He survived, if that matters to you. And no, he wasn't drinking."

"So...try...blame? Roads...ice...treach...erous. B..." she stopped just short of uttering Beth's name. *Brea's dead. What's your point? Don't you think I feel horrible enough?* The weight of her grief washed over. "Go...away."

She dropped into the nearest chair, pain shooting through her limbs and gripping her stomach. Jeffry stood in front of her, challenging her to make him leave. She pointed to the door and fixed her gaze out the window. *Why is he telling me this? Does he know something I don't? Bastard.*

"Well, then," he said. "If you're set, I'm going for a quick run."

Brea stared into her mug. Last night, the garage. Now, a run.

CHAPTER ELEVEN

Brea

BREA COLLAPSED ON THE BED LATE FRIDAY AFTERNOON. What a week. She'd probably tackled too much. Between the three physical therapy sessions, and trying to graduate to a cane from a walker, her body protested, as out of sync as if she were a marionette with tangled strings. Using her broken arm again for the first time in weeks, shuffling kids through the minor ins and outs, readying them for school and daycare, settling squabbles—all of the above—almost debilitated her. Talking became easier as her jaw and abraded chin healed, but just stringing sentences together wore her out. Some days, it was easier to remain quiet. And whatever she tried to do, Judith fought her every step of the way. Brea felt suffocated. Trapped.

"Dr. Marks wants me to do these things. You're taxing yourself. You won't get well if you keep trying too hard."

The woman lurked. Always watching.

Brea had embarrassed herself by misreading the clock Wednesday. When Judith arrived to take Ella to school, she hadn't even dressed her yet. Judith treated Brea like the child, hurrying Ella into her clothes and whisking her out of the house. Brea hated Judith's condescending gaze. She made her feel like an imbecile. All too aware of her frailties, Brea longed for a single day where her brain worked and her body cooperated. The knock on the head sometimes made her read numbers backwards, or inside out or something. She was forgetful. Uncoordinated. Not just in Judith's eyes, but in her own, she saw an invalid.

But if not for Judith, and Dana and Derek's help, she might have curled up in a corner and sucked her thumb.

Their help was invaluable. Dana, in particular, was an angel. She understood the kids and was a natural with them. Derek had a bit of an edge to him, and Brea didn't always approve of the way he cut Dana down about silly little things, criticizing the way she sliced the kid's sandwiches, or berating her for making the kids use their manners. "What's the big deal?" he would say. "They're just kids." Then, he'd wink at Brea as if they shared a secret, some hidden agenda. Kind of a weird gesture, but Brea brushed it off. She was out of touch with today's young men.

But Brea could hardly complain. She wouldn't have survived without them. Or without Jeffry for that matter. He'd come home early today and shipped her off to the bedroom, letting Judith go early and convincing Brea some alone time would do her good. He also promised to cook a meal she could eat. Homemade soup. From scratch. The man was a constant surprise. One minute, his eyes bore into her, the next he looked at her lovingly, as if he wanted her to be his wife. Like it or not, she relied on him. If this plan was to work, despite how she felt about him, it was imperative he was on her side—saw her as a good mother, a stellar household manager, didn't question her judgment but looked to her for answers and support. Yes, indeed, she had made a deal to lie with the devil. If not literally, then in companionship and management of this family they had created.

"You seem awfully tired tonight. Maybe you're overdoing. Judith reports to me, remember?"

"I can't stand that woman looming around. She's a nuisance. And I walked all the way to the mailbox with Jack today. The fresh air felt great. Oh, there's a bill from Ella's preschool. They charged a $325.00 fee for snacks. Is that possible?"

"Where's the bill?"

"On the kitchen counter."

As he busied himself in the kitchen, Brea closed her eyes and rested. She drifted off, savoring a moment of serenity and warmth. Less and less she missed her clients, but the tugs continued to come at expected times, when the kids were crying or bickering. In spite of herself, Brea found it easier and easier to hold the memories at bay. Old patterns of sucking up her feelings and forging ahead came in handy. Little by little, she made this work. She was a mother to her niece and nephew. She kissed their boo-boos and wiped their noses. She read to them at night. In spite of her broken body and her misfiring brain, she decided she was doing the best she could.

"Are you still interested in supper?" Jeffry asked sometime later.

Brea awakened to his voice. He stood before her. "I must have fallen asleep. Smells. Great."

Jeffry, clad in a jeans and a V-neck sweater, guided her to a dining chair, leaving a hand on her shoulder for a long moment. She rested her head against his hand. He left the table to bring more wine and returned with the bottle and a paper. "Looks like your mind's playing tricks on you. That bill from the preschool? The fee is $25.00. Maybe the dollar sign looked like a 3 to you. Here, see?"

Brea scrunched her face, trying to make sense of her mistake. The numbers thing again. "Why would I misread it?"

"Concussions sometimes cause the brain to transpose numbers. I'm paying the bills, so no worries."

"Is this permanent? I have to be able to read things accurately, write checks."

"For now, I've got it. In fact, I paid Dana yesterday. I explained your confusion about numbers lately and she and Derek mentioned they'd noticed too. We'll keep an eye on this. If you continue to have a problem, we'll see the neurologist."

Brea's head dropped. She could hardly trust herself with routines and schedules. Now this. People talking about her behind her back made her stomach twist and her head pound.

"Are you all spying on me? Comparing notes? How long will this last?"

"You're overreacting," Jeffry said as he patted her arm. "I see this fairly often. The confusion usually fades over time. If not, I can handle things."

"How much time?"

"Depends on the individual. We can make an appointment with Harvey, if you'd like."

"Harvey?"

"Berman. He's a colleague of mine. You know his wife, Barb, from the club."

Brea nodded. "Right." Her words fell flat. She had no idea who these people were, and the idea of seeing someone else she was supposed to have a history with but had never even met, made her shudder.

She glanced up at Jeffry in time to see him checking his phone. He kept it turned away from her, his hand surreptitiously shielding the screen from her eyes. His secretive manner chilled her to the core.

A second later, he lifted his glass and toasted. "To us." He clinked her glass. "Just so you know. Six months is too long for a guy to wait to have sex with his beautiful wife."

Brea couldn't escape the madness, no matter how hard she tried.

CHAPTER TWELVE

Brea

JEFFRY SUGGESTED A WHEELCHAIR. THE TREK FROM THE front door of Muehlig's Funeral Home to the viewing room, where Beth's remains waited, was a good distance away, at least for Brea. Walking still proved excruciating, even when aided by a cane. But Brea insisted, "I'll handle the steps."

Ken Muehlig, the funeral director, and his son, Jason, hovered close as she and Jeffry neared the visitation room. Brea excused herself and made the painstaking trip inside to spend some time alone with her sister.

Her throat tightened as she limped forward. The photo collages Dana and Derek had constructed were in place on easels next to Beth's remains. Dana had been right. Derek, odd as he was, did have an artistic eye. The displays were beautiful, but she couldn't bring herself to study a single image. Not yet. She had to stay strong today. Grieving would have to wait.

Suddenly, the room swam. Brea stood frozen to the floor, a flashback slamming into her—the pain in Beth's gaze as Brea zipped her coat, her hand on Beth's as they eased down the road headed back to the cottage. Blinding lights. The icy slide. Metal striking metal. Screams.

I'm sorry, Beth. So sorry.

More alone than she had been in her entire life, Brea forced her way to the urn. She struggled for balance in every way, summoning her role as the steady twin. Just like the night of the accident, shifting the balance now was wrong. With one hand on the top of the chair placed close beside the display table, the other on the urn, she planted her feet. The closer she could be to Beth right now, the better. And she didn't trust her legs to hold her. She longed to talk to Beth, to say the words aloud, but for now, thoughts would have to be sufficient.

Hi Sis. She inhaled a ragged breath and swallowed over the lump in her throat. She struggled to sit and leaned forward on her cane. *There's so much I want to say. I hope you understand. Being here for the kids is the only way I know to make up for the accident. I won't go back on my word. I'll be supportive of Jeffry. I'll help him be a good father. I promise I'll be the best darn mother to your kids you could ever ask for. But here's the thing. I need your guidance. First of all, I can't find a damn thing in your house. Did you have to rearrange everything after I moved to South Carolina? Could you just be an angel on my shoulder and show me the way? And when the kids are cranky and I'm at the end of my rope, you're going to need to lay some patience on me. And how did you ever cope with Judith? No wonder you fired her.*

Tears rimmed her eyes and she rubbed her nose.

Grant Fulton stopped by. Remember him? He looks great, and he's as sweet as always. Too bad I let him go. Truth was, I was afraid to trust him. No one had ever cared that much about me.

Brea caught herself rambling, as she often did with her sister. She sat back for a moment and gazed at the ceiling. She'd spent so much time pushing away the loss, she'd almost convinced herself the denial had worked. But as she studied the urn and allowed herself to contemplate her sister's ashes laid to rest inside, she turned inside out. How could this be real? How could any of this have happened? She glanced at the photos, and smelled the sickeningly sweet scent of the abundance of flowers. Reality gripped her in its clutches. Why won't my legs work? I need to get out of here.

I just want you back. Every day I wake up and hope this has been some kind of nightmare. But it's not. It's real. I'm lost without you. I've tried convincing myself I was the strong one, but I'm not. I'm sad. I'm broken. I miss you. Brea's shoulders hunched under the weight of her grief. Tears poured down her cheeks like a burgeoning stream.

Help me. Please.

Saying goodbye to Beth and Brea at the same time gutted her.

What have I done? She was on her feet and moving instantly.

She turned and struggled to focus on the urn as she approached the doorway.

Don't leave me, Sis. Stay with me. Breathe with me.

Jeffry, turned dutiful husband, waited outside the door. "Need help?"

"No," Brea said, speaking through uncontrollable tears. "Need. Time. Alone."

The funeral director pointed down the hall. "There's a private restroom just beyond the coat rack."

Brea met his eyes with a grateful glance.

Each footstep was like slogging through a bog. At last, she reached the restroom, locked the door behind her and slid onto the toilet with the last of her energy. Every blessed thing was so damned impossible. With the wires clamping her jaw closed, she couldn't even have a decent cry without choking. But this time, she didn't try to stop the tears. She let them flow down her cheeks, drip off her chin, soak her blouse. Frustration. Loneliness. Anger. Desperation. *I can't do this, Beth. Save me.*

Minutes later, a knock on the door interrupted.

"Yes," she muffled through her wired jaw.

"Sorry," a voice said. "I'll wait."

The only thing left to do was splash water on her face and blow her nose. She couldn't hide all day. Mourners would be arriving soon. Brea straightened her skirt, swallowed, and attempted to set her shoulders back.

When she opened the door, Grant stood in front of her. A cry escaped her. Tears welled and tightened her throat again. Grant wrapped his arms around her and held her close. She sucked in his strength.

"I'm sorry, Beth. So sorry."

Brea wept, struggling for air, as the blood drained from her face, dizzying her. "Too. Much," she muttered into his chest.

"I know." His hand pressed into her back, letting her know with certainty he had her. "Everything will turn out. Not today. Not next week. But eventually."

He backed away a fraction of an inch and gazed at her, gently pushing her hair back from her eyes.

The fierceness of their connection shocked her, but it shouldn't have. In this moment, in the throes of profound grief, when she'd numbed out to pretty much everything, he touched her soul. Permeated the shroud of armor she wore 24/7. Grant was her friend. He knew her. Her heart flickered. In an instant, she backed away, blinking like a frightened toddler. Far too dangerous to let those feelings in.

"Thank you," she murmured.

Grant studied her with an intense stare, as if he didn't want to look away for fear of breaking the link.

She stumbled backward, sliding into the door. Grant caught her and held on tight.

"I…have to go." Brea studied the hallway, as if averting her focus would break the bonds that linked her to Grant. Jeffry's frame filled the space, and Brea heaved a sigh.

"Detective Fulton," he said, offering his hand to the detective.

"Hello, Dr. Marks. Good to see you. Not under these circumstances, but…"

"Thank you for coming," Jeffry interrupted. He peered at Brea. "Looks like you could use a hand. Shall we head back inside? Guests will be arriving soon."

Brea rubbed her nose, then nodded.

Grant did a double take, his face registering a quizzical

expression. Oh, no. She'd rubbed her nose. Her tell. She quickly grabbed a tissue and raised it to her face, hoping to hide her mistake.

"See you inside," Jeffry said to Grant as he helped Brea down the hall.

Grant agreed, a hesitation in his step, then slipped inside the restroom.

Panic filled Brea. If Grant figured things out…

Jeffry gripped her elbow, and eased her down the hall. "I'll be right by your side. All day."

A woman, her nurse's garb covered by a heavy wool coat, rushed forward and possessively latched onto Jeffry's free arm. "I'm sorry to interrupt." She rested her hand on Jeffry's chest as she spoke to him, "but I have to be at the hospital soon, and I didn't want to let this day go by without sharing my condolences."

Brea had no idea who the woman was, but the voice sounded vaguely familiar. She sought Jeffry's gaze, hoping he would intervene and make introductions, but when she found his eyes, they were fraught with shock. Not that Brea knew him well, but she read his unease and didn't miss the fact that his legs, as well as his gaze, seemed abruptly unsteady.

He simply muttered, "Thank you. Now, if you'll excuse us, my wife and I need to head inside."

He spun around with such force, Brea felt as if she'd met a sharp turn on an amusement ride. She tumbled into his arms.

"Who…?" The question escaped before she made the connection.

"She caught me off guard," he muttered. He cleared his throat. "Shall we go inside?"

Brea scarcely nodded, barely breathed, and allowed Jeffry to guide her back inside and settle her in a chair in the front row of the visitation room. The voice finally registered. The mistress. The woman who wanted her dead. Her heart hammered inside her chest.

Jeffry stood sentry beside her as the first of the mourners trickled in. On autopilot, she found herself able to shake hands, accept condolences, and block out any semblance of feeling.

The line of mourners stretched into the hall. Jeffry did an impressive job playing macho husband, and Brea was thankful. She fell short of trusting him, but welcomed his hand as it rested on her shoulder while he spoke to friends and colleagues on her behalf, explaining his wife's injuries and how they kept her from talking to them more. Dozens of sad stares offered their sympathies. Brea sat stone-faced, with no idea how much time had passed.

A grating exclamation broke her escape. At first, she couldn't place the voice, even though she'd heard the irritating cacophony before. Then recognition hit her like a wrecking ball. Cynthia Magness. Peter's wife. A knot grew in her chest, constricting her breathing. She fought to catch her breath and struggled to stand, wanting to run from the room. Startled, Jeffry spun around and helped her to her feet. His eyes questioned her, but there wasn't time to talk before Cynthia spoke.

"There you are," she said, looming next to Beth like the Wicked Witch of the West. "The poor grieving sister. Pitiful little Beth. You've lost your slutty sister. How sad Brea spent her short little life trying to steal my husband. If you ask me, she got what she deserved."

Brea cleared her throat and set back her shoulders as she clutched Cynthia's arm. "You are leaving," she said with surprising clarity. Jeffry backed away, and Peter, who stood behind Cynthia like a lost sheep, scuttled up to intervene. "Stay back," Brea warned, her voice rising. Then, to Cynthia, she said, "Come with me."

Through the grace of a thousand angels, she turned on her heel, her grip digging into the flesh above Cynthia's elbow.

"Ouch," Cynthia whined. "You're hurting me."

"Not yet, but I'm about to." Brea shoved Cynthia ahead of her, not stopping until she reached the entrance to the funeral home. Hushed voices filled the air, and when Brea finally lifted her head, she witnessed Peter and Jeffry flanking either side of her and Cynthia.

Peter stepped forward and moved between them, then held Cynthia at bay. He rested his free hand on Brea's arm. "I'm so sorry. We shouldn't have come."

Brea glared, forgetting who she was for a moment. When the realization hit her, she averted her eyes and sought Jeffry's protection, reaching out for him, and locking his gaze.

"Please," she said. "Be sure these people leave."

The funeral director stepped forward and spoke to Peter and Cynthia, offering some lame excuse for Brea's behavior. "Sometimes the bereaved…"

Brea's face flushed with rising anger. Jeffry held her arm as he spoke sharply to Peter. "Get her out of here and don't come back." Then, he leaned in to Brea and spoke softly, "I'm sorry. I should have been paying more attention. What would you like to do? We could take a break in the director's office if you like."

"No," Brea said, her face on fire. "I want to be with my sister."

When they headed back to the viewing room, the first person Brea met was Grant, sympathy etched in his eyes, and a heap of understanding too. She looked away.

She couldn't help but wonder if she'd overreacted. If she had doled out clues that Beth was indeed Brea. If Jeffry suspected, or if he decided to off her as Beth and not Brea, the funeral would be a fine time for him to put a plan into motion. Tammy had arrived to share her sympathies, and Jeffry seemed truly shocked, but what if her visit was part of a plan? What if she had hoped to signal him somehow, that she was ready to take Beth's place? They could stage a suicide. The distraught identical twin too destroyed to continue life without her other half. The devastated weaker link that would sooner check out than live without her lifeline. The lost soul too depressed to envision a future.

Would Jeffry act now? And if he did, if she were out of the picture, could she see him harming the children? Not really. Then again, she could be fooling herself. Blinded by who she wanted him to be rather than seeing him with clear vision. Her thinking had been scattered to say the least. Maybe now that the day had come to say goodbye to Beth, truly close the lid on this part of her life, Brea, living as Beth, had gone over the edge. She gripped her cane as if it would support her mind, not just her broken body. As if it would restore her sanity.

What if he didn't have Tammy? What if she weren't part of the scenario? Could the man live as a single dad raising his two kids? She could see him alone. Jack and Ella might wind up as one of her childhood friends had. Motherless with a steady stream of love-hungry women spending the night with their dad, drinking until the wee hours, leaving them to raise themselves.

Oh, here she was going off on a wild tangent again. The Xanax was to blame. She'd never seen Jeffry do anything questionable around the children. He was a good dad. She had no reason to doubt his love and devotion to his kids.

A memory bolted from out of the blue. Little Ella's dislocated shoulder. According to Jeffry, she had lost her footing on the steps and he yanked her arm to keep her from falling. Beth had been furious. Was it evidence of an abusive husband and father? Or more Beth drama?

Brea could have dissolved right then and there. As if she were bleeding out, sounds faded, the world receded. Her pulse slowed and dizziness stole her thoughts and strength.

Jeffry rushed to her. She crumpled in his arms. A lost soul, drowning in grief, she sobbed.

CHAPTER THIRTEEN

Peter

PETER WRAPPED HIS OVERCOAT AND SCARF TIGHTLY AROUND himself and positioned the umbrella over their heads. The wind whipped icy shards of sleet and rain as he hurried Cynthia to the car. Once onto William Street, he turned the wipers on high and tried to swallow his embarrassment. Seeing Beth, watching Cynthia with her, had been terrifying. His wife was a dragon, and he pictured video of the whole scene playing out on the late news.

"Pining for your dead lover is futile," Cynthia spat.

"You promised to behave. You could've shown some respect."

"I wish there had been an open casket. Then I could be sure she was dead."

Peter had visions of Cynthia clawing Brea's eyes out as she laid to rest and a shiver pierced his spine. He'd only allowed her to attend the wake because she had such a hissy fit when she learned of Brea's death. Her anger meant a nightmare for him, and she insisted she needed to see Brea with her own eyes.

He wasn't in the mood for a fight, so he tried changing the subject. "Are you hungry? We could stop for a bite to eat."

"Or we could go shopping. I'll need a dress to wear to the funeral, so we can say a proper goodbye to your mistress. One final farewell. I bet you'd love to kiss her urn, wouldn't you?"

"We're not going anywhere near the service tomorrow."

"Can't you call off the rest of your appointments for the day? I really would like to do some shopping."

Peter spun away and rolled his eyes. Reminding her that his patient appointments were what kept her in shopping money would only escalate things.

"There's a new boutique on Main Street, and if we're going to New York for a few weeks, I'll need something to wear. I'll bet they have just the thing at Threads. Amber Martin, you know, from the club, was there the other day. She says their clothes are to die for. You remember Amber. Her husband, Tom, is the new CEO at Ford Motor. We really should do more with the business types. Expanding your social circle would be a definite enhancement to your career."

Peter counted to ten, took a breath. "Give Amber a call. Arrange an outing. Tomorrow afternoon is perfect."

"An outing? You make me sound like a child. Like you're arranging a play date to get me out of your hair so you can weep at your girlfriend's grave. I won't have it."

Peter stifled a sigh. This woman was beyond unmanageable. Another migraine threatened. With a full evening of appointments ahead of him, spending another minute placating his wife would make the headache that much worse. "I'll drop you off at home. I'm to call my agent with an answer by three o'clock, and I have notes to read before my appointments. We're agreed, right? We'll be in New York from the first of April through the twenty-first. I'll have John make arrangements for us to stay someplace nice near Central Park so you can walk while I'm busy, or go shopping. Your preference."

"Well, if you expect to stay married, the Ritz is my favorite."

His throat constricted and his airway tightened. He'd never be free of her. She was the noose around his neck, strangling every last molecule of oxygen from his lungs, squeezing every last dollar from his pocket. The best he could do would be to appease her and deal with the fallout later. You'd think since Brea was dead, Cynthia would shut up and let him off the hook, but no. She would never forgive him because she squirreled away all his transgressions like golden dollar signs to be used against him.

He reached out to touch her hand, reconsidered, and gripped the wheel.

There was a time when they'd first met that holding Cynthia's hand was all he had wanted to do. She made him feel like a prince. Cynthia had been carefree and up for any adventure he suggested. Surfing at La Jolla, daylight skinny-dipping, sex in the glass elevator of that little hotel in Paris, strip poker on the cliffs at Torrey Pines. What had happened to his spontaneous, athletic partner? Was this his fault? Had he turned her to stone with his countless affairs? If only she understood. Sexual addiction was as real as any other disease. Treatable too. *If you weren't a marital therapist running the risk of a ruined reputation.* Damn it. He could have healed. If only he'd had her support.

"Amber just found out she's pregnant. Her fourth in vitro, but the little bugger finally took. The new doctor she's seeing is a miracle worker. Maybe we should try her. Don't you think we'd be happier if we had a child?"

Peter choked on the suggestion. "We've been there, tried that. Why bring a child up now? I thought we were past this."

"Having a baby is all I've ever wanted."

She'd lost her mind. Clearly, she'd forgotten the months of pain and heartache they'd gone through.

"I don't mean to be insensitive, but you're forty-four years old. The risk of having a child with Down syndrome increases incrementally once a woman reaches forty. Your chances are 1 in 30-something. I'm not willing to take the chance. Plus, with your history of miscarriage…"

"And at forty-eight, being mistaken for the grandpa at Kindergarten Round-Up wouldn't agree with your image." She paused and let out a heavy sigh. "Yes, my body is a failure. My womb rejects fetuses. Your fetus, at least. Forget I said a thing. I'll simply continue to serve as your arm candy."

His temples throbbed. "You're right. It could be me. There's new evidence sperm may cause miscarriages—if an egg is fertilized with abnormal sperm, there's suggestion the morphology can play a part."

"I'll agree with you there. There's certainly nothing normal about your sperm. Not that you haven't spread it around enough."

Pain radiated across Peter's chest. This woman would never rest. He pulled the car over onto a side street and parked, turned off the ignition and faced his wife. "Why do you stay married to me? What's in this for you?"

Her mouth tightened into a thin line and she clasped her hands in her lap. Her eyes filled with tears. "Aren't you sad? Peter Magness, master magician, the expert who cements fractured marriages back into place, the wizard who comes home at the end of the day and lives a lie with his wife. We're pathetic."

"Then let's stop. Let's repair the damage and start over. Or get a divorce and give each other a chance at happiness."

Her eyes narrowed. He could see she didn't believe him, and he couldn't begin to understand why those words had flown out of his mouth. True, a divorce would do his career no favors, but staying with this woman would certainly kill him.

"You can't be serious."

A challenge. Or maybe her deepest desire. He'd been distanced from her so long he couldn't tell which.

"About what? The reconciliation or the divorce?" He cleared his throat and lowered his voice, his gaze catching hers and holding it. "Why do you stay with me?"

She arched her brows and sighed. "Good question."

They sat in silence for several long minutes.

"Truth? I'm scared of being alone. I haven't worked since we lost the baby. A mistake on my part, I'll admit, but what would I do? Who would I be other than Dr. Peter Magness's wife?"

Peter looked at Cynthia, really looked at her for the first time in many years. She was a strikingly beautiful woman. She lacked gentility and warmth, but maybe he was to blame—her heart had frozen to ice long ago. He recognized the pain in her eyes, had seen it in his office many times, and knew he'd been the cause of much, if not all, of her heartbreak and disappointment. He made himself a promise. *I'm going to be a husband from now on. Devote myself to my wife. I said I wanted a simpler life. The poor woman just wants me to love her. Maybe this is the answer I've been searching for. Granted, I've been looking in all the wrong places, but I'm as capable as the next guy of being blinded by my ego. I can do this for her. Maybe it's what I need, too.*

As hard as Peter tried to muster a way to state his promise aloud, he couldn't force out the words. *I'm an ass and an idiot. Bad combination for a smart guy like me.* After several hems and haws, he spoke. "I'll try," he said. "You?"

She tipped her head back and forth, contemplating his question. "Let's commit to six months of concerted effort. Then, if we can't make a go of things, we'll say goodbye. Should we see a therapist?"

His tongue went dry as dust and stuck to the roof of his mouth. He blinked hard and grabbed for the water bottle in the console, slugging down a long drink before replacing the bottle cap. "Why don't we try working on our own first? We're intelligent people. Divorce isn't the answer. We should be able to figure this out." Indeed. He was insane, but a divorce would ruin him. "We'll start tonight."

The ringing of his phone interrupted their conversation. He pulled the cell from his pocket and studied the screen. "It's Ann Arbor P.D. I need to take this."

Cynthia looked perturbed, but coalesced.

"Peter Magness here."

"Dr. Magness. We need your help. One of your patients…hold on, I have the name right here, Jim Kerfoot."

"Yes?" Peter said, confused and startled. Why would the police be contacting him about Jim Kerfoot, and how did they know he was treating him?

"He's here at the station with us. He just shot and killed his wife. His attorney has asked for you to come to the station. We of-fered to call and let you know what the situation is."

Peter swallowed hard. How had he missed this? He had never imagined… Jim wasn't a violent person. He had no history of abuse, not even a traffic violation. Ann had once compared him to black coffee in the morning—boring.

"Are you sure?" He'd shot her? Killed his wife. Impossible.

"Told me himself, Doctor. Can you come down?"

"Give me twenty minutes." He hit the end button, scrubbed his face with his hand, and fired up the ignition.

Cynthia cleared her throat. "Let me guess. You have to go."

"It's an emergency, Cynthia." His stomach roiled.

"What else is new?"

He shook his head. "I know the timing sucks, but this is a true emergency. I can't share the details with you yet, but I'm guessing you'll hear the story on the five o'clock news. I'll drop you off at the house, and call Martha and have her cancel my remaining patients."

"Focusing on your marriage isn't an emergency, but this is?"

"Cynthia, I'm begging you. If we have any chance of repairing our marriage, you're going to have to understand. In my line of work, true emergencies occur. At those times, my presence is required."

"True emergencies," Cynthia snarled.

He stepped on the accelerator, whipped around Packard St. and headed for home.

"Yes," he said, defeated. "True emergencies."

CHAPTER FOURTEEN

Brea

BREA DONNED THE BLACK DRESS JEFFRY HAD DELIVERED
from Beth's closet, loose, but good enough, and slipped her
feet into a pair of sturdy flats. Still struggling about whether
or not to take Jack and Ella to the funeral, she toyed with options
for the umpteenth time. For the life of her, she couldn't make one
blasted decision. If she took them, they might be traumatized. But
as a psychologist, the answer was clear. Beth's ashes were in an urn.
They wouldn't see a body, or have those questions that might pro-
duce nightmares later. And she had to come to grips with ulterior
motives as well.

At every turn, she worried about giving herself away. Ella's savvy
eye, a moment of forgetfulness on her part, the fact she couldn't
locate a mixing bowl while Dana witnessed her shuffling through
cupboards. Derek, with his superior smile, forced his way in front
of her to grab something from a shelf she couldn't reach. He was
being kind, true, but she couldn't shake his condescending attitude.
Judith with her constant haughty expression. She arched her brows
at every move Brea made, questioning her sanity and intelligence. In
the end, if she were discovered, no one would ever forgive her for
leaving the kids at home, for depriving them of a final goodbye with
their mother. She couldn't be so selfish. She knew better.

The realization sealed her decision. She leaned out of the guest
bedroom door, wishing she could call out for Jeffry. Instead, she rang

the stupid dinner bell he had left for her in case she needed him. He didn't answer the first time she sounded the bell, so she waited a moment, then shook the damn thing again, harder and longer this time.

"Coming," he called from some distance away.

She waited for him to appear at the far end of the long hallway and prayed for strength, stopping for a breath between each word. "Changed. My. Mind. Kids. Come." Her lie became real. Palpable. Yet, the reality of not following through seemed worse.

She swallowed her pain and despair, but could hardly keep down the contents of her stomach. She recalled an old adage from grad school—you're only as sick as your secrets.

She desperately needed the kids, and couldn't survive without Jeffry's support. She had no choice but to dismiss whatever leftover suspicions she held about him for the time being. She needed to be wrong about him. He hadn't killed her yet, and he spent more time at home. These people were her family now. Without a doubt, they needed her, too. Her knees grew weak. None of this made sense, yet the decision she had made loomed, as immovable as the gate of a prison.

A former client had once stayed with her husband so she didn't have to risk the chance of her kids spending time alone with him on visitation weekends. She did the right thing for the right reason. Or was it the wrong decision for the right reason? Why couldn't she think clearly? Would this last forever?

Jeffry stood in front of her. "I'm sorry. I didn't catch that. Here," he said, guiding Brea to the chair by the window. "Sit down. Relax for a minute."

Brea choked back tears as she repeated, "Kids. Come."

He pulled up the footstool and sat before her. "If you want the kids with us, they'll be there. Dana can dress them. I'll have her bring them inside before the service starts, and then drive them home afterward. Derek's here too. He can help. Judith went to help with the luncheon and organize all the meals being delivered."

Tears spilled down her face. "I can't...do this." She longed to tell

Jeffry the truth, but when she gazed into his deep blue eyes and read the empathy in them, caution tempered her once again.

He wrapped his arms around her as she cried. "Shh. Don't worry. I'll be with you every step of the way."

She leaned back to look at him. Her mascara had streaked his white dress shirt, and she fixed her gaze on the dark stains. "I ruined your shirt," she cried softly.

"I have other shirts."

She gasped for air, her heart racing as he gripped her hands.

"Relax," he coaxed. "Try to breathe. In, through your nose." He looked panicked. "I'll get you some water."

She gradually calmed, but only after several minutes. Jeffry stayed with her, stroking her arm until her respirations finally slowed to normal and the tears eased.

He awkwardly mopped at her wet cheeks with a tissue, and she lifted her chin to look at him. "Thank you."

He rested a hand on her leg. "No problem."

"How long have we been here?"

"A few minutes. Don't worry. We have plenty of time."

"Freshen. My. Makeup."

Brea struggled to her feet, searching the room for her cane. Her hips ached, her body dreadfully out of sync. Walking promised to be a special challenge today.

Jeffry pushed to his feet and watched her. "Your cane is upstairs. Jack was pretending his leg was broken. I'll get it for you."

"Thank you. You're the best." Her words were staccato, but she'd managed an entire sentence. Since her confrontation with Cynthia yesterday, she seemed to have gained some ground. Anger and determination produced startling results. She clutched the foot rail of the bed, wishing for a crutch as she limped sans support to the bathroom.

She washed her face and repaired her makeup, all the while avoiding so much as a glimpse in the mirror. She knew what she'd see in her reflection. Hollow eyes, sunken cheeks. Her last vision of Beth.

Deceit took a tawdry toll.

As she limped to the hallway, she discovered her cane propped against the doorframe. She tipped her head to the ceiling and pressed her lips together, wondering if Jeffry would be this kind to her if he knew the truth.

She also couldn't help but wonder about his and Beth's marriage.

There were two sides to every story. Maybe Beth and Jeffry had both withdrawn from their relationship. She would never know. But one thing was certain—Jeffry had been kinder to her in the past week than any man since she'd dated Grant, way back in high school. She needed time to make sense of what she did and did not know about her sister's husband. But not today.

At the funeral home, Brea asked Jeffry for a few moments alone with her sister and stepped inside the viewing room.

Jeffry looked concerned, even worried. "Are you sure?"

"Quite," she said, conviction in her voice. She steadied herself on her cane and hobbled forward.

Brea fixed her focus on the rose-colored upholstery of the Queen Anne chairs near Beth's remains and the wooden folding chairs assembled in rows behind them.

She struggled to kneel before her sister's ashes. For the first time since the accident, she inhaled a steadying breath and studied one of the portraits, just the two sisters, ornately framed and sitting sentry to the right of the memorial table. Brea as maid of honor, Beth as the blushing bride. Beth was a beautiful woman, eyes full of promise and possibility, a hint of mischief behind them. If only Beth had escaped the accident and run off to a new life. She'd been so unhappy the night she died.

Despite seeing and touching the urn the day before, somewhere in the back of Brea's mind, she'd envisioned approaching a casket and seeing a stranger lying within the satin folds. But Beth had opted for cremation, and even though never seeing her sister again left Brea with a gaping wound, she understood. The twins had made a pact after being shocked at the plastic display of their parents' bodies at Muehlig's twenty-two years ago. Mourners had seemed to spend hours commenting on how their parents looked, and the girls decided, then and there, they'd never put themselves through such scrutiny. Death was about honoring and remembering, not about archaic customs. Knowing she and Jeffry had honored her sister's wishes, Brea relaxed, and in the stillness, a presence filled her.

The night she arrived Up North, the last time she and Beth were together, she'd relaxed in untold ways. Once in Beth's orbit, she was home again. Whole again. The same peace and contentedness filled her now. If she could hold onto this, retrieve a dose when she needed it most, maybe she could do this.

She shuffled away from Beth's urn, her vision blurred, and a moan escaped her throat. Her heart broke at the thought of leaving her sister's side. Sharp as a shrapnel wound, the pain of the loss became real. Not just for Beth, but the unborn child. Jeffry had been cool when he shared the news that "Brea" was pregnant at the time of her death, so she had to assume he'd had no knowledge of his wife's pregnancy.

Then there was Jeffry's odd comment about waiting six months to have sex. In a weirdly sane moment, she wondered if he meant he wouldn't wait that long, or if it had been that long since he'd been with Beth. Brea turned her thoughts to that lost little soul. The urn held two lives, not one. After a ragged breath, she wondered if it wasn't strength but shock that shored her up and supported her. Hard to know.

Brea paused as she entered the lobby to scan the crowd, searching for Jeffry.

He appeared moments later. "How are you holding up?"

"Doing my best."

They sat in the front row of the funeral home's chapel. The comfort of the upholstered chairs did nothing to ease Brea's grief. The fabric bit at the back of her legs as mourners filled the room and filed past the urn for the last time, their image closing her throat. The pungent aroma of flowers threatened to knock Brea flat.

Jeffry strode to the front of the room after the last of the mourners passed, and asked for everyone's attention.

"As you know," he said to the guests, "my sister-in-law, Brea Watson, was tragically killed in a car collision. My wife was with her and fortunate enough to survive, but this is a tremendous loss for her. For our entire family." He gazed at Brea, and tears rimmed his eyes. She shivered and dropped her chin to her chest. A knot grew in her throat. "Unfortunately, Beth is still recovering from her injuries. She's asked that I read this for her."

He cleared his throat, unfolded a piece of paper, and began. "My sister was my life. My other half. My better half. We balanced each other like the moon and the sun, the rain and the snow. When I was a waltz, she was a jive. When I was a curtain, she was my window. When I was a screaming banshee, she was a lamb.

"Not only did we share our mother's womb, but one reflection, one heart, and, I like to think, the same soul. I can't imagine moving through life without her. I know better than to think life won't go on, but I'll carry a huge void wherever I go. Thank you for being here today. My sister would have loved knowing how many of you care, and how many of you support us in our loss."

He stopped reading and glanced up at the crowd. Then, he folded the paper and tucked the slip back inside the breast pocket of his suit. Only the sound of sniffling touched Brea's ears. She knew what Jeffry hadn't read. She could recite the words in her sleep.

My sister's death has gutted me. I can't imagine waking up one more day knowing I can't pick up the phone, dial her on Skype, have her finish my sentences, or see her set a bowl of cereal in front of me before I realize I'm hungry.

A million silky threads attached us, invisible to most, but as strong and sturdy as a spider's web for us. There's a hole in my heart that can't be filled.

Jeffry sat down next to her, placed a strong arm around her shoulder and gathered her in a hug. "I'm so sorry," he whispered. When Brea lifted her head and gazed into his eyes, she saw sympathy and sadness.

Dana and Derek appeared with Jack and Ella, each holding one of the children's hands. Jeffry escorted them to the front of the chapel. Brea met them and bit back tears as she guardedly guided them to the memorial display and urn, Jeffry firmly planted at her side, explaining Aunt Brea had gone to heaven to be with their Grandma and Grandpa Watson. They seemed to accept the explanation without any obvious distress, but that was because they hadn't a clue their mother's body had been burnt to ash and laid forever inside the vessel. If the truth ever emerged, they would always know she had tried, in her own feeble way, to allow them to see Beth one last time.

When she glanced back at the mourners, Derek approached, his hand reaching for Jack. "I'm sorry your sister died, Brea. I lost my mom a few years ago. Never gets easier."

"Beth," Brea corrected. "I'm Beth."

"Right, that's what I meant. My mistake."

CHAPTER FIFTEEN

Brea

BREA AWOKE EARLY THE NEXT MORNING TO AN UNUSU-
ally cold house. She shivered, rolled out of bed and
smoothed the covers. Moonlight shone through a slat in
the blinds. She made her way to the window, raised the wooden
slats, and gazed heavenward, loving the way the soft light filled
the sky on a starless night, the stunning peace the scene created.

New day, new life. Today, she would officially take Beth's
place. *Be there for me, Sis. Guide me though each day.*

As she turned, reality slammed her. This was a scene out of
a horror novel. Bizarre. Impossible. Not some simple babysitting
job.

That Derek had called her Brea still gave her the shakes. She
shook off a tremor. Common mistake. Nothing to worry about.
Except for that look as he'd walked away...

It was incredible no one suspected she wasn't Beth. Not Jeffry.
Not Grant, although his ignorance at least made some sense.
None of Beth's friends, neither Jack nor Ella. Then again, they expected her to be Beth. Maybe the answer was simpler than she
imagined.

She shuffled into the bathroom and prepared for the day. If
luck prevailed, the kids would sleep for another hour or two, and
she'd remember to breathe. She didn't know Jeffry's schedule, but

doubted she would need help fixing breakfast. She negotiated the trip down the hallway and limped into the kitchen to start coffee.

At least she could perform simple tasks. The coffee beans were where she expected, and she'd made coffee at Beth's many times before. Mesmerized by the stream of coffee filling the clear glass carafe, she was startled by a quick movement, then lips pressed against her neck.

"Good morning, sunshine," Jeffry said.

She jerked in surprise.

"Sorry," Jeffry said, seemingly embarrassed. "I thought you heard me coming."

Brea gripped the counter's edge. "No problem," she managed, ignoring the kiss. "Coffee?"

"Sure, sounds great."

He leaned casually against the counter, the edges of his mouth curving into a grin. No way to deny or ignore his muscled chest, even though she'd buried her sister the previous day. She couldn't change the course of her thoughts. Why hadn't she noticed Jeffry's appeal until now? Because he was married to her sister. And maybe because she'd been involved with Peter. But this was not the Jeffry she had known as her sister's mate—a distant, flirtatious philanderer. This Jeffry was kind and compassionate, an attractive combination. The tingle that ran up her spine scared the shit out of her. Then again, her history with men had proven disastrous. Who was she to accurately size up a man? She filed away her thoughts under lock and key. Another day.

"I need coffee," she said.

"I'm going to check my mail, then go for a run."

Her momentary mood dissipated at the speed of sound, causing her to clutch her coffee mug and scowl. If only she could hop in the car and follow him. On Beth's behalf, she craved revenge for his infidelity.

Five minutes after Jeffry left, the phone rang.

Brea grabbed the handset without glancing at the caller ID. "Hello?"

"I saw him leave. Can you talk?"

"Who is this?" She measured her words as she recalled the resonant voice. "Peter?"

"Of course. Who'd you expect?"

Shock held her immobile. "Why are you calling me?" she finally asked, her breathing so shallow she feared she might pass out.

"Why wouldn't I call? I'm worried about you. You didn't respond to my text. Plus, I owe you an apology. I never should have allowed Cynthia to attend the visitation with me. She promised to behave, or I wouldn't have. I swear to God, I think the woman's under control, and then boom, she's off on a nut again.

"I didn't have a chance at the visitation to tell you how truly sorry I am. I can't imagine what this is like for you, losing Brea. Maybe there was a small blessing with her moving away. You're not used to having her around like you were. Day to day, her death won't seem real for a while. Your regular schedule won't seem so empty. There are positives to consider. I know you're grieving, and I'll be here for you, whatever you need...I love you."

"This. Is. Not. A. Good. Time," she managed, and disconnected the call.

She searched for the nearest chair and almost stumbled sitting down. Peter said he'd seen Jeffry leave. He was watching the house? Stalking her? Wait. He said, "I love you." *To Beth. Not me.* Had she misheard him? The implications staggered her. Not in a million years would Beth have become involved with Peter Magness. Not possible, especially since Beth had known her history with Peter. Impossible thoughts leapfrogged to foolish conclusions.

Beth's cell phone buzzed on the counter. She hesitated, uncertainty nibbling at her. Jeffry wouldn't be texting now. Curiosity finally got the better of her. She studied the display. White letters on a blue background. *Dr. P.* Below, in smaller script, the message: *Call when you can. Love, P.*

Beth would never have had an affair with Peter. Never have replaced *her*. The irony pierced her. But *I'm doing the same thing.* Taking Beth's place. *Calm down, Brea. Your brain is getting the best of you.* There must be some kind of explanation. Maybe Beth and Jeffry had seen Peter for marriage therapy. Now she was rationalizing. Lying to herself. Losing her mind.

A wave of dizziness rolled over her. Bile rose in her throat. She leaned over the sink, trembling, gripping the counter. "Momma?" Ella called. "What's wrong?"

Brea held on with all her might. She had to remain calm. "Just. A. Little. Dizzy."

"Want me to find Daddy?"

"No," Brea said after she caught her breath and forced herself to utter a complete sentence. "Daddy's gone for a run. Just give me a minute." She made her way to the chair.

Ella approached, rubbing Brea's leg with her plump little hand. "I got dizzy one time, remember? You're supposed to put your head down."

Brea smiled down at the round face filled with hope and promise. "Thanks, sweetie." She patted Ella's hand and lowered her head as far as her stiff joints would allow.

The room stopped swirling, and Brea began to feel steadier. Ella handed her a tattered length of cloth, the blanket remnant she carried around like a shield of protection. "Here, Momma, this will make you feel better."

"You're right." Brea accepted the offering and leaned over to rest her head atop Ella's. "The magic is working already."

Brea vowed to get to the bottom of Peter's call. No rest until she found the truth.

Jeffry returned from his run and retreated to the bathroom for a shower while Brea served breakfast to the kids. Halfway through the meal, an idea occurred to her. Peter might have suspected her true identity. His call could have been a fishing expedition. Doubtful though. Instinct told her something more complex was involved. But she couldn't control the trembling of her hands or her legs turning to butter. *What if Peter somehow knew she was Brea?*

Brea barely functioned through the morning routine, saw Jeffry off to work, and sent the kids to wash up and dress. Jack brought his clothes down to her, needing help to don his jeans and long-sleeved t-shirt. She pulled up some toddler games on the computer for him, and then mixed paints and set out paper and brushes for Ella.

Meanwhile, she mentally planned her next move. She would go through all of Beth's belongings—her wallet, purse, bureau, closet, and laptop. Maybe she would discover some evidence of what, if anything, had happened between Beth and Peter. She said a silent prayer. "I love you," flashed through her mind like railroad warning lights. Peter possessed the morals of an alley cat, while Beth…had not been happy. Maybe unhappy enough to have an affair with her identical twin's lover. Maybe distraught enough to throw caution to the wind and become pregnant. God, she hoped not. For so many reasons. But still, in some ways, Beth and Peter having an affair was somehow preferable to Peter suspecting Brea posed as Beth.

In the background, Judith fussed with laundry. Brea urged her off to the grocery store, insisting that she'd need Judith's help later in the day. As soon as she left for shopping, Brea climbed the stairs to the marital bedroom despite pain shooting through her hips and legs. The simple trip wore her out. She inched herself gingerly onto the bench at the end of the bed, and regained her breath before lifting her eyes. She'd not set foot inside this room since the previous summer. In her dead sister's bedroom, the loss slammed into her chest. Beth. Gone. A tightening chest constricted her oxygen and tears clogged her throat. She longed to see her sister's face, watch her mouth turn into a grin, hear her raucous laughter, feel the touch of Beth's fingertips sweep across her cheek.

Enough. Get on with it.

Like Brea, Beth had always stuffed secrets into the backs of drawers.

Brea left the door ajar so she could hear Jack and Ella if they called to her. The phone in her pocket vibrated. She pulled out the cell. The screen read: Can you talk yet? P.

Had the man lost his mind? Brea stabbed the delete button. She intended to ignore Peter until further notice. If he and Beth had been lovers, she hoped they'd had the courtesy to wait until she left Ann Arbor. As if struck by a lightning bolt, she recalled once she'd decided to break off things with Peter and relocate, Beth had not encouraged her to change her mind. In fact, she had discouraged her, saying things like, "I don't want you to leave, but I know the move is for the best."

For the next ten minutes, Brea ransacked the bureau drawers, finding nothing. Nothing about Peter, and no clues about Jeffry. Frustrated, she exhaled. Then, she jammed the contents back into the drawers and sighed, the lack of evidence weighing on her. With Peter trying so desperately to contact her, she decided the best approach would be to meet with him and ask him some questions face-to-face. Not today. Not tomorrow. But one of these days.

As she listened for the kids, she heard the garage door open. *Shit. Judith was back.* She didn't want the woman to know she'd been upstairs, especially when the kids were downstairs. And she couldn't possibly hurry back down. As she frantically lurched to the bathroom, she saw that she'd dropped socks on the floor. Rushing to pick them up, she lost her balance.

Judith's footfalls sounded on the stairs as Brea lay splayed on the bathroom floor like a bear rug. *That damn Judith is right. I'm not safe by myself.*

Brea kicked the door shut and army crawled to the bathtub

to pull herself up, her stocking feet sliding on the slippery ceramic tile. Finally, she was on her feet. As she grabbed a brush from the sink to take to her room, Judith barged into the room with an armful of sundries.

"You should not be up here."

"I'm fine. Just need to grab a few things."

"Have you any idea what the kids are doing?"

Brea limped into the closet. "They're fine. I want to grab a few of my favorite blouses. It's time for me to get back to normal."

Judith's critical eyes peered over her shoulder. "I can get what you need. Besides, if you're getting back to normal, wouldn't that include sleeping in your husband's bed?" She backed away, but just a smidge, tucking in the blankets sticking out from the comforter.

"Stop hovering. I'm more than capable of choosing a few things." Brea felt heat rise up her neck, tossed some of Beth's blouses over her arm and headed for the stairs. She made her way down, struggling not to yelp with each agonizing move.

Judith stayed hot on her tail, "tsk, tsk, tsk-ing" all the way.

Brea stumbled to a stop in the kitchen doorway, stunned by the sight before her. The kitchen was a cloud of dust. Two small children sat on the floor, covered in what looked like snow. The empty bag on the floor had contained flour. Not anymore. Fine white powder had settled everywhere.

Jack and Ella's impish grins greeted her.

"We were going to make you cupcakes, Momma," Ella said.

Jack giggled. "Yeah, Momma. Cupcapes."

Judith's voice rose as she looked accusingly at Brea. "See what they've done? Ella, Jack, you clean up this mess right now. You little heathens! God will smite you…"

"I've got it, Judith."

"As you should. These children should not be out of your sight. They could have hurt themselves. If you can't be responsible, you shouldn't be their mother."

"Jack, Ella, come with me." Brea marched the kids to her

room, desperate to get away from Judith's ridicule. How dare she speak to the kids that way. How dare she speak to anyone in this house that way! In desperation, she disrobed them and stuck them in the tub, turning on the shower and hosing them off. Within seconds, they were giggling and splashing. She tempted them out of the shower with heated towels and the promise of a snack. Next on her agenda was tackling the "cupcape" disaster, and dismissing Judith for the day.

By the time she made it back to the kitchen, the pain from the stairs was less and Brea's shoulders had straightened. She sat the kids at the table with paper and crayons, and shuddered at the energy she'd require to clean up the impossible mess. Adrenaline fueled her, and as she stepped into the laundry room for a broom and dustpan, she found Judith tucked in the corner, writing furiously in a small notebook.

Brea strode within an inch of Judith, peering over her shoulder. "What are you doing?" She ripped the pages from Judith's grasp and began to read the scrawled notes. "Irresponsible. Leaves kids in danger…" She flipped the page. "Kids unkempt. Jack's fingernails could scratch out an eyeball." Further back. "Can't remember where she keeps things. Unsafe." The next thing she spotted made white heat crawl up her spine. "Child Protective Services," and a phone number. *How dare she!*

Judith ranted, and pushed Brea as she fought to pull the notepad from Brea's tight grasp. "My notes are none of your business. This is between Dr. Marks and me!"

"Get the hell out of my house and take your high and mighty judgments with you," Brea ordered, her hands shaking more than her legs. She shoved the notebook in her back pocket, shuddering at the thought of the other notes Judith had recorded.

"Dr. Marks wouldn't like that," Judith said, planting a hand on her hip, then waving a finger at Brea. "I'm meant to be here until five o'clock."

"I'm in charge, not Dr. Marks. This is my home and I'm

telling you to go. Permanently. Not just for today." Brea's voice rose to a shrill pitch.

Judith huffed on her way to the door. "He's right about you," she snapped. "He said you were sick, and I don't mean your physical ailments. You can't be trusted. You're careless with the children, unstable, and an emotional basket case. God help you. I'm phoning Dr. Marks as soon as I leave." She stormed off, slamming the door behind her.

Ella began to cry. "I want my mommy. My real mommy."

Brea stroked Ella's head, made promises to read her favorite story, offered to bake cookies when they woke from a nap.

"I want Daddy. Where's Daddy?"

"He's at work. He'll be home at dinnertime. Here, send him a text. When I say 'go,' recite your message."

Brea held the phone out to Ella, the blood rushing out of her and threatening to flatten her. Would this day never end?

"Daddy, you need to come home. Mommy isn't acting right. She's scaring me."

Brea turned her back and deleted the message. "There, I sent it to Daddy. Now, listen." Brea gathered Ella into her lap. "I'm sorry I lost my temper with Judith, but Mommy needs some alone time. Not from you and Jack, but from other adults."

"Daddy?"

"No, not Daddy."

"You love Daddy?"

"I love Daddy," Brea recited like a pledge. "I love Daddy very much."

At last Ella offered a half-smile at the words as she wriggled off Brea's lap.

At one o'clock, Brea joined Jack and Ella for a three-hour nap on her bed. She could no more climb the stairs again and search for evidence than she could climb Mt. Everest when she was able-bodied.

When she awakened, she found another text from Peter. An

"I'm sorry." She stared at the ceiling, thinking about the day having turned to shit. The last thing she felt like doing was looking for proof but... She slid out of bed, careful not to disturb the sleeping children.

She made her way to the bottom of the stairs and hesitated. If Beth had held onto evidence of an affair with Peter, the last place she would have hidden mementoes was in the master bedroom. What a relief. Despite her nap, she couldn't muster the energy to climb a single step.

Jack began to cry. Her investigative work would have to keep. Besides, tomorrow would mark the end of strained communication—the remaining wires would be removed from her mouth. She could hardly wait for the opportunity to open her mouth wide and scream at the top of her lungs. Soon perhaps, she could take a step without pain.

In the meantime, a steady diet of Cabernet might mask the pain of her sister's likely betrayal.

CHAPTER SIXTEEN

Jeffry

JEFFRY SAT IN TRAFFIC FOR THIRTY MINUTES. NORMALLY, THE ride home took fifteen at most. He hit the steering wheel with the heel of his hand. It had been a grueling day. The old guy whose stent he'd repaired had led a self-destructive life. Amazing he was still alive. An alcoholic and chain smoker who refused to give up his vices despite his COPD and a failing liver. Hell, half his teeth were gone. The man had promised Jeffry umpteen times that he'd smoked his last cigarette, downed his last beer. The vow lasted about five minutes each time. The man's son wasn't ready to let go of his dad. He'd jump off a ledge for his father, rather than watch the man do himself in. That kind of love was rare, and it made Jeffry think of little Jack. He'd never do that to his kid.

When Jeffry finally strode through the door at half past seven, Ella and Jack clutched his leg like burrs. "Daddy, you're home!"

Jeffry patted Jack's head and swept Ella up in his arms and gave her a kiss.

"Did you get my message?" she asked.

Jeffry gave Brea a quizzical look and she shook her head. "I had a really busy day, sweetie. What did you want?"

"My other Mommy. The one who's nice." She shot an accusatory glance at Brea. "Mommy yelled at Judith. Mommy doesn't like people. She said so."

Jeffry frowned, took a seat, and took both pajama-clad children into his lap. Confusion etched his brow. "Sometimes when people get bad head boo-boos they act a little strange, but after a long time they sometimes get better."

Brea stood and stomped away as well as she was able. Before she left the kitchen, she turned on her heel, lost her balance and clutched at the chair rail to keep from falling. "Judith is not coming back. Not tomorrow. Not ever. I will not be second-guessed, judged, and micromanaged like a brain-injured moron."

"I'll be in to talk to you after I tuck the kids into bed," Jeffry said with measured calm.

Brea slammed the bedroom door behind her and sunk down on the bed, holding her head in her hands. How could he take the side of a five-year-old? And for him to suggest her feelings were part of a head injury? To tell Ella her mother might never get well? To suggest that Ella didn't have to listen to or respect her?

Flames of anger wicked at her skin, as if she couldn't get away no matter where she turned. She'd have the locks changed tomorrow. Judith couldn't get in, nor Dana or Derek. She'd run this house the way she saw fit. To hell with Jeffry and the kids.

She flung herself back on the bed and wailed, crying until exhaustion consumed her. She curled into a ball, but sleep wouldn't come.

A knock on the door. "Beth? It's me."

"Go away."

Jeffry opened the door a crack and stuck his head inside the room. "It's going to be okay. She's a little girl. She's not accustomed to anger."

Brea seethed, but held her words. *Not according to your wife.*

"This won't last forever. It's just your head injury, the loss of your sister, your other injuries. You've been through more than most people deal with in a lifetime. Give Ella some time, and yourself too." He assumed a seat on the side of the bed and stroked her arm.

"I won't be placated."

"I'm trying to be supportive and encouraging."

"You want to be supportive? Leave me alone."

Jeffry stood, sorrow and sympathy in his gaze, a hint of frustration behind his eyes. He turned and left the room with the slightest click of the door.

Brea listened to his footsteps trail down the hall and into the kitchen. She fully expected him to drive off into the night. Grab a scotch at the neighborhood bar. If anyone needed a drink, she did, and a slow fuse started to burn inside her gut.

She mused at the irony of him leaving her alone with the children when he thought she was incapable of caring for them. Calling after him in a rage, her entire body shook with anger, "Oh, so now you trust me? When you need a drink?"

Ella began to cry from outside her bedroom door, her wails growing louder with each passing second. "I want water!" Brea listened to Jeffry's footsteps hurry down the hall, the calming murmurs, and the padding of feet on the stairs. Then, the quiet.

Minutes later, Jeffry entered the bedroom. "You need to calm down. You're upsetting the kids. I won't have it."

"You won't have it? What are you going to do? Toss me to the curb?" She wondered if he'd treated Beth this way. Had this kind of behavior driven Beth into Peter's arms? Had he demeaned her? Beaten her down? Made her feel small and insignificant? Her rage for her sister took over. "You can't treat me like this. I'm not an imbecile, I'm injured."

"You sure don't act like it. And not just since the accident either. I've been patient, Beth. More than patient. You changed some time ago. Lost your fire. Turned cold and mean. I'm doing my very best."

"Doing what? Being king of the castle? Your wishes and wants are the only ones that matter. Your career takes precedence over me, the kids, this house. You hire someone to watch my every move. Did you do that before the accident, too?

"Get out. Just get out. I'm the one who belongs here. Not you. Go to your mistress and enjoy a relaxing evening. That's what you want, isn't it? For the kids and me to disappear?"

114

Jeffry stormed out.

Within seconds, Ella began to wail again. Moments later Brea heard a door slam, then a muffled crash. A huge thud followed.

Brea rose and called for Ella to come downstairs. She bribed her to quiet by allowing her to climb in her bed, then told her she needed to check on Daddy, leaving the television turned onto a recorded cartoon program. Ella immediately calmed and snuggled down in the covers.

Brea made her way to the garage, and stepped into a terrifying scene. The space looked as if it had been ransacked, or worse, the aftereffects of a tornado. Jeffry stood with hunched shoulders, shocked and surprised to see her, his hair standing on end, a wild look in his eyes, mouth agape, and sweat dripping from his brow. Before him, on the cement floor, lay a pile of broken china, shattered pieces scattered everywhere. He held a sledgehammer in his hand.

"What's going on?" Brea asked as she backed toward the door. "Put the hammer down."

Jeffry studied the tool as if it was the first time he noticed it in his hand. As if he had no idea how it had wound up in his grasp. Then, Brea realized he'd smashed her mother's china, the place servings she'd left with Beth before she'd moved to South Carolina. One of the last mementoes of her childhood. Sheer adrenalin allowed her to fall to her knees, unconcerned about injury, and sob as she lifted a remnant to her chest.

"Get out!" Brea cried.

Jeffry spent the night at the hospital, and called Brea every hour on the hour until midnight. She refused to pick up the phone. For two days. He showed up at the end of the third day with a bouquet of flowers and a bottle of wine. Funny, Brea thought, how he expected simple gifts would smooth things over. She made him sit down and wait. The kids were dressed, fed, and the house in perfect order.

Jack and Ella delighted in seeing their busy, overworked father and climbed on his lap for cuddles. After the kids went off with Dana and Derek for an outing, Brea was tempted to go nose to nose with him about Beth's reality. She cautioned herself to temper her words. His outburst could serve as fuel for divorce. That's what he most likely wanted, and a separation would certainly make her deceit easier to manage, but he surprised her by apologizing until his face turned gray with desperation. She had no history to refer to, no past arguments or tirades. Instead of continuing to berate him, she took a seat. Then, a deep breath.

"Let's call a truce. For the meantime, you stay in your world, and I'll stay in mine," Jeffry offered.

"I don't need you," Brea said. "I don't need anyone's help."

Sadness filled his eyes. "Allow Judith back, just until we find someone you like."

"Absolutely not. I'll hire a housekeeper. One of my choosing."

A chainsaw couldn't have cut the tension.

Brea stewed for two entire days, unrelenting in defense of her capabilities. Only when she dropped an entire pot of spaghetti sauce, nearly burning Ella as she played on the floor in front of the sink, did Brea finally acquiesce. She had little choice, and Jeffry heaved a sigh of relief. Brea made the call. Judith was the only available housekeeper. Jeffry agreed to sit down with the two women and spell out new rules for Judith. No more hovering. No more notebook. He convinced Brea that she could find someone of her choosing, but Judith would have to do for now. She'd rather have her jaw wired shut again than deal with that woman, but there was no choice.

His schedule indicated a busy morning, thanks to a glut of patients admitted over the weekend. Monday topped the list as the most popular day for heart attacks, but Saturday ran a close second, which meant back-to-back mornings of angioplasty procedures. He lost himself in his work for the next few hours. A welcome distraction from home. Well past two o'clock, he had a chance to stop for lunch. He headed down to the cafeteria to grab a quick sandwich and a cold drink.

After he wolfed down his sandwich, he stretched and glanced at his cell. No calls. A week had passed since Tammy showed up at the viewing. Not like he'd been expecting a call, but still he was surprised. Maybe she'd gotten the message he was focused on home. No more playing around.

He did miss her, though. The fun—the sex, the relaxation. Tempted as he was to send her a quick text, he clicked to his home screen and checked his email. Best to leave the Tammy door closed, at least for a while. He convinced himself he missed her because of the added stress of helping Beth at home. His wife's recovery was slow. She was exhausted by the time he reached home at night. The more time that passed, the more forgetful and moody she seemed. He made a mental note to check in with the neurologist. She should be better by now, but considering her grief and other injuries, this could be normal. He was too close to Beth and her situation to be objective.

He thought about calling home. There was an idea. If every time he thought of Tammy, he called home, he could replace a vice with an appropriate behavior, like an addict trying to quit. But mid-afternoon, Beth and the kids might be napping. Frankly, he didn't relish speaking with Sergeant Judith any more than Beth, even though Judith delighted in giving him her daily report after he'd told her he neither needed nor wanted one. "Beth is having difficulty controlling her emotions. She often hugs the children more than necessary. She's unfamiliar with the home. She's forgetful and seems lost. I worry for the children's safety." He had enough to worry about without her exaggerations.

His next procedure was scheduled for 2:45 p.m. After he finished the angioplasty, he would call. He needed to work with a clear head. Jeffry stuffed his cell back into his pocket and leaned over to retrieve the napkin, which had slid off his lap.

"Fancy meeting you here."

Jeffry glanced up. Tammy stood before him, her blonde hair cascading well below her shoulders, shiny curls caressing her soft, rounded, perfect breasts.

"Hi," was all he could muster in the midst of clustering thoughts and emotions. A sharp inhale helped him to refocus.

"Mind if I join you?"

"For a minute."

Even though he struggled with immediate and undeniable warmth at seeing her, he knew what he intended to do. Avert his eyes and remain faithful to his wife. Shove the demon right off his shoulder. Tammy had frightened him with her unveiled threats toward Beth. He didn't need his reputation in the toilet because of an affair with a jealous, homicidal woman.

Jeffry waved his hand toward the seat opposite his. Tammy approaching him here had never occurred to him. They had stopped conversing on hospital grounds months ago, lest someone suspect their affair. Both had done their best to keep their relationship under wraps. Then he remembered the night she'd shown up in Beth's room. His shoulders tensed.

"I know we agreed not to talk here," she said, glancing over her shoulder. "Believe me, I'd rather not see you right now either, but there's something you need to know."

"What's that?"

Jeffry focused on the hospital's surveillance camera. His physical attraction was easier to control if he blinded himself to her beauty, which led to the lure of her milky skin, her touch. The temptation was much harder to ignore than he imagined. Out of sight, out of mind was one thing, but seeing her...the pull was magnetic. She appeared almost willowy, her body slim. He flashed on her long legs wrapped around his neck...

Even in her operating room scrubs, she beguiled him. She looked far more like a lingerie model than a nurse. He couldn't help but wonder if she'd let her hair tumble around her slender shoulders purposefully before she walked in.

"We need to talk," she said. She set her tray on the table, but didn't touch her food.

He glanced down at his watch.

"I have a procedure in five minutes. We'll have to talk another time."

"When?" She pleaded.

He squinted over her shoulder, avoiding her gaze. "I'm not sure." He pushed back his chair, and piled his tray with his leftover drink and garbage. Abruptly, he headed toward the door. Then, thinking better of a hasty departure, he faced her. This might be the last time he'd see her for a while. He wanted to burn her image into his memory. "Beth needs me right now. We just buried her sister, and her body is still a wreck. The kids are demanding. We have a lot going on. I can barely catch a break."

"It's always about you," she answered.

"Not now."

"I'm tired of coming in second. Even before this happened with Beth, I'd made up my mind. It's me or her."

Jeffry tensed. "Look, I'm not trying to be a prick, but I thought I made things clear. I have to give this a try. My marriage and family are important."

"I'm trying to tell you something," she said in a huff. "I'm seeing someone."

Her words caught him off guard. He'd never expected Tammy to dump him. She had seemed so head over heels. So committed, so…his. Maybe she was playing games.

"Who? Are you sleeping with him?"

Tammy's jaw tightened. "That's none of your business. You're the one who wants to be home. You're the one who needs to focus on your family. We're over, Jeffry. I need to move on." Satisfaction rang in her tone.

The world tipped off its axis. Jeffry found himself stunned and speechless. He strode off, dumped his trash in the bin, tossed his tray on top of the pile, and marched out of the cafeteria.

His mind raced to the phone call from her over a week ago—the one he'd ignored. His heart rate quickened. Blood rose up his neck and he felt the flush warm his cheeks. Tammy had found someone else.

Considering Tammy was a romantic, she'd probably called to give him one last chance.

He couldn't make heads or tails of anything. How he felt about Tammy. How he felt about his wife. How he was going to keep his hands steady and perform surgery after this unexpected tailspin.

When Grant Fulton had shown up at the hospital, he'd told Jeffry about Beth's accident. He hadn't said anything more. Jeffry remembered how he had wanted, at least momentarily, to hear she'd died. Her death would have been a relief and eliminated a multitude of problems. He'd thought about marrying Tammy, they'd talked about it, but none of the past year made any real sense now. Looking back, he might have been out of his mind.

At the time, he'd created a long list of reasons to choose Tammy over Beth. Because he laughed when they were together. Because she complimented him, not just now and then, but all the time. Because the sex was great. Because she was gorgeous and smart. He was proud of her. He wanted to take her out in public and show her off to the world. He wanted other men to be envious, because he had snagged such a spectacular woman.

He had once been as crazy about Beth. As in love. Somewhere along the line, those feelings had faded. Before the accident, she left him cold, their sex life expiring a long time before. When Jack was born, he guessed. Certainly not the little guy's fault. Maybe Jeffry had dropped the ball. He disliked the discomfort of facing his failings.

He pushed those thoughts out of his mind, thrust open the swinging door to the scrub room, turned on the water, and lathered up.

CHAPTER SEVENTEEN

Jeffry

JEFFRY SQUINTED IN THE HARSH LIGHT AS SUNSHINE streamed through a cloudless sky. He strolled through the towering oaks, which shaded the driveway, and flipped down his sunglasses before taking off at a trot. Conflicting emotions overwhelmed him. He hadn't experienced a stir of attraction for his wife in ages, yet this morning, he'd wanted to hold onto her for dear life. He needed her. The reality shocked him. His ability to reason clearly faltered, too. He couldn't make sense of his emotions, nor talk himself out of them. One minute he was self-assured, the next minute, looking for a place to hide. Decisive one day, unable to choose a necktie the next. Struggling was uncomfortable for him. He desperately needed to get his head on straight.

He blamed it on hormones. He missed sex. And Beth seemed so vulnerable. He wanted to give her an injection. Fill her up with a piece of him.

Beth had been furious this morning, but when Jeffry considered what she had been through, he guessed he should have expected it. Considering also that they hadn't been close since Lincoln was president, he had to forgive her. He knew she wouldn't consider therapy or even a grief group. She'd made her opinions on psychoanalysis all too clear years ago. Considering her twin was a shrink, it surprised him. Maybe he should go alone. At least get some of his questions answered about her current state. It could be normal, or might be a sign of severe depression. Hell, he felt depressed and it wasn't even his sister who died.

As he ran, his heart rate sped up and then slowed, his respirations evened out, his body settled into its pace. After the first mile, he broke a sweat, and the endorphins started to work their magic. The world became clearer, the uneven ground smoother. He was surprised he was so drawn to Beth again. She seemed different somehow. He tried to remember the last time she'd said something nice to him before the accident, when she'd last gazed at him lovingly, playfully. He couldn't recall. Years, perhaps.

With Tammy, the sex was great. Exciting. Being with someone so captivated by him made him happy. So did the chance to truly relax. Whenever he arrived at her apartment, wine glasses were out and ready. He'd kick off his shoes the moment he strolled through the door, pop open a bottle of Cabernet, grab a few slices of cheese, and the world became just about him for a few hours.

He loved Tammy. He had at first anyway. Or maybe he suffered from lust intoxication, and testosterone ruled his brain.

Now, their relationship seemed like a risk.

He'd been given a mulligan. His wife could have died, but instead, his marriage had been given a second chance. If they worked hard, he and Beth could reclaim their passion. He'd caught a hint of desire in her voice, or maybe he'd imagined it, but in any case, she looked good. Better every day. And man, had he witnessed colleagues' divorces over the years. The guys might have substituted a younger model, but had strained-to-non-existent relationships with their kids, and alimony and child support payments up the wazoo.

Jeffry picked up his pace. His lungs burned and he dripped sweat. He slowed, stooped, and placed his hands on his knees. Grappling for breath, his vision blurred. He forced some measured breaths and waited for the moment to pass.

His heartbeat finally slowed and the world stopped spinning. He ambled toward the river's edge. Naked trees tunneled the water trickling through the frigid channel, and he mused at its beauty and breadth. Always moving, flowing past obstructions, rocks, brush, or the occasional fallen tree. Forward momentum. A lesson there. The warm sun abated the chill in his body. Soon his joints relaxed, soothed and rejuvenated.

He resumed his run, thoughts of reconnecting with Beth landing with every step. A bottle of wine. A cozy dinner for two. If he fed the kids and tucked them into bed early, he could offer Beth a simple meal and sit with her and talk. Get to know her again. They had grown apart quite by accident. He'd become wrapped up in his work, and she'd been busy with the kids. If he made the effort, maybe she would respond in kind. Maybe she still wanted to be with him. Maybe she still loved him.

Jeffry ambled along, hands on his hips, all thoughts on his long forgotten birth family. He'd been estranged from them for so many years he couldn't imagine how he might feel if he heard of his parents' or brother's passing. He didn't even know if they were still alive. But the estrangement was their fault, not his.

His family had made clear early on, his ambitions were more than they thought he could handle. He had no reason to believe he could become a highfalutin' doctor. He must think he was better than them. The family business was good enough for his brother, so roofing houses should be good enough for him. The old dialogues stung as he replayed them. He was never good enough, and he supposed he had decided to become a physician as a way of proving himself to them. Or proving something to himself. He'd left for college when he was eighteen and never looked back.

Jeffry lingered and listened to the squirrels' chatter. A gentle breeze ruffled the branches, and he noticed the first buds on the oaks and maples. If he ever did hear of the death of his parents or his brother, he couldn't imagine grieving for them.

Brea's passing would play differently for Beth, though.

Jeffry remembered an identical twin he'd treated during his residency. When his patient did poorly, the healthy twin reported matching symptoms—racing heartbeat, clammy neck, sweaty palms—like their heartbeats were linked, as if they were conjoined, rather than separate individuals. He'd lost sight of their closeness over the years, but the memory was as vivid as a flashing neon sign in this moment. He thought of his wife. And her excruciating heartache.

He released a puff of air. The death of Beth's parents had been traumatic enough. She'd shared so much early on about how Brea had helped her through the grief, posing as her, attending classes, writing papers, taking exams, while Beth lay in bed, hardly able to do more than sob.

She'd need the security and love of her family to get through this grief. And losses like this could cement or destroy a relationship. Bottom line, Beth and the kids were all he had. He didn't want to lose them. Couldn't lose them.

His ass was on the line.

❧

Fate had a way of intervening and Jeffry slowed as a car pulled up next to the curb. He leaned down to the passenger window of the red Mercedes, well aware of the driver. This car had visited his home on more than one occasion. Peter leaned across the console. "How's it going, Doc?"

"Peter. Good to see you. I was just thinking about you, or your profession to be precise."

"When I noticed you running, I thought I'd offer an apology for my wife's behavior at your sister-in-law's funeral."

"Tough on Beth. That's actually why I was thinking of you."

"Hop in," Peter said. "I have a few minutes. Coffee?"

"Why not?"

Jeffry slid into the car, mopping the sweat off his brow with a handkerchief and apologizing to Peter for perspiring on the plush leather seat.

Peter waved a hand in Jeffry's direction. "Life's too short to worry about that."

Two minutes later, Peter pulled into the lot of a local coffee shop. They strode inside, each ordering a cup of black coffee, then assumed a seat at barstools in the back corner of the shop.

Peter adopted a well-practiced listening stance, holding his cup in both hands, eyes locked on Jeffry, leaning forward ever so slightly.

"I'm guessing it's common to sink into depression after losing a family member, especially an identical twin. Beth's angry and she's put up walls. I try to break through the barriers, but mostly it's impossible."

"You're in a tough bind. There's a balancing act a spouse plays when their partner experiences a loss. You want to be there for her, but she's stuck right now and won't let you in. The more she pushes you away, the more she needs you." Peter paused. He was talking about the Beth he knew and cautioned himself to choose his words carefully. "Keep at it. Beth's a good woman. Don't give up on her. Let her know you're there for her no matter how ugly she gets."

Jeffry sipped his coffee and took a moment to absorb Peter's words. "Good advice." After a moment, he continued. "Should I suggest a grief group? Maybe offer to go with her? I know she won't consider therapy, but there must be some value in those groups. Some of my patients' families have spoken quite highly of them."

"Be careful. You don't want to give her the message she can't handle things. Offering to go with her is a great idea. She'll feel supported even if she doesn't want to go. Best thing, though, is to let her talk to you. Whenever and wherever. Don't turn her away. She needs you."

"Thanks, man. And by the way, I know you and Brea were tight. Sorry about your loss."

"I appreciate that, but this isn't about me." He glanced down at his watch. "I'd better be going. Drop you off at home?"

Jeffry checked his watch. "That would be great. Beth has to be wondering where I am."

Minutes later, the Mercedes pulled into the circular drive of the Marks' estate. Peter caught Beth peering out the living room window as Jeffry jumped out of the car.

"Good luck with everything."

Jeffry gave him a nod of thanks before heading inside.

CHAPTER EIGHTEEN

Brea

PETER WAS OUT IN FRONT OF HER HOUSE WITH JEFFRY? What the hell? The hectic pace of a "normal" life had left Brea both weary and weepy. After two weeks packed with doctor's appointments, dodging Judith in the kitchen and child-rearing supervised by the Gestapo's wandering eye, even after she'd promised to leave the trusty notebook at home and not write lists for Jeffry, Brea felt a bit paranoid. This was her house, but it wasn't her home. Now this.

Before lunch, Judith had left for the weekend to attend her niece's wedding in Grand Rapids, a welcome reprieve from her continual hovering and smothering. Physical therapy progress was much slower than Brea had expected. While having the prison bars off her teeth and the casts removed from her arm and ankle liberated her, she feared biting down on anything solid, still gummed her food, and stepped tentatively throughout the house. Her body was stiff, sore, and uncooperative. Like it or not, she was still prisoner in an armed camp. Her face was no longer bruised or swollen, but the weight loss had left her with hollow cheeks and dark circles beneath her eyes. Not only did she feel like a prisoner, she looked like one. All that was missing was the orange jumpsuit.

The strain of adapting to the hectic pace of kids and taking care of a home left her dizzy. She didn't have her own life any longer, and barely managed a clear, reflective thought. She moved through the days numb in body and mind. Losing her sister, losing herself and her identity, had left her adrift and desperate, running like a hamster on a wheel. Getting nowhere.

Dammit. What was Peter doing here? And what had he been talking to Jeffry about?

A soft knock on the back door interrupted her panic attack. Jeffry must have forgotten his key. Brea set her coffee mug on the table and went to open the door for him.

"Hey," she said.

"You okay?"

"Sure."

"What's wrong?"

"Peter. What's that about?"

"Nothing. He happened to drive by when I was running. Just gave me a lift home."

Brea's mind started to spin. Maybe they were comparing notes. *Maybe they're on to me.*

Jeffry wrapped his arms around her and held her close. She molded into his chest. He led her back to the couch and sat her down, cuddled her against him. She leaned her head on his shoulder. They sat in peaceful silence for a good fifteen minutes.

"Don't you have to work?"

He gave a sheepish grin. "There's that." He kissed her on the forehead and trotted off to the shower.

Suffocated beyond belief, she needed a way out. A reprieve. A breath. Peter's arrival had put her over the top. Too much. Too close.

She could travel before long, and in all logic, she needed to clean out her condo. She could milk that for at least a week. Dana's spring break had to be right around the corner. If she could enlist Dana to watch the kids between the time Judith left for the day and Jeffry arrived home from the hospital, she'd drive to Hilton Head. The sooner she got out of town, the better.

Energy and motivation zipped through her veins. For the first time since coming "home," she crossed the threshold to untraveled territory: Beth's laptop. She Googled UofM's spring break. Two weeks from now, mid-March. If Brea pushed herself, she could be ready. The forty-five minute drive from Savannah airport wouldn't be a problem. Her flexibility and mobility would improve the more she moved, and the lingering pain should abate more each day. She'd talk to Jeffry over the weekend and persuade him to hire Dana for the week, maybe even for the summer, to act as their au pair. Their time with Judith should wind down now that she could navigate the house, drive and perform all the household tasks. She wouldn't miss the ball and chain for a single minute. The kids would be fine. They knew and liked Dana. Then, she would create a bit of a life for herself. Maybe even figure out a way to go back to work, not in her previous role, but something—anything—to give her a sense of autonomy.

The day passed quickly as her mind busied itself making plans. After tucking in the kids, she poured a glass of wine and put her feet up, exhausted.

She was just beginning to relax when a knock on the back door interrupted.

Brea huffed as she hobbled to the door and peeked outside. The neighbor, Susan, a friendly sort, although Brea hadn't seen the woman lately except for the funeral. Brea pasted a smile on her face and opened the door. The full moon, shining over Susan's shoulder, explained everything.

"Susan? Is something wrong?"

Susan held a glass of wine. "Let me in. I've been trying so hard to leave you alone the past few weeks. I can't imagine how devastated you are, but I never should have stayed away. I'm not one to avoid uncomfortable situations, but well, to tell you the truth, Ben and I are having our share of problems. We've decided to split up, and I desperately needed to get out of the house."

She eyed Susan. Trim and gorgeous, she moved with the grace of a gazelle. What Brea would give to move with such ease. She cursed under her breath.

"Come on in," Brea said. "Have a seat."

Once Brea turned and faced Susan her heart beat like a jungle drum. Just what she needed, another chance to screw up.

But Susan didn't seem suspicious or curious at all, and yammered on about her failing marriage. After a good twenty-minute diatribe, during which Brea fell into psychologist mode, listening and mirroring Susan's words, Susan peered at her.

"You're a much better listener since the accident."

Brea chuckled nervously. "Guess wearing those wires on my teeth for almost two solid months proved useful." She stood, twisted away and refilled her glass.

"So," Susan said, "how are things with Jeffry? Is he still MIA?"

Brea took mental notes. Susan might be the key to sorting out Beth's marriage and Jeffry's seeming changes of behavior since the accident.

"He's been home more." She paused, filtering through her options, then opting for the truth. "Actually, he was home a lot more when I first came home from the hospital. But the past couple of weeks, he's back on his hectic schedule. I try to understand, but I'm tired. The kids are a ton of work, the house is a mess, and I can't seem to find a thing."

"You never should have done a major overhaul after Brea moved. I know you rearranged everything in an attempt to reorder your life, but seriously, honey, you went a bit overboard."

"What do you mean?"

"Well, none of this is my business, but Brea moving away was harder on you than you thought. I worried when you started seeing Peter…you made the move like a teenager on the rebound. Just trying to fill up the space Brea's leaving left." She waved a dismissive hand. "Don't mind me, I'm playing amateur shrink."

Brea wished she could corral this woman and pick her brain all night. She stood and plucked a bottle from the wine rack, removed the cork and refilled Susan's glass.

"You're not mad, are you?"

Brea rubbed her arms, hoping to hide her goosebumps. "Of

course not. And you're right. B…Brea moving away was horrid. I hadn't put together why I'd gone into overdrive rearranging. Funny how far we'll go to avoid our feelings."

"Don't I know," Susan said. She gulped her wine. "I'm just hoping Ben leaves me the house."

Brea fished. "You seem resigned to a split."

"Like we've said a million times, honey. Who needs a man?" Then, she stopped and rolled her eyes. "Well, I do. I can't live without sex. And I've been lucky enough Ben's never suspected anything about Chuck. Not to say I see myself with Chuck long term. I'd rather wait and see who's available when the divorce is final." She stopped and swallowed more wine. "You look a little pale."

"Just tired."

Susan hopped up from her chair. "I'm sorry. I'm a bad friend. I'll stop by in a few days and see how you're doing." She wrapped her arms around Brea. "I love spending time with you, honey. And while I'm sorry about Brea, you seem more centered than you have in a long time. You'll miss your sister for the rest of your life, but make the best of what you have."

Brea rubbed her nose. "Thanks for stopping by."

"They're never far away, are they, even when they're gone. You reminded me so much of Brea just then, rubbing your nose like that." She paused. "Oh, I almost forgot…the woman's club is due for lunch here on Friday. Remember, it's your turn.

"Judith said you've been forgetful, so I thought I'd better remind you. Do you even read your email any longer? Not that I'm judging, really, and those women can be a pain in the ass. Do you have a caterer? Moveable Feast is probably already booked this close. Maybe I can find someone last minute or, better yet, have Judith run to Whole Foods."

"How many people?"

"Twelve, darling. And serve some wine. That always makes the afternoon go by in a flash. Did you know Cynthia Magness joined the group? Reinforce your armor. The woman is a snake. An absolute reptile. And she's already got her teeth in you. Between your affair with Peter and the scene at the funeral home, she's probably planning to have you for lunch."

"God help me."

"Yes," Susan said, grasping her arm. "You should pray."

Once she ushered Susan out the door and returned to the table, Brea held her head in her hands. She took a long moment with her thoughts. What a night. Susan knew Beth had been seeing Peter. She hoped her face hadn't revealed her shock, but Susan seemed oblivious to all but her own problems. One of those women who prattled on with her opinionated musings. Brea didn't have much use for people like Susan. She'd had enough of them as clients and they drove her to study the clock's secondhand, willing it to move faster. Then again, she could benefit from this woman's insight into her sister. She had to be careful though, sorting out the nuggets from the crumbs. *Crap. A luncheon in two days. With Cynthia. Wonderful.*

Brea sipped her wine as she entered the study. In a feisty mood, ready to take on the world, she checked Beth's favorites bar at the top of the computer screen. Fairly organized with matters of the house and kids, Beth had bookmarked a folder entitled "Bills." A place to start. Especially the cell bill.

She located a file containing usernames and passwords. Both she and Beth had done this a long time ago, before the computer did it for you. She merely typed a "B" into the user name for the cell phone provider sign-in, and the whole shebang popped up.

Brea started with January, discovering twelve calls and sixteen texts before the fifteenth of the month, their birthday. Then she went back six months further. She had left Ann Arbor for Hilton Head in June. As she clicked on the June statement, she inhaled sharply. She closed her eyes and guessed Beth was already seeing Peter when she left town. After counting to ten, slowly and deliberately, she opened her eyes, and began to make tally marks when Peter's number appeared under calls. Then, she scrolled down the page to texts.

The June statement included most of May. Twenty-seven

messages in all. Maybe Beth contacted Peter because she was upset about Brea's departure. A professional relationship. Or maybe Peter cried on Beth's shoulder and lured her into his orbit. He could be enigmatic and sexy as hell. Brea put the brakes on the impulse to blame Peter. Beth was just as guilty. She tamped down her spiking anger. Investigate first, put the facts together, decide what happened. Then, get pissed.

She continued to dig backward, discovering contacts between Beth and Peter well before she expected them. The innumerable calls and texts made her weary. She switched screens to check Beth's email account, only to discover Beth had been vigilant about keeping her mailbox uncluttered, to the point of deleting everything prior to the accident. Beth left nothing questionable behind.

Brea recognized the value of thorough research and pressed her lips together with conviction, then inspected Beth's mailbox folders. *The deeper you dig, the more you find.*

The back door slammed. As Brea listened for footsteps, she shut down the computer. Strange. The house was silent. Jeffry was a creature of habit. In the evenings, he strode in, shut the door with a determined thwack, clip-clopped to the liquor cabinet, clinked a rock glass onto the counter, and glugged a couple of shots into it.

Brea heard none of the familiar sounds. Her breath caught and she shuddered. She stood slowly, her stocking feet moving soundlessly along the carpet. She entered the hallway, leaned around the corner, and peeked into the kitchen.

Jeffry sat in the easy chair, the grand tub of upholstery facing the heavily forested yard. His long arms dangled over the chair arms, his legs splayed in front of him, his chin drooped against his chest. A small overhead light above the sink illuminated the room, the light Brea always left burning in anticipation of his arrival.

He looked gloomy.

"Jeffry, are you okay?"

"Huh? Oh, yeah, hi," he said. "Tired. Exhausted, really."

"Can I get you anything?"

"No, I don't want to bother you."

"I'll just warm your dinner. I fixed you a plate."

"Thanks." He didn't move a muscle, not even the slightest shift of his frame.

"Want to talk about your day?" Curiosity fed her as much as anything.

"No."

She pressed the reheat button on the microwave and waited as the fan whirred and the aroma of roasted chicken, beans, and mashed potatoes filled the air. She considered what she might do to be helpful. Old habits die hard. Even though she didn't know her brother-in-law well, his behavior struck her as out of character, and a bit alarming. She retrieved his glass, poured several fingers of Scotch over ice, and placed the tumbler in his hand.

"Thanks," he mumbled.

Brea placed his plate on the table and limped away.

CHAPTER NINETEEN

Grant

GRANT PUT IN FOR CHIEF, GLAD HE'D FINALLY MADE A DE-cision. He tossed back a shot of bourbon, pushing away the pit-load of what-ifs and if-onlys he'd been carrying around like a hundred pound rucksack. He'd dreamed of having a home and a family, so he always let the other guys go for the promotions, thinking a steady job and regular shift was better suited to family life. Now, he looked forward to the added responsibility, the crazy hours, the chance to change all the shit he'd hated for far too long.

His partner, Shaun Davis, sat at his side and took a long draw of beer. He patted his round belly. One thing about Shaun, he enjoyed the simple life. "You're right, buddy, marriage isn't in the cards for a guy like you. But don't worry. You get this job, you'll get laid plenty."

Grant blew out a puff of air, his momentary pride shifting to anger. "What the hell is that supposed to mean?"

Shaun tapped a cigarette out of the pack and tucked it behind his ear. "You made a mistake splitting up with Mary. Now you're living like a priest. This is simple. The reason you're such a crab ass is you haven't gotten laid in a while."

"Shut the hell up."

"Well, let's think about the bachelor life. You're not one to settle down, but you're a man. You have to take care of yourself."

"Where the hell is this coming from?"

"Maybe you're one of those guys who can't commit. Okay, so

you've never met a girl you thought worth marrying. Clue one, buddy. Clue one."

"Asshole. You have no idea," Grant shot back.

"Oh, so there's someone special you haven't mentioned in the last two years? In the day-in, day-out partnership thing we share? Didn't have time to tell me about her? Hmm. Must be the blow-up girl you keep hidden in the closet." Shaun's next sip nearly showered Grant with the beer spray of self-induced pleasure from his own weak joke.

"I don't know why I even talk to you," Grant muttered.

"Aw, c'mon, I'm just messin' with you."

Grant folded his hands beneath his chin. "You wanna really know what's bugging me?"

"'Fess up, buddy."

"What really bugs me are icy roads. Cold, senseless deaths. The damn semi-drivers never die. Only innocent women and kids. I'm fed up with the injustice."

"Whew. You need a day off. Or maybe a few vacation days. A little R&R."

"I'm serious. The freaking monster semis decide who lives and dies. And the weather. There's no order to life. None of us have any control." A lightning bolt struck Grant. He'd never called about the vehicle inspection. Maybe he did need a break. Then again, black ice explained the accident. Still, no stone unturned and all that.

"This spring storm's got you in its grips, my man. Many a guy goes squirrely in the middle of a Michigan winter. Head to Florida for a couple of days. Visit your mom. Snowbirds love it when family comes to visit. How long is she staying down there anyway?"

"Last thing I need right now is my mother. I'd rather chew glass."

Shaun shoved Grant's arm, almost knocking him out of his chair. "I'm going out back for a smoke. Be here when I get back?"

"No. I'm heading out."

"Suit yourself, man. Hey, there's Brad and JT." Already a little juiced, Shaun waved enthusiastically to gain their friends' attention.

Grant stood and threw a few bills on the table. "I'll tell 'em you're over here. Catch you later."

Grant passed the word to the two veteran detectives, then ambled into the slushy March evening where a typical late snowfall was making a sludgy mess of the streets. He hunched his shoulders, trying to stay warm as he headed into the bitter wind. He couldn't shake the chill inside or out, and his dissatisfaction carried a wicked bite.

A picture popped into his head. Junior year of high school. The large red crayon heart with the initials M.F.E.O. Made for each other. Brea's homemade Valentine.

As he strode toward the parking garage on Liberty, head down in a reflective trance, he shook as if trying to bust out of the horrid abyss he had plunged into. He glanced up to distract himself, reading the signs on office doors. Every other entryway announced some Ph.D. or another. Lots of shrinks in these parts. Gotta love a university town. The trained docs stayed right there, next to the weight loss center and Bikram yoga. Shrink your body or your mental problems right down to their bare bones. If the hour weren't so late, Grant might have considered stopping by to see if they had drop-in appointments. When a guy felt the end of the world coming, it might be time to get a few things off his chest.

He didn't want to contemplate his life, too many years spent going nowhere, but he couldn't shift his thinking. He'd avoided serious reflection for way too long. Living a prescribed life. Doing a noble job. Predictable, yet risky. Getting all the kicks he needed from his career rather than a satisfying home life. Now he felt a little desperate.

He couldn't get his mind off Brea and replayed his time at the funeral home. Brea's ashes in the copper urn and the emptiness when he knelt in front of her remains and prayed. His brief conversation with Beth. The comforting hug he gave her when she came out of the restroom.

By the time he climbed into his Jeep, his feet were frozen. He drove over to the station and made a quick call to the Northport PD and asked for the vehicle inspection to be emailed. While he waited for the report, he reheated a cup of decaf that had been sitting on his desk from earlier in the day. Minutes later, an email notification popped up on his computer screen. Grant scanned the report until he found the answer to his looming question. "Damage to the front end of the passenger car was cataclysmic. Impossible to determine if mechanical/hydraulic tampering had taken place. No evidence of tampering in the rear. Evaluation of electronics does not indicate tampering. Overall conclusion of tampering is undetermined." As expected, a dead end. At least he'd done his due diligence.

He zipped the four miles to the condo and heaved a sigh as he shut the door tight behind him. He hung his coat on the rack, kicked off his shoes, and rubbed his hands together. Hard as he tried, he could not warm up. He flipped the wall switch, and waited for the fireplace gas to connect. Flames flickered and flew, but he still carried a nasty chill.

He'd hoped to lock his feelings outside by latching the door. Worked before. He sat, propped his feet on the coffee table, flicked the TV clicker to a game, and grabbed the evening paper. Five minutes later, he realized he hadn't read a single word. He popped up and headed to the kitchen. The fridge stood at attention like a soldier without a mission. Grant smacked the door with an open hand.

Taking out his aggressions didn't help him shake the unease either.

Something wasn't right. He stopped. Closed his eyes. Blinked. Then, he remembered. Beth had rubbed her nose. At the funeral home. Right before Jeffry met them by the restroom.

Brea's nervous tic. Every time she was anxious. Grant had teased her about the tell constantly. She'd pretend everything was fine, then he'd see her rub her nose with the tip of her middle finger—like Pinocchio, telling a lie and hoping it wouldn't grow. It was how he knew something was bothering her.

Still, he had a tendency to over-think. Everybody touched their nose. It was in the middle of their face, for God's sake.

He grabbed a beer and headed into the bedroom. Deep in the

back of his tunnel-like closet, he found the cardboard box he hadn't dared to open in ages. He held a musty yearbook in his hands and ran his fingers over the worn pages.

He recognized the rush, the shortness of breath. Whenever he was in the middle of an investigation, on the track of a hunch, his blood caught fire like a match to dry grass. He retraced his steps to the living room, perched his beer on a cushion then leaned back. The yearbook fell open naturally to the middle—to the card Brea had constructed especially for him.

His breath evened out, as if her presence—real or remembered—made him more whole.

Inside the homemade valentine, Brea had placed a photo of the two of them taken the previous summer, right before the start of senior year. Clad in swimsuits, they stood with their arms snugly nestled around each other's waists. Grant's eyes struggled to adjust to the muted light, but his reading glasses were in the other room. He recalled the faint discoloration in the shape of a crescent that interrupted the tan on Brea's belly. A spot that didn't tan. He'd discovered the birthmark one afternoon at Kensington Park. A huge group of kids had gone to the beach, Beth included. He'd been proud of himself for pinpointing a clear and undeniable difference between the two girls, the only visible sign to set them apart.

He couldn't ignore the chemistry between himself and Beth at the hospital, and again at the funeral home visitation. He'd never experienced a connection with her before. No way Brea would take Beth's place…right? An impossible thought. He was being silly. Living on wishful thinking.

Still, he'd love to see Beth in a bikini. Just to be sure.

He couldn't help himself. Deep down, he was a cop. Solving puzzles was in his blood.

CHAPTER TWENTY

Jeffry

YET ANOTHER LONG DAY. THE PRESSURE, CELEBRITY, AND work used to pump him up. Now, Jeffry couldn't keep track of a single thought. More than anything, he just wanted to get in his car and drive. No destination. No constraints. No Tammy.

She'd had the nerve to pass him in the hall, flipping her hair off her shoulders like she was flipping him off.

And imagining her with someone else—what a kick in the balls.

He'd never anticipated her moving on. True, he had been about to do the same, but she beat him to it. He'd underestimated her, never dreaming she'd go after another man. His ego felt the blow as swift and sharp as the strike of a tire iron.

While he could intellectualize her right to replace him, he couldn't shed the sting of rejection. The burn went deep, seethed beneath his skin, churned a cavern in his gut, and slashed deep internal wounds.

Double standards sucked. Especially when they worked against you.

Reflective thought wore him out.

Jeffry refilled his drink and wandered into the study. He needed a distraction and reached for the laptop. World of Warcraft used to work. When his eyes settled on the screen, curiosity took over. Beth hadn't been on the computer since her return home, not so he could tell. He examined her recent history. He'd never studied her cell phone bill before, so he spent a minute or two to figure out the layout. Once he determined where to click, text messages lit up the screen. He scrolled the page and found a lot of messages to one particular number. He Googled a reverse search on the number.

Peter Magness.

Well, now. Peter. He glanced at the bill once more and began to scroll. Brea had left town last June but the texts reached as far back as he could scroll. Brea and Beth must have traded phones. In the past, they'd done silly things to cover for each other. But that didn't make much sense. Brea lived alone and had no reason to hide her affair with Peter from anyone except Peter's wife. And from what he witnessed at the funeral home, Peter's wife was well aware of the affair. Brea and Peter had visited the house upon occasion. Their secret affair was out in the open with him and Beth. Maybe it hadn't been a secret after all.

Maybe they'd accidentally switched phones. No, not for such a long stretch.

Jeffry scratched his head. He remembered offhand conversations about drama of one kind or another between Brea and Peter. Beth, the ever-involved sister, could have spoken to him on Brea's behalf. Jeffry counted the number of texts and phone conversations. Too many for simple intervention. Beth spent her days with the kids and rarely had an evening to herself. Beads of sweat formed on his brow. Was it possible Beth had had an affair with Peter Magness too? No, she'd never betray Brea. And Peter, the snake, had been so congenial when they ran into each other the other day.

Then again, they were twins; some men had that fantasy. He pictured Peter's smile and the self-assured way he eased into a room and assumed all the attention.

Damn. Magness and Beth?

The more he thought about it, the more he was certain Peter had slept with his wife, the mother of his children. Which made Peter a goddamn asshole. Magness had crossed the line. Jeffry pushed trembling fingers through his hair, muttering curses.

The bastard slept with my wife!

It was one thing for him to have an affair, but for Beth to do this? Jeffry swallowed hard as bile rose in his throat. Heat rose up in him.

Damn Peter Magness!

He downed the rest of his drink, and poured another. Once he pulled the lukewarm plate in front of him, he sat in the dark, thinking.

CHAPTER TWENTY-ONE

Brea

Afters Jeffry left the house and Brea dropped Ella off at preschool, she and Jack returned home. As she settled Jack with a tub of building blocks, the doorbell rang, followed by the sharp rap of the knocker. Brea's heart skipped a beat. She hoped her visitor was someone she knew and not someone she didn't… but that as Beth, she should. Being it was the front door and not the back, must be a delivery. Brea opened the door.

Cynthia the Magnificent, Peter's wife, stood on the stoop. Caught completely off guard, Brea managed, "What are you doing here?"

Cynthia scowled for a second, then her look softened, like a puppy who had been caught chewing a slipper. "I came to apologize."

"No apology necessary."

Brea double-clutched, praying Cynthia couldn't read the panic behind her eyes or hear the pounding of her heart. She avoided looking at the woman. It wasn't like Cynthia had known her or Beth well enough to tell them apart, but being around her former lover's wife still made her cringe with guilt and shame—as if an imaginary Scarlet Letter might appear on her chest.

Peter had shared his disdain for Cynthia with one nasty story after another every time they'd spent time together, claiming venting lightened his mood. Peter suspected she hated him, and blamed him for their eventual inability to conceive after five miscarriages. He said she'd been furious when he refused to see an infertility specialist.

Brea had held her tongue but she guessed spreading sperm in too many places might limit your comfort in seeking professional help.

Peter's pattern was to spend hours moaning about his problems, right before he led her to bed to make love. Looking back, Brea realized she'd been played, as if he were constantly saying, "Feel sorry for me. Take pity on my bruised and battered ego." With hindsight and 20/20 vision, Brea reassessed Peter. In the time she'd spent with him, he'd recovered repressed memories from a troubled childhood. Abusive parents who beat him daily and called him names. His father belittled Peter, teased him mercilessly about his sensitivity, and assured him he would wind up in the arms of a controlling woman who would whip his organ into hamburger if he didn't develop a spine.

Peter falling for the beautiful Cynthia, for the softhearted Brea, for the needy Beth, all of those relationships made sense. Yet the same phrase repeatedly flashed in her mind, "What a crock of shit."

As Brea scrutinized Cynthia further, she saw someone different than the woman she'd imagined, or the one Peter had presented. This was a real woman, clearly in pain. Agony etched her empty eyes. Her body, once fit and trim, was bony, a mere shell. Pasty skin stretched unnaturally over her cheekbones—a too taut facelift or too many Botox injections. If Brea didn't know better—and maybe she didn't—she would have guessed Cynthia suffered from some debilitating disease, far more than depression.

For an instant, Brea's heart went out to the woman, and her loathing of Peter rose to the surface. He'd left at least three women in his wake. But in cases like this, initial estimates always ended up growing exponentially as the truth came out.

Brea surprised herself by inviting Cynthia in. "Would you like a cup of tea?"

"Decaf if you have it." Cynthia entered the hallway and studied the house. "You have a beautiful home."

"Thank you. Please, come into the kitchen." Brea led her down the hall and gestured for her to have a seat at the table. Her mind worked double-time thinking of ways to pump her for information.

"I want to know why she left," Cynthia spoke softly.

Brea took a calming breath. There was no reason on earth to feel obligated to this woman. "I thought you came to apologize. Perhaps I've made a mistake inviting you in."

"I need to know," Cynthia insisted.

A chill crept up Brea's arms. Piercing pain lived in the woman's eyes. Not only did she know about Brea and Peter's affair, but seemed truly wounded. Brea had to look away. The pain of facing her sins, her guilt, and her shame, seemed insurmountable.

"I don't know," Brea lied.

"Did he end the affair, or did your sister?" Cynthia stood and locked eyes with her. "Please understand, I love my husband. He's flawed, but so am I. He's grieving now, like you, but he's coming back to me. I can tell. I should thank your sister for dying. If she hadn't, Peter would still be lost to me."

Brea glared for a moment, but then her mind cleared. If she were in a similar position, she was sure the death of a mistress served as a wife's chance to save her marriage.

"If I knew why she left, I could decide if Peter really loves me. Maybe he told her our marriage was more important than their affair."

Poor Cynthia. She could understand the woman's need, but the fact that Peter was involved with Beth, too, was more than she was willing to share. "I'm sorry. I can't help you."

"Please," Cynthia said, desperation palpable in the thin thread of her voice. "Am I just the token wife? Some men have affairs because they can't help themselves—they can't turn away from the adoration, the sex. Was it like that with Peter?"

Her eyes pleaded for Brea to erase her pain but only Peter could answer her question. Brea didn't know.

Her eyes stayed locked on Brea's. "I'm pregnant," she whispered. She covered her face as she choked out an aching wail. After an excruciating moment, she exhaled a ragged breath. "I need to matter. You know what it's like to have a child. I want to be more than a mother."

A distant cry reached Brea's ears. "Momma," Jack called.

Brea clamped her lips shut, afraid to speak for fear of what might tumble out. Words of shock, words of hate. Not aimed at Cynthia, but at Peter.

She stared at Cynthia's middle. No way to tell. *Peter told me he's sterile. How did she get pregnant? How come I never did? Wait. Beth was pregnant too. Was that child Jeffry's? But he'd said they'd gone six months without sex. Who else had Beth slept with?* Locked in a soap opera she didn't want to watch, she grabbed onto the seat of her chair. *Was this some kind of sick cosmic joke? If I'm the one who's sterile…*

Brea stood, her legs barely functioning, shuffled to the side door and gestured to Cynthia. "You can let yourself out. I need to check on Jack."

She limped out of the room, hating her physical vulnerability when she needed to appear strong and in charge. Her slow burn would take root soon, like flames licking dry wood. The woman had a hell of a lot of nerve showing up here so soon after Brea's funeral.

She stopped dead in her tracks. This was the first time she'd thought of herself as Beth. She was mentally becoming Beth. Losing herself. She leaned against the wall, choked for air, grappling to calm down, center herself, and gain some balance. Prickles of fear ran to her toes, through her fingertips, and up to the throbbing in her head.

What the hell was I thinking? What have I done? She'd come to Michigan to celebrate her birthday, not to change her life. *Unintended consequences. Seeds planted early. A full-grown tree over time with deep and tangled roots.*

"Momma!" Jack called.

Brea took a labored breath, straightened, and squared her shoulders. "Coming."

When she returned to the kitchen ten minutes later, Cynthia Magness was gone.

Damn Cynthia. Damn Peter. Damn Beth. Damn us all.

CHAPTER TWENTY-TWO

Brea

BREA PUT THE EVER-NOSY JUDITH TO WORK ON THE LUN-cheon, after giving Jeffry hell for telling Susan she was up to the task. Evidently, he thought the time had come for her to rejoin the human race and disseminated that information to their neighbor. Little did he know, the less his wife interacted with others, the safer she remained. But if he hadn't figured she wasn't his wife in the three months since the accident, chances were she was in the clear. Who the hell knew?

Judith eagerly put her party-planning skills to use, and Brea was more than happy to get the woman out of the house for a few hours. Judith made long lists, including a theme for the luncheon, ideas for decorations and food. Brea left it all to her. Why not? Judith would sabotage any agenda that wasn't her own. No matter, Brea could not have cared less.

Cynthia's final message, "I'm pregnant," had somehow set her nerves on edge. But then, Peter had always spoken of his wife's con-niving ways. Brea had to admit, even though she was 99.9% sure Cynthia had been lying and just tacked the pregnancy on as a last ditch effort to deliver a final blow, the saber sharp stab had hit its mark. She dreaded the return of Cynthia Magness to her home, but she had a hunch Susan would be her ally against Peter's unstable wife, who imagined a pregnancy with a sterile husband.

Brea conjured up a vision of Hilton Head. She couldn't plan a trip fast enough.

Using old coping skills, Brea pushed Cynthia's announcement to the back of her brain. Two hours later, she retrieved Ella from preschool, prepared lunch, and tucked in the kids for a nap. When both fell asleep, she stepped out of Jack's room and pulled the door closed behind her.

Five minutes later, Ella's delicate little body appeared in the kitchen doorway, a bejeweled tutu pulled cockeyed around her waist, turning pirouettes. "Momma, look at me!"

Brea turned to face her. A smile made crooked by haphazard lipstick strokes, and dimpled cheeks plastered with streaks of blush met her gaze. She should have chastised Ella for being up from her nap and getting into makeup, but her heart melted at the sight of the tiny ballerina. "Just a minute, sweetie, I have to finish up these dishes."

Ella ran up behind Brea, threw her arms around Brea's legs and kissed her on the back of the knee. "I love you, Momma. You're the best momma in the whole wide world."

A transformation took hold. Nothing tangible, but resembling an invisible branding on her heart. Ella was her child now. She'd sealed the adoption.

She couldn't pick Ella up, although she longed to, so she pulled a chair out from the table and asked her to climb up into her lap. Once she snuggled in, she reached for a lock of Brea's hair.

"When your Auntie Brea and I were little," Brea explained, "we used to take our naps together. Grandma Watson would read us a Dr. Seuss story and we would laugh and giggle. We would hold hands when we fell asleep and sleep for exactly the same amount of time every afternoon."

"'Cuz you were twins."

"Yes," Brea said. "We were just alike. Once, when we were your size, almost five, we went to the store with Grandma Watson and a lady came up to us. She said she couldn't tell us apart. Your Auntie and I studied each other for a long time, a little puzzled at first. We didn't understand we were identical. From then on, we were always checking the mirror, comparing our eyes, or nose, or teeth."

"Did you lose your teeth at the same time?"

Brea tossed her head back and laughed at the memory. "We figured out if one of us had a loose tooth, the other could wiggle theirs and we would lose them at almost the same time. Once we figured out we looked exactly alike, we didn't want anyone to be able to tell us apart."

Ella cuddled even closer, yawned and closed her eyes.

Brea kissed the top of her head and inhaled her purity. "You're sleepy."

"I like that story. Will you tell me more stories about you and Auntie Brea?"

"Right after your nap. Now, I'll let you sleep down here today. Come on, I'll tuck you in." Brea led her down the hall and kissed her on the forehead after she snugged the blanket up around Ella's shoulders. "Sleep tight."

"I love you, Momma."

"Love you too, angel." Brea's heart swelled as she went back into the kitchen. She hurried through the clean-up and considered shortening her trip to Hilton Head, dreading being away from the kids any longer than necessary.

Her phone rang.

"Hi," Jeffry said. "What are you up to?"

"Making plans for Hilton Head actually. Much as I hate to do this, I need to take care of Brea's things."

"I don't envy you."

"Me either. But maybe I'll be better able to move on after it's taken care of."

"So when? And how are you going?"

"There's a flight that goes through Charlotte, but then I land in Hilton Head rather than Savannah. Saves me a drive."

"Are you sure you can handle a layover?"

Rising heat flushed Brea's neck and face. "Yes, I'm sure."

"Can you send me the information? I want to put your flight times in my planner so I can drive you to the airport."

"No, you're checking up on me. It's Judith again, isn't it? I'm better with numbers now, you can stop worrying. US Airways flight 5029 to Charlotte. US Airways 4837 to Hilton Head. Go ahead, verify the flights." Brea regretted snapping at Jeffry, but the words were already out there.

"Thanks for clearing that up," Jeffry murmured.

"I've printed two copies of my itinerary. One for each of us."

A long silence filled the line.

"Are the kids sleeping?"

"Yes, actually. Why?"

"I wanted to talk to you about something and I have a break. How about if I stop home for a bit?"

Brea's shoulders tensed. Things always seemed to happen in twos if not threes. First, Cynthia's visit, now Jeffry wanted to talk. She could hardly wait. "Um, sure."

"Good," he said. "I'm already on my way. I'll be there in ten minutes. Maybe five."

Brea decided to dust the table, reaching for a tad of control. Just this morning she'd prided herself on how seamless this whole identity switch had gone. Foolish notion.

She'd just finished the final polish when Jeffry strode through the door, looking as serious as she'd ever seen him. She held her breath for a long moment. "What's up?" she finally managed.

"Have a seat, Beth."

Shit. He never used her name when he spoke to her. Not unless he was calling her from upstairs or something.

As if she'd just been caught cheating on a test, or overspending on the grocery bill, she did as he asked, folded her hands, and waited for the wrecking ball to land.

Jeffry paced a path on the kitchen floor. Brea counted. Six steps one way, six steps back. All the while, he kept his gaze glued to the floor, hands stuffed in his pockets, as if he hadn't yet decided what to say.

He finally stopped about three feet in front of her and stared.

Her knuckles turned white, she gripped her hands so hard, but she dared not look away.

"I'm not comfortable doing this," he said, "but I think we need to clear the air. Trust me, I've been over this again and again. You've been through hell these past three months, the accident, losing Brea, the funeral, and now you're planning to handle Brea's personal effects. This is a ton to manage, plus you've been working double-time to be a good mom to the kids. The thing is," he paused and paced another six steps, "I've found some evidence you've been having an affair with Peter Magness."

Brea opened her mouth to speak, to call him on his affair, but her gut churned while the hair on her nape rose. Her hands went cold. Jeffry's eyes registered sympathy. He sat down in front of her and took her hand. Brea remained motionless. She'd never expected this. She sat frozen to her chair.

"The thing is, I've been unfaithful too. We lost our way, honey. I'm sorry. I don't know if we can get past this, but I'm willing to try if you are."

The implications staggered Brea. She needed an answer, fast, but her instincts told her buying time meant more than anything. "I...don't know what to say."

"I know. This is beyond awkward. We can talk about it if you want, go back over the past few years, I guess. Or we can just move on. I've ended my relationship, and from what I've seen since the accident, you have too. I'm willing to forgive and forget if you are. What do you say?"

"I need some time with this."

"Can we both agree to give it some serious thought? I've already made my decision, and I realize I have a lot to make up to you. How about this? You go to Hilton Head and take some time to yourself.

You've been in over your head since you came home from the hospital. Take a break."

"Closing up my sister's condo and sealing her life in boxes is hardly a break."

"Sorry, I sound insensitive, and I don't mean to. I was hoping, in spite of the fact your trip to South Carolina will be enormously difficult, you could catch your breath."

"Yes," Brea said. "You're right. I am exhausted."

A smile lit up Jeffry's face and shivers ran down Brea's arms.

"Thank you," he said.

"Can I have a minute?" Brea asked. "I'm a bit overwhelmed."

"Of course," Jeffry said as he checked his watch. "I need to get back to the hospital." He leaned over and kissed her cheek. Brea's heart sank. She'd wanted to hate him. She really had.

Breathe, Brea, Breathe. Was this a ploy? Would she ever stop second-guessing this man? C'mon, Beth. Give me a clue.

Before he walked out the door, he turned to her. "I have to work late tonight, but maybe tomorrow we can put the kids to bed early and spend some time together, real time. Date night, just like old times."

Date night?

CHAPTER TWENTY-THREE

Brea

By 11 A.M. Judith had adorned the house with fresh flowers and dainty place settings for the luncheon. While she bustled between the kitchen and dining room, Brea spent the morning primping, her best defense against crossing paths with the housekeeper or Cynthia. She spent a good hour hiding in the study and investigating the background of the club's members. Other than at the funeral where Brea had trouble identifying the women who would soon be sitting in her dining room, she hadn't ever seen most of them. Beth had handled the doctor's wife social functions on her own. Once Brea found the list of names and addresses in Beth's inbox, she Googled each of the women and committed their names and faces to memory.

She waltzed into the kitchen twenty minutes later to check on Judith.

"Everything looks lovely, Judith. Thank you so much."

"I'm glad my work meets your standards."

"It seems we need to clear the air. Please understand it's been very difficult for me to lose my sister and recover from my injuries. I'm very appreciative of your help, and apologize for being short with you. I've made so many physical improvements lately, I think your work here is about to come to a close. I'm almost able to take over the household again."

Judith's eyes narrowed to slits. "Oh no, you can't get rid of me so easily."

Brea registered a jolt. What did this woman have in mind?

"I see what's going on. You want the house free so your precious Dr. Magness can visit. You underestimate me. I'm a very thorough housekeeper. And you probably aren't aware, but Gina is my best friend."

Brea looked at her quizzically.

Judith stepped within inches of Brea. "Your former housekeeper. The one you let go before me. She filled me in before I started here. We share everything about our clients."

Brea backed away. "What on earth…?"

"All you fornicators are bound for hellfire and damnation. I pray for your soul. And for your poor children."

"And you think I'm crazy?"

"I'd advise you to keep me on."

Is she trying to blackmail me?

"Let's discuss this later. We have company coming soon. You can take the afternoon off. We'll be fine here without you."

"No ma'am. I'll be available to serve and remove the dishes from the table."

Could Brea not rid herself of this woman? What Judith said made absolute sense, but she once again had Brea in her clutches. Brea didn't have the strength to fight without time to think. She sighed and palmed the side of her head, trying to pry loose some brainpower. Nothing.

Brea left the room and walked into the kitchen, pouring herself a glass of wine and downing it in a single gulp. Her nerves steadied, or at least deadened to the point where she released the tension from her neck. She peeked out the back door to watch for Susan.

The doorbell began to sound thirty minutes later as Judith scurried about. Brea ignored her and allowed her to answer the door and greet the guests.

Overwhelmed but almost managing, Brea accepted another

round of sympathy from Beth's friends, and herded them into the dining room where everyone met their wine glass with delight, tittering, "The best part of the afternoon."

Brea swallowed over the rising bile.

The first half-hour, the ladies caught up on kids and hospital gossip. Brea secretly delighted in seeing Cynthia Magness' spot at the table remain empty. But as Murphy's Law had a tendency to rear its ugly head, the doorbell rang again. Cynthia made a grand entrance, standing in the doorway of the dining room with her hand tucked protectively over her abdomen, making her grand announcement. "I'm so sorry to be late, but my morning sickness won't seem to pass much before noon."

Susan's eyes rounded like donuts, and several of the ladies rose to Cynthia's side to congratulate her and ask for details about the blessed event. Brea couldn't help but notice a slight protrusion from Cynthia's middle. Susan leaned over and whispered, "I thought Peter shot blanks."

Brea felt blood drain from her face as Judith led Cynthia to her place at the table and offered her a cup of decaffeinated tea, shooting daggers at Brea. Cynthia held court for the next ninety minutes, before Susan came to the rescue and suggested they finish dessert and leave Brea in peace. "Beth's had it. I'm afraid we've been more than enough company for one afternoon."

With pained effort, the women dragged themselves away, one by one, apologizing to Beth and suggesting they bring meals and offer more support to her than they had since the accident.

Susan suggested an alternative. "I'll coordinate a schedule and be the intermediary. Now, let's give Beth some time to rest."

"Thanks for taking the reins. I'm in desperate need of a nap."

"Go," Susan said. "I'll take charge of Judith. Her holier than thou stance seems to be getting under your skin today. You can't take her seriously. Those zealots are always preaching. But I get it. Between her and Cynthia, you have to be over the top."

Brea barely made it to the bedroom. She locked her door and fell into bed for a solid hour before rejoining the world.

After an exhausting dinner, messy bath time, endless bedtime stories, and the final, final, final kisses goodnight, Brea staggered to her room and donned her flannel pajamas. Jeffry had the TV on in the living room, but shortly after she lay down in bed, she heard him turn off the set. His footsteps padded down the hall, and she heard the door creak open, then latch. She stayed still, breathless. He climbed into bed with her, spooning up behind her and draping an arm over her middle before cuddling her close. He nuzzled her neck and she inhaled his scent. They slept.

CHAPTER TWENTY-FOUR

Brea

THE PLANE TOUCHED DOWN IN HILTON HEAD DURING A thundershower. Brea managed to drag the carry-on bag out of the overhead bin. Her strength had improved on a daily basis. Her spirits lifted at the thought of a week entirely on her own. No children to shuttle, feed, or bathe. No housekeeper spying on her every move. No horror stories about her former lover impregnating his wife. She would miss the nightly story and tucking the children into bed, but Jack and Ella loved Dana and Derek, and could hardly wait for the small outings they'd planned. Plus climbing on Derek as if he were a jungle gym delighted both of them.

Brea would clean out her place, arrange to ship the things she wanted to keep, tidy up the last of the bills, close her bank account, and empty her safe deposit box. She'd handle the tasks in a perfunctory way. Crossing items off the list, she decided, would make things manageable and hopefully keep her emotions at bay. If she let her feelings run rampant, she might never return to Michigan.

She drove along 278 toward Folly Field Road as the rain ended and the sky filled with sun. A welcome sign.

What about Beth? How would she have felt about Jeffry showing up at bedtime? She'd been so pissed off the night of the accident, but had been carrying on with Peter for quite some time. The old "what's good for the goose" hurt more when you were the "gander," she supposed. Beth's rage, although potent, was misplaced. And what about this pregnancy? Peter's child? Maybe the infertility story was just that, a tall tale. Did she and Peter just get lucky?

Considering the kids, Brea guessed Beth would have welcomed the chance to recreate a life with Jeffry. *Then again, I didn't know Beth as well as I thought.*

But what did she want? As Beth? As Brea? Jeffry had offered her a gift. With his left-handed proposition, she could assume her place as the children's mother. But could she become his wife? Maybe. Beth was dead. She wasn't coming back.

If she accepted his offer, would she be able to continue her deception? He'd come clean with her. She could hardly resist the urge to wash away her sin and find the peace she'd been longing for her entire life. But did she love him? Didn't he deserve to be loved?

Didn't she deserve to love someone? To be loved in return? As Brea and not as Beth.

Jeffry's level head had surprised her. So had his arrival in her bed.

But the entire scenario—him showing up at home to discuss Beth's affair with Peter. She couldn't recall a single client who had handled mutual affairs with such grace and dignity. He'd become a stand-up guy, if not in the past, certainly now. Although this could be another sign in the endless list of too-good-to-be-true Jeffry. Something still didn't ring right. Brea went over it again. Thought about what she'd learned from her married clients. Accommodating men sometimes seethed with anger and control beneath their benign outward affect. Her mind ricocheted like a boomerang. She couldn't help but wonder what Jeffry was like in bed. Did his desire for control come out in the bedroom? He had oodles of control as a surgeon. The ultimate purveyor of life and death. Maybe he was playing nice so he could off her when she least suspected it. No, she didn't buy that. He'd changed. Otherwise, she wouldn't have slept last night. Her radar had always been pretty good when it came to safe havens.

Part of her had relished every minute of his embrace. She felt comfort. Secure in his arms. Cared for. Already, she longed for that feeling again.

Brea cleared her head.

Her life was here, in Hilton Head. She'd established her practice. The condo was home. Going back to Michigan was a step backward.

Did giving up her entire life for her twin really make sense?

If a client had sought her advice—does it makes sense to give up my life to honor a promise I made to my sister?—her answer would have been a resounding, "No." Not even a close call.

She swallowed over the growing lump in her throat and rubbed her nose as she glanced at unfamiliar scenery, then realized she'd missed her turn. The car grew uncomfortably warm. She rolled down a window and shed the light sweater she'd worn on the plane. During her time in Michigan, she'd forgotten the luxurious feel of radiant energy.

She pulled into her parking space at the condo, the hair rising on her arms and a chill overtaking her. She was home. Her head fell to her chest. Nausea rose from her belly. She missed Beth so desperately.

She braced herself, then stepped out of the rental. There was plenty of time to sort out her life. Not today, or even tomorrow, for that matter. Spanish moss hung in delicate waves from the old oaks. Brea inhaled. The infusion of green lifted her spirits.

"Brea?" a voice called. "Is that you?"

Brea's breath caught and her cheeks flushed with duplicity. She took her time turning around. "No," she said quietly. "I'm her twin, Beth."

The tall older gentleman bowed slightly and offered her his hand. "How do you do?" he said. "I'm Mr. Mangioni, her neighbor."

Brea shook his hand, clasping it for a long moment. "So nice to meet you." He seemed a little more stooped since the last time she'd seen him, and her temptation was to ask about his arthritis and his rose garden.

"Why, you're her spitting image. I haven't seen your sister in quite some time. I thought maybe she'd moved."

"No," Brea answered. "I'm sorry to tell you Mr…" she purposely stumbled on his name. Frightening, how easily the lies came.

He steadied his cane, his faded brown eyes peering directly into hers. "Mangioni," he offered. "It's a little tricky."

She loved Mr. Mangioni. He was such a gentle sort and always willing to help if he spotted her laden with packages. She found herself beginning to tear up.

"Yes, well," Brea struggled, "my sister was killed in a car accident." In an instant, she blurted out the rest of the story.

Before she knew what was happening, Mr. Mangioni's age-splotched arms shrouded her like a protective cloak.

"You poor thing," he murmured soothingly. "I'm so sorry."

Brea's body shook as she sobbed into the stooped man's chest, burrowing into his creaky body like nestling into a cave. He rocked and soothed her, and in that desperate moment, miles away from herself, she peered out from Mr. Mangioni's torso, and wondered if there really was a place for her in this big, wide world.

After a few minutes, she wiped her nose and backed away. "I'm sorry," she said. "I don't know why…"

"It's part of grief," he said. "After I lost my Gracie, I'd find myself crying in the most unexpected places, at all the wrong times, of course. In the checkout line at the grocery, pumping gas, meeting a stranger who reminded me of Gracie in some way. Moments like this can knock you for a loop, but sorrow needs an outlet. Now, would you like me to show you around, help you find your sister's place? Anything you need during your stay, I'm happy to help."

"You're too kind," she managed. "But I've been here before. I think I can find my way." She mopped her face with a tissue. "I can't thank you enough for your shoulder. And again, I apologize for falling apart."

"I'm in 1202 if you need anything, young lady," he offered. "Anything at all, you just knock on my door."

CHAPTER TWENTY-FIVE

Brea

BREA RUMINATED ABOUT THE GROSS REFRIGERATOR AND countless dead plants awaiting her as she climbed the stairs to the third floor. She unlocked the door and stale, musty air assaulted her. She heaved her luggage through the front entrance, bolted the door behind her, threw open the patio doors and windows, and welcomed in the weighty Deep South humidity and sweet scent of magnolia blossoms.

Her head throbbed. Her heart raced. Brea gripped the door handle and told herself to breathe. She turned and took in the living room, then counted her steps as she made her way to the bathroom where she eased herself down the wall and sat on the floor, lifting the toilet seat. Nausea rose in her throat.

The room reeked of musty fabric. Dust bunnies had gathered in the corners. Brea hung her head over the toilet and vomited, sweat beading on her forehead, her hands clammy yet sticky with perspiration. She somehow managed to stand and pull out a washcloth from the linen closet. After she ran cold water in the sink, she soaked and pressed the cloth against her forehead, praying the nausea would pass.

She focused on breathing. Several minutes later, the queasiness eased, and she was able to hobble into the kitchen. She found a bottled water and stepped outside. Fresh air might quell the rooted nausea.

Brea guzzled her water, grabbed another and located several clear plastic storage bins at the back of her bedroom closet, along with some drawstring trash bags. She began to sort, separating items into several piles: keep, recycle, trash. As time went on she delved deeper into her belongings, and became curious about the contents of boxes she hadn't examined in months, perhaps even years. She discovered photos of herself and Beth, albums they and their mother had assembled of their elementary and high school years.

Tears streamed down her face. She had forgotten, or pushed away, her love for her home, her love of Beth. How she missed her. She unearthed a photo of them making a video. They had modeled themselves after the Olsen twins from Full House, and pretended they were one person, one on screen while the other filmed. When they showed their masterpiece to their parents, Mom and Dad couldn't tell the difference between them. The sisters had swelled with pride.

Another photo showed them sitting next to each other at a band concert, Beth's flute poised under her bottom lip while Brea taunted her with a crazy face. Then, the pose at the beach. She and Beth had traded places one day, so Brea could kiss Michael Spencer, the dreamy quarterback Beth was dating. Since Beth claimed he was the best kisser in the entire school, Brea gladly forked over Beth's demanded fee: five bucks for ten minutes with the guy.

They traded bikinis in the bathroom, and Brea sauntered over to Michael, wrapped her arms around him and planted a lip lock on him. He didn't flinch, just kissed her back with the ease of his next breath, and moaned as his hand slid down her back and into the bottom of her swimsuit. Brea backed away, startled. She flushed with embarrassment and raced off to the restroom. There, she searched frantically for Beth, fearing her twin would be ruffled she'd allowed Michael to take such a liberty with her. When Brea explained, Beth had tossed her head back and laughed. "Seems we've found the difference between us, Sis. I'm fun, you're a prude."

"Am not!"

Brea smiled at the memory.

The tissue box soon emptied, and Brea took a break to make a sandwich and give her shattered heart a moment's rest. After lunch, she plunked down in an outside chair to soak up the sunshine. She had grabbed a small box on her way out the door, one whose contents she couldn't recall.

Brea opened the cardboard folds and found envelopes. Letters from Peter during their first years together.

The perfect researcher and author of self-help books, Peter was also a talented poet and letter writer. He fancied himself as somewhat elite, superior to everyone else, and more than that, an artful wordsmith. Some people found his attitude off-putting, but Brea had thought him sweet and endearing in his excitement over his accomplishments. His magnetic personality left her speechless at times, in awe of his talent, raw sensuality, and mesmerizing effect on her.

Her eyes widened as she read.

My dearest Brea,

The moment I laid eyes on you, I knew. The depths of my being had been touched in a way not previously known. At least a power of this sort had not yet been unleashed within me. My heart, a tender and sheltered place, was for the first time opened and anointed by your love…

Silly girl. She had been hypnotized by the letter's content, had fallen for every word. Peter was a narcissist. Pure and simple. This was self-aggrandizing crap.

She stuffed the letter inside the envelope, closed the box, and marched down to the trash receptacle, sweat dripping in tiny rivulets down her spine. Without ceremony, she tossed the container inside, brushed her hands together in relief, and trudged back upstairs to unscrew the top of her first, but certainly not last, beer of the day.

CHAPTER TWENTY-SIX

Peter

HE'D BEEN DISTRACTED AND MISSED HIS TURN. PETER slammed on the brakes and spun around, pulling the rental car into the parking lot at Fiddlers Cove. Damn Beth, making him travel all the way to Hilton Head for answers. If she weren't still ignoring his texts, he wouldn't have had to make the trip. The grief over Brea's death might be explanation for her detachment, but he'd have never guessed she possessed the fortitude to stay away from him, or what they shared, no matter what current crisis she faced.

Peter reduced his speed through the complex, searching for building A. Although the buildings were labeled with the letters of the alphabet, whoever had engineered the site had mixed up the order so the letters were out of sequence. Between the moss-covered units and the lush lagoons he spotted through the sea of parked cars, he might be driving around in circles for a while. He glanced at his watch. He had time, but not all day.

Once he located building A and pulled into a nearby parking spot, a tug of common sense nagged him. He'd agreed to focus on his marriage. His career demanded it. But only once he got the answers to Beth's hasty departure from his life. If he had closure, he could move on. Maybe he could talk her into a quick roll in the hay for old time's sake. His hormones fired, raged even. The thought of doing Beth in Brea's apartment fueled his desire.

He slammed the door of the red Dodge Avenger, and headed

in search of 1322. He considered texting Beth that he was here, but then reconsidered. She'd successfully avoided him since the funeral. A warning could provide her with the chance to hole up inside and deny him the answers he so desperately wanted. Plus, cautioning her of the photos, the threats, and his plan to thwart any chance of their affair reaching daylight was only fair.

As he circled the building in search of the correct house number, a stooped octogenarian struggling with a heavy trash bag stopped him. The old guy studied him. "Can I help you?"

Peter pushed a hand through his hair and weighed his options. The last thing he needed was for anyone to know he'd been here. The schedule he'd laid out to Cynthia had been vague. Meetings out of the office all day. A bit of shopping—a new suit for his first appearance on GMA next week—then dinner and drinks with a colleague after the five o'clock symposium at the U. The fictitious schedule allowed him plenty of time for a short visit with Beth, the return trip to the airport, and a ten o'clock arrival at home. He shot a lie at the old gent, "No, thank you. I know where I'm going."

The man continued to block his path. "Not seen you around here before," the man said. Then, he paused and cocked his head. "Wait a minute. You look just like somebody. Um, that guy…?"

Great. The geezer recognized him. Peter turned away, dropped his head and tried to mask his panic. He attempted to skirt around the senior citizen by sidestepping into the landscaping and brushing him off with a wave, but the old man grabbed his arm. Peter froze. The guy kept yammering. "Wait. I know. You're the doctor guy. The guy who tells people how to be married. The big wig who's gonna be on the TV morning show…Bright Morning America. No, that's not right. It's Good Morning America. You look just like him. Not like I'm one to pay attention to self-help baloney. Back in the day, when I married, we committed for life. No promises of happiness, just solid commitment. Sickness, health, better, worse. Bunch of hogwash if you ask me, people thinking they need to be happy one hundred percent of the time. If you count the little things, your blessings…"

"Guess I have a twin," Peter murmured as he twisted away from the man's grasp and ducked out of sight. His nerves frayed further as he investigated the row of condos and finally spotted Brea's door. A wreath hung on the entrance, one of those welcome-to-my-life wreaths. Just like Brea, always warm, always making friends wherever she went. That was one of the reasons he hadn't worried about her after she moved away. He shook off another pang of guilt. An unfamiliar and difficult feeling to manage.

Peter shook his trembling fingers and balled them into a fist. He'd come for answers and he planned to stay until he got them. He rapped on the door. No answer. He rapped again.

"Who's there?" Beth called from inside.

He couldn't answer. If she heard his voice, he feared she wouldn't open the door.

"Who's there?" she called again, impatiently. An instant later, he heard the deadbolt lock from inside. "Go away," Beth said. "I don't want to see you."

Damn. She'd spotted him through the peephole. "I came all this way. Please, let me in. I don't have much time." Peter peered over his shoulder and off to his right. He worried the old man would show up and become suspicious to see him still standing outside. "Please," he pleaded. "Five minutes."

For her own reasons, he supposed, Beth hesitated. He couldn't blame her. Because he was still anxious about drawing unwanted attention, he stood absolutely still after cramming his hands back in his pockets and tipping his head toward the welcome mat at his feet. He counted silently, one-one thousand, two-one thousand, three…"Beth, you left me no choice. You won't take my calls. You don't answer my texts."

No response. He raised his gaze to the peephole. Maybe if she caught sight of his sad, pleading eyes, he would succeed in softening her resolve. He waited, biting his bottom lip, determined to get what he came for.

Finally, after an impossibly long moment, he heard the deadbolt slide. Beth inched open the door and peered out at him through a sliver of light. "What are you doing here?"

"Please, Beth. Let me in."

She sighed. A deep, weighty, full-of-capitulation sigh. "Five minutes." She backed away from the door, extending her hand toward a chair in the front room. He took inventory. The place was all Brea. Totally homey, totally comfortable with pastel-colored walls and flowery upholstered furniture finished with ivory wood accents. Watercolor prints complimented the patterns on the sofa, and the ceiling fan resembled a swaying palm tree. Southern, light and airy. For a minute he missed Brea, then he checked himself and reminded himself of his mission.

In deference to Beth, he fixed his eyes on the braided jute rug beneath the glass coffee table, focusing only on his words, "This has to be difficult, being at Brea's place. You okay?" He leaned forward then reached out to touch her knee as a show of sympathy and support.

"Do. Not. Touch. Me."

"What's wrong?"

Her gaze bore into him. If venom could be transmitted through a stare alone, he'd be dead already. He paused and studied her. She looked different. True, she'd been to hell and back, but there was something in the way she slanted her head, she reminded him so incredibly of Brea. His mind was playing tricks.

"Peter, we're over. I can't for the life of me understand why you'd show up here. Oh, wait, I forgot. Your freaking ego is in charge. Your inability to consider anyone but yourself. You're so hungry to be 'the one' for countless women you forget your mistresses are human beings with real emotions and real lives. Being with you was the biggest mistake of my life. I've lost almost everything I can possibly lose, but losing you isn't one of them."

"But...we have plans. Everything's in place. I'll be in New York for the next month or so, and there may even be a permanent position for me on a talk show, my agent's working on a deal as we speak. I have a guest appearance on Dr. Oz in three weeks. If I can land a show, I'll move, divorce Cynthia—she won't mind staying in Ann Arbor with the house and the money—and we can be together. Permanently, like you wanted."

Beth's face turned green, as if she were going to be ill. "What on earth?"

"What? What's the matter?"

She glared at him. "Now, you can leave your wife and not lose your credibility?" Then, a look of resignation dawned. "You know your wife is pregnant, right?"

Peter's eyes widened. He darted to his feet and began to circle the room. "What are you talking about? Cynthia isn't pregnant. I had a…vasectomy. Where did you hear such a ridiculous rumor?"

"She told me when she stopped by last week. This is news? Or can't you keep your lies straight anymore? You told me you were sterile. Today, it's a vasectomy. Which is it, Peter?"

He squeezed his fists and beads of sweat covered his brow. His wife, more calculating than he had ever dreamed, had stepped out of line. Again. "She's lying. There's no possible way. I had a vasectomy. That means I'm sterile. Right after her last miscarriage. I told you that. I couldn't risk fathering a defective child. Cynthia's well over forty. Our chances for a normal baby…besides, you know how I feel about kids. They're great as long as they aren't mine."

"You're quite the guy." Beth marched to the door, pursed her lips, and rested her hand on the knob. "Please leave. I let you in against my better judgment."

"Wait. We need to talk. Come. Sit with me. Just take a breath and hold my hand. You're stirred up. Understandable, considering all you've been through. You know how things are between Cynthia and me. If she said anything to you about being pregnant, she lied in a feeble attempt to hurt you because she can no longer hurt Brea—you're the closest she can get to her. She doesn't know about us though." At least he didn't think she did. With luck, he could keep the secret buried.

He flushed as he recalled the photos and letter, the demand for cash, the deadline. If Cynthia knew about his affair with Brea, she might have found out about his affair with Beth. Holy hell. Maybe Cynthia had visited the Marks' home because she knew about Dana, too. His wife, amateur spy. This changed everything. He fought for a measured breath, hyperventilating instead.

Beth cleared her throat. "I asked you to leave. There will be no further discussion. Jeffry and I have reconciled. We're making a life together—a life I should have been committed to all along."

Peter rose to leave, an about-face climbing up his throat. Sick of women making demands, thinking they could control him, his eyes met Beth's in a fiery glare. He had a far-fetched idea, but one certainly worth his time.

"Listen, Brea. I don't know who you think you're fooling. You act arrogant, like you know what's best, that no one's the wiser. You make landmark decisions without considering my feelings, my commitment to you. Anyone's feelings, for that matter. How do you think Jeffry would feel, knowing his sister-in-law decided to stand in for his wife?

"Just know this. My time with Beth was a mistake. I'm committed to you. When you're ready to come clean, let me know.

"In the meantime, I need to borrow some cash. New York won't be cheap, and Cynthia spends every dime I make."

Dizzy and stunned, Brea's heart bounced in her chest. How could he know? If Jeffry and the kids hadn't been able to tell…

"Just so you're aware, I'm not the only one who's noticed. I stopped by the house one day when you were out. Dana and Derek remarked you were acting odd and how much you'd changed. Dana thinks you got a serious bump on the head in the accident. She says you put things in strange places and fold the laundry different than before. Derek thinks maybe Beth was killed in the accident and you decided to take her place."

This could not be happening.

"My brain has been a muddled mess since the accident. You, as a psychologist, know better than anyone how trauma affects the psyche. I understand you're desperate, but don't let your despera-tion play tricks on you." Beth's jaw muscles bunched as she stamped her foot. "Get out."

He tried to lock on to her gaze, but she stared over his shoulder at the wall. Seeing her proved what he suspected. She was different. Too different, even considering all she had been through. None of this made sense. Before the accident, things had been a little tense, true. He was juggling an impossible schedule, which made making some of their dates difficult.

She'd been frustrated by his lack of attention, and reminded him more than once that being slighted by him was unacceptable. While being ignored wasn't foreign to her, more like part of her daily routine, she hadn't expected such treatment from him, and missed their last date. He had thought the move was in retaliation for his last-minute cancellations, but maybe there had been something more.

When he ambled out, he turned to catch her eye. But as soon as he faced her, she slammed the door.

Women.

CHAPTER TWENTY-SEVEN

Brea

BREA ROLLED ONTO HER BACK AND STRETCHED HER ARMS above her head, scowling at brilliant sunshine. Her mood darkened further as she recalled the unexpected visit from Peter. She grimaced and berated herself for having opened the door. *He can't possibly know. He's a manipulation expert, pure and simple.* Bullshit ploy on Peter's part, calling her Brea. Still, the earth shook. Dana, Derek, Judith, all might be suspicious. They knew Beth, her routine, her habits. But they had no solid evidence to prove she had taken Beth's place. But like it or not, their wary eyes posed a serious problem. Thank God she had leftover Xanax from the doctor. If she hadn't popped two of them last night, she never would have slept.

She couldn't allow Peter's misdirection to brew. *Bastard. The nerve of him. Shut him down. Move on with your life.*

Still, her arms tingled.

The issue boiled down to trust. And Peter couldn't be trusted. Plus, he'd asked for money. Why? He had money. Book deals, a successful practice, and, soon, segments on a national TV show. A self-involved master, he'd been lying to her for years. Add the fact that he'd told Beth he'd had a vasectomy, but not her, the woman he'd slept with for eight years. Rage twisted her gut. He'd probably lied to both pregnant women, so he didn't have to suffer the discomfort of a condom. Maybe the sterility issue lay with her. Not Peter. *Goddamn it.*

While Jeffry had transformed overnight, Peter, in some sick comforting way, proved to be the same snake he had always been. She had been a fool to trust him in the past, and thanked the stars in heaven she knew better than to trust him now. In retrospect, the distance of the last nine months had been useful. Once her raw emotions were boxed and shelved, she could afford to be objective.

The questions raised by Dana and Derek were far more concerning. They were detached enough to be keen in their observations. Allaying their misgivings might be a challenge, but since Peter had brought the matter to her attention, she was certain she could convince them otherwise. She bristled just thinking about Dana. The nerve of the girl allowing Peter inside the house. To have not mentioned his visit seemed deliberate. Then again, Dana might have been privy to Beth's life in a way Brea had never dreamed.

And the other day, she'd been searching the kitchen drawer like a crazy loon, sick to death of being unable to find a single utensil she needed.

"You looking for the immersion blender?" Derek asked, wedging his muscled torso in front of her and opening the drawer below the one she shuffled through. He pulled the damn appliance out and held it up like a master teasing a dog with a treat.

She'd grabbed the blender from him with a sharp "thank you," knowing her own consternation was at fault.

His unusual familiarity with her continually made her angry. At first, she'd written it off as odd behavior from an odd generation, admitting she had a hard time understanding the Xers and millennials, and everyone in between. But more than that, she'd always required personal space, and he'd stepped inside her circle. And sometimes his touch lingered. Disturbing, to say the least. It creeped her out.

She was over-thinking this, letting Peter's words fester. She knew better.

She picked up the phone and called home. Jeffry answered on the second ring.

"Hey there," he said.

"I miss you guys." There. She'd said it. She meant it. And she needed Jeffry now more than ever.

"We miss you too. I'm trying to distract the kids, but they're complaining I don't do anything like Momma."

Brea's heart swelled with pride. She had made a home for the kids. She had become their mom.

"Should I talk to them? Or will I make matters worse?"

"Maybe later. I'd rather deal with them missing you at night than when we're starting the day."

"Absolutely," Brea said. "Makes perfect sense."

"Hey," Jeffry said. "Thanks for calling."

"You're welcome. And thanks for holding down the fort."

"Wait," Jeffry said. "Good luck today. I'm thinking of you. And don't worry about a thing, Judith has the day off but Dana and Derek will be here soon. The kids will be much happier with them than they are with Judith or me. Besides, I miss you. I can't wait to have you back home."

"Once I'm home, we need to rearrange some things. I'm feeling so much better. Coming down here has helped. I'm laying my sister to rest. While this may not make much sense to you, my soul is healing, my body is healing. This is the closure I need."

"We can make all the changes you want."

"Thanks." Brea's stomach twisted as she ended the call. Getting Judith, Dana and Derek out of her house would provide her with a needed safety net.

She faced an impossible day ahead, with hardly any time to worry about the dreaded D's as she was coming to think of them. She cracked open the patio doors inviting in the early morning scent of dewy moss. The peaceful sway of tall marsh reeds against the background of a clear blue sky delivered the perfect distraction. Brea stepped into a pair of flip-flops, poured a mug of coffee, and hit the deck. Her feet seemed magnetically drawn to the railing. Parking them on the sturdy wooden slat, she pulled her sweats above her knees and let the sun drench her legs. Sourness rose in her throat.

Who was she kidding? Denial was a great coping skill, but only when time was on your side. In the midst of saying goodbye to her life, she felt the noose tighten with every word, each step.

She needed Jeffry on her side. She needed to believe he loved his wife, and had become newly invested in his family. How on earth could she manage this toppling tower all at once?

First, she'd make the trip to the bank to retrieve her important papers stored in her safe deposit box. While she mulled over the order of her errands, she showered and dressed, procrastinating at every step of the process, dragging her body through the motions, reciting each step of every task. Mousse. Blow dryer. Mascara. Keys.

Losing track of her agenda, she drove straight to the clinic where she had worked for the past six months, and parked near a stand of pines. When she went inside, people would mistake her—for herself. A chill raced down her spine. Somehow this was more real than anything she'd done so far.

She slumped in the driver's seat, exhaustion draining her resolve—*lies have a way of wearing you out*—and rested her head against the steering wheel. She didn't have the strength or courage for any of this. Not today. Without another thought, she put the car in reverse. But a woman scurried forward in black utilitarian pumps—her boss, Peggy Gray. Peggy's salt and pepper bob, the only hint of her advancing age. She stepped with a youth and assuredness that warmed Brea's heart. Peggy had been a friend and confidante. She realized now how much she'd missed her.

Brea stomped on the brake, jerking the car to a stop.

"Brea?" the woman asked, disbelief fixed in her eyes.

"I'm her sister, Beth."

"I'm Peggy Gray," the woman said, sympathy etched in her eyes. "Brea's boss."

"Let me park." Brea pulled forward, eased the sedan into a slot and stepped out. As she approached, she reassured herself that people believed what they wanted to believe. Peggy would not recognize her. Houdini couldn't have done a better job.

She offered her hand. "Nice to meet you," she said. "My sister spoke highly of you."

"We were shocked to hear of Brea's passing. Her death still doesn't seem real." Peggy's fist pressed against her heart. "I'm sorry no one could attend the service."

"I understand," Brea acknowledged, seamlessly stepping into her alternative identity. "The accident, my recovery, the memorial service taking place so long after Brea's death. The last few months seem surreal. Especially to me."

Brea startled. The words flowed off her tongue like water running downhill. She rubbed her nose.

Peggy's hand gently settled on her forearm. "Would you like to come in?" she asked. "We could have a cup of tea and chat."

Just like Peggy. When Brea had arrived at the island, on her first day of work, Peggy's hospitality immediately won her over, assuring her the move had been the absolute right decision.

Brea teared up. Taking Beth's place was agony. She missed her quiet condo, her colleagues, and her clients, especially little Billy, the autistic five-year-old who had said his first word in their last session together. She envisioned his little round face, bangs framing huge blue eyes, wispy blond hair tickling his brows. He had gazed at her when he spoke, "Truck," unaware he'd given her a gift.

"I can't get over this," Peggy said. "I'd swear you're Brea. Other than being a few pounds lighter, you're a dead ringer for your sister."

Brea's eyes widened.

"Oh my gosh," Peggy said, her face blooming to a bright shade of crimson. "I can't believe I said that. How insensitive of me. I'd bet you'd never guess I'm a clinical psychologist, now would you? Please forgive me."

"Don't worry," Brea said as she gripped Peggy's warm hand. "I'm afraid I have a knack for putting my foot in my mouth as well. I can relate."

"Funny, your sister always alluded to foot-in-mouth disease, too. But, honestly, I only heard stories. I never witnessed any major blunders." Peggy stopped and held Brea at arm's length. "The resemblance is uncanny. The cadence of your voice, your mannerisms, everything. Even your facial expressions."

Brea stood in dangerous territory. She needed to tightrope the fine line between the desire to relax and fall back into her friendship with Peggy, and the necessity of protecting her new life. The draw to be at home with a familiar friend, with someone who knew her, was like being trapped in a force field.

In Peggy's office, professional books, journals and magazines were stacked artfully on built-in bookshelves. Her desk though, typical Peggy, remained strewn with post-it notes and pens. A staple remover was precariously hooked to the handle of a mug.

As she perused the recognizable and comfortable surroundings, she recalled conversations with Peggy about Beth, Jack and Ella, her parents, and Peter. Her words had fallen like heavy rain, and she'd never censored herself when she and Peggy were together. Peggy knew as much about her as almost anyone.

The urge to confess overwhelmed her. It was happening more and more frequently and her inability to quell the impulse flashed like a caution lamp. Thankfully Beth held up her hand, just like she used to, and Brea swallowed the words.

Peggy set a hot mug of tea in front of Brea. "Too late in the morning for tea?"

"A cup of tea is perfect."

The woman assumed the role of listener, advocate, and confidante. "This is a difficult time for you."

"I'm managing." Brea attempted a half-hearted grin.

"What's the hardest part?"

"Survivor's guilt." She sat contemplating the concept, biting her lip. "I carry a boat load."

"Accidents are no one's fault. You mustn't hold yourself responsible."

Brea clenched her teeth. "I'm working on that." The admission strangled her. She fought for breath.

"So," Peggy said, shifting gears, "tell me about your family."

She sketched a brief scenario of disrupted kids, an overcompensating husband, endless pain, everyone missing Brea. Then she glanced up at the clock. "I've taken too much of your time already and I still have a ton of things to do." Brea placed the empty mug on the coffee table, strode to the door, and looked back at Peggy. Brea's skin burned. Her muscles ached. Her bones cried out in pain. "I can't thank you enough for your hospitality. My sister spoke so highly of you. She appreciated all you did for her when she first arrived on the island, and I know she considered you a dear friend."

Tears filled Peggy's gentle brown eyes. "She was a friend. I miss her. I really do. To say nothing of the fine addition she made to our practice here. Your sister was a talented therapist. She helped many clients in her short time here."

Brea wrapped her arms around Peggy and hugged her friend goodbye, flattered by the compliments but also afraid to let them in. Lying to Peggy made everything real. She envisioned nailing a coffin shut. Peggy gently released Brea from her embrace and wiped her eyes.

"All right." Peggy turned the conversation to business-like concerns. "Let's gather your sister's belongings. I'll help you carry them out to your car."

They loaded the two lightweight boxes into the rental. Brea gave Peggy another brief hug and drove off to the bank.

Moss-draped trees canopied the narrow winding road as sun danced through the windshield, muting the harshness of its rays, but Brea didn't see a thing. Sorrow shrouded her in gray.

At the bank, she gathered the will and death certificate, and double-checked that she had the safe deposit box key, aware that she was about to do something fraudulent. Even worse, about to take the irreversible step of erasing her past. She rested her head against the steering wheel, tempted to bang some sense into her brain. Images of Jack and Ella flashed in her mind. The sound of Jack's gravelly voice, calling her, "Momma."

Then, Beth's hand again—she scolded this time, "Quit being such a pansy."

Brea set her shoulders back and strode into the bank.

As she stepped through the door, she spotted Mr. Bradley, the bank manager. Instead of acknowledging him, she dropped her head and went to a teller's window to state her business.

"Since these are joint checking and savings accounts and both you and your sister are named on them," the teller began, "we can remove her name from the accounts and the monies will revert to you. You have the death certificate?"

"Yes." Brea struggled to quash her nervous stomach.

With each step, each word, each lie, reality gripped Brea. *I'm about to put my future in a vise.* She handed the envelope to the clerk without removing the document. The less she viewed anything official, the better. "I'd just like to close the accounts."

"I'll need some identification and a copy of the Will, which names you executor," the clerk said.

Brea handed over Beth's driver's license. She breathed a deep sigh of relief as she went about her business, glad she did not personally know the young woman. "Would you like a cashier's check?" the teller asked.

"Please," Brea's voice cracked. "Yes, please."

Less than thirty seconds later, the bank manager came over and introduced himself. Brea's throat went dry as he chastised the teller for requiring a copy of the will. "Documentation isn't necessary in the case of a joint account. You've put this woman through unneeded red tape." And to Brea he said, "I'm sorry for the inconvenience," then finally signed off on the transaction. Flushed, the clerk returned Brea's documents and presented her with the checks. Blindly, she checked the numbers. Her breath became so shallow, she worried she might faint. *Breathe, Brea, breathe.* Then she corrected herself. *Breathe, Beth, breathe.*

"Thank you," she said. "I also need to retrieve some papers from my sister's safe deposit box."

"Of course," the clerk said. "Just let me get my keys."

When Beth had helped Brea move, she had signed the access to the account. In Brea's wildest dreams she had never imagined she would come to appreciate that July morning so much. With renewed confidence and courage, Brea squared her shoulders. She'd made the right decision to close up shop in Hilton Head. Although impossible to reason why, there were those times she and Beth had discussed trading places.

You always want the life you don't have. You imagine the mountains less steep, or a certain set of circumstances—someone else's life—will make you happier. In the end, what matters is that you live your life for others. True happiness lies there. *More bullshit lies.*

Signing everything over to Beth in the event of Brea's death had ended up being an omen, a crystal ball moment, a harbinger of things to come. If you believed in that sort of crap.

She gathered the contents of the metal box, and left the secured room.

"Thanks again," she said to the cashier as she slid the key inside the teller window. She moved as if her feet slogged through wet cement, the exit door seemingly miles away. When she finally reached the door, she was able to move again.

Her head pounded as she pulled out of the parking lot.

She barely blinked, unaware of the drive home. All she wanted was to put on some sweats, pour a drink, and disappear. She wandered into the kitchen, splashed a few inches of Basil Hayden's into a glass of ice, and went out to the deck, where she settled into her favorite chair. Without a doubt, she'd ship a few things back to Ann Arbor. There were pieces of her life as Brea that would bring her comfort. Still, she couldn't shake the hollowness.

Her phone pinged. She'd missed a call and a message had gone to her voicemail. Jeffry.

"Hi honey, it's me. Just wanted to check in and see how your day was going. I hate to think about you wrestling with Brea's things all alone. Just want you to know I love you more than ever. You've changed since the accident. Don't think I haven't noticed. And by the way, I love the changes. And I appreciate all you've done to keep our family strong in spite of the fact you've lost so much. Call me if you feel like talking."

Brea drained her drink and went inside to pour another.

There were so many things to consider. When the topic of survivor's guilt had come up earlier with Peggy, the notion hit her with the weight of a lead pipe. Funny how guilt reared its horns, twice that she could recall, but she'd never dwelt on culpability, choosing instead to shelve the blame. And once the decision was made, she had put Peter out of her mind without much turmoil too. Maybe she didn't feel things as deeply as others did. Maybe she was different, or maybe she'd learned a long time ago how painful feelings could be, so she simply shut them out. *Maybe I died with Beth.*

Leaving her career didn't seem like such a big deal. Fulfilling as her work had been, there were also the painful reminders of her past. The single years. The childless years. The wasted Peter years. She would file those memories away. Better left in the drawer. Locked up tight. Or even better, shredded to bits.

But a twinge of regret tugged at her. Offering up what had given her life direction through all the madness added another loss to what seemed like an endless list of heartache.

Leaving her home. No biggie. Home was where your "stuff" lived. She could take her favorite possessions with her, right?

No one would ever call her Brea again.

No one would hold Brea.

What have I done?

CHAPTER TWENTY-EIGHT

Grant

Grant groaned as he opened his eyes. The damned phone had interrupted dreams of Brea.

Another ring.

"Fulton," he managed, groggy and irritated. He glanced at the digital clock on his nightstand. 2:30 a.m.

"Got a fresh one for you," the desk sergeant said.

"Anyone I know?"

"Maybe. A guy named Peter Magness. Wife is the reporting party. She found him dead at the entrance to their home. Claims she heard a pop. It woke her. When she realized her husband wasn't in bed, she went looking. Front door was standing wide open. She found him on the front stoop with a GSW to the chest."

Grant couldn't place the name Peter Magness, although he was sure he knew the guy from somewhere.

"Give me the address." Once he heard the street number and name, he calculated. "I'll head there directly. Tell Shaun I'll meet him at the scene in thirty minutes."

As Grant wound his way through the quiet streets he recalled his dream. Brea had been trying to tell him something. He scowled. If he'd been able to stick with the dream a few minutes longer, he'd probably know. His thoughts circled back to the car. The vehicle inspection yielded nothing. The electronics hadn't been tampered with, and the car had been too damaged to be sure about the hydraulics.

Why couldn't he let go of this? Something didn't fit, but what? In his dream someone was after her. She'd raced toward a ravine, away from an accident, calling his name.

Seconds later he cursed the absence of coffee, and the decedent's name replayed in his head. Magness. Peter Magness. The guy from the funeral. The guy with the crazy wife. Beth had practically hurled the woman out of the place, while Magness trailed like a benign pet.

Ever the cop, Grant had made sure to find out who the folks were. Guess there was more to the story than the original explanation, "guy's an author, wife's a nut job." Lucky Grant, he was about to find out.

He flipped off his brights as he pulled in front of one of the nicest homes in the Underdown Road neighborhood. No expense spared here. An ambulance and police vehicle were parked just ahead of him. All was quiet but for the murmuring of voices near the front door. For the time being, the body lay covered on a raised semi-circle of cement gracing the entrance of the home. The medics had hoped to revive the man, but now were returning some of their gear to the ambulance. The forensics team needed to do their job before he could release the body for transport to the Medical Examiner's office.

Grant surveyed the property, two acres or more. The house itself was an old English Tudor showpiece and appeared to be at least six thousand square feet in size. They didn't build them like this anymore.

One thing for certain. Peter Magness was somebody.

With ties to Brea.

And maybe Beth.

He made his way into the scene.

Crime tape created a perimeter surrounding the circular drive and the entrance. Grant ducked under the tape and approached two uniformed officers.

"Mason, what've we got?"

"A doc. Peter Magness. Gunshot wound to the chest. Gone by the time we got here, probably pretty quick."

Grant reached inside his coat pocket for a pair of latex gloves. His rule was always to check the details for himself, the position of the body, the obvious wounds, the face of the victim. The victim's expression often told him a few things. When he peeled back the blanket to examine Magness's face, Grant saw shock and terror. A large pool of blood so possibly a through-and-through. Fair-sized wound to the chest, blood blossoming over a white T-shirt. Paramedics and fire personnel couldn't have helped this guy no matter how quickly they'd arrived.

Grant shook his head and re-covered the victim. Patrol officers P. Mason and his partner, N. Bartholomew, stood in the entryway of the home. He'd worked with them before. Both knew not to muck up a crime scene. They were efficient at taking down initial information, securing the scene, and waiting for the forensics team and detectives to arrive.

"What do you know so far?"

Bartholomew flipped a few pages in her spiral. "I spoke with the decedent's wife. We figured she might relate better to a woman," she said with an offhanded shrug.

Grant waited for her to continue.

"She claims she was sound asleep, woke to sounds coming from downstairs. She wasn't clear about what she heard. First, she thought she heard a pop, like a firecracker. A bump and a thump afterward, was what she said. When she went to wake her husband, she discovered he wasn't in bed. Says they keep a gun in the nightstand drawer, so she grabbed the weapon and headed downstairs. Said a cold breeze through the hall led her to the front door, where she found her husband lying on the stoop. She called 911 right away. The guys were here in seven minutes, but said he didn't have a pulse."

"Did she check for a pulse?" Grant asked.

"Don't know. The woman's a basketcase. Says she's pregnant and worried the shock will cause her to lose the baby. She's been clutching her belly since we got here, so I had the medics check her out. She isn't in labor or anything. Doesn't even look to be more than a few weeks along. The EMTs are keeping an eye on her. I knew you'd want to talk to her, so I didn't press the details. John Moore is sitting inside with her."

"You have the gun?"

"She says it's in the house."

"Get it. Shaun's not here?"

"No sign of him," Mason said.

Grant huffed and grimaced. "Probably kissing the wife goodbye," he said with a hint of sarcasm.

Shaun and his wife still behaved like newlyweds, even though they had three kids. The thought of the two lovebirds tugged at him.

Headlights swept across the porch area.

Bartholomew tipped her head toward the driveway. "Here he is now."

"When the forensics guys get here, fill them in. Until then, hold the scene. Once they take over, canvass the neighbors. See if anyone saw or heard anything. You know the drill."

"Anything else?"

Wind whipped through the brisk night. Grant pulled up his collar as he waited for Shaun to catch up. "What do you know about this Magness guy?"

"You don't know?" Bartholomew said. "He's a psychologist, a big wig authority on marriage. Couple of bestsellers, going to be the new feature on GMA. Was going to be, anyway."

"Disgruntled client?"

Officer Mason cocked his head. "Remember that killing a couple months ago? The guy who shot and killed his wife? Kerfoot— weird name's why I remember."

"Yeah. Why?"

"I saw Magness at the station after the murder. The suspect was a patient of his."

"Sounds like he could have used a different doc."

Mason nodded.

"Hey," Grant greeted Shaun. "What took you so long?"

"What, you been here all night or something?"

"How'd a bald fat guy like you land a fine looking woman like Amy?" Grant asked with a wink. "Makes no sense to me."

"The green-eyed monster is rearing its ugly head again, buddy. Jealousy looks shitty on you."

Grant groaned. "Let's get this done."

"Fine by me."

Grant hated the way Shaun looked at him sometimes. Like he pitied him. He turned around and entered the home. A curved arch separated the foyer from a long hallway. A spiral staircase with cream-colored walls took center stage beneath recessed lighting. Fresh flowers stood in an ornate vase, casting the scent of lilies throughout the entry. Grant crossed into the main living area of the house, noticing a set of double doors to his left. Not the typical Ann Arbor crime scene.

He guessed the Oriental rug beneath his feet was the real deal. Queen Anne wingback chairs were situated in front of a marble fireplace with a mahogany hearth. A detail person through and through, he'd seen a lot of hellholes in his life. This was so far from the mainstream he couldn't stop taking in the opulence and glut of wealth. The room itself, nearly the size of a football field, seemed more like royal palace than a home.

On the far side of the room, almost to the opposite end, he spotted a uniformed officer and a petite forty-something woman. She wore a silk embroidered bathrobe cinched tightly around a tiny waist. Her hair hung in haphazard platinum streaks around a tear-stained face. The officer stood nearby, supporting but not touching.

Grant had to study closely to see the same woman who had affronted Beth at Brea's memorial. But, after a moment, beneath the mascara smudges and the tinny voice, he spotted her.

He strode directly to the center of the room while perusing the place. Shaun occupied himself with similar matters. Once the two assessed the scene and Grant noticed the team had arrived, he took control of the situation. Shaun stood on the perimeter, taking his own notes.

"Mrs. Magness?" Grant asked.

"Yes," she whispered. "Cynthia." She gazed up at him with blank, red-rimmed eyes.

"I'm Detective Fulton. First of all, I'd like to tell you how sorry I am for your loss." Even though he'd witnessed this woman at her worst at the funeral home, he experienced a stab of compassion. He well knew the pain of losing someone close.

"I'm sorry, but we need to perform a routine test on your hands."

"What?" Shock cemented her face.

"Before we ask you a few questions, our forensics team needs your fingerprints and to check your hands for powder residue. It's a formality. The test will help us to eliminate you as a suspect. Will you give us permission?"

"Yes," she replied, blankly holding out her hands. The forensics team moved in and worked quickly. They handed Mrs. Magness a wet towel when they were finished. She wiped her hands and handed the cloth back.

Grant tipped his head to the team, who excused themselves, and then glanced at Cynthia Magness. She sniffled a bit and dabbed her nose with a shred of tissue.

He sat in the wing chair opposite Mrs. Magness, which allowed him a clear view of her body language and facial expressions. He reached inside his pocket for his spiral notebook and a pen, and decided to hold off on the matter of her pregnancy unless she broached the topic. Avoiding sensitive issues would allow him to gather the information he needed as quickly as possible.

"I apologize, but as a matter of record, I need to ask you some questions. Do you feel able to answer them?"

"I think so." A vein swelled in the middle of her forehead.

Stress, he figured. But due to the dead husband or having to answer questions?

"First, I'd like you to state your full name."

"Why?" Cynthia asked. "Am I under arrest?"

"No, ma'am, I just need your name for the record."

She looked puzzled. "My name is Cynthia Ann Magness."

"Thank you. Now, can you tell me what happened? Try to give me all the details, anything at all you remember. Even the tiniest particulars could be helpful in finding your husband's killer."

"Well, I guess it was about one-thirty. Peter and I turned in early. He had a symposium at the clinic, and seemed quite tired when he arrived home. Peter's a marriage counselor. He's written several books and teaches at the University School of Social Work. Anyway, he arrived home about ten. We had a quick drink together. Mine was soft." She laid a hand on her abdomen. "We always have an evening cocktail when Peter returns home." She sniffled again. "We went to bed shortly before eleven."

The guy was barefoot, wearing thick sweats and a T-shirt. Did he wear that every night? Had he merely gotten up to use the bathroom, or had he heard something? Had he been expecting someone? Not likely he was heading out without shoes. In order not to interrupt the flow now that he had her going, Grant made a note to ask later.

"And then what?"

"We went to sleep." Tears streamed down her face.

"What do you remember next?"

"I heard something. I reached out for Peter, but his side of the bed was empty. He wasn't there. At first, I thought he had gotten up to use the bathroom."

"Did you get up then?"

"No, not right away. I lay there for a minute and listened. You know. Sorting things through."

Grant noted her earnestness, then waited for her to continue.

"But I didn't hear him. It seemed to be taking longer than usual for him to get back to bed."

She stopped and stared off into space. Grant watched her, then his gaze strayed to something out of place in the all too perfect room.

A desk drawer, slightly ajar. A bank envelope stood at attention, saluting out of the top. He took brief note, and then drew his attention back to the wife. She fingered the tissue in her hands, then began to shred the Kleenex into pieces.

"I called his name," she remembered.

Grant waited.

"Yes, I called his name, but he didn't answer. I lay there waiting for him. The house was totally quiet. Eerie quiet. I sensed there was something wrong."

She became more anxious as she spoke, fraying her tissue to lint and wringing her hands. "Then I heard something. Like a thump. Like someone dropped something. Then mumbling almost, like the bass of a drum. Voices. Deep voices."

"Did you hear one voice? Or more?"

"I'm not sure, but I think more. I only heard mumbling, you know? Like low booms."

"How long did the voices go on?"

"Not long, maybe a few seconds or so. All of a sudden there was a thump, then mumbling, then a pop, like a firecracker. Then another thump."

Grant took notes. He had a good guess what the last sound signified.

"A man's voice? A woman's?"

"I couldn't tell. Just voices."

"What did you do?"

"I froze. I was scared to death."

"What did you think had happened?"

"I didn't know what to think, but I started to call Peter's name, louder and louder, but he didn't answer. So I reached into his nightstand drawer and grabbed the gun."

"The gun." Grant repeated her words.

"Yes, we keep a gun for safety reasons."

"Do you have reason to be concerned about protection?"

"There were some robberies in the area a couple of years ago. Peter said it's important to be prepared for every eventuality."

"Do you keep cash and valuables in the home?"

"Oh no," Cynthia said dismissively. "Never cash. We use credit cards and pay bills online. My jewelry is in a safe deposit box at the bank. You know, Peter has been threatened by clients before."

Grant agreed as he wrote. "Tell me what you did after getting the gun."

"I removed the safety, like Peter trained me," she said, rushing her words.

"Did he keep the gun loaded?"

"No, never." Then, confusion knit her brow. "I don't know, I don't remember. I think so," she repeated with growing conviction.

"What happened after you removed the gun from the drawer?"

"I threw on my robe and came downstairs. The house was dark. That scared me, too. Why would Peter get up during the night and not turn on the lights?"

"Maybe he didn't want to wake you."

Cynthia released a gust of air. "Trust me, Peter isn't a quiet man. Or a consid—" her voice broke off.

Grant watched her face redden. "Ma'am?"

Cynthia straightened her shoulders. "Peter's noisy, is all."

"So you came down the stairs."

"Yes." Her expression remained oddly detached. "I came down slowly. Quietly. Listening."

"Um-hum."

"The house was unusually cold."

"Cold?"

"Yes. I felt the breeze as soon I made the turn. The staircase curves," she explained. "I realized then the front door was wide open. The hum of the wind whizzed through the hallway. I got curious then."

"Curious?" Grant asked.

"I thought maybe the wind had blown open the door, and Peter had forgotten to lock up."

"Did Peter always lock the doors?"

"Well, yes, when he's home. Otherwise, I lock them."

"He's not always home by bedtime?"

"He works late on occasion."

Grant nodded. "So you went to check the door."

Cynthia's face paled as she relived the scene. "That's when I saw him." She dabbed at her eyes with a tissue.

"Saw him?"

"Peter. He was lying on the stoop. On his back. The porch lamp acted like a spotlight," she wailed. "His eyes were open. Staring at me. Not moving."

"Yes, ma'am."

"I turned away. I know I did. I shut the door. I ran to the phone and called 911."

"Yes, ma'am," Grant repeated.

"I knew he was dead."

"Did you check for a pulse?"

"I don't know. I don't think so. I don't remember." She stopped and inhaled a sharp breath. "No. I didn't check."

"Did you touch him at all?"

"No," Cynthia said.

"Are you sure?"

"Yes. No. I'm not sure."

"That's all right, ma'am. One more question. Did Peter usually wear pajamas to bed? Or sweats and a t-shirt as he did tonight?"

"Peter slept in the nude." The tone in her voice startled Grant. She sounded put off by Peter's lack of clothing.

So either he'd heard something and thrown on clothes, or he was expecting someone.

Grant stood, reached for the glass of water on the table between them, and offered her a drink, averted his gaze to the drawer once again, and noticed cash protruding from the envelope. He couldn't decipher the denomination. As the only item out of place in the perfect room, he couldn't help but imagine Peter riffling in the dark before he answered the door. A planned meeting? A thwarted robbery? He searched for footprints on the high gloss cherry floor entrance to the room. There were none. Cynthia took the glass from him and sipped, then placed the water back on the table and gasped a ragged breath. She eased back on the sofa, small and defeated.

"Sorry, ma'am," Grant said again. "Just a couple more questions."

Cynthia vaguely nodded, resigned.

"Did anything appear disturbed, as if someone had entered the house? Taken anything?"

"Well, no. I never thought to check. The door was wide open. Peter was lying there. I was shocked."

"We'll want to do a full search of the house. I recognize your husband's death occurred outside the residence, but we can't overlook the possibility that this was a robbery gone wrong."

Cynthia waved her arm in dismissal. "Go ahead. I have nothing to hide."

Interesting comment, Grant noted. Blackmail? Robbery? He could hardly sit still. He couldn't get a search warrant fast enough. Or…

"Did your husband owe anyone money? I can't help but notice the bank envelope in the drawer."

"Where?" Cynthia appeared genuinely surprised.

Grant stood and made his way over to the desk. "Would you mind taking the envelope out of the drawer? Just count the money for me and make sure none is missing?"

"I've never seen that envelope. I had no idea there was money in the house. This is Peter's doing."

"It's not a problem, ma'am. Having cash in the home is fine." He couldn't make sense of her reaction, but it did make his antenna rise.

"Bring it here," she ordered, a sharp edge to her voice.

Grant snapped on a pair of latex gloves and opened the drawer. What he discovered inside pinned his brows to his hairline. Eight envelopes. Fat. So fat the glue wouldn't hold them shut. Beneath that, two empty envelopes.

He gathered the packet in his hands and delivered it to Mrs. Magness, setting them next to her on the sofa. She looked up at him, unsure what to do next. "Can you count the contents for me, please?"

"I knew nothing about this. I swear."

"Mrs. Magness. As I stated before, you are not in trouble. Please understand, your home is a crime scene, and we need to cover all our bases. I can and will get a search warrant. We want to solve your husband's murder, and the sooner we can put the pieces together, the better."

Cynthia's fingers trembled as she removed cash from the first envelope and began to count. Mixed bills, mostly twenties, but some fifties. Not new bills. Drugs?

As Cynthia counted, Grant counted along with her, waiting after she counted the contents of the first envelope to jot down the amount. It was then that he noticed the scribbling on the outside of the envelope. "Is that Peter's writing?" he asked.

Cynthia looked puzzled and Grant led her gaze in the direction of the note. "Yes," she answered. "It looks like he wrote the amounts on the outside of all of these. This one says "$1500.00, but I only counted $700.00."

Grant assumed as much. "Could you please count the others for me?"

The same held true for each pouch. The outside sum didn't match the contents. Half of the supposed twenty grand Peter had, now missing. Interesting. He knew the answer, but had to ask. "Are you sure you don't recall the cash? Maybe you kept it upstairs for an emergency and it was moved downstairs some time ago?"

"I already told you. We don't keep cash in the house."

Unless Robin Hood had decided these folks needed a windfall, Grant was sure no one had delivered the money before killing Peter. Unless… Maybe it *was* drugs. Peter got paid and returned to the front door with the goods. But who wouldn't run in and grab the cash before taking off?

"Did Peter owe anyone money?"

"No, of course Peter doesn't owe anyone. He has enough money." She took breath after breath, her inhales short, her exhales ragged and puffy. Frustrated, bordering on downright angry.

"Did he have any enemies? Anyone you know of who would want him dead?"

Cynthia's shoulders slumped. "Just one," she said with conviction.

Again, Grant waited.

"Brea. Brea Watson."

This time, Grant exhaled sharply, as if he'd just been sucker-punched.

CHAPTER TWENTY-NINE

Grant

GRANT IGNORED HIS INITIAL SHOCK AND REMAINED IN cop mode. A woman didn't often spit out another woman's name with such malice, not without good reason.

Shaun studied him with a puzzled expression. Grant gave a barely discernible shake of his head.

"Could you state the name again?" Grant asked.

"Brea Watson," Cynthia said, her voice hard. "I believe her full name is Breanne."

Okay, this was bizarre. Cynthia had been to Brea's visitation, and even staged a tirade at the funeral home. She clearly knew Brea was dead, yet she insisted on blaming her for Peter's murder. Grief could scatter clarity, but she was accusing a dead woman of murdering her husband. He couldn't help wondering…Cynthia had motive. Jealousy. Revenge. Maybe a case of 'if she couldn't have him'…? Her state of mind was certainly in question. She might be just plain bonkers, or shocked silly from finding her husband's dead body. Maybe she had seen something and blocked it out. And what about Beth? Would she have had reason to kill Peter?

Grant proceeded with caution. He knew better, but there might be two Breanne Watsons from Ann Arbor.

"Tell me what you know about Breanne Watson," Grant urged.

"Peter was having an affair with her." Cynthia's words erupted like hot lava.

Grant noted the heat of her spite. "And?"

"When Peter ended the relationship, she wasn't happy. She didn't want to believe the affair was over."

"Why do you believe this to be true, Mrs. Magness?"

"I checked the phone bill. She continued to text and call him even after he told her they were through. Even after he told her he was staying with me."

"I beg your pardon, ma'am, but how do you know she initiated the texts and calls and not the other way around?"

"Trust me," Cynthia said firmly, "I know my husband. When he came home, he came home for good."

Grant made a mental note to check those records. "Then you were separated?"

"Not physically. We were living together when Peter was involved with the sl—" she stopped short, "—with the woman."

"I see," Grant said, taking notes. "Again, I apologize for having you run through this tonight, but collecting as much information as possible while the specifics are fresh in your mind will be helpful."

He glanced at Shaun and arched his brows. Shaun acknowledged the cue and stayed put. Always proved best if the two of them remained in the room.

Grant turned back to Cynthia. "I gather you don't like Brea Watson. Any reason other than the obvious?"

Cynthia leaned forward, vicious and more in control. "I loathe her."

"How long was your husband involved with Ms. Watson?"

Cynthia Magness's lips thinned. "Quite a long time."

Grant sat back, remaining silent.

"Seven or eight years."

"You mean months?" he clarified.

"No," she faltered. "Years. Peter admitted his indiscretion. He was extremely sorrowful. We saw our pastor for a while."

"So, I'm safe to assume you and Peter had put your marriage back together."

"Absolutely. We…" She began to sputter, "…are expecting a child."

"You didn't harbor any ill will toward your husband?" Maybe he needed to check the details of the accident once more, thinking a woman scorned… Thinking this woman may have tampered with Brea's car. Thinking how perps returned to the scene. The memorial…The cash. Had she staged the scene? Killed him in cold blood?

She laid a protective hand on her stomach. "I forgave him. Totally and completely."

Grant weighed his options. He still didn't have a clear indication this woman had not killed her husband. But there was something off about this scenario that he couldn't put his finger on.

"Ma'am. Just wondering. You said you had possession of a gun when you came down the stairs to find your husband. Where is the weapon now?"

Cynthia straightened and surveyed the room, searching for the misplaced gun as though hunting for a missing grocery list. "Hmm, I must have set the gun down next to the landline, in the kitchen. That's where I made the 911 call."

She began to stand.

Grant waved her back. "That's all right, ma'am. We'll find the gun."

Shaun left the room, returning less than a minute later. He nodded at Grant.

Grant leaned forward to peer into Cynthia Magness's eyes.

"Ma'am, the first forty-eight hours are crucial in a murder investigation. If you don't mind, we'd like you to come downtown so we can get some additional information."

"Why? You don't think I killed Peter, do you?" Cynthia's tears resumed.

"Just routine. You are not under arrest. I'm not going to read you your rights or anything." Grant tried to sound reassuring. In truth, he wondered if this woman had shot her husband and left him on the front porch to die. Maybe she'd killed Brea then finished off by killing Peter. "Is there someone you'd like to call? Your older children, perhaps?"

"We don't have other children."

"Anyone else you'd like to notify?"

"An attorney?" Her hands trembled in her lap.

"No, ma'am, that's not necessary," Grant said quietly. "We'd just like to ask you a few more questions at the precinct. Are you feeling well enough to come to the station?"

"In the middle of the night?"

"Yes, ma'am." Grant stood, indicating the seriousness of his request.

"May I get dressed?"

Her face ashen, her hair mousy and stringy, Cynthia no longer looked like the resident of a million dollar neighborhood. She looked crushed.

Something was up. He just didn't know what.

CHAPTER THIRTY

Grant

"WHAT'S WRONG WITH YOU?" SHAUN ASKED AFTER Cynthia Magness exited the room. "You're jacked up."

Grant marched over to the built-in bookshelves in the corner of the room. Next to a stack of books, Peter Magness's bestselling book covers were artfully displayed inside ornate frames. Grant peered at the titles: *Six Steps to a Better Marriage*. Next stood *How to Guarantee a Lasting Marriage*.

Grant stifled a laugh. "Get a load of this."

Shaun sauntered over. "This guy's a piece of work."

"Apparently so." Grant agreed. "He's no Dr. Phil, that's for sure."

Then he remembered he had seen Magness's name in the *Ann Arbor News*. Several years ago, he recalled, when the University of Michigan had made a big deal about having a nationally renowned author on its payroll. Newscasters would have a field day with his murder. Add the recent murder of a patient and news of his affair with Brea, and a media frenzy would ensue. Not much scandal in town. Folks would eat this story up.

Grant shook his head, disgusted.

"What?" Shaun asked.

"After icons like Schembechler and Carr, we're certainly not attracting the cream of the crop any longer."

"The dude's a marriage guru, not a coach."

"I know, just sayin'…"

"You got a problem with this case, or is something else bugging you?"

"I'm fine."

Shaun knitted his brows, headed toward the hallway, and peered around the door in search of Cynthia Magness, then back at Grant. When his partner's eyes widened, Grant strode into the hallway to make sense of Shaun's reaction.

The woman had taken the time to apply makeup and twist her hair into some kind of knot. She wore a straight skirt, tight sweater, and heels, dressed like she was off to play bridge at the country club. Pregnant, she did not look. Murder suspect, nope. But did she have motive and opportunity? Hell, yes.

She dabbed at her eyes with a tissue. "I need to find my handbag," she announced, parading toward the kitchen.

"We'd better take her out the back," Grant said. "Maybe walk along the driveway. I'm not sure if forensics is done outside."

Just in case she hadn't been the one to kill Magness and always aware of cross-contamination, he didn't want her passing near the crime scene. He also didn't want her to see her husband's corpse. That seemed unnecessarily cruel.

Shaun agreed. "Want me to take her?"

"Sure. I'll check on the progress out front then follow you."

As Shaun ushered Cynthia out the back door, Grant checked again to be sure his guys had secured the gun before he made his way to the front door. He opened the entryway to find a half dozen folks—the coroner, the State Crime Lab guys, and the first responders. The media had arrived, their trucks parked on the street, and he spotted Officer John Moore handling those details. Good. Moore would keep them busy with the vaguest of facts.

"Any news?" He eyed Mason and Bartholomew for answers.

"Not much. A neighbor who lives a few doors down said his dog started barking some time after midnight. Says the dog only kicks up a ruckus when there's someone in the yard," Mason said.

"Did he do anything?"

"He flipped on the light and checked over the backyard from the window, but he didn't see anyone. Also said deer sometimes come up toward the house, but the dog usually leaves them alone."

"Find a weapon? Any casings?"

"No," Bartholomew chimed in.

"I'll leave the house open in case you guys need to get inside. We're taking Mrs. Magness to the precinct to ask her a few more questions. And the gun she claims she had when she came looking for her husband? Check it into the lab."

"Sure thing, boss."

Grant's shoulders ached, his upper back tensed as if pulled tight as a bowstring. He rotated his shoulders to ease the tension.

He itched for answers. Peter Magness had pissed off someone royally enough to shoot him dead on his front stoop. Pretty cold-blooded. Robbery a possible factor, as well as revenge, or a drug deal gone south. Nothing like a long list of suspects with motivation to keep him on his toes. Hell, the wife had motive and opportunity. Once he eliminated the Mrs. from the suspect list, he guessed there might be quite a few other contenders.

Maybe he'd have good fortune and the team would uncover a murder weapon. Or figure out Cynthia killed him. He could lock that down tonight. If not, the dogs might be able to track the killer. Fresh body, fresh tracks.

He considered the list of questions he still needed to ask Cynthia Magness.

After he finished her interrogation, he'd learn more about Breanne Watson, now that he had cause to ask.

Grant pulled into the precinct and parked. He lumbered inside with hunched shoulders, still unable to shake off the tension or the cold. He wanted this night to be over.

He spotted Shaun outside an interrogation room.

"We should put our heads together before we go in," Shaun said.

"Yeah," Grant agreed. "I need a cup of coffee first."

"I'll check and see if the wife wants something, be the good cop," Shaun said.

At the door to the interview room, Grant glanced at Shaun. "Give me five minutes." He donned his game face and strode in. "Sorry to have kept you waiting." He took a seat in the vinyl chair across the table from Cynthia Magness.

Haggard in the bright light, she shivered—legs crossed, one foot jiggling.

"I understand my partner is grabbing you a cup of tea." A sympathetic look crossed his face. "Again, I apologize for bringing you down so late, but I'd like to gather a bit more information and perhaps have you sign a statement so that we can move forward with the investigation."

"I understand," Cynthia said.

The color had drained from her face, and Grant couldn't decide whether she looked more green or gray in spite of the make-up. Her mask seemed to be shattering. "You feeling all right?"

Cynthia lifted her head, as if distracted from a trance. "Morning sickness."

Grant noticed she kept a protective hand over her abdomen. Instinct, he guessed. "Just a couple of things." He leaned forward in his chair and rested his spiral notebook on the table. "You mentioned an enemy of your husband's."

"Yes. The woman he had broken off with, the slut." Cynthia became more animated, the anger in her voice hissing with each word.

"I'd appreciate any information you have about her." Grant watched her face grow tense and brittle. "I don't mean to upset you, but even the simplest detail may prove to be important."

"Her name is Brea. Breanne Watson."

"Yes, thank you, I have her name. Do you have an address or phone number? We'd like to speak with her."

"Good luck." Her sarcasm cut like a cleaver.

"Excuse me, ma'am?"

"She's dead."

The words stabbed Grant but he played along. "I don't understand."

"She was killed in a car accident a few months ago."

"I'm aware someone by that name recently died. So how do you think Brea was involved in this crime tonight?"

"It's her fault."

"I'm sorry, I know this is difficult, but I need to understand. You indicated this woman was an enemy and she harbored ill will toward your husband. If she's dead, how could she have killed him?"

"You're right. Naming a dead person doesn't make sense. But I'm blaming her because she's to blame. Not for Peter's death, perhaps, but for everything else."

"Perhaps someone who knew and loved her harbored some resentment toward your husband. Was she married? Could her husband or another family member have been angry with Dr. Magness?"

"She has a sister. A twin. Identical, in fact. You should talk to her. Her name is Elizabeth, she goes by Beth. Maybe she wanted Peter dead. Maybe she blames him instead of herself."

Grant frowned. "What do you mean?"

"Perhaps she blames Peter for the accident that killed her sister. She was at fault, she was driving, but she probably twisted things and blamed Peter. You know how irrational people can be."

"Let me be sure I understand. You think Brea's sister, Beth, may have had something to do with Peter's death."

"Yes. Her full name is Elizabeth Marks. She was driving, and her sister died. If you want to find her, she lives in Barton Hills and she's married to a doctor. Jeffry Marks."

"Do you have reason to think Mrs. Marks had something to do with Peter's death? Did she threaten him?"

"Well, I can't be certain, but I did speak to her a week or so ago, and she was quite defensive and evasive. I've been to her home twice. Let's just say she wasn't happy to see me either time."

Grant studied Cynthia Magness, wondering if she might be a little bit crazy. She'd certainly gone on a nut at the funeral home. But for Beth, injured and debilitated the last Grant knew, to simply show up at the guy's front door and shoot him made no sense whatsoever. It wasn't as if he knew Beth well, or the circumstances of Brea's affair with the marriage guru, and he'd do his due diligence, but his best hunch told him Beth wasn't the killer. The Beth he'd known some twenty years ago was a softie, weak, needing constant care. Brea had fussed over her like an orphaned kitten. The Beth he knew, even now, didn't seem like someone capable of murder.

The cell phone on his belt vibrated. "Excuse me. I'll be right back."

Shaun stood outside the door, a cup in each hand. "How's the interview going? You seemed to be doing all right in there, so I took a call."

"I don't know." Grant's eyes narrowed as he checked his cell. He didn't recognize the number, so he silenced his phone and hooked the handset back on his belt.

"Let me drop off her tea. Be right back."

Shaun rejoined Grant in the hallway a moment later.

"You want to tell me what's going on?"

"No," Grant answered bluntly.

Shaun squinted at him. "I hate to say so, partner, but you look like you're circling the drain. All the color's left your face."

"Come with me," he said, gesturing down the hall. He strode to a bench and took a seat. Shaun sat beside him. "First of all, I think the Mrs. is a little off. Maybe more than a little. Also, the person of interest she's naming is an acquaintance of mine."

"Well, now…"

"Yeah." Grant's neck muscles tightened, he took a sip of coffee, and tipped his head toward the ceiling.

"So this is personal," Shaun said.

Grant sighed again. "Long story."

"Sure you don't want to tell me?"

"Not really."

CHAPTER THIRTY-ONE

Brea

EARLY MORNING SILENCE. HER THOUGHTS WERE CLEARER. Emotions deeper. More profound. Days like today, Brea wished she could avoid both, but reality wouldn't stop its incessant niggle.

Grant's face rose in her memory.

If only she could ignore the connection. When he hugged her at the funeral home, her heart had opened, as if she'd been hibernating the past twenty years.

She stared at her phone.

One quick call. He could join her in South Carolina, she could confess to impersonating Beth, and never go back to Ann Arbor. End of story. He'd be horrified, she was sure. Cops liked the truth. They lived to uncover lies. Detectives especially.

A chill ran up her spine. A lump in her throat threatened suffocation.

Tucked in the bottom drawer of her dresser, she found the memento Grant had given her, the keepsake for her seventeenth birthday. A little rectangle of wood with a heart carved into the grain. He had burned the words "Love you," on the back, and signed his name. She clutched the treasure, small enough to slip into her pocket. A touchstone.

Brea plopped down on the side of the bed. Standing required

more energy than she could muster. These deep thoughts were too much to tackle first thing in the morning.

Brea lay on her back and stretched, lengthening her hip to keep the morning stiffness from overtaking her. Hard as she tried, she couldn't wrangle her thoughts, her ping-ponging emotions, or control her body. Nausea rose in her throat and her arms tingled.

Beth had led her to believe she spent every waking moment nurturing: feeding, clothing, bathing, reading, playing, toting, and soothing. But Dana must have provided opportunities for escape, chances to hook-up with Peter. If Peter had lied about the vasectomy, then Beth had that piece of him that she—Brea—had wanted more than anything. Not a noble thought to crave the child of a married man, but true nonetheless. But if Peter actually had the vasectomy, and if she were to believe that Jeffry and Beth hadn't had sex for six months, neither of the men were the father. Whose baby had Beth been carrying?

The nerve of Peter. He'd most likely been the one to snare Beth. With Beth's suspicions of—and anger at Jeffry—she would've been easy prey. Plus, Beth had worked diligently to return to her pre-pregnancy weight after Jack's birth. She'd matched her workouts to Brea's until the scales read the same at both their houses. She'd been proud of her toned body. Maybe she'd been anxious to show it off as well.

Brea knew all about getting in over one's head. There were no do-overs. Maybe Beth became caught up in the relationship with Peter before she knew what happened. Momentum was the only answer, or at least one she could reason. She couldn't fathom her sister intentionally hurting her. But Beth had betrayed her. No way around it.

Brea clenched her jaw. She was trying to cram jagged puzzle pieces into square holes. Nothing fit. Not really. Spitting angry at Peter and Beth, she shot a look at the clock.

7:00 a.m. The whole damn day lay ahead of her. She peered through the blinds to search for the sun. Clouds dotted the sky in puffs of white, casting shadows over spring lawns and colorful flowers, mirroring her state. Coffee might help.

Her hip ached more than usual today. Maybe she'd slept funny. She climbed over several packed boxes on her way to the kitchen, a feeling of unease heavy on her chest. Not much left to do here. Find a realtor, settle on a price, and list the condo for sale. Maintaining two separate lives made little sense now.

She polished the granite countertops while the coffee brewed, opened and closed drawers to take mental inventory of what she would pack and what she would donate to charity. The ring of her cell phone startled her.

She glanced at the number. Unfamiliar. The readout didn't provide a name.

"Hello?"

"Beth, darling, how are you?"

Her breath caught in her throat. The voice didn't sound familiar either. Thankfully, the caller filled in the blanks.

"It's Julie, darling. Your neighbor."

"Oh, sorry. You caught me waking up," Brea said.

Julie wound up to a full chatter. "I've tried to leave you alone, and respect your privacy since Brea's death, you know, as you recover and take care of the kids. I knew if you needed anything, you knew you could count on me. But last evening I stopped by, brought over a casserole, the turkey recipe you gave me. Anyway, Jeffry said you'd gone to Hilton Head." She sounded horrified. "By yourself! To close up Brea's place and all. Honey, you should have called me. I would have come with you. I gave Jeffry a hard time, I'm afraid, for letting you go alone. What could he have been thinking? This is too much for you right—"

"Thanks, Julie," Brea interrupted, "but really, I'm fine. Taking care of Brea's belongings and tidying up her business affairs has been cathartic. I needed to do this. But thanks so much for being concerned. I'll be home in a few days and we can catch up then."

"Are you sure? This must be agony for you."

"Honestly, I'm fine." She rolled her eyes as she reassured Julie. "How are things at home? Things with you?"

The best defense with people like Julie was a good offense. Keep her talking about herself and deflect the onslaught of questions.

"Oh, things here are fine. The kids run me ragged, as usual. I'm a full-time taxi driver at this stage of their lives."

Brea chuckled. "Something I have to look forward to," she replied. "Seems I do a fair amount of taxiing already, but I'm sure the chauffeuring is bound to get worse. Anyway, I think I hear the realtor at the door. I'd better let you go."

"At 7:30 in the morning? Certainly it's too early for visitors," Julie said.

"I asked her to come when the day was fresh. I have a million other things to accomplish today."

"I'll let you go then. But, Beth, one last thing."

"What?"

"You won't believe what's happened. Pe…" The connection cut out. "…was murdered."

"A murder? In Ann Arbor?" Impossible. Murders, other than the convoluted domestic violence tragedy of a few years ago, were rare in the quiet college town. "Who did you say?" she asked.

"Peter. Magness. Your Peter. I feel horrible being the one to tell you, but I guess the news is better coming from a friend."

Brea's chest tightened. "Who?"

"I gathered you moved on. I haven't seen him around, just once…maybe twice, when Dana was watching the kids. Here, let me grab my laptop."

Stunned, Brea made note of the fact Julie provided a better neighborhood watch than security cameras ever could. Still, she couldn't process Julie's words.

"Who?" Brea asked as she heard Julie come back on the line.

"Peter Magness."

Brea slid down the wall to the ceramic tile floor.

"Beth?" Julie asked. "Are you there?"

"Yes," Brea whispered. "I'm here."

She inhaled deeply to suck back the oxygen Julie's news had knocked out of her. "Sorry, Julie, I really have to go. The realtor is going to leave if I don't answer the door. We'll talk soon."

Brea gasped for air. Dropped her cell phone. Spinning room. Racing heart. White noise.

Peter. Murdered?

She edged up. Propped against the cupboard. Shock rolled across her. In waves. Dead? He was just here.

Breathe.

She aimed her gaze at the cabinet door handle. Focusing helped. Her heart eased its gallop, and her respiration slowed. After several minutes, her vision cleared and the knifing pain in her gut began to recede. She twisted, shifted onto her knees, and gripped the counter edge to pull up to her feet. Brea reached for a glass, turned on the water. She splashed her face before filling her glass and sipping slowly. Bile eased back down her throat. She finally inched her way across the room to the sofa in the living area.

Where the hell was her laptop? She couldn't move her head for fear of puking. Peter had killed himself? No. Julie said murdered, and Brea had been too dumbstruck to ask questions. Peter was extremely confident, bordering on narcissistic, if she were being kind. Hardly a candidate for suicide.

Brea made her way to the bedroom, and pulled her laptop close. She Googled: Peter Magness. Murder. Ann Arbor, Michigan.

After an eternity, Brea scanned a short article on MLive:

Peter Magness, renowned psychologist…

murdered at his home…gunshot wound…

homicide…no suspects…

Women flocked to Peter. He had a list of enemies longer than an NBA player's wingspan. Her mind shifted to Cynthia's venomous behavior at Beth's funeral, malice dripping with every word.

Nausea returned full force. A murder equaled an investigation. Everything would come out. Peter's visit. Her affair with Peter. Beth's affair with Peter. Things would get ugly quick. Panic gripped her. Violent chills racked her body. After all this, there was every chance she would be exposed.

Her legs quivered. Hands trembled. Tear choked sobs filled the silence.

Sometime later, she made her way to the kitchen, filled a glass with ice, and poured three fingers of bourbon.

I wasted eight years of my life on this man.

CHAPTER THIRTY-TWO

Brea

THE WHISKEY TOOK OFF THE EDGE. BREA SHUFFLED TO THE patio doors and opened the blinds. Sunshine flooded the room, a stark contrast to the storm brewing inside her. Panic overwhelmed her. A prisoner of grief and guilt, she huddled on the floor, knees to her chest, rocking. She saw Peter just yesterday. She'd been cruel, unforgiving.

Her cell phone chirped. A telltale ring.

"Hey, Beth, it's me," Jeffry said.

"Hi," Brea replied in a whisper, emotions still paralyzing her.

"How are you?"

"Um, good. How about you?" Brea sunk back to rest against the wall. She gulped whiskey, wiped her mouth with the back of her hand, and braced herself.

"Just wanted to check on you. How are you holding up?"

Jeffry. Her last resort, she realized. She had no one now but the children and him. Her family. Her salvation.

If Peter were still alive. If she could turn back the clock… But she couldn't. His death seemed a prophetic twist of fate. She was meant to be with Jeffry, Ella and Jack.

"All of this is…unimaginable," she finally admitted, biting back tears.

"I'm sorry."

"How are the kids? I wanted to call again, but I didn't want to make things harder for you. I remember when B... I remember when I came to visit Brea, how they whined and cried for me. I hate to leave you with the aftermath."

"I told you the other day, call whenever you want. But we're all fine, really. I just wanted to make sure you're all right," he said gently. "I've been worried about you."

"Thank you," she said, grateful for his concern. Lonely. Desperate. Not good to be alone right now.

"Beth." Anxiety in his voice.

"Yes?"

"Something's happened."

Brea's heart stuttered in her chest. *He's calling to tell me about Peter.*

"What?"

"Peter," Jeffry said his name and waited. For a reaction, Brea supposed. She stayed quiet. After a moment, he continued. "Peter Magness was found murdered last night at his home."

Brea met Jeffry's words with silence.

"Beth?" he asked. "Are you still there?"

"Yes," she managed, not knowing what else to say.

"Listen. We've both made a lot of mistakes. I just want you to know I understand this is devastating news. Even though you're not seeing him any longer, I realize you cared for him." *Was he for real?*

She couldn't speak. Her breath came in short, shallow spurts. He was forgiving her. Forgiving Beth. On this call. Right now. Moreover, offering his love and support. This had to be a ploy, some kind of covert manipulation.

"Beth?"

"Yes?"

"We can deal with this."

Maybe he'd killed Peter. Men didn't like to think about their wives putting out. Especially when Beth had denied him. "Uh-huh," she choked out, fear gripping her words.

"Can we talk when you get back?"

"Yes," Brea whispered.

"I'll let you go. I know this is tough news, and understand you need some time to process Peter's death. I thought the news would be best coming from me."

Brea couldn't think, or talk. She could barely breathe. So she kept her mouth shut.

"Call if you want to talk," Jeffry continued.

"Thank you." She ended the call.

CHAPTER THIRTY-THREE

Grant

GRANT DROVE TO THE PRECINCT AND DOVE INTO THE break room. He lay down on a narrow cot and closed his eyes, thinking a power nap would clear his head, but Cynthia fingering Beth and Brea kept him tossing and turning. He threw back the blanket and headed into the locker room. After a tepid shower, he dressed and headed out to his favorite haunt for a large coffee. As he fastened the lid on his cup, the Marks' residence flashed in his mind like a lighthouse, beckoning him. Getting a take on Beth might help put things in perspective. In any event, he needed to check out links to Peter, if only to rule out any involvement.

He took note of the time. Catching the family in the midst of their normal early morning routine made perfect sense.

He made the drive and knocked on the door, noting a dilapidated Ford Focus in the driveway. A dowdy woman answered, wearing a turn of the century dress with old lady shoes, tight gray curls framing her fleshy face, even though she couldn't be more than fifty years old. As he flashed his badge, she leaned her dust mop against the wall, clutched at her apron, and clucked her tongue. "What's she done now?"

"My name is Detective Fulton from the Ann Arbor PD. I'm investigating the Peter Magness murder."

"That man has been in this house."

"May I come in?"

"The family isn't home. I no longer work here. I was only called in to clean before Mrs. Marks' returns from her trip. Seems like I'm the one soul willing to take on this family. Dr. Marks took the children to breakfast. It's sinful how he spoils them."

Grant stepped into the vestibule and closed the door behind him. "And you are?"

"Judith Buckholder. I used to be the nanny."

Grant's eyebrows furrowed, hearing a story behind the answers. "I'd like to ask you a few quick questions. Can we sit?"

Judith fidgeted, nervous as a mouse, eyes darting to and fro, flitting this way and that, as if lost.

She finally slowed and led him to the kitchen, taking a seat at the table and folding her hands in her lap, her lips pursed.

"Mrs. Marks is traveling?"

"You're the detective. I don't know where she is, but I assume so if Dr. Marks is picking her up from the airport." Judith shot daggers at him, and Grant couldn't help but wonder if the look was permanent.

"She's a horrid woman. She claims to have memory loss since the accident, and scrambles through closets and drawers all the time, like she has no idea where anything goes. She acts like she's in a foreign place, or from one."

Grant nodded and waited for her to go on. For some reason, she'd decided to focus on Beth, and the hostility she harbored couldn't be ignored.

"She fired me because I was doing my job. Keeping track of her. She couldn't find a single thing she needed, she'd forget to dress the children for school, and the mess these children make, it's despicable. Parents today have no rules. And the oversights she made were endless. It took me hours to record everything for Dr. Marks. All these people are fornicators."

"First, I'd like to know where you were last night."

"Not that it's any of your business, but I was home, in my bed. My husband can verify my whereabouts."

Grant jotted notes. "Do you own a firearm?"

"Of course not. I'm a woman of God. God takes care of sinners as He sees fit."

"You mentioned fornication. Can you tell me why you suspect that of the Marks?"

"The doctor takes an overnight bag with him when he leaves for the hospital. God only knows what he does there. And Mrs. Marks, well, she's had visitors, like Dr. Magness. She hasn't moved back to the marital bedroom yet, even though she's healed from her injuries. It doesn't take a genius to sum the numbers."

"Have you seen Dr. Magness and Mrs. Marks together?"

Judith's face soured, as if the thought of telling the truth was like sucking on a lemon. Her goal seemed to implicate Beth, if not for murder, certainly for worst mother and wife. "Well, no. But the doctor stopped by at least twice since Mrs. Marks returned from the hospital. Why would he come here, except to see her? You know, Dr. Magness had an affair with Brea Watson, Mrs. Marks' sister. And he's a married man."

"Yes, ma'am." Grant wrote furiously in his notebook, but kept his eye on Judith, not wanting to miss a second of the woman's body language. Grant looked for fangs, sure he'd spot them.

"Follow their evil trail and you'll find who you're after. Sinners always find their due. Now, if you'll let me finish my work. I have no desire to lay eyes on any members of this family today or any other day. I need to be out of here soon."

Grant excused himself and added mental notes to the interview, asking himself a question or twenty. Did Judith hold spite toward this family for any justifiable reason, or was she just another viper tangled in the wheel? Would she have reason to kill Peter?

Would Jeffry, or Beth? He'd check on Beth's trip. Verify Jeffry's schedule from last night. Find out where Peter fit in the mix.

Jeffry

Jeffry pulled into the airport cell lot then double-checked the status of Beth's flight. Still on schedule.

Truth be told, Peter's death had come at a good time with Beth away and not privy to all the gossip. The local morning news shows had carried stories about the murder, telling and retelling the same stories for hours, and nurses at the hospital had gathered in little knots all day, nattering, conjecturing who might've done such a thing. Jeffry wondered if GMA had done their homework before broadcasting the story of Peter's murder. They'd aired the usual 'he was a good man, loved everyone' pap. Loved everyone, indeed. Guys like Peter gave men a bad name. The stories he could have supplied would have made The National Enquirer blush. Jeffry found mustering sympathy for a miserable guy like the so-called "marriage guru," difficult.

On second thought, he was no better than Peter. The realization hit him like a sharp kick in the balls. He was no better than a cockroach—an unimportant, scared, floundering shell of a man who couldn't grab hold of his emotions if his life depended on it. House of glass. Two stones. He'd become wrapped up in his professional power, just like Magness, and strayed. Looking back disgusted him. How easily he'd become removed from what really mattered. Could've just as easily been him as Peter.

These past few days, home with the kids while Beth was away, he'd actually been happy, centered and at peace in a way he hadn't been since he and Beth tied the knot. Yet he'd wandered away from his marriage without a blink. At least there was time to make things right. Especially now that Peter was so conveniently out of the triangle.

The kids sang in the back seat. The same song, over and over again. Screeching at the top of their lungs. His head throbbed. Childrearing was not a vocation he wanted to tackle solo. He couldn't wait to see his wife, and hand the little cherubs over for a while.

☙

Brea

Brea slept until jarred awake by the plane's wheels as they kissed the runway at Detroit Metro Airport. Her phone returned to life and she texted Jeffry while heading for the exit door.

The phone vibrated a few seconds later with a message: "On our way."

As she stood on the sidewalk outside the terminal, shivering despite the unseasonable warmth, a horn beeped. She waved and smiled when she saw Ella's face pressed against the window of the van. Swells of love rose inside her.

Jeffry pulled up and rushed out of the car. His warm gaze felt genuine and a smile lit up his face. He jogged around to meet her, practically sweeping her into his arms. The force of his embrace surprised her, but she cuddled into him. And when his lips brushed her cheek, she relished his touch. Within a second he held her at arm's length and took inventory. "You look great, maybe even a bit rested."

Brea blushed at his compliment. "Good to see you, too."

He placed a happy-to-see-you kiss on her cheek, and hugged her again.

Brea savored his touch, ashamed at how hungry she was for human contact. "Let me see my kids," she interrupted. "I've missed them."

"Of course," Jeffry said.

He stepped out of her path, rushed ahead and opened the rear door of the van to load the baggage. Both Jack and Ella yipped and shouted, "Momma! Momma!"

Car seats restrained them, but Brea gathered their chubby little hands into her own. "I'm the luckiest mom in the world." She leaned in and kissed their cheeks. Such softness.

"Did you bring us prizes?" Jack asked.

Jeffry piped up, "Now then, let's not worry about the prizes."

Brea twisted around and did a double-take. "Who's kidding who? Prizes are the most important part of Momma coming home."

Jeffry arched his brows as Brea buckled up in the back between the two car seats. He climbed into the driver's seat.

"Chauffeur Daddy, at your service. Let's hurry home so we can check out what Momma brought you." Jeffry smiled in the rear-view mirror then pulled out into the line of traffic and headed for the freeway.

Brea couldn't keep her face off the kids. She delighted in their antics, pretending her hand was a puppet, and using a tinny high-pitched voice, asking each of them about their favorite song. They each made their own hand puppet and changed their voices too.

She began to sing "The Wheels on the Bus." Jack and Ella joined in without skipping a beat.

Then, as quickly as the pleasant scene began, the entire situation fell to pieces. Jack began to screech uncontrollably.

"What's wrong, sweetie?"

Jeffry offered an explanation. "I'm afraid we were up past our bedtime again last night."

In spite of Brea's attempts to calm Jack, his wails escalated. The half-hour ride home lasted an arduous eternity. Her head began to pound. Jeffry, his usual speed-demon self, didn't help matters, although she assumed he sped in an effort to shorten the agony. He parked in the garage, then lifted the rear door to retrieve Brea's luggage while she unbuckled the kids and unloaded them from the minivan.

"Inside, you two," she said briskly.

Jeffry came up behind her and patted her bottom. She jerked in surprise. Married habits were far more curious than she'd imagined.

Jeffry brought her luggage and bags into the family room, placing the souvenir package at her feet. Already seated on the floor with Jack and Ella, she carefully untied the bag and lifted out the sturdy box with the train set, followed by a bubble-wrapped baby doll. She placed the box before Jack as he jumped up and down.

Jeffry helped Jack undo the packaging while Brea pulled away the paper on the doll and gently unwound the wrapper from its body. Ella's hands flapped with anticipation, and Brea's joy rooted in her heart. In spite of her hectic arrival, she was home, with her family.

The kids quickly became preoccupied with their new toys. Jeffry excused himself and strolled out of the room, looking like a Cheshire cat—all knowing, smug, secretive. He returned a few moments later, toting a bottle of wine, a corkscrew, and two stemmed wine glasses.

A shiver trailed down Brea's spine, a grateful shiver. Jeffry wasn't just attractive, but kind. A genuinely thoughtful guy who appeared to love his kids and his wife. He'd spent time in the house while she was away, setting out flowers and buying some of her favorite snacks. He'd handled the final details of discharging Judith. Brea soaked up the comfort and the freedom. She took in the scene as he poured the ink-colored liquid into goblets. The kids played happily in front of a roaring fire, the hominess of the scene both comforting and secure. With practice, she could make this work. And clearly, she'd lost all touch with reality.

When Jack grabbed the remote, she didn't move to stop him. Five minutes of TV and he'd be napping, which was what he needed. The TV blared to life in a CBS Newsbreak. "...Dr. Peter Magness was killed in the early morning hours outside his home—"

Jack's finger hit a button; the squawk of cartoon animals interrupted.

A frightening thought jabbed her reverie. What if Jeffry had killed Peter? She had laid her suspicions about his ulterior motives of wanting Beth dead to rest, but without logic or solid evidence. And Jeffry had never struck her as one to forgive easily. *Step lightly, Brea.*

Jeffry offered her a glass and clinked his against hers. "To a new beginning," he said.

"To new beginnings," she agreed.

Within the hour, she and Jeffry had dressed Jack and Ella in their pajamas and tucked them into bed, Ella still clutching her baby doll to her chest. Brea closed the door, weary and drained. She exhaled a heavy sigh. The day had finally caught up with her.

As she and Jeffry faced each other in the hallway, she averted her eyes.

"Come to bed?" he asked.

The question hung in the air. Her answer would either be a closed door or a portal.

Brea summoned her courage. "I'm going to sit up for a while, sip my wine. I'm afraid I'm coming down from the trip. I'm not sure I made the right decision," she said, buying a little more time. Necessary time.

"About the condo? Look, there's no reason to rush. Holding onto it for a while longer doesn't pose any problems. We're good."

Brea's throat closed. Thoughtful. Respectful. She added those positive attributes to the list of the Jeffry surprises. But even then, she wasn't ready to head off to bed with him. He was Beth's husband, not hers.

"And about sleeping together? I understand I might be rushing things," he added. "I know we have a lot to talk about. And, just so you know, I was talking about sleep, not sex."

Something urged her toward him. Like a lodestone. Not animal magnetism but a need for connectedness, to the kids, to a family, to the world. She grasped his hand and led him back to her bedroom. While he sat on the side of the bed and removed his clothes, she slipped into the bathroom, freshened up and donned a clean flannel nightgown. When she returned to the bedroom and climbed into bed, soft snores filled the room. She snuggled into him and pulled his arm around her middle, intertwining fingers and inhaling a momentary peace.

Becoming Beth.

Far more complicated than she had fooled herself into thinking.

CHAPTER THIRTY-FOUR

Brea

A TEMPTING AROMA ROUSED BREA TO FULL WAKEFULNESS. She opened her eyes, trying to make sense of her surroundings. A mug of piping hot coffee sat on the night table next to her.

She swallowed hard. A moment of embarrassment flushed her cheeks as she recalled her disappointment in finding Jeffry asleep when she came to bed. He hadn't been joking about sleep. The thought brought a grin to her face.

Screw all the suspicions. Screw Beth and Peter.

Thanks to Jack, she climbed the steps a minute later. He called out for her and the day began, doing what she was meant to do. She tousled his hair and brought him into her arms. "Morning, buddy. Hungry?"

Jack rubbed his eyes, nodded, and snuggled his face into her neck.

Brea heard substantial footsteps enter the room. Jeffry, dressed and ready for work, kissed the top of her head and reached out to take Jack.

"C'mon, little man," he said. "I'll carry you downstairs for Momma."

"Breakfast, coming right up," she said.

Jeffry poured more coffee while Brea emptied cereal into a bowl and flooded the circular o's with milk. Weird, but normal.

Be watchful, but settle into this at the same time. Always commit to normal. The new normal.

Ella padded into the kitchen and crooned her good mornings. She climbed into her seat and waited as Brea filled her bowl. She didn't like milk on her cereal. Brea placed a small glass of milk beside Ella's bowl. "Milk on the side, my dear."

"Go get a shower," Jeffry urged. "I've got a few minutes."

"Really?"

"Really." He pulled up a chair alongside the kids.

"Can I thank you again for getting rid of Judith? The woman creeped me out."

"Not a problem. We can hire a new housekeeper in a few weeks if we want. I figured we needed some time alone to regroup."

Regroup. That's one word for it.

Brea took advantage of the chance to get a head start. One of the most difficult challenges she faced was getting the kids ready each morning, especially on days she had to drop Ella off at school without looking like she wore a fright wig in the drop-off loop.

She reappeared half an hour later, showered, hair styled, make-up applied, and peeked in on the kids in the family room. They played quietly with toys while Jeffrey tidied up the kitchen.

"You look nice." Jeffry passed her a nod of approval as he loaded cereal bowls into the dishwasher.

Warmth flooded her cheeks. "Thanks."

He wrapped his arms around her in a lingering embrace. "I've got to hit the dusty trail."

Brea offered him her cheek as he came in for a kiss, not avoiding him exactly, but measuring her encouragement. "I'm looking forward to seeing you later."

"I'll call and let you know when I'm about to finish up."

"Sounds like a plan."

"Don't let these guys run you into the ground."

"I'll try not to." Brea knew the day could go any of six hundred different ways. "I'm going to steal another cup of coffee while they're happy."

Jeffry closed the door behind him as Brea settled in at the table, gazing out at the backyard. The landscape displayed solid signs of spring. Overnight, it seemed. Bright red tulips bloomed along the perimeter, the stunning forsythia painting a yellow background. She swung her legs onto the chair next to her and stretched, lifting her arms above her head, noticing how her body seemed to be co-operating in unfamiliar ways. At last, she was healing. She inhaled deeply, treasuring a moment's peace.

As if on cue, a stentorian thud echoed from the family room. Screams erupted on the following beat.

Here we go.

The shrieks came from Jack, and she prayed there was no real emergency.

Ella sat on the floor playing, ignoring her brother. Jack held his hands over his face, screeching words Brea didn't understand.

"Did you fall?" she asked. She looked over at Ella. "Did he fall?"

Ella chattered to her dolls, oblivious, while Brea soothed Jack. She checked him over, but saw no signs of blood, ran her hands through his hair, and found no lumps on his head.

"You're fine." She brushed him off and gestured to his train. He continued his death grip to her thigh.

The phone rang in the kitchen. Brea scanned the family room for the extension, but didn't spot one. She needed, albeit gradually, to make the house more her own.

She settled Jack. "Play," she commanded him. "Momma has to answer the phone."

Brea checked the Caller ID, but didn't recognize the number. City of AA glowed on the read out. "Hello?"

"Is this Elizabeth Marks?" a male voice asked.

Brea brushed tousled curls back from her face. "Yes."

"This is Grant Fulton. Sorry to phone so early…"

Brea cut him off, the quick fluttering in her chest nearing explosive proportions. "Not a problem."

"I wonder if I could stop by in a little while. I have some questions for you." An awkward silence followed. "About Peter Magness."

Brea's heart battered her ribs.

"Sure," she said, gulping in a quick slug of air, "but I have children. Talking around them may prove challenging, if you know what I mean."

"I understand."

"Why don't I make arrangements for a sitter and call you back?"

"Thank you," Grant said before reciting his number.

Brea hung up, then inhaled a steadying breath. The thought of satisfying his questions, those she had no answers for, made her wish she still fit under the bed. After all, she didn't know when the affair between Beth and Peter had begun. An idea sparked: Be sure of the timeline before Grant's interview. Act confident.

Brea willed herself into motion. She hurried into the family room and turned on the TV. Keeping the kids occupied while she researched proved essential. Then, she entered the study, reached for the phone, and scrolled down to Dana's number. She punched the dial button. As she waited for the call to connect, she pulled up Beth's phone records on the computer.

She remembered what she'd found the last time she looked them over. A year ago May, there had been twenty or more calls. Because she didn't have much time, she accessed the preceding January's records, six months before she moved to Hilton Head.

"Hi, Mrs. Marks." Dana's answer startled her.

"Any chance you could watch the kids in an hour or so? I have to run some errands."

"Sure thing. I don't have classes today."

"Perfect." Brea glanced at the clock to assess the time she needed. "Does forty-five minutes work?"

Brea hung up the phone and returned her attention to the computer screen. She recorded the timeline on her notepad, just to let it sink into her brain. A notion occurred to her. Check Beth's calendar. That way, if Grant asked, she could tell him what she was doing. Brea pulled the schedule up on the screen. February. February. What was Beth doing on Valentine's Day? Had she met with Peter, too? Her heart sank. Initials. P.M. Sure, the abbreviation could have meant she had something in the afternoon, but Brea knew better. Way better.

Between her, Beth, and his wife, Peter Magness must have been a busy, busy man. The psychologist in her guessed he must have distanced himself after she made the decision to move away. Perhaps in anticipation of her departure, he'd hooked up with Beth. A fitting replacement. And also a possible explanation she could give Grant. He would almost certainly ask when and how she'd become involved with Peter. Their texting had begun later in March and ramped up in April. By June, when Brea moved to Hilton Head, the texts leveled off to one or two each day.

Grant would want to know, if he didn't already, where they met for their trysts. Doubtful she could coax the information out of him before he asked her. No good detective would reveal what he knew. Grant was smart and savvy. He always had been. Thank goodness she could prove she'd been in Hilton Head when Peter had died, and verify her whereabouts. Her goosebumps disappeared. At least she could supply him with a valid alibi.

But he'd have questions about Peter's visit. The truth actually worked in that instance. Imagine. The truth. Peter had come to coax her back into a relationship. She turned him down. End of story.

After jotting down the months and calculating the number of phone calls and texts for each, she Googled the local newspaper for the details of Peter's death, to discern what the police knew so far. Early reports indicated the homicide investigators conjectured the killer might be a disgruntled client of Peter's. A likely scenario, she agreed. Or Cynthia. Surely, Grant would look into the possibility.

She clenched her teeth.

She shut down the PC and scurried to check on the kids. The quiet alarmed her.

Their eyes stayed glued to the TV set. Brea dressed them while they remained in their cartoon-induced stupor. "I need to go out for a little while, and Dana is coming over to play with you," she said. They absently agreed.

She returned Grant's call, her stomach in loops as she arranged to meet him at the Starbucks on Main Street. After a quick check of her hair in the bathroom mirror, she set out lunch supplies on the kitchen counter.

Five minutes later, the doorbell rang. Dana. Brea let her in.

"How are you?"

Dana set her things down without answering. She seemed… distracted.

"Is something wrong?" Brea asked.

"I feel so bad about Peter." She bit her lip, then corrected herself. "Dr. Magness, I mean."

"Yes, what a tragedy," Brea said, "very sad news."

"I know he was…a friend of yours. I'm sorry for your loss."

"Thank you," Brea said, then hurried through instructions, her brain churning. Something about the girl's face. Sadness and grief etched there.

Jack hugged her leg and she kissed him goodbye. On the drive to Starbucks, she cautioned herself to listen to Grant before jumping to answer, and to respond to his questions generically without too much detail—and pray to God he didn't see through her lies.

She parked in the city garage and speed-walked, as quickly as she was able, the city block to the coffee shop. Grant sat at a corner table near the back of the store. He wore a navy blazer and khaki trousers. With his blond hair trimmed short, he looked like a cop. As Brea drew closer, she detected a sliver of silver at the edge of his sideburns and caught herself smoothing her hair. His eyes crinkled at the corners when he saw her, and her heart melted a little, seeing the young man he once was in the curve of his smile.

Grant stood as she approached. "Buy you a cup of coffee?" he asked.

"I've had enough coffee to fuel a tanker, but water would be great." She fidgeted uncontrollably as he excused himself, rubbing her nose, jiggling her leg.

When he returned, he set a bottle of water in front of her. "Thanks for meeting with me," he said.

"No problem."

Brea gazed into his pale blue eyes and relaxed. This was Grant, not some cop she didn't know. Then, her gaze dropped down to his hand. No wedding ring.

"I know you're just coming off of your own tragedy here. And I'm sorry for your loss."

"Thank you," Brea replied.

"I have to admit, your sister's death has been a blow for me, too. I'm sure this might not make sense to you, but as I mentioned at the funeral, your sister meant a lot to me."

"And you meant a great deal to her." Brea's eyes softened, and she took a moment to study Grant. He was the guy she'd been most in love with. In the entire world. In her entire life. Even though they were young at the time, their relationship had been something special. This was a problem. Of gigantic proportions. She might still be in love with him.

Brea distracted herself and looked around. This Starbucks resembled every other one.

"Unfortunately, I need to ask you a few questions regarding Peter Magness."

"I understand," Brea said, fixing her gaze on him. She sipped her water as he opened his spiral notebook and reviewed his notes.

He offered her a nervous smile. "This is a little awkward since we know each other, but I hope we can get through the interview without too much discomfort."

Brea clutched her hands in her lap. "I'm sure you want to know about my association with Peter."

"Yes," Grant said, his surprise at her directness evident. "I do need to know about your relationship."

A beam of sunlight landed on her, as if she'd been singled out by a laser. "As I'm sure you've already figured out, my sister was involved with him for several years. Not only did they share a professional relationship, but a highly personal one as well."

Grant scribbled notes in his spiral.

"And then I'm sure you've discovered Peter and I were lovers, too."

His eyes widened.

Brea shrugged. "If you already know, there's no sense...forcing you to beat the sordid details out of me."

"Right," Grant said, shifting in his chair. "Want to fill me in?"

"Understandably, I'd rather this didn't become public. The gossip wouldn't serve anyone well. Things with Peter ended some time ago."

"Since the accident?"

"Pretty much."

"I imagine, considering both you and Brea were involved with Dr. Magness, your relationship with your sister became complicated at best."

Her stomach lurched. Grant couldn't hold her-as-Beth responsible for the accident. Her mind sped like a runaway train. He thought she caused the accident. Got rid of Brea. So she could have Peter all to herself. She had never imagined this scenario.

"Um, no, I don't think so," Brea answered slowly, hesitantly, as she ran her fingernail along the grooves of the bottle cap.

"No?" Grant asked.

Brea took a deep breath. "I don't believe B ... Brea was not aware of my relationship with Peter."

"What makes you think so?"

Brea met his gaze.

"Peter and I initially got together around Beth's—I'm sorry—Brea's departure. Sorry," she added, biting her lip, "I've been making that mistake since the accident. Getting Brea's and my names mixed up...twins, I guess, overlapping identities, the hit on the head..." Her voice trailed off, and she laughed unsteadily. "He was upset with Brea for initiating their break up. It was over a year ago." Tears began to stream down her face, as involuntary as breathing.

"I'm sorry," Grant said, reaching across the table and then stopping abruptly before he touched her. "I've upset you."

Brea rummaged through her purse for a tissue, blew her nose, and regrouped.

She cleared her throat. "I feel guilty about my relationship with Peter," she admitted. "At the time, I was lonely, things were tough at home, but I should have known better. What I did was wrong. I can only hope…she never suspected."

"Would she have confronted you?" Grant leaned forward. Not threatening, but focused. "Families differ a lot. Some siblings go at each other like boxers in a ring, while others seethe silently or talk about each other behind their backs. What were you and Brea like?"

Brea sat back in her chair and took stock, wrapping her arms tightly around her chest. What an interesting question. Now she really had to put herself in Beth's shoes and wonder what Beth's life had been like. The Beth who'd had an affair with Peter. Beth would have worried Brea would discover the truth. But if confronted, Beth would have lied. No question.

Not a subject she ever wanted to think about. But now she had to.

A shiver sliced down her arms. "What were we like?" she asked, repeating his question.

"Did you fight?"

"We were best friends." Sadness spilled throughout her voice. "I thought we were. But best friends don't do things like this to each other, do they?" Her question was introspective. The thought hit her like a gut punch. Brea's face burned with shame. "Not much of a way to treat my sister. Or Jeffry for that matter. Guess we were all a mess. Maybe we still are. All clamoring for a meaningful connection, but in all the wrong places and in the most convoluted ways. This must sound like a soap opera to you. A cluster of gigantic proportions."

Grant waited. Brea had sunk back into her chair, either pondering the unanswered question, or closing in on herself.

She peered at the ceiling. "We didn't ever really fight," she continued. "We had this idealistic relationship, like harmony in a song, we told ourselves we were more perfect than any other twosome as we were growing up. We said we complemented each other perfectly…like salt and pepper. The same but different, both bringing something special to whatever we did. As if the two of us together were better than either of us alone."

"You were so identical," Grant said.

Brea straightened with tension.

"Hardly anyone could tell you apart," he added.

Brea couldn't control the goosebumps on her arms. "I guess not."

Grant could. He always knew. Even before he'd become a cop.

"I didn't know you as well as your sister, but I remember you fighting."

Brea's mouth gaped. "You do?"

"There were times Brea turned an unattractive shade of green."

Speaking of green, Brea felt her skin turn inside out. "Probably typical teenage stuff. Can't say I remember that…"

"Did you feel the brakes were working properly the night of the accident?"

Brea double-clutched. Did Grant consider her responsible for Beth's death? She fought her memories. She remembered hitting the brakes. Hard. She couldn't recall if they'd worked.

"Everything happened so fast."

"Right," Grant said, an air of suspicion in his tone.

"You had other questions about Peter?" Brea prompted. She could hardly control the shaking of her legs, even when she placed her hands on her knees and pressed with all her might.

"Yes. When did you last see him?"

"I can't lie, and this is incredibly awkward considering Peter's death, but he came to Hilton Head to see me the day he died." She sank back into her chair and the air rushed out of her.

"Really?"

"Yes," Brea said. "I figured you'd already discovered his trip."

"Tell me more. Was this an arranged meeting?"

"No, not at all." This was her big chance. Time to be as truthful as she possibly could. "I'd been ignoring Peter's attempts to contact me since the accident. Jeffry and I are trying to put our marriage back together, and my sister's death put things into perspective for me. Not unusual for anyone who's lost someone so close, I suppose."

Grant's eyes grew concerned, like those of a sympathetic friend.

"I can't even begin to describe the loss. It's like I've sliced off a limb, and sometimes, a piece of my sanity as well. I'm still struggling with my physical challenges, the demands of raising two small children, trying to find a moment to grieve, but I don't even know how. After my parents died, I…" Brea stopped herself. She was speaking as Brea, this was dangerous territory. "Wait, I'm going to tell you the truth instead of pretending. I fell apart." She explained how Brea had taken care of her, seen to it she got through school. "I'm the weaker of our twosome." Brea stared at her water bottle and noticed goosebumps rise to welts on her arms. Before long she'd break out in hives. "I feel so guilty about the accident." She swallowed hard and fought to continue.

"Take your time," Grant said.

"I have to be strong now. I have no choice. When Peter showed up, I saw him differently. Guess you could say I finally took off the rose-colored glasses. I was past playing the cheerleader role for him any longer. Plus, his wife is pregnant. I don't need any more drama in my life. I want to focus on my family, not some torrid affair. I'd derailed for a while, but I'm back on track."

"How do you know his wife is pregnant?"

"She dropped by. Delivered the news personally. She followed up a day later by attending a luncheon at my home. Through some awkward twist of fate, she joined the Women's City Club and it was my turn to host the group. She didn't miss the chance to broadcast her pregnancy."

"You know Cynthia well?"

"Not really," she answered truthfully. "Mostly just through Peter's woe-is-me stories and her ugly display at my sister's wake. Her recent membership in the Women's City Club seemed a bit coincidental, considering. She made it her business to be in my home, which doesn't make much sense, unless she was on a treasure hunt, but she didn't seem to know I'd been involved with Peter, just about Peter and Brea having been lovers."

Brea took a minute to recall the conversation. "She accused my sister of ruining her marriage."

"How did you feel about that?"

"Relieved."

"Because?"

"Because she didn't seem to know about my affair with Peter, but she did want to know who broke off the relationship, Brea or Peter. She became a tad hysterical, which was understandable considering the circumstances, but I thought she was a bit over the top. And she made a point of telling me she was pregnant. She used the information like a weapon, a dagger plunged straight into the jugular."

"Why?"

Brea became thoughtful. "I don't know. I guess she wanted revenge. She wanted her husband back."

"Did she get him back?"

"I have no idea," Brea said. "When I saw Peter in Hilton Head, he didn't seem too keen on her, but he has a penchant for lies."

"When did you and Peter call it quits?"

Brea didn't know what to say. She hesitated. "I tried breaking things off with Peter several times," she said, her tone confiding. "Not only was I having an affair with my sister's lover, but both Peter and I were married. Things became far too complicated. Believe it or not, much as I'm to blame, I struggled to distance myself from the relationship. But I cared for Peter. He was quite remarkable." A cleaver sliced her open. *If Jeffry knew of Beth's pregnancy, did Grant as well? Is he trying to trick me? Does he think I somehow set up the entire accident? Did he imagine I'd tried to kill us both, but my plans were ruined and I miraculously survived? Calm down, Brea. You're letting guilt play tricks on you. Too many Dateline episodes.*

"In what way?" Grant's eyes narrowed.

Brea shifted in her chair, and struggled to regain her composure. "He was brilliant. I found his intelligence quite alluring. Magnetizing, really."

"So he was a smart guy," Grant said.

"You're understating his abilities."

"A ladies' man?"

"Certainly."

"Do you think there were other women?"

Brea winced. "From a logical perspective, yes. If I had to guess, I'd say several." Tears gathered on her lashes as anger began to slice through her. "Sorry. This is far more difficult than I imagined."

"I know. And I'm sorry to be the one to put you through more heartache, but I thought…better me than a total stranger."

Brea bit her lip and brought her hand to her mouth.

"I have one more difficult question."

"Yes?" Brea asked, the color draining from her skin.

"Was Dr. Marks aware of your affair with Peter?"

"Jeffry?" Brea's eyes read the grain of the table. "Yes, but just recently. He confronted me, not confronted really, but told me he knew. He was quite gentle really. Jeffry strayed too, you see. He was involved with a nurse. I believe her name was Tammy. Tamara Hawthorne, at least that's my theory. She's a nurse at the hospital." Brea toyed with telling Grant about Tammy's threats, but decided that might lead to more questions about Jeffry. As Beth, she couldn't risk setting Jeffry up for undue scrutiny. If Grant thought Tammy and Jeffry were complicit in a scheme to kill her, then he would also think Jeffry wasn't above murder. "Jeffry and I are trying to be married again, and he's been beyond understanding."

Brea fell silent, the seconds growing to minutes as she stared down at the table.

"That's quite an extraordinary reaction. Most men wouldn't understand, even if they had drifted. Do you find his reaction puzzling?"

"Surprising."

Grant wrote furiously in his notebook.

Brea sat quietly, pensively, saddening with every passing moment.

Grant finally looked up, and Brea locked onto his gaze.

"What's wrong?"

She picked at the table edge with a nail. "I miss my sister."

"I miss her, too," Grant said. "As a matter of fact, I've just come to realize how much." He paused, took a breath. "Let's consider the interview over. I'd like to ask you something. Person to person."

Brea's eyes met his.

"Was she happy?" Grant asked.

Brea took a moment, then answered. "As happy as she could be, I think. She made the best of things after our parents died. Really, I think she blamed herself, like all kids do when something bad happens to their parents."

"But they were killed in a car accident. I told her it wasn't her fault."

"I don't know what to tell you. I just know she took responsibility for their deaths."

"Did she ever get past it?"

"Sort of, I guess."

"Sort of?"

"I think their deaths were one of the reasons she became a therapist."

"Really," Grant said. "I suppose a tragedy could lead to such a choice."

"She may have thought psychology would help her find her way, figure herself out. And maybe, at the same time, she was giving back what she thought she had taken away."

"I'm not sure I follow."

Brea couldn't imagine she had anything to lose by sharing this part of her life with Grant. The story poured out of her, her mom's affair, how her dad found the letter.

"Dad was so angry, he barely said goodbye. And then, well, then they had the accident. Both of them died instantly." Brea stopped, searched inside her bag for a tissue, and dabbed at the tears streaming down her cheeks. "You knew."

"Yes. I can't tell you how sorry I am. I know the pain of losing someone close."

"You do? Who? Your parents?"

"No. My partner. A while ago."

"How long?"

"A few years." Grant stopped and calculated. "Two years, eleven months and six days to be exact."

"Not so long ago," Brea said. "What happened?"

"Domestic dispute," Grant said. "Dave Johnson, my patrol partner at the time…was a gentle giant. A guy you didn't want to cross, although he had a heart the size of Texas. Dave got between the man and his wife, wrestled with the guy. Dave's gun went off. A couple of times. I was hit in the leg, but Dave took one to the chest. He made it to the hospital, but they couldn't save him."

The lump in Brea's throat grew. She could imagine the pain Grant must have gone through. She ached for him, and wished she could tell him the truth. "Were you able to say goodbye?"

Grant instinctively rubbed his leg and nodded. "Once I got the scene under control, I called for help. I held him while we waited for the paramedics. Told him to hang on, told him help was coming. But it was too late." He stopped and scrubbed his hands over his buzz cut. "There's something about being there and feeling so helpless…. The worst part was telling his wife…relaying his last words, 'Hey, tell Gloria I love her forever.' He always told her that, whenever they spoke on the phone, 'Love you forever.'"

Tears spilled from Brea's eyes. "I have nightmares. Every night. And then I climb out of bed and put on my game face." She paused.

"I hear the crash of metal on metal. If I could have a do-over…" She wiped the tears away with the sleeve of her blouse.

Grant's lips pressed into a thin line. "The replay. I know. You have to let yourself off the hook."

"You, too." Brea swiped a tissue across her nose, gazing at him sympathetically.

Grant reached for her, squeezed her hand, and then settled back in his chair. "Can I ask you one more thing? Then I'll let you go."

"Sure."

"Did she ever talk about me? Ever miss me?"

"All the time," Brea said, speaking from her heart. "Losing you was one of her greatest regrets."

CHAPTER THIRTY-FIVE

Grant

GRANT LEANED BACK IN HIS CHAIR AFTER BETH LEFT. FLOODED with a mix of emotions, he questioned his intelligence. He was somehow never completely objective after spending time with Beth Marks. Visiting with her today had caused his heart to flop like a fish on dry land.

Everything about her spoke of Brea—her looks, mannerisms, the inflections in her voice. As soon as he spotted her rushing down the street toward the coffee shop, the shared past between him and Brea had swept over him like a tidal wave. The same catch in his heart from twenty-three years ago—whenever he spotted her in the football stands, or in the school hallway when he was on his way to class—happened today. He'd always been somewhat indifferent to Beth. Telling them apart had been innate. As natural as breathing. They'd been able to fool others, but not him. He had the same reaction earlier today.

He longed to turn back time, but to be a few years older and wise enough that they could have built their puppy love into a life-long match. As hard as he tried to shake his reaction, the heartbreak lingered and tormented him. He pored over his notes, realizing the heartache in Beth's answers.

He couldn't imagine the pain of losing an identical twin. Beth's guilt, living with the fact she'd been the driver, would follow her the rest of her life. Grant knew too much about survivor's guilt not to feel compassion for her.

Beth probably felt as if she'd lost an enormous part of herself. And her obvious symptoms of post-traumatic stress syndrome—she faced so many hurdles. He didn't envy her.

Grant returned to his exhaustive notes.

Judith's alibi had checked out, she'd been home asleep the night of the murder. Her husband had verified that, and Grant had no reason to doubt the man. They lived in a small ranch on the west side of Ann Arbor, and the guy had no registered weapons. He'd been inundated with religion during his visit, enough to last a few hundred years.

Beth was indeed out of town as she claimed to be at the time of the murder, Grant had checked her whereabouts after interviewing Judith, so she wasn't a suspect. Somehow, he needed to assess if Beth was back with her husband. Really back with him, considering Judith said she hadn't been sleeping in the master suite. And then pursue questioning Jeffry. Jealousy served as the perfect motive for murder. Grant made a note to check Jeffry's alibi. He knew Jeffry was supposed to have been at the hospital on the night of the slaying. But, the good doctor had apparently known about his wife's affair with Magness. No guy liked to admit his wife had slept with another man. And maybe the decision to play things cool was part of his plan to kill his wife's lover.

Grant remembered seeing Beth with Jeffry at the funeral, noticing their heads together a couple of times. But experience told him never to assume. He'd need a warrant to check Jeffry's cell records and learn when the texts and phone calls to a woman named Tamara Hawthorne had ended. Killing his wife's lover after breaking up with his mistress made no sense. But people routinely did inane things.

And then there was Cynthia Magness, the widow. He disliked the woman. So did Shaun, but his partner was an opinionated guy. Shaun detested people with money on general principle. Grant tabled thoughts of Cynthia…for now, even though she'd landed a top spot on the suspect list.

Checking Peter's schedule was a good place to start. Had he gone to Hilton Head, or been at a symposium as Cynthia stated?

Beth's answers required his focus. Maybe she could lead him to the killer. Plus, he wouldn't mind spending a little more time with her. He found the closeness, the physical proximity in and of itself, soothing in a weird and inexplicable way.

He was pleased Beth had been so forthright about her affair with Magness. Confirming facts proved much speedier than unearthing them. He gave her points for being candid. What wowed him about Beth, though, was the fact she had slept with her sister's ex-lover. Peter must have been one happy man, living every guy's fantasy. Grant didn't know whether to hate guys like Magness or admire them.

One thing he did agree with Peter on was his choice to become involved with Brea.

Grant's last memory of her, still painfully vivid, included a forced smile as she spun around to wave goodbye after their mutual break up. Brea's sad grin turned up at the edges, dimpling freckled cheeks as her green eyes glistened with tears. Smiling in the face of heartache. The image tugged at him even now. And their hungry kiss before the goodbye—the heat of her lips on his—returned this minute in the twist of his pounding heart.

Then he thought back to the telltale mark, which distinguished one twin from the other, all those years ago. The faint crescent moon birthmark on Brea's stomach, which he had keenly discovered long before he'd become a detective, when they wore their bikinis. Telling them apart was almost impossible. Maybe Peter couldn't really tell the difference, or talked himself into believing Beth was Brea. He might have become involved with Beth as a replacement. Hell, Grant realized, *I'm fighting the same inclination.*

Get your head back in the game, man. The money. He checked his phone. He'd better hustle back to the station and get caught up on the investigation. Maybe Shaun had some luck on his end.

CHAPTER THIRTY-SIX

Brea

A LIGHT DRIZZLE CAUSED BREA TO QUICKEN HER PACE AND hurry to the parking garage. After tucking herself into the car, she called home. "Hey, Dana. How are things?"

"Fine," Dana said abruptly.

"Are you sure?"

"I'm fine, the kids are fine."

"You don't sound fine," Brea said, the therapist emerging.

Dana remained quiet for a second, as if composing herself. "I'm having some personal problems. Things with Derek aren't going well. I'm sorry if I sounded curt."

Brea relaxed her grip on the steering wheel. "No worries. I'm sorry about your man trouble. Relationships are never easy. Anything I can help with?"

"Don't worry," Dana replied. "I'll be okay. He's stopping by in a few. We'll work things out. And if we don't, that's fine too."

"I just phoned to be sure all was well with the kids. Would you mind if I took another couple of hours? I'd like to run a few more errands."

"I have all the time in the world." Now she sounded sarcastic.

"Right, then I'll be two, three hours at the most."

Brea heaved a sigh, made a left hand turn after paying the weathered attendant, and wondered what to do with her time. The unexpected rain took away the option of sitting on a park bench to compose her thoughts. She was kidding herself. Fighting to control her emotions was the real issue.

She cracked a window as she drove north on Main Street, and breathed in the scent of the spring rain shower. Seeing Grant had been difficult. Instinct had told her to spill everything, confess her decisions, and ask his opinions. And forgiveness. She wanted so badly to confide in someone, someone who really knew her. As if the witness relocation program had whisked her off, she'd had little-or-no time to prepare before disappearing.

There were so many things in her life she regretted. Back at Starbucks when she told Grant she regretted having missed her chance with him, she'd never been more serious.

Grant sensed their connection, too. She could feel it.

She pushed out a breath and drove aimlessly, losing track of time and place. By the next time she glanced at her dashboard clock, she realized she'd been driving for almost an hour.

The Lifetime movie she lived was headed for a dreadful ending. Tears leaked down her cheeks. She yearned for a relationship without guilt and desperation like with Peter, and without obligation like with Jeffry. She wanted to touch and be with a man out of simple love and need the way she felt with Grant.

She pushed the Bluetooth dial on her dash. Then she tapped Jeffry's name. A soft ringtone did its work.

"Beth?" he answered. "Is something wrong?"

"Um…maybe. I'm not sure yet. Don't panic. I'm fine. The kids are fine. I'm just having a serious off day. I'm out running errands." She stopped herself. "No, I'm not running errands. I just met with Grant Fulton, the detective who is working on the Peter Magness case. He had some questions for me. I'm not sure how you feel about any of this, but talking to Grant was unnerving, and made me realize I'd like to…I don't know…I wondered if you'd eaten lunch yet."

She'd start with lunch, then arrange a time to be alone with Jeffry, come clean and enlist his help in sorting out the entire disaster, stopping the madness before her ruse reached epidemic proportions.

"Lunch sounds great." Jeffry paused. "Hold on a sec. Let me check my calendar." After a few moments of silence, he said, "I have a few more appointments before I get a break. Want to meet here? Whatever's bugging you, we can sort out. Together."

"Why don't I pick up something? Bring lunch to the office." Brea asked, the knots in her gut twisting.

"Zingerman's? I'm craving a deli sandwich."

As Brea inhaled a measured breath and slowly exhaled, the weight lifted from her shoulders. "Sounds great. What would you like?"

"The usual."

Brea bit her lip. She had no idea of his "usual" choice. "I was actually thinking of trying something new. They have a sandwich of the month. Feel adventurous?" She had seen the ad in an online sidebar. Worth a shot.

"Just get me a corned beef on rye, instead. With Swiss."

"Mustard?"

Jeffry's laugh was lighthearted. "Must be your other husband who likes mustard. Mayo, remember? I'm the mayo guy."

Brea's eyes widened, glad Jeffry couldn't see the relief on her face. "Mayo, mustard, they both start with 'm.' See you in an hour or so." Soon, all the secrets would be out. Soon, she could live her life, and be free of the self-inflicted chains. She exited at the next ramp and turned around. By the time she retraced her route, picked up sandwiches, drove to the hospital, and located Jeffry's office, time would be up.

She repeated the old adage: *Live the life you want.*

CHAPTER THIRTY-SEVEN

Grant

MICHIGAN WAS ENJOYING A GENUINE SPRING FOR ONCE, the kind of spring Grant recalled from his childhood. They didn't come along so often anymore, with climate change and all. The scent of lilacs traveled with him as he jogged to the parking lot in the light rain. He experienced more energy and enjoyment than in weeks. Maybe something to do with Beth Marks, but he wasn't quite sure he could admit to his growing crush.

Shaun's text beeped as he put the car into gear. Grant read the display.

—News—

—?— He texted back.

—Bring coffee—

Twenty minutes later, Grant slid a cup of coffee and a bag of sweet rolls onto his partner's desk. "Go ahead," he said. "Put your brag on and tell me."

"Got the gun." Shaun nodded smugly as he chewed on an oversized bite of cruller.

"No way." Grant struggled with the disappointment he hadn't uncovered the weapon first. He hoped his distractions weren't costing him an edge. "Way to go. How?"

"Just this nagging feeling, a hunch really. The weapon had to be somewhere. I took Jake and his dog back to the neighborhood first thing this morning. Seemed like we'd missed something."

"Not like we have a murder weapon each and every time," Grant reminded.

"Duh."

"So, you had a hunch and you didn't call me?"

Shaun ignored him. "You know the path along Barton Pond?"

"Yup." Grant bit the inside of his cheek. The discovery of the gun was good news no matter who found the damn thing.

"Jake's dog has a nose like a…" Shaun paused to laugh at his own joke. "Right," he finished.

"So," Grant said, removing the lid of the insulated cup and sipping his black coffee, "this story's gotta be better than just finding the gun."

Shaun leaned back in his chair and folded his arms above his head, his Cheshire cat grin biting into Grant's pride. "Wanna guess?"

"No." Grant had fallen into that trap before. He shot his middle finger at Shaun with a leer. "But thanks."

"Not only did we recover the weapon, but the registration record is going to make you happy. Goddamn blessed happy. Belongs to Jeffry Marks. Dr. Jeffry Marks. Registered in 2017. Ballistics matched. We've got him."

The air rushed out of Grant. "Jeffry Marks." Made total sense. He'd dismissed the notion at one point, but after his conversation with Beth, it made perfect sense. The guy had motive. His wife was having an affair with the decedent, and the good doctor was used to having things his own way. Emotions roiled inside his gut. The city fathers would cringe at the thought of their bus bench campaign model being arrested for murder. He could hear the mayor now. "You better make goddamn sure…"

"Hey!" Shaun's voice boomed. "Where the hell are you? Got an idea?"

Grant shook off a rush of thoughts. "Nothing." He fought the urge to bang his forehead against the top of Shaun's desk.

"Motive?" Shaun asked.

"Yeah, plenty."

"Opportunity?"

"Not sure yet, but maybe."

"Too easy?"

Grant scrubbed his jaw with his hand. As convenient as pinning this on the wronged husband and tying up the case with a bow might be like grabbing the gold ring…"Right, and he's got way too much to lose. The guy's an icon. The heart campaign, his family; he's at the top of the food chain, for Christ's sake. I don't buy this. Too damn simple. And what about the money? Could be a robbery, a drug deal gone wrong, a blackmail payoff."

"Agreed," Shaun said. "But we've got to start somewhere. You're the one who always says we shouldn't ignore what's up in our face."

Grant grimaced, slumped in his chair and took a long swallow of coffee. He didn't like thinking Beth would have to suffer another crisis on the heels of her recovery from the accident and Brea's death. But everything happened for a reason, and he wouldn't mind seeing Beth again. Not one bit.

Shaun hopped up and clapped his hands together. "Let's get busy."

Grant eased out of his chair, stretched for a minute, and sat back down in front of his computer. He knew what this meant. Shaun would be conducting initial interviews while he did the grunt work. Fine with him. He'd have time to get his head back into the case.

After he rolled up his sleeves, he spent the next hour drinking bitter coffee and checking databases, calling up templates, filling out paperwork. He devoured every piece of information he unearthed about the illustrious Jeffry Marks, and printed off a few reports. He checked the criminal files, the DMV. The guy was squeaky clean. Grant neatly piled the slim stack of papers, snagged a clean manila folder, and placed everything inside. He wrote Marks' name on the tab, then tucked the sleeve in his file drawer. He checked for a lab report on the bank envelopes. Peter's prints. Cynthia's prints. Another set too. Not in the database. Probably a damn bank teller. Fine. If Marks was the guy, so be it.

Last, he established where the doctor had purchased the gun. He pulled on his jacket and drove to Howell, thirty minutes north, to speak with the owner of Gunsmith M.D., Chuck Bronson.

"Hard to forget him," Bronson said, arching heavy brows.

Hard to forget this guy, too, Grant thought. Bronson looked every bit the part. Military style haircut. Tattoos across the back of his neck and covering his bulging forearms.

"Nice guy. Doing good stuff out there. Hell, my kid ran track with the young man who keeled over and died of that undetected heart condition the doctor's campaign is all about." Bronson shook his head. "Dr. Marks was looking for protection for his family after a rash of robberies in Ann Arbor."

Nothing suspicious there. Grant thanked the man and exited the store. He'd already spoken with Shaun on his way to the gun shop, after verifying Jeffry had been signed in at the hospital the night Peter was killed. Somehow, had he left the hospital, killed Magness, and returned without anyone noticing? Could happen. There were exit doors all over the place and a lighter security staff at night.

Shaun had already spoken with the doctor's former lover, Tammy Hawthorne. She said she had broken things off with Jeffry before Peter Magness was killed, at least a month ago. Shaun was verifying her statement.

Grant glanced at his watch. Twelve-thirty. With Shaun busy, he grabbed a sandwich at a local hangout and drove back to the precinct. As he sat at his desk and took a bite of his ham and Swiss on rye, his thoughts drifted back to his conversation with Beth, her mannerisms, her slip up with her name. If he didn't know better, he would have sworn on a stack of bibles.

Beth was Brea.

He grunted in self-disgust. If only he had a bottle with a genie inside.

His cell phone vibrated. He pulled the mobile out of the tangled web of change and bills in his pocket and checked the number. "Hey," he answered.

"Hey," Shaun said. "Nothing much here."

"No?"

"Everything checked out. No bells or whistles going off."

Grant bit the inside of his cheek. "That leaves Marks. Where do you want to catch him? At the hospital or home?"

"I think his hospital office makes the most sense. Private. Professional."

Grant stood and jiggled the keys in his pocket. "Meet me there."

CHAPTER THIRTY-EIGHT

Brea

BREA SQUARED HER SHOULDERS. TIME FOR LUNCH. SHE JUGgled the Zingerman's bag, a tray of drinks, her purse, and a steady case of nerves.

Someone had done her a favor and punched the elevator button, but waiting for the doors to open in the damp chill of the concrete parking garage still made her uneasy. A few passersby acknowledged her, and Brea responded in kind, not knowing if she should be familiar with them or not. She rode the elevator to the second floor and traveled the covered bridge to the hospital offices. Jeffry's office number was listed on the business directory next to the elevators inside the main building.

"Mrs. Marks?" a sweet voice said.

As Brea studied the list of offices, the voice didn't quite register.

A hand tapped her shoulder. "Mrs. Marks?"

Brea turned. "Yes?"

She studied the young nurse. The girl couldn't have been more than twenty-five, her dark brown hair shocked with red streaks spiking from the top of her head like the cherry on a hot fudge sundae. Tiny pink elephants covered her cheery uniform jacket. A pediatric nurse. The face, the body, the demeanor…nothing seemed familiar. Her nametag had rotated on the clip, so Brea could only see blank white plastic in a clear sleeve. Panic set in.

A split-second later, she apologized, "I'm sorry. I have some memory problems since the accident. Some days I can't even re-member my own name."

"I'm Quinn," the girl said. "I heard about the accident. I'm so sorry about your sister."

Brea closed her eyes for a brief moment. "Thank you."

"How are the kids? I miss seeing them."

She must be a babysitter. "They're great. Thank you for asking. Sorry I don't have time to chat, but Jeffry's schedule is limited today and we're having a quick lunch."

"You two are so special. You instill hope—a couple so in love."

Brea masked her confusion with a weak smile. Clearly, this girl didn't know them well, but perhaps she knew something Brea didn't. Maybe she'd known Beth and Jeffry when they were first married. Back when they were in love. She shifted her purse strap on her shoulder, catching Jeffry's office number out of the corner of her eye. Fourth floor.

"Great seeing you," the girl said. "I'll have to stop by and see the kids soon."

"Please do, Quinn." Brea committed the name to memory. "Take care."

Brea followed a corn maze of directions, following the yellow line on the hallway floor to the next bank of elevators, which went to the 4th through 6th floors and waited with the other visitors for the car to arrive. A shiver ran up her spine. She exited the elevator at the fourth floor, searching for another sign. She found Jeffry's of-fice, which took up the entire corner and, she guessed, proved to be one of the largest offices in the building.

Brea stood at the entrance, unable to open the heavy glass door while balancing the packages and drinks. A patient inched up from behind her and let her in. She slowly eased inside, then, as confi-dently as she could muster, made her way to the reception desk.

"Hi," she said, glancing at the woman's nametag. "Good to see you, Diane."

"Mrs. Marks," Diane replied. "So nice to see you. Your husband mentioned he was expecting you. Let me get the door for you."

"Beth," Brea said. "Please call me Beth."

Diane rushed around the reception partition to open the door for Brea. As Diane led her down the hall, she came to an abrupt halt. "Oh," she said. "They're still here."

Brea asked, "He's with a patient?"

"No." Worry lines creased her brow.

"What's wrong?"

Diane wrung her hands. "Two gentlemen are speaking with your husband."

"No problem. I can wait. I'm in no rush."

The woman chewed her lip.

"Diane," Brea insisted. "What's wrong?"

"Nothing, I'm sure."

"Tell me."

"The police," Diane whispered. "I can't imagine why they're still here. I hate to interrupt."

"No, don't disturb them. I'll wait for Dr. Marks. No problem, really. I don't mind."

Diane took the drinks from Brea's hand and set them on a nearby table, then headed back to her desk. Brea watched, certain the woman was accustomed to important people visiting Jeffry. Even the police, when certain causes of death required answers from a medical professional.

Jeffry's office door snapped open. Brea twisted in her seat. She recognized the first man as someone she had seen before, but didn't know personally. He was bald, of average height, and thickly built, with piercing dark eyes. His stern expression made her flinch. Jeffry stepped into view, staid and unsure. Grant emerged last, the pain of their morning meeting still etched in his eyes. Grant and the other man were flanking Jeffry. She wasn't imagining this.

Brea stood. She studied Jeffry, reading the worry carved into his face. Her heart raced. "What's going on?"

Jeffry kissed her cheek. "Hi, honey," he said, clutching her arm.

The other detective, not Grant, muscled between her and Jeffry. He didn't seem to want them to touch or talk.

Brea gripped Jeffry's hand. The tension in the air palpable, she glanced at Grant, her eyes questioning.

An apology radiated from his gaze. Sad and sorrowful for the pain he'd caused her.

"What's happening?" she asked. "What's wrong?"

"Call Brock," Jeffry said, his shoulders slumping. He read her confused look. "Brock Bulham. And ask Diane to cancel my afternoon patients."

Bulham. Bulham. Brea committed the name to memory. "Where are you going?"

"He's coming downtown with us, Mrs. Marks," Grant replied.

Brea studied Jeffry. His arms hung free. No handcuffs. No restrictions. He was cooperating. Bulham must be a lawyer.

Brea could only guess what might happen next.

She trailed the men into the hall and watched Jeffry step onto the elevator. Hurrying from window to window, she found the front of the hospital and watched them head toward a black Crown Victoria. While she couldn't see perfectly, Jeffry looked stoic, brave... and stunned. Once she gathered her wits, she hurried to the parking structure, reclaimed her car and raced home, lunch forgotten.

Brea tried to act normal and put on a happy face as she entered the back door with cash in hand. Paying Dana and having time to sort out details was paramount right now.

Dana met her with a glare and Brea couldn't help but notice a bruise forming around her eye.

"What happened? Are you all right?"

"Derek happened. To you. To me. And God knows who else."

"He hit you? Dana, we should call the police."

"And tell them what? That you slept with my boyfriend? That I slept with yours? That the entire world is fucked up? I think they know that, don't you? Peter is dead. His wife will be a single mother. Do you ever feel the least bit guilty about the life you live?"

"I have no idea what you're talking about."

"Great. Go ahead and pretend." Dana stepped close. "Beth Marks, you are a filthy whore. I feel sorry for your children and your husband. Poor Judith couldn't stand you. You are the single most selfish, narcissistic woman I've ever met. I don't know what any man sees in you. I stayed on because I felt sorry for Jack and Ella, but make no mistake, I will not watch them any longer, not while you're out slutting it up. If you want to be an STD queen, you're on your own. I don't know if you're aware or not, but you're not safe. Not in this house. Not in this town."

"Dana, please sit down. You're upset and that's understandable, but I think you have me confused with someone else."

"Your sister?"

All the breath left Brea and her arms prickled with fear. Her time was up. Too many people were suspicious and she was about to come undone. What had Beth done? Peter? Had Brea lived in an imaginary world all along? Was no one who she thought they were?

Dana stormed out of the house. When the door slammed, it nearly shook off the hinges.

Brea stared at the wadded up cash in her hand and swallowed the bile that filled her throat.

After Dana sped off, Brea double-checked all the doors to be sure they were locked, then ransacked the junk drawer for Beth's address book. Coming up empty, she headed to the laptop. She Googled Bulham's name, located his number, and dialed.

Inexplicably, he answered the phone. For certain, not an everyday thing in legal offices. "Brock Bulham."

"Hi, Brock. This is Br…" She stopped herself and breathed. "Beth…Beth Marks. Jeffry's wife."

"Oh, hi, Beth. How are you? I owe you an apology. I missed your sister's funeral. Kathy and I were out of town. I'm sorry."

"Thank you." Brea cleared her throat. "The reason for my call is… Jeffry's been taken to the downtown precinct. By the police. They're questioning him." Erupting tears choked her voice. "He needs you as soon as possible."

"What's this about?" he asked, surprise and alarm in his tone.

"I'm not really sure, but I think their questions have something to do with Peter Magness's death."

"Magness…the murder." Brock's voice now sounded rock-steady. "Peter Magness, the psychologist?"

"Yes. Listen, this is all a bit tricky. More than that, things are a real mess."

"How about you explain the mess to me before I head across the street?"

Brea sighed in relief. Jeffry would be getting some help. Guilty and scared, she explained the situation anyway. "I, um, had an affair. With Peter Magness. Our relationship ended after my sister died, but the affair is probably the reason Jeffry is being questioned. I spoke with a detective, Grant Fulton, this morning. He and his partner took Jeffry to the police station."

Anger welled up inside her. How could Grant do this to her?

"I see," Brock replied.

Awkward silence followed. Brea couldn't think of anything else she could safely add. Was it pertinent to say she, Brea, had also had a long-term an affair with Peter before Beth's involvement with him, and she was posing as her sister? No. She couldn't reveal to a stranger what Jeffry didn't yet know. A catastrophe from every possible direction. She wanted to come clean, but not now, not in this way.

Brock cleared his throat. "Did Jeffry know? About the affair?"

"Yes, he did." Tears streamed down Brea's face.

"I'll head down to the precinct and then let you know where we stand once I know more."

"Do you need a check? A retainer?"

"Beth, relax. I'm a friend, remember?"

No, I don't remember.

"Sh-should I meet you there?" Brea stammered, afraid of his answer.

"No. Here's my cell number in case you need to contact me, but wait for my call."

Brea jotted down the number. "Thanks."

The line went dead. Bile rose in Brea's throat. She inhaled a steadying breath and waited for nausea to pass before pushing herself off the chair. She climbed the stairs, tiptoed down the hall, and eased the bedroom doors ajar. Blessedly, the kids remained sound asleep.

Brea headed toward the study, sat cross-legged on the floor, and began to rummage through desk drawers. She had done this before heading to Hilton Head, searching for any hint of Jeffry's childhood, but had found few personal items in the desk. The entire house seemed more like Beth's domain than his. But then, Jeffry had an office at work. Perhaps he kept personal items there.

Brea dug further this time, and leafed through the hanging files, all efficiently labeled. House, Bills, Cars, Health Insurance. At the back of the top file drawer, she discovered a thick, unlabeled file. Inside were a few simple greeting cards. Brea shuffled through them, checking signatures and tossing them onto the floor in front of her. Many were from her. Birthday wishes, simple "love you" notes, sister notes.

At the back of the file, she discovered a thin manila envelope. The dog-eared edges suggested age. She peered inside. Newsprint, a narrow column Brea recognized immediately, then removed with reverence and pain. Her parents' obituary.

Her faced flushed with fury. She hated the niggling guilt, detested the years spent shielding Beth from pain and heartache. Anxiety and worry had preoccupied her life—fretting about Beth getting married, having a family, being happy. She'd worried far more about Beth than herself. Now, she'd stepped into Beth's shoes to rescue her children. An unimaginable sacrifice, and for what?

The irony pierced like a nail gun to the heart. She had stepped into what she had imagined as Beth's perfect life, the dream life Brea had always wanted—married to a successful doctor, two precious kids, the security of a substantial home and a solid financial base, when in actuality, Beth's life was a total cluster.

Brea tucked the death notice back into the envelope.

Her mother had betrayed her father, betrayed their family. And the apple hadn't fallen far from the maternal tree. Beth had betrayed her family. Jeffry too. But Brea knew better than to think she was above scrutiny. While she wasn't quite the home wrecker her sister, Jeffry, or Peter had been, still, she had to face the truth. She was no better than any of them.

Brea set the envelope on the floor and swallowed the rising bile in her throat. She leaned against the wall, thoughts racing back over the years. Thunder boomed outside. Rain fell in torrents. She cracked open the window and breathed in the fresh smell of a cleansing rain, which seemed to seep through the walls and offer her a brief moment of solace.

"Momma?" Ella's disheveled curls framed her face as she hovered anxiously in the doorway. Thunder had always frightened her.

Brea opened her arms to the little girl. Ella crawled into her lap, resting her small head against Brea's breast. She wrapped her arms around Ella's soft little body and held on.

Brea's safety wasn't paramount, but the children's well-being was.

CHAPTER THIRTY-NINE

Brea

BREA SETTLED THE CHILDREN WITH A COMPUTER GAME. As the kids sat transfixed by the image on the screen, she ransacked drawers and cupboards, praying she wouldn't overlook something important.

Ella's tenderness stayed with her, strengthening her resolve to connect the dots. Then a memory hit like a beam of light. Beth's journal. She had started making entries when she was pregnant with Ella, recording her changing body, her rush of longing, how she spoke to her unborn child so the baby would recognize her voice, how she worried whether she'd have enough love for both her new little bundle and her husband. Later, Beth had said she hadn't kept up with regular entries, especially after she was caring for an infant, but maybe this last year or so, since she had been involved with Peter, she had resurrected recording her thoughts and feelings. And when she found out she was pregnant again though she'd always thought Jack would be the last.

Brea searched her memory. A simple composition book, the journal had a felted cover Beth had purchased on their annual trek to the Ann Arbor Art Fair. She had fallen in love with the design, especially the colors, soft peach with pale blue accents. Perfect for a baby, she'd said.

Where on earth would Beth keep something so private? She

used to keep the journal inside Ella's closet, on the back of the top shelf. Was there a chance…?

Brea hurried to Ella's closet, reached above her head and fingered the felted cover before she saw the colors. She clutched it to her chest, peeking in briefly on the kids before she hurried to the den.

She blew out a deep breath as she eased into the desk chair and swiveled away from the door. When she opened the pages at the back of the book, photos slid to the floor. Five by seven glossies. Photos of Peter. Photos of Beth and Peter. She recognized the sweater Beth was wearing as a gift she'd given her a year or two back. Peter and Beth embracing in the rear doorway of the house. Peter's hand cupping Beth's breast, their lips parted in a deep kiss.

One in particular reminded Beth of The Kissing Sailor photo—their unguarded passion reached out and grabbed her by the throat. There was no denying the love, or at least the lust.

Really, Beth? You could do this to me?

Her eyes filled with tears. Her vision blurred. Facing reality hurt, but she couldn't afford to let the emotions sweep her away now. Couldn't afford to feel the ax blade cleaving chunks from her heart. *Force yourself to think.*

Who took these?

She wracked her brain. In her few months with Jeffry, she had never seen him with a camera capable of taking high-quality photos. He had snapped a couple with his smart phone every now and then when he wanted to capture Jack and Ella's antics. She recalled how she'd softened toward him, and she remembered a gentle smile had crossed his lips as he clicked a proud papa photograph.

No. Someone else had taken these.

Her mind raced like a runaway train. She'd seen this quality before, this style. These photos resembled the ones pinned on her wall in the hospital. Jeffry had packed her belongings in a small duffle before bringing her home. As the quintessential neatnik, he would have returned the bag to its proper place: the closet in the master suite.

After she checked the still rapt kids, she hurried upstairs.

She stepped inside the spacious walk-in closet, looking for the standard issue gym bag. Blue. Although organized, the closet was jammed with a dense collection of clothes, shoes, boxes and luggage. She groaned at the overabundance of stuff, then bent to the task. She began at floor level, slowly working her way up to the hanging clothes suspended from a multitude of rods.

She stepped back in frustration, scanning the area. Nothing.

Then she looked up. A blue gym bag set on the top shelf. She wrestled a step stool from behind a clothing rack, and reaching high, she tugged, letting the bag fall to the floor.

She carried the bag into the bedroom, and unfastened the zipper. With a simple sweep of her hand, she located the photographs that had hung in her hospital room.

The top photo showed Ella, her impish grin captured in a sea of grays. The photos were intimate, as if someone had stolen a secret and committed the moment to memory. In Jack's photo, a severe case of bedhead blended with his devilish smile. The look of pure little-boy spunk. The photos were gallery quality. Brea didn't need an expert eye to appreciate the talent of the artist.

Who was the photographer?

Brea steadied herself against the edge of the bed as she arranged the photos of the children and those of Beth and Peter side by side. The artistic style was unmistakably the same, but the photos of Peter and Beth must have been taken without their knowledge. The photographer had to have hidden to catch them in such an intimate moment.

These were Beth's photos, but clearly taken without her knowledge. Did Peter have them taken as some kind of surprise or...? No, he wouldn't have. He'd been paranoid and rigidly discreet about photos during their long relationship.

Brea wondered why anyone would photograph Jack and Ella in the same unposed fashion as those of Beth and Peter. The real mystery. These, like the others, were candid works of art. Definitely not the shoot and run work of a private investigator. She inspected the backs of the photographs. No stamp, no ID tag to reveal who had taken them.

Brea struggled to fit the pieces together. Jeffry hadn't taken the pictures. Neither Beth nor Peter would have posed for them. Which left Dana, until today the most down to earth and genuine person on the planet.

There had to be a connection, a meaningful connection between the two sets of photos. Confusion began to wear on her. Then her mind turned to the kids. She couldn't believe she hadn't checked on them. She hurriedly stacked the photos, slipped them and the journal into the envelope, and hurried downstairs. Too much to do, too much to think about. Too much responsibility.

Hoots and hollers came at her as she reached the staircase. She rushed to investigate. A peek into the family room made her smile. Jack and Ella had pulled the cushions off the couch, lined them up on the floor like train cars, and now were taking turns jumping from the couch onto their cushion cars. After a sharp inhale, she sighed with relief.

Sunlight bathed the room. The rain had finally ended. Outside, the patio table had a pool of standing water on its top, but the deck had nearly dried off. She could take the kids outside, watch them play while she tried to figure this whole thing out.

"Hey, guys. Let's go outside. You can monkey around in the yard. In fact, how about playing in the sandbox?"

"Yay!" They shouted and darted for the wide glass door.

Brea made short work of gathering up towels, drying off the patio furniture, removing the sandbox lid, and settling in at the table. She arranged all of the photos while Jack and Ella scooped and sifted sand with their plastic buckets.

Brea glanced over at Jack and Ella and froze. She turned all of the photos facedown, except for a few. "Ella, sweetie, could you come here for a minute? Momma wants to ask you a question."

Ella bolted upright, shooting a spray of sand on top of Jack. Brea clutched fisted hands to her chest, taking a sharp breath. Thankfully, Jack giggled. Crisis averted.

She scooped Ella into her lap, and tapped her finger on a photo of the little girl. "I love this picture of you, kiddo. One of my favorites."

Ella beamed as she twirled a curl with her index finger and cuddled into Brea.

"Do you remember who took this picture of you? Momma can't remember."

"Derek," Ella answered as she scrambled off Brea's lap and raced back to the sandbox to rejoin her brother.

Derek. Of course. The answer had been in plain sight all along. Derek had pulled out his fancy camera the day after she'd arrived home, ready to take a photo of her and the kids. She'd nixed it. A memory of her broken body held no appeal, to say nothing of a memory of the day she took Beth's place. How had she missed it?

What intrigued her more though, Derek had snapped innocent shots of the kids, then intimate poses of Beth and Peter. Why? She couldn't imagine Jeffry hiring Derek to catch the two lovebirds in a lip lock, or Beth asking Derek to photograph her and her lover.

Her mind raced. At best, Derek could be a peeper, or worse, he could've been trying to blackmail Peter. And Peter would have been terrified the photos would somehow get out.

If she turned over the photos to either Grant or to Jeffry's lawyer, she might be incriminating herself. Either as Beth or as Brea. She needed to proceed with caution. She should tell Jeffry about the pictures, if he didn't know already. But, until she was certain he had not killed Peter, keeping the information private might be wiser.

Back up. What made the most sense? Maybe Derek had taken the pictures, and showed them to Beth, who couldn't bring herself to part with them. Maybe Derek had blackmailed Beth. Brea had never liked the kid. Something about him made her skin prickle.

But blackmail seemed like a stretch. Beth wouldn't pay a blackmailer. No need to if Jeffry already knew the truth. Besides if Beth knew of Jeffry's affair, neither of them would have been any guiltier than the other.

If only she knew more. Like whether Jeffry had known about Beth's affair with Peter when they were hooking up, or if he'd just recently figured things out. After Peter's death he had said, "Couldn't have happened to a nicer guy." Then again, when Jeffry acknowledged that both of them had strayed during their conversation before she went off to Hilton Head, he was sure. He hadn't asked her probing questions, just stated the information as fact. And he had been calm.

The photos prompted another web of confusion. Twists and turns she couldn't know as Brea. Her head spun new threads at each lead. There was no way she could solve this mystery on her own. And there were a multitude of reasons not to.

If she gave Grant the photos, he would want information. She could claim ignorance. She could ask Jeffry if he knew about the photos but she could hardly trust him to tell her the truth if he were involved. On the other hand, if the police were just questioning him, and nothing came of it, she had nothing to fear. If, however, the media got hold of the news, Jeffry might lose face with the hospital. Lose his reputation. Because of her. She couldn't bear being the cause of further heartbreak. Even if nothing came of things with Jeffry, she couldn't live with herself knowing she'd cost him his career or his children. She'd done enough damage for a lifetime.

She longed for a confidant. Anyone. If not Jeffry, who? Maybe she should find a shrink, someone sworn to keep her confidences. Maybe Brock Bulham. A lawyer would be more helpful than a shrink. But she wanted to tell someone who would understand, someone… *Why did you have to die, Beth? Why?*

Her gaze turned toward the table. She realized she'd left the phones in the house. Brock or Jeffry could have called while she was busy playing detective. She hurried inside, grabbed both her cell and the landline, and raced back to the rear deck. Times like these, accidents happened. After checking on Jack and Ella, she sank into her chair at the table. She checked both phones for missed calls. Nothing.

No news was good news. She hoped.

Her mind strayed back to Grant. Maybe the time had come to tell him the truth—about the pictures at least. She'd stumbled upon them while trying to sort things out for herself. She could even claim she might have seen them before and had blocked out the memory. The accident had left her mind with empty pockets.

Or maybe she should let the dice fall where they may, quit trying to orchestrate life. Perhaps that was the better answer. If she was discovered, the possible repercussions were too numerous to count. The risks too great.

She could call Derek, meet with him. Sort out the details. No. Stupid idea. Even the thought of being near him raised goosebumps.

She could ask Dana. Explain she had forgotten some of the circumstances surrounding the photos. Another dumb idea. Dana was no longer someone she could turn to for help. Still, she wondered if Dana had ever seen the photos of Beth and Peter. Or if the photos played a part in his death. In any case, the likelihood of ever speaking to Dana again was nil.

Peter had mentioned that both Dana and Derek were suspicious. They'd deduced Brea was posing as Beth. Too risky for her to speak to either of them under any circumstances.

The only idea that contained any semblance of logic was handing over the pictures to Grant, explain she hadn't remembered them until now, and leave matters to him.

Worst idea ever.

CHAPTER FORTY

Brea

TWO HOURS PASSED AND STILL NO WORD FROM BROCK. Beside herself with worry, Brea paced a path in the carpet. Staying home made no sense. Any decent wife would be standing at her husband's side. She clicked on the news, careful to make sure the kids were occupied. No word about Jeffry. No news on the investigation into Peter's murder. Thank God.

Brea picked up the phone. *Ring, dammit. Give me some news.*

She stared at the screen for a full thirty seconds, but much like waiting for a pot to boil, her efforts produced no results. She set her phone on the counter, double-checking to make sure the ringer was operational and the volume set to high in case Brock or Jeffry called, then rested her hand on her stomach in a feeble attempt to calm the jitters. She tried not to let her thoughts carry her off to a darker place.

She cooked macaroni and cheese for the kids, and shifted into mindless Momma-mode, tidied up the kitchen, switched the laundry, relaxed the kids with a long bath, and read a fistful of storybooks to them before tucking them into bed. A bit early perhaps for a spring evening where daylight stretched into night, but they cooperated without protest. Brea pressed her palms to her eyes as she closed the bedroom doors after kissing them goodnight. In the midst of the flurry of activity, she'd checked and rechecked her phone. Nothing. The wait was excruciating.

She placed the cell back in her pocket and descended the stairs.

Thuds came at her. Dull thuds. More dull thuds. Not recognizing the sound, she picked up her pace. The clunking finally registered. Someone was at the front door, banging with that sneering knocker.

Brea ushered Grant into the foyer and bolted the door. She swallowed over the knot filling her throat. "You must be here to deliver bad news. How's Jeffry?"

"Cooperating."

"No one's called. What's going on?" She could hardly disguise her confusion, her rising anger and frustration, in spite of the fact she knew she should try.

"I don't know anything. Not yet."

Brea couldn't say why, but she marched down the hall to the kitchen. He followed with a direction. "Sit down and tell me what's going on."

"I have a couple of questions for you."

"What a surprise."

Grant took a seat across from her. "About the gun."

Brea's fingers turned to ice. "Gun?"

"Your husband's gun. He says he kept the weapon in the nightstand next to his bed."

Beth had never mentioned a gun. Jeffry had never mentioned a gun.

A wife should know if her husband has a gun. "Let's go look," Brea said, all the while praying Grant wouldn't have further questions.

Her heart hammered against her ribs as she climbed the stairs. Grant thought Jeffry killed Peter. Her legs went to rubber and white noise filled her head. She focused on her breathing and gripped the stair rail. Maybe this was why she was meant to take Beth's place. Jeffry was a murderer. Ugly scenes flooded her mind. Horrific headlines. Being stalked by news media and peppered with throngs of questions from badgering reporters. Trying to protect the kids.

Grant's question interrupted her nightmares. "Have you seen a gun? Any guns? Jeffry had more than one perhaps."

Brea led Grant into the bedroom and pointed at the nightstands. Truth be told, she had no idea which side of the bed was Jeffry's, and knew nothing of a gun's existence. She evaded his question. "Please," she said. "Feel free to check anywhere you'd like."

Grant eyed her apologetically as he strode over to investigate one drawer and then the other, shuffling through items, removing them, and even taking out the drawers and flipping them upside down.

For a brief moment, she considered asking him to wait, to give her time to call Brock and ask his advice. But instinct told her to cooperate. Calling Brock might raise more suspicion.

Her finger reflexively traveled to her nose, but she caught herself in the nick of time and scratched her chin instead. "I'm concerned about my husband. Worried I'm doing something wrong by letting you go through his drawers without a search warrant."

"There's no reason for a warrant. I'll just have a quick look around. I don't expect to find anything, and from all accounts, you and Jeffry seem to be in the process of working things out. Neither one of you seem to be harboring any ill will toward the other."

"No, we aren't."

Grant continued to investigate the room. Under the beds, in the dresser drawers, a cursory inspection of the closet.

Brea stood in the doorway, numb, waiting.

"I'm done here," he said.

"Then let's go downstairs." She wrestled with showing him the photographs. If he found them first, she could only imagine him taking them as evidence of Jeffry's anger, and motivation to kill Peter. Thank goodness, she'd stuffed the envelope into the slim cupboard where she kept the cutting boards. Not only out of sight, but in an unobtrusive location.

Back in the kitchen, Grant sat forward at the table, pensive, placing his elbows on the table. "Do you remember Jeffry's gun?"

Brea shook her head. "No. I mean I don't know. I don't recall. The more time passes, the less I remember." As she said the words, she startled at their truth. She understood less and less about her life. She couldn't even trust her memories.

Grant sat back, took a long drink of water, and set his glass on the table. "I probably shouldn't tell you this, I'm overstepping my bounds, but he said you knew about the gun."

"If he said I know, then I must know."

"Listen, I realize you've been through a ton lately, and I'm not trying to make matters worse. I'm simply trying to verify the facts."

"You're right. I'm overwhelmed. I don't know what to think about anything right now."

"Do you trust your husband?"

"I'm not sure what you mean."

Grant sat quietly for a time. "Let's drop this," he said finally. "I was wrong to come. This isn't an official visit. I'll let you get some rest, and then we can talk tomorrow."

"What's Jeffry's status?"

"We're holding him."

"He's been arrested?"

"No, but we have probable cause to hold him."

"Because?"

"Because his gun was the weapon used in Peter Magness's death."

"I see," Brea said, taking a sip of wine. "Did our attorney show up?"

"Yes," Grant replied. "But formal charges won't be filed until tomorrow. There's really nothing a lawyer can do for him until then."

"Can we keep this out of the press?"

"They don't know anything yet, but word will get out pretty quick." Grant reached across the table and settled his hand atop Brea's. "I'm sorry."

Brea nodded. She sat frozen, dazed. But worn out as she was, the warmth of his hand had lit a spark.

"This is a lot to absorb."

"You have no idea." Brea stared at him. "Too much."

"I can see you're in no shape to do this now."

"Is anyone ever in shape for this?" A thought struck her. "Wait. You said it was Jeffry's gun. Do you have the gun?"

Grant's gaze dropped. "Yes."

Brea's eyes shot angry daggers. Her arms flew up in a "what the hell" gesture. "Then what are you doing here?"

"Trying to exonerate your husband." His gaze softened. "Could we take a break from this, officially as well as unofficially?"

Brea's eyes met his, fury and exasperation furrowing her brow. "Friend to friend?"

Brea stopped and took stock. Friend to friend might entail 'fessing up.

"I'm exhausted. Right now I need some rest."

Grant stood without a word. He headed to the front door and Brea locked up behind him. She leaned against the door, tipped her head to the ceiling and exhaled. The feel of his touch lingered.

If I had let him stay, he'd be in my bed.

CHAPTER FORTY-ONE

Brea

BREA COLLAPSED ON THE BED AFTER GRANT LEFT, overcome with exhaustion, and feeling more like a trapped animal every minute. A long breath later, she opened her eyes and stared at the ceiling, only able to make out the slightest curve of the swirled paint caught in a single sliver of moonlight. *The last thing I need is a murderous husband.*

Another rap came at the door. That damn doorknocker again. Pissed her off every time. The scorn of the gargoyle's eyes, the anger in its tone, the imprisoned woman she'd become.

Grant

Grant had hoped to find more, bloody clothes, socks, shoes…something to tie Jeffry irrefutably to the murder. The gun excuse was just that, a way into the home. As he drove toward the Magness address to check the mileage, he thought about Beth. She didn't seem either comfortable or familiar in the master bedroom, the way she'd stood back observing, looking very much like the new kid on the block, unaware of the location of drawer possessions or soiled laundry. She had strode directly into the closet, then stopped in her tracks and scratched her head. To him, enough time had passed for these memory lapses to have subsided. And, she'd seemed pretty darn together when they'd met to talk about Peter. She picked at her fingernails too. Nervous.

At the point when he'd asked, "You don't know where Jeffry puts his dirty clothes?" she'd remarked that she'd been sleeping in the guest room because of her injuries. When they'd met at Starbucks, she said she and Jeffry were making a go of their marriage, but she no longer wore a cast or used a cane.

Clearly, the man still resided in the master bedroom and hadn't moved to hers; his razor lay on the bathroom counter, as well as a man's hairbrush and cologne. If a guy moved downstairs, making up with his wife, he'd certainly not leave his deodorant behind. Not a guy like Jeffry.

A cell phone ping interrupted his assessment. He groaned as he realized the message meant a trip back to the station.

Brea

Brea stormed to the front door, angry and adrenalin fueled. Grant must have had one more question to ask, one more thing to torment her with. She threw open the door. "What is it?"

Derek stood in front of her. Every nerve in her body stood on end.

A chill ran up her spine. Tempted to warn him she'd called the police to report his assault on Dana, she checked herself. Provoking a violent man always proved a bad idea. *Summon logic, Brea.*

"It's late, Derek, and I've had a long day."

"I just need a minute."

"Tomorrow. Not tonight. I hear Ella. I have to go."

She slammed the door shut and bolted it, fastened the chain, and tore through the first floor in the dark, double-checking every window and door lock.

She hurried upstairs and latched each window.

She went downstairs and headed into the kitchen, ready to wind down with a glass of wine, but stopped with a jolt, the hair on her nape spiking. Derek. He'd always seemed more at ease in the house than she, had known the exact location of the damned immersion blender when Brea was making gravy for dinner. She remembered hating how he knew the location of items she couldn't ever imagine he would use.

Then, as if struck by the weight of a falling branch, an idea stunned her. Even more than a notion, she heard Beth's voice. "He hits sometimes." She grabbed her wine and took a stiff drink.

Something took hold. A premonition. A hunch. Intuition.

The click of the kitchen door jarred her. When she looked up from the table, Derek stepped inside.

Brea struggled to will her nerves calm. "Derek."

He dangled his keychain from a finger. "Still have a key for the deadbolt."

Her eyes threatened to give away her fright, but she glanced quickly at the phone in her hands and hit Grant's number and the speaker button, hoping he would hear the conversation and hurry back.

"What won't wait until tomorrow?" she asked.

"I need money."

The kid's hair was wild, and his hands, squeezed into fists, were parchment white. She recalled the part of his day she knew about.

"I can lend you a few dollars."

He blew out a disgusted breath and paced the floor like a cornered animal. "Real money."

"How much?"

"Ten grand. I'm leaving town. Tonight. I can't wait."

"Sit. Try to relax." Brea patted the seat next to her, then rose to get him a glass of water. She had to rest one hand on top of the other to quell the shakes, and placed the glass in front of him half-full. She'd been in situations like this before. Crazed kids, jazzed with emotion, hard to talk down. The best defense was to radiate a sense of peace. Listen sensitively. Not react.

"Peter's dead. I can't get money from him. It's on you now, bitch."

She sat back down and sipped her wine. "Here's the thing. I don't keep that kind of cash in the house. I'm happy to loan you some money. But we can't do it right now. The bank is closed."

"Are you stupid? I'm not talking about fun and games like last time. This is the real deal. It's not a loan. It's time for another payment. The ATM," he said, still tracing a path on the floor.

"An ATM won't give me that much. How about this? Jeffry called a minute ago. He's due home in…" She pulled out her phone to check the time and noticed the connection to Grant's phone had been lost. Her heart sunk. *C'mon, Brea. Keep up the act.* "…any minute. I'm assuming you don't want Jeffry involved."

He raised his chin in acknowledgment.

"Come back in the morning. The bank opens at 9 A.M. I can meet you there."

"Write me another check."

"I can do that, but we need to hurry. And it's traceable. Do you want that?"

"Yes. No."

Brea rose and stepped back. "Everything will be all right. I can write you a check now or meet you at the bank in the morning. But if this is between us, you'd better leave." She backed away, turned to the stove clock and pointed. "Any minute."

Derek's eyes went wild and he lunged at Brea, grabbing her around the throat, fingers squeezing. "You better not be lying, bitch. I'll be back at 9. No cops. If I even smell blue, I swear you're next. No Jeffry either. You, me, and the kids go to the bank. You go in. I stay with the kids. You say a single word to anyone, I'll take the kids. You'll never see them again. You got that?"

Brea could barely breathe. Her hands clutched at his. "P..l..ease. Let…me…go."

His grip on her neck loosened. He slung her away.

"I mean it. Screw this up, your kids' lives are over."

The sound of a car engine revved outside. Derek's eyes narrowed. He was at the door in two steps. "9 A.M. And I'll be watching you."

"Hurry. It could be him. And leave the key."

"Fuck you."

Derek's stare cut through her, but he left. She rubbed her neck as she raced to bolt and chain the back door. She recoded the alarm and raced to see who was in the driveway, peering out the front window from behind the drapes, knees knocking and breath coming in sputtered ragged gasps. There wasn't a sign of anyone out front. She could have sworn she heard a car.

Brea somehow made it back to the kitchen, grabbed her phone with trembling hands, and headed into the study, firing up the computer, and dialing.

"Grant Fulton."

"Why didn't you pick up? Where are you?"

"Who is this?"

Panic closed her throat, the fear of the last minutes taking a firm grip.

"Who is this?" he repeated.

"Brea. Brea Watson."

"Brea…?"

"Please, hurry. He tried to choke me."

"Where are you?"

"At Beth's. Hurry. He's watching. Pull into the garage. I'll lift the door when I see your car. What are you driving?"

"A green Jeep Cherokee. Who's watching?"

"I'll explain when you get here."

"I'm fifteen minutes away. I can send a patrol car."

"No. Just you. Don't flash your lights, don't beep your horn. Just drive in like you live here. Be careful. He might have a gun. Please… please hurry."

"On my way," he barked.

Brea struggled to calm her speeding heart. Derek was watching and she ached for Grant's safety. She had little time. She rubbed her bruised neck, fighting to push away the feel of Derek's hands closing around her throat.

She had no idea of the spelling of his name. Derek. Derrick. Derick. Deryk. The list was endless. And, hard as she tried, she could not recall ever hearing the young man's last name. *Send me a message, Beth. Give me the kid's last name.*

Maybe Beth had written his contact information in the phone book. She hurried into the kitchen. No luck. Maybe his name and number were recorded in her phone and she'd never put the two together. Shrouded in panic, she scrolled through the phone, even checking Dana's information to see if Beth had added his number there. No luck.

Wait. Another check, he'd said.

Beth's checkbook. The hair on her arms prickled. Beth must have paid him for the photographs. Brea had seen duplicate check receipts when she had done her initial search to learn more about Jeffry. Now, if she could just remember where. She checked the file drawer in the study. Nada. The desk drawer. Nope. She sat down at the computer desk and asked, "Where would Beth have kept them? Where would I have kept them?" After a deep exhale, Brea took inventory of her surroundings. Above her head was a cabinet built into the wall unit. *Of course.*

She stood and tugged on the cupboard handle. Just inside she spotted six boxes of checks. She held her breath. *Please be there.* She set the boxes on the desk. Opened one. Then another. Riffled through.

The background in the photos was summer. She began to check dates. June. July. There. A check to Derek Browning dated May 1st. For three thousand dollars. Whoa. Three hundred made sense. But Brea hadn't moved until June 14th. That was well before she'd broken off with Peter and left town. Apprehension simmered in her chest.

This didn't make sense. Jeffry would have noticed a three

thousand dollar check passing through their account. Beth couldn't explain spending a small fortune on photographs.

Brea studied the checks again. This was Beth's account. Not joint. A personal account allowed her some independence. From Jeffry. From Brea.

She remembered once asking Derek where he was from. Ann Arbor he had said. Easy to check and see if he had a Facebook account or a local address listed through the University.

Instead of guessing until her head exploded, she turned to Google.

Not only did a Facebook link pop up, but several other links to various men with the same name. She almost skipped the link to a newspaper article, but the words "Browning" and "murder" appeared in the same line and snapped her to attention.

Brea waited as the article loaded. The headline and a photo appeared first.

MAN SENTENCED IN BIZARRE HIT MAN MURDER SCHEME

Ann Arbor businessman Joseph Browning was sentenced to 90 to 260 months in prison for admitting he tried to arrange the jailhouse killing of his wife's murderer, Ken Cockler. This is the latest twist in the bizarre murder mystery that gripped Ann Arbor in 2014.

Browning had long been regarded as a person of interest in the death of his wife, Jill Browning, who was found stabbed in her garage on Christmas Day. When his long time business partner, Ken Cockler was arrested and convicted of the crime, Browning threatened to kill him, but those threats were initially disregarded as the words of a distraught husband.

A year after the conviction, Browning admitted to police that he paid Tom Turret, a local drug store owner, $2000 to help him find a hit man. Turret wore a wire from police, and recorded Browning asking for his help.

Browning also asked Turret for a receipt for the down payment.

Jill Browning left behind two sons, Derek and Jacob, both students at Pioneer High School. The boys have vowed to raise money to appeal their father's conviction.

Brea flushed, her temperature rising. Derek must have set Jeffry up. Stolen his gun and shot Peter. He must have blackmailed Beth because he needed cash. And Peter. Peter had always been nervous about his reputation...

CHAPTER FORTY-TWO

Grant

GRANT WHIPPED A FAST U-TURN, HIS ADRENALIN SURGing. His suspicions had become reality. Brea *was* alive. And in danger.

Grant made the trip in quick time. His heart hammered, thinking of Brea in danger. He couldn't wait to lay eyes on her. Make sure this wasn't some kind of sick dream. He needed to make sure Brea was safe. And keep it that way.

The garage door lifted as he pulled into the drive, then, lowered behind him. He pulled his gun, scanned 360 to make sure he was alone, and made his way to the door.

Clad in T-shirt and sweats, Brea met him, her copper curls pulled back at the nape of her neck, frightened green eyes big above pasty, freckled cheeks. He took in the discolored throat, her shaking hands. Grant had seen the same look on too many domestic violence victims.

He paused. He wanted to pull her into his arms, but he had to be a cop now, and a man, later.

She pulled him inside and closed the door, fastening locks as if she were vaulting them inside. "I told him you were Jeffry and almost home."

"Who? I need a name."

"D-D-Derek Browning."

"And you're really Brea?" he asked.

"Yes." Her voice cracked.

"You're sure he's gone?"

"Yes. He's not in the house."

Panic written in her eyes, she tugged on the neck of her shirt. Her fingers were trembling so they seemed to dance against her skin. The bruises were beginning to deepen.

Grant keyed his cell phone. "What was he wearing?"

He peppered Brea with questions, which she answered as best she could, and listened while he ordered dispatch to put out a BOLO on Derek.

"That means if they see him, they'll detain him," he explained in answer to her question. "Be on the lookout."

Outside, the wind picked up and shrubbery brushed against the house. A shiver ran up Brea's spine. She could feel eyes on her.

"We can't stay in this room. Too many windows."

"In a minute. I need to look at you."

"I'm serious. We're in danger. Me. The kids. You. Let's go upstairs. I need to be near the kids."

Brea grabbed a pile of papers from the counter. Grant followed her upstairs. She checked on the kids then pulled him into the master bedroom. Brea laid the photographs out on the bed along with the duplicate check Beth had written to Derek, and pulled up the article about Derek's dad on an iPad.

She sank down on the bench and recited the details of Derek's visit, becoming more distanced with every word, reliving it as if she were in a trance.

Grant's eyes hardened as he studied her.

"Thank God you're okay. Thank God you're you."

She tried to stand, but her legs wouldn't hold her. Grant steadied her. Brea trembled as the shock took hold. "You need to sit and tell me more. Who is Derek? Where does he fit in your life?"

"I need to catch my breath first."

Grant headed into the bathroom and filled a glass of water. "Here," he said. "Drink this."

Brea took a long drink and several deep breaths. "All of this is conjecture, but Derek, the guy who was just here trying to kill me, is our babysitter's boyfriend." She told Grant all she knew or had pieced together and then pointed to the photos. "They're all professional shots, and look as if the same photographer took them. I think Derek blackmailed my sister after he snapped these photos of her and Peter in…let's say a compromising position. This is a duplicate check of the payment. What if he took Jeffry's gun?" She waited for Grant to respond.

"Sorry." Grant blinked several times, fighting his emotions, and trying to fit together the leaps in logic Brea had made. He paced into the hall and made a loop around the landing, out of Brea's sight.

"Grant?"

Wrapped up in his thoughts, Grant didn't respond.

"Grant! Don't leave me!"

Grant turned and kicked the toe of his shoe into the carpet, wrestling with focus, unable to turn down the heat growing in his gut. He stood in the doorway and locked eyes with Brea.

Brea's gaze pleaded with him. Her shoulders rattled like a skeleton, nose ran like a faucet, tears staining her cheeks. "Derek has a key. He'll come back. He'll hurt us."

Grant went to her side, resting a hand on her back. "I'm not going anywhere." He sat to her right, staying close, and moved the photos around like puzzle pieces, then eased the iPad closer so he could read the article about Joseph Browning. He had worked the case, so didn't need to read the details, just perused the article to confirm the name.

Brea wiped away her tears and regained her composure.

"Can you tell me more?"

"Peter was about to start a stint on GMA. He had an agent, a publisher, a wife, and above all, a reputation. And Peter was all about keeping up appearances. Sure, he said all the right things to his mistresses, but history proves he never intended to leave Cynthia."

Grant slid the pictures and check copy back into the envelope.

"I appreciate all the legwork you've done here. I'll take these with me, all right?"

"You're leaving? Derek knows this house better than I do. What if he comes back?"

Grant studied her face. She was still in shock, mind jumping around, repeating things to make sure he understood. "I'm not leaving, I promise. I'll be sure on Derek before I go anywhere."

Grant narrowed his eyes, wanting to press Brea for more information, but she seemed too spent to continue. He rested a hand on her shoulder. "Can you tell me more?"

Brea slowly nodded and continued her story. "I'm not sure if this matters or not, but Beth was pregnant when she died. Peter told me the night he visited Hilton Head that he'd had a vasectomy. If that's true, he couldn't be responsible for either Beth or Cynthia's pregnancies. On the other hand, Peter is—was—an accomplished liar. And he asked me for money when he came down to see me. Money might be the connection between Derek and Peter."

"Got it." Grant didn't want to move his hand away from Brea but duty called. He pulled out his phone and held a finger up to Brea. "This is Detective Fulton with an update on the BOLO for Derek Browning. He is now wanted as a suspect in the Magness homicide. I need backup at my location. Have them set up a perimeter. He's possibly hiding on the grounds." He recited Brea's address. "Also requesting a K-9 unit. Suspect may be armed. Unclear at this time. I'm in the residence with one female and two juveniles and will remain here. Suspect has a key."

As soon as he disconnected he explained to Brea. "When the dog arrives, if Derek is still here, they'll find him."

Brea nodded numbly.

"It shouldn't be long." Grant turned off the bedroom light and strode over to the back window, peeking through the blinds and surveying the yard for activity—shadows, any movement.

Minutes later, Grant's cell rang. "Fulton." He listened for a moment. "He left out the back door off the kitchen. He is in possession of a key, so it's possible he'll return there and attempt to regain entry. The door is located to the west of the garage about five yards." He disconnected the call and explained to Brea. "They're bringing the dog around back to catch Derek's scent. Once he has it, they'll release him."

Grant's gaze dropped to Brea's neck. "Does it hurt?"

Brea touched her neck, wincing from the memory as much as the pain. "A bit."

"Swallowing hurt? We can call the paramedics."

Brea offered him a half-grin. "I'm fine."

"You don't have to be brave, you know."

Brea ran fingers over the raised rope of bruises around her throat. "It's tender, but I'll be okay."

She pulled the blanket tight around her shoulders and joined him at the window. While it was difficult to see much, they were able to decipher the officer and dog as they made their way to the door. The K-9 officer then shouted, "Sending in the dog." And a few moments later, "Bruno, get!"

Brea huddled into Grant, holding her breath as the dog darted toward the woods, pulling his handler. Bruno's growls grew fierce as he made his way further into the trees. His threatening bark continued to swell as searchlights cut through the woods, crossing each other like a spinning web. The dog's sound rose to a howl, then finally, baying. Brea jumped as Grant moved closer to the window, pulling her out of a panicked trance. Her heart raced at breakneck speed. She hid her head in Grant's shoulder, attempting to block out the frightening sounds.

A prolonged scream hit her ears. Another yelp and then a howl. But from Derek, not the dog.

Brea shuddered, unable to control bottled up emotions. Seconds seemed like hours and sweat beaded on her brow.

"It's all good," Grant whispered. "They got him."

Brea swiped away tears that trickled down her cheeks, her flimsy armor giving way. Grant sat her down and handed her water. Brea sipped as he hurried back to the window.

Within a minute, Grant's phone rang again. Derek was in custody. Shortly, several officers accompanied him out of the woods, across the lawn and toward the back door.

Grant hurried down the stairs and stepped outside to meet the arresting officer. "Book him for assault for now. I'll be there soon."

As the officers left via the side yard and the radio traffic faded, Brea let Grant in the back door and fell into his arms.

"They'll take him to the precinct and book him. I have a few minutes, but then I have to head out. Derek and I have some serious talking to do." He smiled down at Brea, wiping the tears from her cheeks before wrapping his arms around her and pulling her close again.

"Can I tell you something?" Brea sketched out for Grant what had happened the night of the accident. "After the crash, I was too injured to speak and correct the mistake, and something in my heart…either gave up, or gave in, or wanted to spare Jack and Ella their mother's loss. I had promised Beth to care for them. I couldn't go back on my word. I moved to Hilton Head with the intention of finding myself. Instead, I gave all that up in a heartbeat and became someone else. Looks like I took Beth's place for no real reason at all. Just that I'm a co-dependent freak, imagining I'm far more important than necessary. I'm not trying to offer an excuse, but an explanation. I'm crazy."

Grant caressed her cheek. "Not crazy, human." He checked his watch. "I have to go. My partner will be waiting to be filled in." He locked her gaze. "Call me, text me, email, drop by. I love you, Brea. Always have. Always will."

CHAPTER FORTY-THREE

Grant

G RANT HEADED INTO THE PRECINCT, A LIGHTNESS IN HIS step that overcame the worry that Brea would somehow escape from him again. Something told him he needn't worry, but to a cop's way of thinking, the only sure thing was yesterday. Still, he'd fight for her with every breath.

Before he headed into the interrogation room, he poured himself a fresh cup of black coffee and stretched his arms over his head, loosening up for the ordeal ahead. Eager for the opportunity to interview Derek, he could hardly control the bounce in his step. The exhaustion he'd felt as the adrenalin overload left his body was replaced by anticipation. Locking down a killer made him happier than anything.

Grant entered the room and observed the young man, his hand bandaged from the puncture wound he received from the dog, his hair matted and his face drawn. The kid was built like a linebacker, about 5'11," dressed in a leather jacket and jeans. "Can I get you something to drink? Water? Coffee?"

Derek shook his head and dipped his chin toward his chest, his shoulders slumped.

"Look kid, right now we've got you for the assault on Mrs. Marks but we've also got you for the Magness murder. We've got the gun. We have photos, cancelled checks, enough evidence to book you for that now. So you might as well lay it out straight. It'll go easier for you in the long run."

"It's not what you think."

Grant leaned forward in a show of sympathy. "What do I think?"

"That I killed Dr. Magness on purpose. It was an accident. I didn't mean to shoot him. He was waiting for me. The door was already open. I didn't break in or anything."

"Why were you there?"

"The doc offered to lend me some money. I went to collect. When I got there, he changed his mind. I just took the gun as insurance. I never meant to shoot him."

"Why did you need money?"

"My dad's in the slam, man. I owe his lawyer lots of dough. We're trying for an appeal, and if I don't pay what I owe, he's going to drop the case. Lawyers don't come cheap."

"Here's the thing, kid. I know you were blackmailing Dr. Magness because of his affair with Mrs. Marks. I have evidence that you were blackmailing her too. So why don't you just cut through the bullshit. I can't help you if you're going to lie to me."

Derek stared, clearly trying to choose his next lie.

"How long were you blackmailing Dr. Magness and how much did he pay you?"

Derek shrugged. "About ten grand. But it was a loan, man. I swear. I wasn't stealing from him. I was supposed to get another five grand that night, but he said he didn't have it. He lied. I know he had it. I watched him go to the bank."

"So what happened?"

"We argued. I pulled out the gun, just to convince him to give me the money. He tried to grab it. I'm not sure how, but the thing just fired. I guess I pulled the trigger during the tussle. But I swear to God man, it was an accident."

"Where did you get the gun?"

"I found it."

"At the Marks' home. In Dr. Marks' nightstand drawer. It was reported missing."

"No, I found it, I tell you. It was on the ground in their yard. Just lying there."

"Nice try. Sit tight. Someone will be in soon."

A piece of Grant felt sorry for the kid—or would have—right up until he made the decision to put his hands on Brea. At the moment, he was fighting the urge to grab the little weasel by the collar and shake the snot out of him. Scare him to death. He'd check with Brea and see if she wanted to press charges, but his gut told him she had enough juggling to do. Adding Derek's assault to the mix might not be on her list.

Grant asked for Jeffry to be moved to an interview room and re-filled his coffee while he waited. When Jeffry was ready, he went in to share the news. He explained the new developments, Derek's arrest and the certainty of his guilt. He left out Brea's confession, and told Jeffry he'd be released within the hour. Jeffry let out a sigh of relief, regret following quickly on its heels. "I can't believe I let that kid in my house. Thank God the kids are all right. Thank God Beth is okay. What a mess."

"This part is under control. You go home and get some rest."

Grant's emotions jockeyed for position as he sipped his coffee. Elation that Brea was alive, a deep ache in his gut that she wouldn't be his, and daydreams of what life would be like if she... Oh, hell. Any sensible cop knew you didn't live on hopes and promises. He inhaled, reliving the feel of her, the all-consuming desire his heart held for her.

When Shaun stepped into the office, he caught Grant grinning from ear to ear. "You've had quite a night."

"You don't know the half of it."

Brea

Brea eased her head back as she curled up on the couch. The past months seemed surreal, like something out of a novel, not real life.

She couldn't imagine how she'd begin to sweep up the mess she'd made of everyone's lives. Or how she would keep her head together explaining things to Jeffry. Too many thoughts to wrangle, considering the events of the past twenty-four hours. The clock chimed six times and Brea rose to make coffee.

Her shoulders shook reflexively upon entering the kitchen and she had to talk through the steps of coffee making to maintain her focus and sanity. Her phone rang as she filled the carafe with water, and she grabbed it from her pocket and peered at the screen. Jeffry.

Her heart sped up before catching for a beat. She answered but couldn't speak.

"Beth?" Jeffry asked.

"Hi," Brea finally said.

"I'm coming home."

She planted her feet firmly on the floor, to keep from crumbling. "Thank God."

"They've released me. There's been a break in the case."

"I'll come and get you."

"No need," Jeffry said. "I've already called a cab."

Brea noticed movement out of the corner of her eye. A sleepy Jack rubbed his eyes with balled-up fists and shuffled beneath her waiting arm.

"I can't wait to get home," Jeffry added.

"Be safe," she said, cuddling Jack closer.

She'd barely ended the call before the phone rang again. "Hello?"

"Brea," Grant said. "Have you heard from Jeffry?"

"Yes, he just called."

"I wanted you to know that I explained we now have Derek in custody. I didn't tell him about Derek's visit to your house last night. I didn't share your news."

"Thank you," she said. "I'll be in touch. It may be a while, but…"

"I'll let you go."

Brea hung up the phone and held tight to Jack.

She wouldn't be able to breathe until she told Jeffry. She wished she could be cavalier about the whole thing. Adopt a "whatever happened, happened" attitude. But her stomach flipped, knotted and contorted in ways she had never experienced before.

Jeffry would be exhausted after being questioned and detained all night. Worried, too. And he had to juggle the hospital, appointments and procedures, and possibly the media. How she could blurt out the truth in the midst of all that craziness, she had no clue.

She swept Jack into her arms and hugged him tight.

"Momma," Jack whimpered. "You're squishing me."

"Sorry, sweetie." She eased her hold on him. "I love you so much."

He stroked her cheek with a chubby hand.

"Let's get you something to eat."

Her legs went leaden as she lifted Jack into his booster seat at the kitchen table. She kissed the top of his head, ruffling his hair afterward. She couldn't bear the pain of losing him and Ella.

Brea withdrew Jack's favorite cereal boxes from the cupboard and placed them on the table with a bowl, spoon, and carton of milk. When he pointed to the one he wanted, she filled his bowl, poured milk over the top, and sat at his side as he clumsily fed himself. She hoped beyond hope when Jeffry arrived, she could find the right words, a way to help him understand her decisions and actions since Beth's death.

What she wanted more, though, was to seek his forgiveness, not just his understanding of what had motivated her to deceive everyone.

Brea heard his key slide into the tumbler. She stood, frozen, waiting for him to push open the door and step inside.

Jeffry offered her a relieved nod, made his way to her, and draped his arms around her. He drew her close, held on for what seemed like forever, and reassured her as tears streamed down her face and wet his shoulder. "The entire nightmare is over," he soothed. "We're okay. Everything's going to be all right."

Those were the words Brea longed to hear, but she knew better.

Things weren't anywhere near all right, and probably wouldn't be for a good long while.

Concern overtook Jeffry's gaze as he traced a finger over her bruises. "Your neck. What happened?"

Brea tugged self-consciously at the nape of her t-shirt, not wanting to relive a minute of last night. "I'm fine."

She backed away from him, gripping his forearms with both hands. His five o'clock shadow had already progressed into a shallow beard. His hair was disheveled and his dress shirt wrinkled. The relief in his eyes made him look all the more human—and vulnerable. Sadness washed over her. For all she had done to him. For what she was about to do.

"We need to talk," she said. "Can I pour you a cup of coffee?"

Jeffry gave her a puzzled glance, which soon became a panicked look, as Jack waved his spoon, flinging milk across the table. "Daddy, look at me."

"I'll settle him with cartoons so we can have a few uninterrupted minutes."

Jeffry scooped Jack into his arms and followed her into the family room. He sat Jack on the floor and punched the buttons on the remote, searching for Jack's favorite program. A local station announced a special report, and Jeffry paused to listen as a news anchor revealed the arrest of Derek Browning—the suspect in the killing of the renowned author and authority on marriage, Dr. Peter Magness. The broadcaster confirmed the authorities had discovered a link between the murder weapon and their new suspect. Homicide investigators also discovered a letter that linked the two men. According to the report, Derek Browning's father was serving time in Jackson Prison.

Jeffry turned toward Brea, his fingers on his temples, his mouth agape. "When Detective Fulton told me, this hit me hard. Derek spent every day here. Thank God you and the kids are all right. I don't know what I would have done…We dodged a bullet. Literally." He let out an incredulous sigh and slapped a palm on his forehead. "Did you have any idea?"

Jeffry inched up behind her as she stared at the television screen, but Brea was too focused on other matters to answer him. She led the way out of the family room and into the study. She perched on the edge of a chair in front of the mahogany desk and slid Jeffry's mug onto the top. He sank into the adjoining chair, rubbed absently at the stubble covering his jaw, took a long drink from the mug, and as if the caffeine had jolted him back to reality, shifted toward her.

Brea willed her pulse to slow and summoned courage. "I need to ask your forgiveness. I've done something terrible. Beyond your worst nightmare," she said.

"Look." He leaned forward and placed a reassuring hand on her knee. "We've both done things we regret. Tammy was my mistake. Peter, yours. All of that's behind us. I've not only forgiven, I've forgotten. I hope you've been able to do the same."

"I'm not talking about the affairs, Jeffry. Please listen."

He waited for her to speak.

"This is about me," she said with a resolve that surprised her. "I'm not who you think I am." Brea bit back tears. She wanted his understanding, not his sympathy.

She took a moment to steady herself. "The night of the accident, Beth and I had a serious discussion. She told me you were having an affair. Because she was distraught, she made me promise to take care of the kids should something happen to her."

Her throat clogged with tears and she fought the urge to run. She saw a spark of understanding dawn for Jeffry. After a long moment, she continued.

"At the time of the accident, a terrible mistake was made—a mistake I didn't correct, even though I should have."

Jeffry's lips thinned. Color vanished from his face.

Tearfully, Brea described the circumstances, Beth's anger, her desperation. "When she confided in me, she'd already had several drinks. She was furious with you. She took off her wedding rings and tossed them into the ashtray on the table. I put them on my finger for safekeeping."

She paused to meet his gaze.

He nodded slowly, shock and understanding meeting like crossroads in his eyes.

"On the way back from the bar, I drove while Beth slept. She was the passenger, not me. I don't think she ever knew what happened."

Jeffry sank back in his chair, clearly stunned. "You're Brea?"

Her sadness magnified the disbelief that registered on his face. A shudder ran through her as the shadow of the semi, the glaring lights, the rending metal flashed to mind. Brea battled for control as she swiped at her tears. "The hospital made the first mistake, or maybe the paramedics… They assumed I was Beth. I was in and out of consciousness, so confused. And then I wanted to be Beth, so I could take care of the kids. Respect her wishes. After what Beth had said about you, I thought you were a total jerk. I thought you hit her. But, I've come to learn it wasn't you Beth referred to. Still, in my mind, you didn't deserve the kids. I believed they would be better off if I could watch over them—as their mother. I don't mean to excuse my behavior. I want you to understand my reasoning, at least I hope you can."

Brea studied Jeffry. She couldn't get a fix on him. His face showed more than shock. Recognition, perhaps, and a slice of anger. What a web she'd sewn.

"You aren't who I thought you were. In the past few months, I've seen what a great father you are, how invested you are in the kids. In Beth's eyes, you'd become distant, distracted, and uncaring. I've seen the opposite. I'm not sure this matters, but I want you to know how I see you. I'm so sorry about Beth. I'm sorry you lost your wife. That we lost her." She reached out to touch Jeffry's hand, but then pulled back, and crossed the room.

"I'll go," she said. "I'm sure you need some time with this. I don't want to leave the kids, but what I've done is wrong. I hope the day will come when you'll be able to forgive me, and maybe you'll even be able to understand. I made some difficult decisions, but out of love for my sister and her children. Maybe someday, you'll allow me to be a part of their lives again."

Jeffry met Brea's tortured gaze, went to speak, then inhaled a choppy breath and looked away. "I don't know what to say," he said finally. "I had these…fleeting questions. You seemed different. But I was going through my own stuff." He tilted his head and paused. "I think I might be in shock."

Tears streamed down her face—her chin quivered. "I'm so sorry."

Jeffry rose to his feet and approached her, stopped short and steadied himself against the arm of the sofa. He looked dazed. Dizzy even. "None of this seems real."

Brea broke into sobs. "No."

Jeffry eased himself onto a couch cushion and held his head in his hands. "As a doctor, I rationalized—not unusual for someone who goes through a major trauma not to be themselves—likely to take you a while to get back to normal. I thought you might suffer from PTSD and look a little different as a result of your injuries, but I never expected you to be anyone but Beth. Now, all the little differences make sense. You acted …kinder toward me." He closed his eyes and his breathing came in shallow gasps as he rocked back and forth. "Beth? My wife is dead? I can't believe this."

Brea inched forward, closer, and hesitated as she saw his jaw clench. "I don't know what to say. I don't know how I could have done this to you."

"To me? I'm no prize." A faraway look came into his eyes. "The accident changed me, too. Blew me off a destructive path, although I admit I spent a good deal of time justifying my affair." He paused for a long moment. "For years, I'd deserted you."

Brea's eyes widened.

He registered her stunned expression and stopped himself. "Deserted Beth, I mean. I ditched my family and did what I had to do to in order to survive. I was selfish. I only hope Beth can forgive me for what I did. What she said about me was right. I'd lost my way.

I drove her to Peter. Trust me, Be…I mean Brea, I've had plenty of time to think about how my marriage played out."

Jeffry's eyes welled with tears. "You don't need to leave," he said. "Besides, where would you go? And what would happen to Jack and Ella without you?"

"You're making this too easy," Brea admitted, unable to decide if she was relieved or more confused.

"It's hardly easy."

Brea rubbed her temples, overwhelmed by exhaustion. "I probably need a lawyer."

"We'll talk to Brock."

"Won't my staying make matters harder for the kids?"

"Leaving won't make life easier for them," Jeffry reminded her. "They believe you're their mother. You are their mother. Besides, Beth wanted you in their lives. The kids are my first concern."

"You seem so…logical."

"That's me. Mr. Logical." Jeffry strode out of the room, leaving Brea to stare after him.

She moved through the day in a fog. Neither she nor Jeffry spoke, but the mood in the house was deeply contemplative. After she tucked Jack and Ella into bed for the night and Jeffry shut the door to his room, she gathered her purse and keys and headed into the soggy night. Soft rain splattered the pavement as Brea pulled Grant's address from her purse and plugged the location into the GPS.

The windshield wipers clapped a steady rhythm as she drove. Brea pulled into the condo parking lot and searched through porch lights for a house number. When she found the correct unit, she parked beneath the streetlamp and stepped out of the car. Rain dampened her hair and face, and she smelled spring's promise in the ripe night air.

Through the window, Brea noticed a single lamp burning. She spotted Grant as he glanced out the window, then hurried toward his door.

ACKNOWLEDGEMENTS

First and foremost, to my husband, for his endless edits, suggestions, and cliff-diving to rescue me when I didn't think I'd finish this novel. Also, to Lori LaBoe, my BFF and partner-in-crime in all things life related. Both Don and Lori have read my books countless times without complaint and have helped me to hone them and make them the best that they can be. Most importantly, I need to thank my editor, Jean Jenkins, who died of cancer in October 2020. She is sorely missed. Jean spent many, many hours editing a number of my books, counseling me and keeping me on track when I faltered, and humoring me with her keen sense of humor. I can't imagine her not being here, so I'd like to think she's shining down on me—I can still hear her voice telling me to keep plugging away.

To my kids for the constant support. To Stacey Blake from Champagne Book Design for the wonderful cover art and formatting.

To Janis, Lori, Connie for Beta reading *Black Ice*. Your feedback is always much appreciated. And to all my friends from the Southern California Writers' Conference. You gave me my start and kept me going.

To all my faithful readers, thank you for reading and loving my books. I can't tell you how much I appreciate your enthusiasm.

ABOUT THE AUTHOR

Claudia Whitsitt is the best-selling author of nine books and has been published since 2012. She is a lover of the written word, mystery and romance, and includes some of each in most of her novels, no matter what genre she is writing.

When Claudia isn't reading or writing, she's spending time with family, enjoying the outdoors, traveling.

Claudia is a also a lover of coffee and cabernet, depending on the time of day, and although she avoids sugar, it's a weakness she has yet to overcome completely.

To find more about upcoming events and releases,
please sign up for Claudia's newsletter.

www.claudiawhitsitt.com
cjw@claudiawhitstt@gmail.com

Made in the USA
Monee, IL
08 January 2022